The Trail of th

A Comedy of the Serious

Sinclair Lewis

Alpha Editions

This edition published in 2024

ISBN : 9789357965910

Design and Setting By
Alpha Editions
www.alphaedis.com
Email - info@alphaedis.com

As per information held with us this book is in Public Domain.
This book is a reproduction of an important historical work. Alpha Editions uses the
best technology to reproduce historical work in the same manner it was first
published to preserve its original nature. Any marks or number seen are left
intentionally to preserve its true form.

Contents

PART I
THE ADVENTURE OF YOUTH

CHAPTER I

Carl Ericson was being naughty. Probably no boy in Joralemon was being naughtier that October Saturday afternoon. He had not half finished the wood-piling which was his punishment for having chased the family rooster thirteen times squawking around the chicken-yard, while playing soldiers with Bennie Rusk.

He stood in the middle of the musty woodshed, pessimistically kicking at the scattered wood. His face was stern, as became a man of eight who was a soldier of fortune famed from the front gate to the chicken-yard. An unromantic film of dirt hid the fact that his Scandinavian cheeks were like cream-colored silk stained with rose-petals. A baby Norseman, with only an average boy's prettiness, yet with the whiteness and slenderness of a girl's little finger. A back-yard boy, in baggy jacket and pants, gingham blouse, and cap whose lining oozed back over his ash-blond hair, which was tangled now like trampled grass, with a tiny chip riding grotesquely on one flossy lock.

The darkness of the shed displeased Carl. The whole basic conception of work bored him. The sticks of wood were personal enemies to which he gave insulting names. He had always admired the hard bark and metallic resonance of the ironwood, but he hated the poplar—"popple" it is called in Joralemon, Minnesota. Poplar becomes dry and dusty, and the bark turns to a monstrously mottled and evil greenish-white. Carl announced to one poplar stick, "I could lick you! I'm a gen'ral, I am." The stick made no reply whatever, and he contemptuously shied it out into the chickweed which matted the grubby back yard. This necessitated his sneaking out and capturing it by stalking it from the rear, lest it rouse the Popple Army.

He loitered outside the shed, sniffing at the smoke from burning leaves—the scent of autumn and migration and wanderlust. He glanced down between houses to the reedy shore of Joralemon Lake. The surface of the water was smooth, and tinted like a bluebell, save for one patch in the current where wavelets leaped with October madness in sparkles of diamond fire. Across the lake, woods sprinkled with gold-dust and paprika broke the sweep of sparse yellow stubble, and a red barn was softly brilliant in the caressing sunlight and lively air of the Minnesota prairie. Over there was the field of valor, where grown-up men with shiny shotguns went hunting prairie-chickens; the Great World, leading clear to the Red River Valley and Canada.

Three mallard-ducks, with necks far out and wings beating hurriedly, shot over Carl's head. From far off a gun-shot floated echoing through forest hollows; in the waiting stillness sounded a rooster's crow, distant, magical.

"I want to go hunting!" mourned Carl, as he trailed back into the woodshed. It seemed darker than ever and smelled of moldy chips. He bounced like an enraged chipmunk. His phlegmatic china-blue eyes filmed with tears. "Won't pile no more wood!" he declared.

Naughty he undoubtedly was. But since he knew that his father, Oscar Ericson, the carpenter, all knuckles and patched overalls and bad temper, would probably whip him for rebellion, he may have acquired merit. He did not even look toward the house to see whether his mother was watching him—his farm-bred, worried, kindly, small, flat-chested, pinch-nosed, bleached, twangy-voiced, plucky Norwegian mother. He marched to the workshop and brought a collection of miscellaneous nails and screws out to a bare patch of earth in front of the chicken-yard. They were the Nail People, the most reckless band of mercenaries the world has ever known, led by old General Door-Hinge, who was somewhat inclined to collapse in the middle, but possessed of the unusual virtue of eyes in both ends of him. He had explored the deepest cañons of the woodshed, and victoriously led his ten-penny warriors against the sumacs in the vacant lot beyond Irving Lamb's house.

Carl marshaled the Nail People, sticking them upright in the ground. After reasoning sternly with an intruding sparrow, thus did the dauntless General Door-Hinge address them:

"Men, there's a nawful big army against us, but le's die like men, my men. Forwards!"

As the veteran finished, a devastating fire of stones enfiladed the company, and one by one they fell, save for the commander himself, who bowed his grizzled wrought-steel head and sobbed, "The brave boys done their duty."

From across the lake rolled another gun-shot.

Carl dug his grimy fingers into the earth. "Jiminy! I wisht I was out hunting. Why can't I never go? I guess I'll pile the wood, but I'm gonna go seek-my-fortune after that."

Since Carl Ericson (some day to be known as "Hawk" Ericson) was the divinely restless seeker of the romance that must—or we die!—lie beyond the hills, you first see him in action; find him in the year 1893, aged eight, leading revolutions in the back yard. But equally, since this is a serious study of an average young American, there should be an indication of his soil-nourished ancestry.

Carl was second-generation Norwegian; American-born, American in speech, American in appearance, save for his flaxen hair and china-blue eyes;

and, thanks to the flag-decked public school, overwhelmingly American in tradition. When he was born the "typical Americans" of earlier stocks had moved to city palaces or were marooned on run-down farms. It was Carl Ericson, not a Trowbridge or a Stuyvesant or a Lee or a Grant, who was the "typical American" of his period. It was for him to carry on the American destiny of extending the Western horizon; his to restore the wintry Pilgrim virtues and the exuberant, October, partridge-drumming days of Daniel Boone; then to add, in his own or another generation, new American aspirations for beauty.

They are the New Yankees, these Scandinavians of Wisconsin and Minnesota and the Dakotas, with a human breed that can grow, and a thousand miles to grow in. The foreign-born parents, when they first come to the Northern Middlewest, huddle in unpainted farm-houses with grassless dooryards and fly-zizzing kitchens and smelly dairies, set on treeless, shadeless, unsoftened leagues of prairie or bunched in new clearings ragged with small stumps. The first generation are alien and forlorn. The echoing fjords of Trondhjem and the moors of Finmark have clipped their imaginations, silenced their laughter, hidden with ice their real tenderness. In America they go sedulously to the bare Lutheran church and frequently drink ninety-per-cent. alcohol. They are also heroes, and have been the makers of a new land, from the days of Indian raids and ox-teams and hillside dug-outs to now, repeating in their patient hewing the history of the Western Reserve.... In one generation or even in one decade they emerge from the desolation of being foreigners. They, and the Germans, pay Yankee mortgages with blood and sweat. They swiftly master politics, voting for honesty rather than for hand-shakes; they make keen, scrupulously honest business deals; send their children to school; accumulate land—one section, two sections—or move to town to keep shop and ply skilled tools; become Methodists and Congregationalists; are neighborly with Yankee manufacturers and doctors and teachers; and in one generation, or less, are completely American.

So was it with Carl Ericson. His carpenter father had come from Norway, by way of steerage and a farm in Wisconsin, changing his name from Ericsen. Ericson senior owned his cottage and, though he still said, "Aye ban going," he talked as naturally of his own American tariff and his own Norwegian-American Governor as though he had five generations of Connecticut or Virginia ancestry.

Now, it was Carl's to go on, to seek the flowering.

———————————————————————————————

Unconscious that he was the heir-apparent of the age, but decidedly conscious that the woodshed was dark, Carl finished the pile.

From the step of the woodshed he regarded the world with plaintive boredom.

"Ir-r-r-r-rving!" he called.

No answer from Irving, the next-door boy.

The village was rustlingly quiet. Carl skipped slowly and unhappily to the group of box-elders beside the workshop and stuck his finger-nails into the cobwebby crevices of the black bark. He made overtures for company on any terms to a hop-robin, a woolly worm, and a large blue fly, but they all scorned his advances, and when he yelled an ingratiating invitation to a passing dog it seemed to swallow its tail and ears as it galloped off. No one else appeared.

Before the kitchen window he quavered:

"Ma-ma!"

In the kitchen, the muffled pounding of a sad-iron upon the padded ironing-board.

"Ma!"

Mrs. Ericson's whitey-yellow hair, pale eyes, and small nervous features were shadowed behind the cotton fly-screen.

"Vell?" she said.

"I haven't got noth-ing to do-o."

"Go pile the vood."

"I piled piles of it."

"Then you can go and play."

"I *been* playing."

"Then play some more."

"I ain't got nobody to play with."

"Then find somebody. But don't you step vun step out of this yard."

"I don't see *why* I can't go outa the yard!"

"Because I said so."

Again the sound of the sad-iron.

Carl invented a game in which he was to run in circles, but not step on the grass; he made the tenth inspection that day of the drying hazelnuts whose husks were turning to seal-brown on the woodshed roof; he hunted for a good new bottle to throw at Irving Lamb's barn; he mended his sling-shot;

he perched on a sawbuck and watched the street. Nothing passed, nothing made an interesting rattling, except one democrat wagon.

From over the water another gun-shot murmured of distant hazards.

Carl jumped down from the sawbuck and marched deliberately out of the yard, along Oak Street toward The Hill, the smart section of Joralemon, where live in exclusive state five large houses that get painted nearly every year.

"I'm gonna seek-my-fortune. I'm gonna find Bennie and go swimming," he vowed. Calmly as Napoleon defying his marshals, General Carl disregarded the sordid facts that it was too late in the year to go swimming, and that Benjamin Franklin Rusk couldn't swim, anyway. He clumped along, planting his feet with spats of dust, very dignified and melancholy but, like all small boys, occasionally going mad and running in chase of nothing at all till he found it.

He stopped before the House with Mysterious Shutters.

Carl had never made b'lieve fairies or princes; rather, he was in the secret world of boyhood a soldier, a trapper, or a swing-brakeman on the M. & D. R.R. But he was bespelled by the suggestion of grandeur in the iron fence and gracious trees and dark carriage-shed of the House with Shutters. It was a large, square, solid brick structure, set among oaks and sinister pines, once the home, or perhaps the mansion, of Banker Whiteley, but unoccupied for years. Leaves rotted before the deserted carriage-shed. The disregarded steps in front were seamed with shallow pools of water for days after a rain. The windows had always been darkened, but not by broad-slatted outside shutters, smeared with house-paint to which stuck tiny black hairs from the paint-brush, like the ordinary frame houses of Joralemon. Instead, these windows were masked with inside shutters haughtily varnished to a hard refined brown.

To-day the windows were open, the shutters folded; furniture was being moved in; and just inside the iron gate a frilly little girl was playing with a whitewashed conch-shell.

She must have been about ten at that time, since Carl was eight. She was a very dressy and complacent child, possessed not only of a clean white muslin with three rows of tucks, immaculate bronze boots, and a green tam-o'-shanter, but also of a large hair-ribbon, a ribbon sash, and a silver chain with a large, gold-washed, heart-shaped locket. She was softly plump, softly gentle of face, softly brown of hair, and softly pleasant of speech.

"Hello!" said she.

"H'lo!"

"What's your name, little boy?"

"Ain't a little boy. I'm Carl Ericson."

"Oh, are you? I'm——"

"I'm gonna have a shotgun when I'm fifteen." He shyly hurled a stone at a telegraph-pole to prove that he was not shy.

"My name is Gertie Cowles. I came from Minneapolis. My mamma owns part of the Joralemon Flour Mill.... Are you a nice boy? We just moved here and I don't know anybody. Maybe my mamma will let me play with you if you are a nice boy."

"I jus' soon come play with you. If you play soldiers.... My pa 's the smartest man in Joralemon. He built Alex Johnson's house. He's got a ten-gauge gun."

"Oh.... My mamma 's a widow."

Carl hung by his arms from the gate-pickets while she breathed, "M-m-m-m-m-m-y!" in admiration at the feat.

"That ain't nothing. I can hang by my knees on a trapeze.... What did you come from Minneapolis for?"

"We're going to live here," she said.

"Oh."

"I went to the Chicago World's Fair with my mamma this summer."

"Aw, you didn't!"

"I did so. And I saw a teeny engine so small it was in a walnut-shell and you had to look at it through a magnifying-glass and it kept on running like anything."

"Huh! that's nothing! Ben Rusk, he went to the World's Fair, too, and he saw a statchue that was bigger 'n our house and all pure gold. You didn't see that."

"I did so! And we got cousins in Chicago and we stayed with them, and Cousin Edgar is a very *prominent* doctor for eyenear and stummick."

"Aw, Ben Rusk's pa is a doctor, too. And he's got a brother what's going to be a sturgeon."

"I got a brother. He's a year older than me. His name is Ray.... There's lots more people in Minneapolis than there is in Joralemon. There's a hundred thousand people in Minneapolis."

"That ain't nothing. My pa was born in Christiania, in the Old Country, and they's a million million people there."

"Oh, there is not!"

"Honest there is."

"Is there, honest?" Gertie was admiring now.

He looked patronizingly at the red-plush furniture which was being splendidly carried into the great house from Jordan's dray—an old friend of Carl's, which had often carried him banging through town. He condescended:

"Jiminy! You don't know Bennie Rusk nor nobody, do you! I'll bring him and we can play soldiers. And we can make tents out of carpets. Did you ever run through carpets on the line?"

He pointed to the row of rugs and carpets airing beside the carriage-shed.

"No. Is it fun?"

"It's awful scary. But I ain't afraid."

He dashed at the carpets and entered their long narrow tent. To tell the truth, when he stepped from the sunshine into the intense darkness he was slightly afraid. The Ericsons' one carpet made a short passage, but to pass on and on and on through this succession of heavy rug mats, where snakes and poisonous bugs might hide, and where the rough-threaded, gritty under-surface scratched his pushing hands, was fearsome. He emerged with a whoop and encouraged her to try the feat. She peeped inside the first carpet, but withdrew her head, giving homage:

"Oh, it's so *dark* in there where you went!"

He promptly performed the feat again.

As they wandered back to the gate to watch the furniture-man Gertie tried to regain the superiority due her years by remarking, of a large escritoire which was being juggled into the front door, "My papa bought that desk in Chicago——"

Carl broke in, "I'll bring Bennie Rusk, and me and him 'll teach you to play soldiers."

"My mamma don't think I ought to play games. I've got a lot of dolls, but I'm too old for dolls. I play Authors with mamma, sometimes. And dominoes. Authors is a very nice game."

"But maybe your ma will let you play Indian squaw, and me and Bennie 'll tie you to a stake and scalp you. That won't be rough like soldiers. But I'm going to be a really-truly soldier. I'm going to be a norficer in the army."

"I got a cousin that's an officer in the army," Gertie said grandly, bringing her yellow-ribboned braid round over her shoulder and gently brushing her lips with the end.

"Cross-your-heart?"

"Um-huh."

"Cross-your-heart, hope-t'-die if you ain't?"

"Honest he's an officer."

"Jiminy crickets! Say, Gertie, could he make me a norficer? Let's go find him. Does he live near here?"

"Oh my, no! He's 'way off in San Francisco."

"Come on. Let's go there. You and me. Gee! I like you! You got a' awful pertty dress."

"'Tain't polite to compliment me to my face. Mamma says———"

"Come on! Let's go! We're going!"

"Oh no. I'd like to," she faltered, "but my mamma wouldn't let me. She don't let me play around with boys, anyway. She's in the house now. And besides, it's 'way far off across the sea, to San Francisco; it's beyond the salt sea where the Mormons live, and they all got seven wives."

"Beyond the sea like Christiania? Ah, 'tain't! It's in America, because Mr. Lamb went there last winter. 'Sides, even if it was across the sea, couldn't we go an' be stow'ways, like the Younger Brothers and all them? And Little Lord Fauntleroy. He went and was a lord, and he wasn't nothing but a' orphing. My ma read me about him, only she don't talk English very good, but we'll go stow'ways," he wound up, triumphantly.

"Gerrrrrrtrrrrrude!" A high-pitched voice from the stoop.

Gertie glowered at a tall, meager woman with a long green-and-white apron over a most respectable black alpaca gown. Her nose was large, her complexion dull, but she carried herself so commandingly as to be almost handsome and very formidable.

"Oh, dear!" Gertie stamped her foot. "Now I got to go in. I never can have any fun. Good-by, Carl———"

He urgently interrupted her tragic farewell. "Say! Gee whillikins! I know what we'll do. You sneak out the back door and I'll meet you, and we'll run away and go seek-our-fortunes and we'll find your cousin———"

"Gerrrtrrrrude!" from the stoop.

"Yes, mamma, I'm just coming." To Carl: "'Sides, I'm older 'n you and I'm 'most grown-up, and I don't believe in Santy Claus, and onc't I taught the infant class at St. Chrysostom's Sunday-school when the teacher wasn't there; anyway, I and Miss Bessie did, and I asked them 'most all the questions about the trumpets and pitchers. So I couldn't run away. I'm too old."

"Gerrrtrrrude, come here this *instant*!"

"Come on. I'll be waiting," Carl demanded.

She was gone. She was being ushered into the House of Mysterious Shutters by Mrs. Cowles. Carl prowled down the street, a fine, new, long stick at his side, like a saber. He rounded the block, and waited back of the Cowles carriage-shed, doing sentry-go and planning the number of parrots and pieces of eight he would bring back from San Francisco. *Then* his father and mother would be sorry they'd talked about him in their Norwegian!

"Carl!" Gertie was running around the corner of the carriage-shed. "Oh, Carl, I had to come out and see you again, but I can't go seek-our-fortunes with you, 'cause they've got the piano moved in now and I got to practise, else I'll grow up just an ignorant common person, and, besides, there's going to be tea-biscuits and honey for supper. I saw the honey."

He smartly swung his saber to his shoulder, ordering, "Come on!"

Gertie edged forward, perplexedly sucking a finger-joint, and followed him along Lake Street toward open country. They took to the Minnesota & Dakota railroad track, a natural footpath in a land where the trains were few and not fast, as was the condition of the single-tracked M. & D. of 1893. In a worried manner Carl inquired whether San Francisco was northwest or southeast—the directions in which ran all self-respecting railroads. Gertie blandly declared that it lay to the northwest; and northwest they started— toward the swamps and the first forests of the Big Woods.

He had wonderlands to show her along the track. To him every detail was of scientific importance. He knew intimately the topography of the fields beside the track; in which corner of Tubbs's pasture, between the track and the lake, the scraggly wild clover grew, and down what part of the gravel-bank it was most exciting to roll. As far along the track as the Arch, each railroad tie (or sleeper) had for him a personality: the fat, white tie, which oozed at the end into an awkward knob, he had always hated because it resembled a flattened grub; a new tamarack tie with a sliver of fresh bark still on it, recently put in by the section gang, was an entertaining stranger; and he particularly introduced Gertie to his favorite, a wine-colored tie which always smiled.

Gertie, though *noblesse oblige* compelled her to be gracious to the imprisoned ties writhing under the steel rails, did not really show much enthusiasm till he led her to the justly celebrated Arch. Even then she boasted of Minnehaha Falls and Fort Snelling and Lake Calhoun; but, upon his grieved solicitation, declared that, after all, the Twin Cities had nothing to compare with the Arch—a sandstone tunnel full twenty feet high, miraculously boring through the railroad embankment, and faced with great stones which you could descend by lowering yourself from stone to stone. Through the Arch ran the creek, with rare minnows in its pools, while important paths led from the creek to a wilderness of hazelnut-bushes. He taught her to tear the drying husks from the nuts and crack the nuts with stones. At his request Gertie produced two pins from unexpected parts of her small frilly dress. He found a piece of string, and they fished for perch in the creek. As they had no bait whatever, their success was not large.

A flock of ducks flew low above them, seeking a pond for the night.

"Jiminy!" Carl cried, "it's getting late. We got to hurry. It's awful far to San Francisco and—I don't know—gee! where'll we sleep to-night?"

"We hadn't ought to go on, had we?"

"Yes! Come on!"

CHAPTER II

From the creek they tramped nearly two miles, through the dark gravel-banks of the railroad cut, across the high trestle over Joralemon River where Gertie had to be coaxed from stringer to stringer. They stopped only when a gopher in a clearing demanded attention. Gertie finally forgot the superiority of age when she saw Carl whistle the quivering gopher-cry, while the gopher sat as though hypnotized on his pile of fresh black earth. Carl stalked him. As always happened, the gopher popped into his hole just before Carl reached him; but it certainly did seem that he had nearly been caught; and Gertie was jumping with excitement when Carl returned, strutting, cocking his saber-stick over his shoulder.

Gertie was tired. She, the Minneapolis girl, had not been much awed by the railroad ties nor the Arch, but now she tramped proudly beside the man who could catch gophers, till Carl inquired:

"Are you gettin' awful hungry? It's a'most supper-time."

"Yes, I *am* hungry," trustingly.

"I'm going to go and swipe some 'taters. I guess maybe there's a farm-house over there. I see a chimbly beyond the slough. You stay here."

"I dassn't stay alone. Oh, I better go home. I'm scared."

"Come on. I won't let nothing hurt you."

They circled a swamp surrounded by woods, Carl's left arm about her, his right clutching the saber. Though the sunset was magnificent and a gay company of blackbirds swayed on the reeds of the slough, dusk was sneaking out from the underbrush that blurred the forest floor, and Gertie caught the panic fear. She wished to go home at once. She saw darkness reaching for them. Her mother would unquestionably whip her for staying out so late. She discovered a mud smear on the side of her skirt, and a shoe-button was gone. She was cold. Finally, if she missed supper at home she would get no tea-biscuits and honey. Gertie's polite little stomach knew its rights and insisted upon them.

"I wish I hadn't come!" she lamented. "I wish I hadn't. Do you s'pose mamma will be dreadfully angry? Won't you 'splain to her? You will, won't you?"

It was Carl's duty, as officer commanding, to watch the blackened stumps that sprang from the underbrush. And there was Something, 'way over in the woods, beyond the trees horribly gashed to whiteness by lightning. Perhaps the Something hadn't moved; perhaps it *was* a stump——

But he answered her loudly, so that lurking robbers might overhear: "I know a great big man over there, and he's a friend of mine; he's a brakie on the M. & D., and he lets me ride in the caboose any time I want to, and he's right behind us. (I was just making b'lieve, Gertie; I'll 'splain everything to your mother.) He's bigger 'n anybody!" More conversationally: "Aw, Jiminy! Gertie, don't cry! Please don't. I'll take care of you. And if you ain't going to have any supper we'll swipe some 'taters and roast 'em." He gulped. He hated to give up, to return to woodshed and chicken-yard, but he conceded: "I guess maybe we hadn't better go seek-our-fortunes no more to———"

A long wail tore through the air. The children shrieked together and fled, stumbling in dry bog, weeping in terror. Carl's backbone was all one prickling bar of ice. But he waved his stick fiercely, and, because he had to care for her, was calm enough to realize that the wail must have been the cry of the bittern.

"It wasn't nothing but a bird, Gertie; it can't hurt us. Heard 'em lots of times."

Nevertheless, he was still trembling when they reached the edge of a farm-yard clearing beyond the swamp. It was gray-dark. They could see only the mass of a barn and a farmer's cabin, both new to Carl. Holding her hand, he whispered:

"They must be some 'taters or 'beggies in the barn. I'll sneak in and see. You stand here by the corn-crib and work out some ears between the bars. See— like this."

He left her. The sound of her frightened snivel aged him. He tiptoed to the barn door, eying a light in the farm-house. He reached far up to the latch of the broad door and pulled out the wooden pin. The latch slipped noisily from its staple. The door opened with a groaning creek and banged against the barn.

Paralyzed, hearing all the silence of the wild clearing, he waited. There was a step in the house. The door opened. A huge farmer, tousle-haired, black-bearded, held up a lamp and peered out. It was the Black Dutchman.

The Black Dutchman was a living legend. He often got drunk and rode past Carl's home at night, lashing his horses and cursing in German. He had once thrashed the school-teacher for whipping his son. He had no friends.

"Oh dear, oh dear, I wisht I was home!" sobbed Carl; but he started to run to Gertie's protection.

The Black Dutchman set down the lamp. "*Wer ist da?* I see you! Damnation!" he roared, and lumbered out, seizing a pitchfork from the manure-pile.

Carl galloped up to Gertie, panting, "He's after us!" and dragged her into the hazel-bushes beyond the corn-crib. As his country-bred feet found and followed a path toward deeper woods, he heard the Black Dutchman beating the bushes with his pitchfork, shouting:

"Hiding! I know vere you are! *Hah!*"

Carl jerked his companion forward till he lost the path. There was no light. They could only crawl on through the bushes, whose malicious fingers stung Gertie's face and plucked at her proud frills. He lifted her over fallen trees, freed her from branches, and all the time, between his own sobs, he encouraged her and tried to pretend that their incredible plight was not the end of the world, whimpering:

"We're a'most on the road now, Gertie; honest we are. I can't hear him now. I ain't afraid of him—he wouldn't dast hurt us or my pa would fix him."

"Oh! I hear him! He's coming! Oh, please save me, Carl!"

"Gee! run fast!... Aw, I don't hear him. I ain't afraid of him!"

They burst out on a grassy woodland road and lay down, panting. They could see a strip of stars overhead; and the world was dark, silent, in the inscrutable night of autumn. Carl said nothing. He tried to make out where they were— where this road would take them. It might run deeper into the woods, which he did not know as he did the Arch environs; and he had so twisted through the brush that he could not tell in what direction lay either the main wagon-road or the M. & D. track.

He lifted her up, and they plodded hand in hand till she said:

"I'm awful tired. It's awful cold. My feet hurt awfully. Carl dear, oh, pleassssse take me home now. I want my mamma. Maybe she won't whip me now. It's so dark and—ohhhhh——" She muttered, incoherently: "There! By the road! He's waiting for us!" She sank down, her arm over her face, groaning, "Don't hurt me!"

Carl straddled before her, on guard. There was a distorted mass crouched by the road just ahead. He tingled with the chill of fear, down through his thighs. He had lost his stick-saber, but he bent, felt for, and found another stick, and piped to the shadowy watcher:

"I ain't af-f-fraid of you! You gwan away from here!"

The watcher did not answer.

"I know who you are!" Bellowing with fear, Carl ran forward, furiously waving his stick and clamoring: "You better not touch me!" The stick came down with a silly, flat clack upon the watcher—a roadside boulder. "It's just a rock, Gertie! Jiminy, I'm glad! It's just a rock!... Aw, I knew it was a rock all the time! Ben Rusk gets scared every time he sees a stump in the woods, and he always thinks it's a robber."

Chattily, Carl went back, lifted her again, endured her kissing his cheek, and they started on.

"I'm so cold," Gertie moaned from time to time, till he offered:

"I'll try and build a fire. Maybe we better camp. I got a match what I swiped from the kitchen. Maybe I can make a fire, so we better camp."

"I don't want to camp. I want to go home."

"I don't know where we are, I told you."

"Can you make a regular camp-fire? Like Indians?"

"Um-huh."

"Let's.... But I rather go home."

"*You* ain't scared now. *Are* you, Gertie? Gee! you're a' awful brave girl!"

"No, but I'm cold and I wisht we had some tea-biscuits——"

Ever too complacent was Miss Gertrude Cowles, the Good Girl in whatever group she joined; but she seemed to trust in Carl's heroism, and as she murmured of a certain chilliness she seemed to take it for granted that he would immediately bring her some warmth. Carl had never heard of the romantic males who, in fiction, so frequently offer their coats to ladies fair but chill; yet he stripped off his jacket and wrapped it about her, while his gingham-clad shoulders twitched with cold.

"I can hear a crick, 'way, 'way over there. Le's camp by it," he decided.

They scrambled through the brush, Carl leading her and feeling the way. He found a patch of long grass beside the creek; with only his tremulous hands for eyes he gathered leaves, twigs, and dead branches, and piled them together in a pyramid, as he had been taught to do by the older woods-faring boys.

It was still; no wind; but Carl, who had gobbled up every word he had heard about deer-hunting in the north woods, got a great deal of interesting fear out of dreading what might happen if his one match did not light. He made Gertie kneel beside him with the jacket outspread, and he hesitated several times before he scratched the match. It flared up; the leaves caught; the pile of twigs was instantly aflame.

He wept, "Jiminy, if it hadn't lighted!..." By and by he announced, loudly, "I wasn't afraid," to convince himself, and sat up, throwing twigs on the fire grandly.

Gertie, who didn't really appreciate heroism, sighed, "I'm hungry and——"

"My second-grade teacher told us a story how they was a' arctic explorer and he was out in a blizzard——"

"——and I wish we had some tea-biscuits," concluded Gertie, companionably but firmly.

"I'll go pick some hazelnuts."

He left her feeding the flame. As he crept away, the fire behind him, he was dreadfully frightened, now that he had no one to protect. A few yards from the fire he stopped in terror. He clutched a branch so tightly that it creased his palm. Two hundred yards away, across the creek, was the small square of a lighted window hovering detached in the darkness.

For a panic-filled second Carl was sure that it must be the Black Dutchman's window. His tired child-mind whined. But there was no creek near the Black Dutchman's. Though he did not want to venture up to the unknown light, he growled, "I will if I want to!" and limped forward.

He had to cross the creek, the strange creek whose stepping-stones he did not know. Shivering, hesitant, he stripped off his shoes and stockings and dabbled the edge of the water with reluctant toes, to see if it was cold. It was.

"Dog-gone!" he swore, mightily. He plunged in, waded across.

He found a rock and held it ready to throw at the dog that was certain to come snapping at him as he tiptoed through the clearing. His wet legs smarted with cold. The fact that he was trespassing made him feel more forlornly lost than ever. But he stumbled up to the one-room shack that was now shaping itself against the sky. It was a house that, he believed, he had never seen before. When he reached it he stood for fully a minute, afraid to move. But from across the creek whimpered Gertie's call:

"Carl, oh, *Carl*, where are you?"

He had to hurry. He crept along the side of the shack to the window. It was too high in the wall for him to peer through. He felt for something to stand upon, and found a short board, which he wedged against the side of the shack.

He looked through the dusty window for a second. He sprang from the board.

Alone in the shack was the one person about Joralemon more feared, more fabulous than the Black Dutchman—"Bone" Stillman, the man who didn't believe in God.

Bone Stillman read Robert G. Ingersoll, and said what he thought. Otherwise he was not dangerous to the public peace; a lone old bachelor farmer. It was said that he had been a sailor or a policeman, a college professor or a priest, a forger or an embezzler. Nothing positive was known except that three years ago he had appeared and bought this farm. He was a grizzled man of fifty-five, with a long, tobacco-stained, gray mustache and an open-necked blue-flannel shirt. To Carl, beside the shack, Bone Stillman was all that was demoniac.

Gertie was calling again. Carl climbed upon his board and resumed his inspection, seeking a course of action.

The one-room shack was lined with tar-paper, on which were pinned lithographs of Robert G. Ingersoll, Karl Marx, and Napoleon. Under a gun-rack made of deer antlers was a cupboard half filled with dingy books, shotgun shells, and fishing tackle. Bone was reading by a pine table still littered with supper-dishes. Before him lay a clean-limbed English setter. The dog was asleep. In the shack was absolute stillness and loneliness intimidating.

While Carl watched, Bone dropped his book and said, "Here, Bob, what d'you think of single-tax, heh?"

Carl gazed apprehensively.... No one but Bone was in the shack.... It was said that the devil himself sometimes visited here.... On Carl was the chill of a nightmare.

The dog raised his head, stirred, blinked, pounded his tail on the floor, and rose, a gentlemanly, affable chap, to lay his muzzle on Bone's knee while the solitary droned:

"This fellow says in this book here that the city 's the natural place to live— aboriginal tribes prove man 's naturally gregarious. What d'you think about it, heh, Bob?... Bum country, this is. No thinking. What in the name of the seven saintly sisters did I ever want to be a farmer for, heh?

"Let's skedaddle, Bob.

"I ain't an atheist. I'm an agnostic.

"Lonely, Bob? Go over and talk to his whiskers, Karl Marx. He's liberal. He don't care what you say. He—— Oh, shut up! You're damn poor company. Say something!"

Carl, still motionless, was the more agonized because there was no sound from Gertie, not even a sobbing call. Anything might have happened to her. While he was coaxing himself to knock on the pane, Stillman puttered about the shack, petting the dog, filling his pipe. He passed out of Carl's range of vision toward the side of the room in which was the window.

A huge hand jerked the window open and caught Carl by the hair. Two wild faces stared at each other, six inches apart.

"I saw you. Came here to plague me!" roared Bone Stillman.

"Oh, mister, oh please, mister, I wasn't. Me and Gertie is lost in the woods—we——Ouch! Oh, *please* lemme go!"

"Why, you're just a brat! Come here."

The lean arm of Bone Stillman dragged Carl through the window by the slack of his gingham waist.

"Lost, heh? Where's t'other one—Gertie, was it?"

"She's over in the woods."

"Poor little tyke! Wait 'll I light my lantern."

The swinging lantern made friendly ever-changing circles of light, and Carl no longer feared the dangerous territory of the yard. Riding pick-a-back on Bone Stillman, he looked down contentedly on the dog's deferential tail beside them. They found Gertie asleep by the fire. She scarcely awoke as Stillman picked her up and carried her back to his shack. She nestled her downy hair beneath his chin and closed her eyes.

Stillman said, cheerily, as he ushered them into his mansion: "I'll hitch up and take you back to town. You young tropical tramps! First you better have a bite to eat, though. What do kids eat, bub?"

The dog was nuzzling Carl's hand, and Carl had almost forgotten his fear that the devil might appear. He was flatteringly friendly in his answer: "Porritch and meat and potatoes—only I don't like potatoes, and—*pie!*"

"'Fraid I haven't any pie, but how'd some bacon and eggs go?" As he stoked up his cannon-ball stove and sliced the bacon, Stillman continued to the children, who were shyly perched on the buffalo-robe cover of his bed, "Were you scared in the woods?"

"Yes, sir."

"Don't ever for——Da——Blast that egg! Don't forget this, son: nothing outside of you can ever hurt you. It can chew up your toes, but it can't reach you. Nobody but you can hurt you. Let me try to make that clear, old man, if I can....

"There's your fodder. Draw up and set to. Pretty sleepy, are you? I'll tell you a story. J' like to hear about how Napoleon smashed the theory of divine rule, or about how me and Charlie Weems explored Tiburon? Well——"

Though Carl afterward remembered not one word of what Bone Stillman said, it is possible that the outcast's treatment of him as a grown-up friend was one of the most powerful of the intangible influences which were to push him toward the great world outside of Joralemon. The school-bound child— taught by young ladies that the worst immorality was whispering in school; the chief virtue, a dull quietude—was here first given a reasonable basis for supposing that he was not always to be a back-yard boy.

The man in the flannel shirt, who chewed tobacco, who wrenched infinitives apart and thrust profane words between, was for fifteen minutes Carl's Froebel and Montessori.

Carl's recollection of listening to Bone blurs into one of being somewhere in the back of a wagon beside Gertie, wrapped in buffalo robes, and of being awakened by the stopping of the wagon when Bone called to a band of men with lanterns who were searching for the missing Gertie. Apparently the next second he was being lifted out before his home, and his aproned mother was kissing him and sobbing, "Oh, my boy!" He snuggled his head on her shoulder and said:

"I'm cold. But I'm going to San Francisco."

CHAPTER III

Carl Ericson, grown to sixteen and long trousers, trimmed the arc-lights for the Joralemon Power and Lighting Company, after school; then at Eddie Klemm's billiard-parlor he won two games of Kelly pool, smoked a cigarette of flake tobacco and wheat-straw paper, and "chipped in" five cents toward a can of beer.

A slender Carl, hesitating in speech, but with plenty to say; rangy as a setter pup, silken-haired; his Scandinavian cheeks like petals at an age when his companions' faces were like maps of the moon; stubborn and healthy; wearing a celluloid collar and a plain black four-in-hand; a blue-eyed, undistinguished, awkward, busy proletarian of sixteen, to whom evening clothes and poetry did not exist, but who quivered with inarticulate determinations to see Minneapolis, or even Chicago. To him it was sheer romance to parade through town with a tin haversack of carbons for the arc-lights, familiarly lowering the high-hung mysterious lamps, while his plodding acquaintances "clerked" in stores on Saturdays, or tended furnaces. Sometimes he donned the virile—and noisy—uniform of an electrician: army gauntlets, a coil of wire, pole-climbers strapped to his legs. Crunching his steel spurs into the crisp pine wood of the lighting-poles, he carelessly ascended to the place of humming wires and red cross-bars and green-glass insulators, while crowds of two and three small boys stared in awe from below. At such moments Carl did not envy the aristocratic leisure of his high-school classmate, Fatty Ben Rusk, who, as son of the leading doctor, did not work, but stayed home and read library books.

Carl's own home was not adapted to the enchantments of a boy's reading. Perfectly comfortable it was, and clean with the hard cleanness that keeps oilcloth looking perpetually unused, but it was so airlessly respectable that it doubled Carl's natural restlessness. It had been old Oscar Ericson's labor of love, but the carpenter loved shininess more than space and leisure. His model for a house would have been a pine dry-goods box grained in imitation of oak. Oscar Ericson radiated intolerance and a belief in unimaginative, unresting labor. Every evening, collarless and carpet-slippered, ruffling his broom-colored hair or stroking his large, long chin, while his shirt-tab moved ceaselessly in time to his breathing, he read a Norwegian paper. Carl's mother darned woolen socks and thought about milk-pans and the neighbors and breakfast. The creak of rockers filled the unventilated, oilcloth-floored sitting-room. The sound was as unchanging as the sacred positions of the crayon enlargement of Mrs. Ericson's father, the green-glass top-hat for matches, or the violent ingrain rug with its dog's-head pattern.

Carl's own room contained only plaster walls, a narrow wooden bed, a bureau, a kitchen chair. Fifteen minutes in this irreproachable home sent Carl off to Eddie Klemm's billiard-parlor, which was not irreproachable.

He rather disliked the bitterness of beer and the acrid specks of cigarette tobacco that stuck to his lips, but the "bunch at Eddie's" were among the few people in Joralemon who were conscious of life. Eddie's establishment was a long, white-plastered room with a pressed-steel ceiling and an unswept floor. On the walls were billiard-table-makers' calendars and a collection of cigarette-premium chromos portraying bathing girls. The girls were of lithographic complexions, almost too perfect of feature, and their lips were more than ruby. Carl admired them.

A September afternoon. The sixteen-year-old Carl was tipped back in a chair at Eddie Klemm's, one foot on a rung, while he discussed village scandals and told outrageous stories with Eddie Klemm, a brisk money-maker and vulgarian aged twenty-three, who wore a "fancy vest" and celluloid buttons on his lapels. Ben Rusk hesitatingly poked his head through the door.

Eddie Klemm called, with business-like cordiality: "H'lo, Fatty! Come in. How's your good health? Haven't reformed, have you? Going to join us rough-necks? Come on; I'll teach you to play pool. Won't cost you a cent."

"No, I guess I hadn't better. I was just looking for Carl."

"Well, well, Fatty, ain't we ree-fined! Why do we guess we hadn't to probably maybe oughtn't to had better?"

"Oh, I don't know. Some day I'll learn, I guess," sighed Fatty Ben Rusk, who knew perfectly that with a doctor father, a religious mother, and an effeminate taste for reading he could never be a town sport.

"Hey! watch out!" shrieked Eddie.

"Wh-what's the matter?" gasped Fatty.

"The floor 's falling on you!"

"Th—th——Aw, say, you're kidding me," said Fatty, weakly, with a propitiating smile.

"Don't worry, son; you're the third guy to-day that I've caught on that! Stick around, son, and sit in any time, and I'll learn you some pool. You got just the right build for a champ player. Have a cigarette?"

The social amenities whereby Joralemon prepares her youth for the graces of life having been recognized, Fatty Rusk hitched a chair beside Carl, and muttered:

"Say, Carl, here's what I wanted to tell you: I was just up to the Cowleses' to take back a French grammar I borrowed to look at——Maybe that ain't a hard-looking language! What d'you think? Mrs. Cowles told me Gertie is expected back to-morrow."

"Gee whiz! I thought she was going to stay in New York for two years! And she's only been gone six months."

"I guess Mrs. Cowles is kind of lonely without her," Ben mooned.

"So now you'll be all nice and in love with Gertie again, heh? It certainly gets me why you want to fall in love, Fatty, when you could go hunting."

"If you'd read about King Arthur and Galahad and all them instead of reading the *Scientific American*, and about these fool horseless carriages and stuff—— There never will be any practical use for horseless carriages, anyway."

"There will——" growled Carl.

"My mother says she don't believe the Lord ever intended us to ride without horses, or what did He give us horses for? And the things always get stuck in the mud and you have to walk home—mother was reading that in a newspaper, just the other day."

"Son, let me tell you, I'll own a horseless carriage some day, and I bet I go an average of twenty miles an hour with it, maybe forty."

"Oh, rats! But I was saying, if you'd read some library books you'd know about love. Why, what 'd God put love in the world for——"

"Say, will you quit explaining to me about what God did things for?"

"Ouch! Quit! Awwww, quit, Carl.... Say, listen; here's what I wanted to tell you: How if you and me and Adelaide Benner and some of us went down to the depot to meet Gertie, to-morrow? She comes in on the twelve-forty-seven."

"Well, all right. Say, Bennie, you don't want to be worried when I kid you about being in love with Gertie. I don't think I'll ever get married. But it's all right for you."

Saturday morning was so cool, so radiant, that Carl awakened early to a conviction that, no matter how important meeting Gertie might be in the cosmic scheme, he was going hunting. He was down-stairs by five. He fried two eggs, called Dollar Ingersoll, his dog—son of Robert Ingersoll Stillman, gentleman dog—then, in canvas hunting-coat and slouch-hat, tramped out of town southward, where the woods ended in prairie. Gertie's arrival was forgotten.

It was a gipsy day. The sun rolled splendidly through the dry air, over miles of wheat stubble, whose gray-yellow prickles were transmuted by distance into tawny velvet, seeming only the more spacious because of the straight, thin lines of barbed-wire fences lined with goldenrod, and solitary houses in willow groves. The dips and curves of the rolling plain drew him on; the distances satisfied his eyes. A pleasant hum of insects filled the land's wide serenity with hidden life.

Carl left a trail of happy, monotonous whistling behind him all day, as his dog followed the winding trail of prairie-chickens, as a covey of chickens rose with booming wings and he swung his shotgun for a bead. He stopped by prairie-sloughs or bright-green bogs to watch for a duck. He hailed as equals the occasional groups of hunters in two-seated buggies, quartering the fields after circling dogs. He lunched contentedly on sandwiches of cold lamb, and lay with his arms under his head, gazing at a steeple fully ten miles away.

By six of the afternoon he had seven prairie-chickens tucked inside the long pocket that lined the tail of his coat, and he headed for home, superior to miles, his quiet eyes missing none of the purple asters and goldenrod.

As he began to think he felt a bit guilty. The flowers suggested Gertie. He gathered a large bunch, poking stalks of aster among the goldenrod, examining the result at arm's-length. Yet when he stopped at the Rusks' in town, to bid Bennie take the rustic bouquet to Gertie, he replied to reproaches:

"What you making all the fuss about my not being there to meet her for? She got here all right, didn't she? What j' expect me to do? Kiss her? You ought to known it was too good a day for hunting to miss.... How's Gert? Have a good time in New York?"

Carl himself took the flowers to her, however, and was so shyly attentive to her account of New York that he scarcely stopped to speak to the Cowleses' "hired girl," who was his second cousin.... Mrs. Cowles overheard him shout, "Hello, Lena! How's it going?" to the hired girl with cousinly ease. Mrs. Cowles seemed chilly. Carl wondered why.

From month to month of his junior year in high school Carl grew more discontented. He let the lines of his Cicero fade into a gray blur that confounded Cicero's blatant virtue and Cataline's treachery, while he pictured himself tramping with snow-shoes and a mackinaw coat into the snowy solemnities of the northern Minnesota tamarack swamps. Much of his discontent was caused by his learned preceptors. The teachers for this year were almost perfectly calculated to make any lad of the slightest independence hate culture for the rest of his life. With the earnestness and

- 24 -

industry usually ascribed to the devil, "Prof" Sybrant E. Larsen (B. A. Platonis), Miss McDonald, and Miss Muzzy kept up ninety-five per cent. discipline, and seven per cent. instruction in anything in the least worth while.

Miss Muzzy was sarcastic, and proud of it. She was sarcastic to Carl when he gruffly asked why he couldn't study French instead of "all this Latin stuff." If there be any virtue in the study of Latin (and we have all forgotten all our Latin except the fact that "suburb" means "under the city"—*i. e.*, a subway), Carl was blinded to it for ever. Miss Muzzy wore eye-glasses and had no bosom. Carl's father used to say approvingly, "Dat Miss Muzzy don't stand for no nonsense," and Mrs. Dr. Rusk often had her for dinner.... Miss McDonald, fat and slow-spoken and kind, prone to use the word "dearie," to read Longfellow, and to have buttons off her shirt-waists, used on Carl a feminine weapon more unfair than the robust sarcasm of Miss Muzzy. For after irritating a self-respecting boy into rudeness by pawing his soul with damp, puffy hands, she would weep. She was a kind, honest, and reverent bovine. Carl sat under her supervision in the junior room, with its hardwood and blackboards and plaster, high windows and portraits of Washington and a President who was either Madison or Monroe (no one ever remembered which). He hated the eternal school smell of drinking-water pails and chalk and slates and varnish; he loathed the blackboard erasers, white with crayon-dust; he found inspiration only in the laboratory where "Prof" Larsen mistaught physics and rebuked questions about the useless part of chemistry—that is, the part that wasn't in their text-books.

As for literature, Ben Rusk persuaded him to try Captain Marryat and Conan Doyle. Carl met Sherlock Holmes in a paper-bound book, during a wait for flocks of mallards on the duck-pass, which was a little temple of silver birches bare with November. He crouched down in his canvas coat and rubber boots, gun across knees, and read for an hour without moving. As he tramped home, into a vast Minnesota sunset like a furnace of fantastic coals, past the garnet-tinged ice of lakes, he kept his gun cocked and under his elbow, ready for the royal robber who was dogging the personage of Baker Street.

He hunted much; distinguished himself in geometry and chemistry; nearly flunked in Cicero and English; learned to play an extraordinarily steady game of bottle pool at Eddie Klemm's.

And always Gertie Cowles, gently hesitant toward Ben Rusk's affection, kept asking Carl why he didn't come to see her oftener, and play tiddledywinks.

On the Friday morning before Christmas vacation, Carl and Ben Rusk were cleaning up the chemical laboratory, its pine experiment-bench and iron sink and rough floor. Bennie worried a rag in the sink with the resigned manner of a man who, having sailed with purple banners the sunset sea of tragedy, goes bravely on with a life gray and weary.

The town was excited. Gertie Cowles was giving a party, and she had withdrawn her invitation to Eddie Klemm. Gertie was staying away from high school, gracefully recovering from a cold. For two weeks the junior and senior classes had been furtively exhibiting her holly-decked cards of invitation. Eddie had been included, but after his quarrel with Howard Griffin, a Plato College freshman who was spending the vacation with Ray Cowles, it had been explained to Eddie that perhaps he would be more comfortable not to come to the party.

Gertie's brother, Murray, or "Ray," was the town hero. He had captained the high-school football team. He was tall and very black-haired, and he "jollied" the girls. It was said that twenty girls in Joralemon and Wakamin, and a "grass widow" in St. Hilary, wrote to him. He was now a freshman in Plato College, Plato, Minnesota. He had brought home with him his classmate, Howard Griffin, whose people lived in South Dakota and were said to be wealthy. Griffin had been very haughty to Eddie Klemm, when introduced to that brisk young man at the billiard-parlor, and now, the town eagerly learned, Eddie had been rejected of society.

In the laboratory Carl was growling: "Well, say, Fatty, if it was right for them to throw Eddie out, where do I come in? His dad 's a barber, and mine 's a carpenter, and that's just as bad. Or how about you? I was reading that docs used to be just barbers."

"Aw, thunder!" said Ben Rusk, the doctor's scion, uncomfortably, "you're just arguing. I don't believe that about doctors being barbers. Don't it tell about doctors 'way back in the Bible? Why, of course! Luke was a physician! 'Sides, it ain't a question of Eddie's being a barber's son. I sh'd think you'd realize that Gertie isn't well. She wouldn't want to have to entertain both Eddie and Griffin, and Griffin 's her guest; and besides——"

"You're getting all tangled up. If I was to let you go on you'd trip over a long word and bust your dome. Come on. We've done enough cleaning. Le's hike. Come on up to the house and help me on my bobs. I got a new scheme for pivoting the back sled.... You just wait till to-night. I'm going to tell Gertie and Mister Howard Griffin just what I think of them for being such two-bit snobs. And your future ma-in-law. Gee! I'm glad I don't have to be in love with anybody, and become a snob! Come on."

Out of this wholesome, democratic, and stuffy village life Carl suddenly stepped into the great world. A motor-car, the first he had ever seen, was drawn up before the Hennepin House.

He stopped. His china-blue eyes widened. His shoulders shot forward to a rigid stoop of astonishment. His mouth opened. He gasped as they ran to join the gathering crowd.

"A horseless carriage! Do you get that? There's one *here*!" He touched the bonnet of the two-cylinder 1901 car, and worshiped. "Under there—the engine! And there's where you steer.... I *will* own one!... Gee! you're right, Fatty; I believe I will go to college. And then I'll study mechanical engineering."

"Thought you said you were going to try and go to Annapolis and be a sailor."

"No. Rats! I'm going to own a horseless carriage, and I'm going to tour every state in the Union.... Think of seeing mountains! And the ocean! And going twenty miles an hour, like a train!"

CHAPTER IV

While Carl prepared for Gertie Cowles's party by pressing his trousers with his mother's flat-iron, while he blacked his shoes and took his weekly sponge-bath, he was perturbed by partisanship with Eddie Klemm, and a longing for the world of motors, and some anxiety as to how he could dance at the party when he could not dance.

He clumped up the new stone steps of the Cowles house carelessly, not unusually shy, ready to tell Gertie what he thought of her treatment of Eddie. Then the front door opened and an agonized Carl was smothered in politeness. His second cousin, Lena, the Cowleses' "hired girl," was opening the door, stiff and uncomfortable in a cap, a black dress, and a small frilly apron that dangled on her boniness like a lace kerchief pinned on a broom-handle. Murray Cowles rushed up. He was in evening clothes!

Behind Murray, Mrs. Cowles greeted Carl with thawed majesty: "We are so glad to have you, Carl. Won't you take your things off in the room at the head of the stairs?"

An affable introduction to Howard Griffin (also in evening clothes) was poured on Carl like soothing balm. Said Griffin: "Mighty glad to meet you, Ericson. Ray told me you'd make a ripping sprinter. The captain of the track team 'll be on the lookout for you when you get to Plato. Course you're going to go there. The U. of Minn. is too big.... You'll *do* something for old Plato. Wish I could. But all I can do is warble like a darn' dicky-bird. Have a cigarette?... They're just starting to dance. Come on, old man. Come on, Ray."

Carl was drawn down-stairs and instantly precipitated into a dance regarding which he was sure only that it was either a waltz, a two-step, or something else. It filled with glamour the Cowles library—the only parlor in Joralemon that was called a library, and the only one with a fireplace or a polished hardwood floor. Grandeur was in the red lambrequins over the doors and windows; the bead portière; a hand-painted coal-scuttle; small, round paintings of flowers set in black velvet; an enormous black-walnut bookcase with fully a hundred volumes; and the two lamps of green-mottled shades and wrought-iron frames, set on pyrographed leather skins brought from New York by Gertie. The light was courtly on the polished floor. Adelaide Benner—a new Adelaide, in chiffon over yellow satin, and patent-leather slippers—grinned at him and ruthlessly towed him into the tide of dancers. In the spell of society no one seemed to remember Eddie Klemm. Adelaide did not mention the incident.

Carl found himself bumping into others, continually apologizing to Adelaide and the rest—and not caring. For he saw a vision! Each time he turned toward the south end of the room he beheld Gertie Cowles glorified.

She was out of ankle-length dresses! She looked her impressive eighteen, in a foaming long white mull that showed her soft throat. A red rose was in her brown hair. She reclined in a big chair of leather and oak and smiled her gentlest, especially when Carl bobbed his head to her.

He had always taken her as a matter of course; she had no age, no sex, no wonder. That afternoon she had been a negligible bit of Joralemon, to be accused of snobbery toward Eddie Klemm, and always to be watched suspiciously lest she "spring some New York airs on us."... Gertie had craftily seemed unchanged after her New York enlightenment till now—here she was, suddenly grown-up and beautiful, haloed with a peculiar magic, which distinguished her from all the rest of the world.

"She's the one that would ride in that horseless carriage when I got it!" Carl exulted. "That must be a train, that thing she's got on."

After the dance he disposed of Adelaide Benner as though she were only a sister. He hung over the back of Gertie's chair and urged: "I was awful sorry to hear you were sick.... Say, you look wonderful, to-night."

"I'm so glad you could come to my party. Oh, I must speak to you about——Do you suppose you would ever get very, very angry at poor me? Me so bad sometimes."

He cut an awkward little caper to show his aplomb, and assured her, "I guess probably I'll kill you some time, all right."

"No, listen, Carl; I'm dreadfully serious. I hope you didn't go and get dreadfully angry at me about Eddie Klemm. I know Eddie 's good friends with you. And I did want to have him come to my party. But you see it was this way: Mr. Griffin is our guest (he likes you a *lot*, Carl. Isn't he a dandy fellow? I guess Adelaide and Hazel 're just crazy about him. I think he's just as swell as the men in New York). Eddie and he didn't get along very well together. It isn't anybody's fault, I don't guess. I thought Eddie would be lots happier if he didn't come, don't you see?"

"Oh no, of course; oh yes, I see. Sure. I can see how——Say, Gertie, I never did know you could look so grown-up. I suppose now you'll never play with me."

"I want you to be a good friend of mine always. We always have been awfully good friends, haven't we?"

"Yes. Do you remember how we ran away?"

"And how the Black Dutchman chassssed us!" Her sweet and complacent voice was so cheerful that he lost his awe of her new magic and chortled:

"And how we used to play pum-pum-pull-away."

She delicately leaned her cheek on a finger-tip and sighed: "Yes, I wonder if we shall ever be so happy as when we were young.... I don't believe you care to play with me so much now."

"Oh, gee! Gertie! Like to——!" The shyness was on him again. "Say, are you feeling better now? You're all over being sick?"

"Almost, now. I'll be back in school right after vacation."

"It's you that don't want to play, I guess.... I can't get over that long white dress. It makes you look so—oh, you know, so, uh——"

"They're going to dance again. I wish I felt able to dance."

"Let me sit and talk to you, Gertie, instead of dancing."

"I suppose you're dreadfully bored, though, when you could be down at the billiard-parlor?"

"Yes, I could! Not! Eddie Klemm and his fancy vest wouldn't have much chance, alongside of Griffin in his dress-suit! Course I don't want to knock Eddie. Him and me are pretty good side-kicks——"

"Oh no; I understand. It's just that people have to go with their own class, don't you think?"

"Oh Yes. Sure. I do think so, myself." Carl said it with a spurious society manner. In Gertie's aristocratic presence he desired to keep aloof from all vulgar persons.

"Of course, I think we ought to make allowances for Eddie's father, Carl, but then——"

She sighed with the responsibilities of *noblesse oblige*; and Carl gravely sighed with her.

He brought a stool and sat at her feet. Immediately he was afraid that every one was watching him. Ray Cowles bawled to them, as he passed in the waltz, "Watch out for that Carl, Gert. He's a regular badix."

Carl's scalp tickled, but he tried to be very offhand in remarking: "You must have gotten that dress in New York, didn't you? Why haven't you ever told me about New York? You've hardly told me anything at all."

"Well, I like that! And you never been near me to give me a chance!"

"I guess I was kind of scared you wouldn't care much for Joralemon, after New York."

"Why, Carl, you mustn't say that to me!"

"I didn't mean to hurt your feelings, Gertie, honestly I didn't. I was just joking. I didn't think you'd take me seriously."

"As though I could forget my old friends, even in New York!"

"I didn't think that. Straight. Please tell me about New York. That's the place, all right. Jiminy! wouldn't I like to go there!"

"I wish you could have been there, Carl. We had such fun in my school. There weren't any boys in it, but we——"

"No boys in it? Why, how's that?"

"Why, it was just for girls."

"I see," he said, fatuously, completely satisfied.

"We did have the best times, Carl. I *must* tell you about one awfully naughty thing Carrie—she was my chum in school—and I did. There was a stock company on Twenty-third Street, and we were all crazy about the actors, especially Clements Devereaux, and one afternoon Carrie told the principal she had a headache, and I asked if I could go home with her and read her the assignments for next day (they called the lessons 'assignments' there), and they thought I was such a meek little country mouse that I wouldn't ever fib, and so they let us go, and what do you think we did? She had tickets for 'The Two Orphans' at the stock company. (You've never seen 'The Two Orphans,' have you? It's perfectly splendid. I used to weep my eyes out over it.) And afterward we went and waited outside, right near the stage entrance, and what do you think? The leading man, Clements Devereaux, went right by us as near as I am to you. Oh, *Carl*, I wish you could have seen him! Maybe he wasn't the handsomest thing! He had the blackest, curliest hair, and he wore a thumb ring."

"I don't think much of all these hamfatters," growled Carl. "Actors always go broke and have to walk back to Chicago. Don't you think it 'd be better to be a civil engineer or something like that, instead of having to slick up your hair and carry a cane? They're just dudes."

"Why! of course, Carl, you silly boy! You don't suppose I'd take Clements seriously, do you? You silly boy!"

"I'm not a boy."

"I don't mean it that way." She sat up, touched his shoulder, and sank back. He blushed with bliss, and the fear that some one had seen, as she continued: "I always think of you as just as old as I am. We always will be, won't we?"

"Yes!"

"Now you must go and talk to Doris Carson. Poor thing, she always is a wall-flower."

However much he thought of common things as he left her, beyond those common things was the miracle that Gertie had grown into the one perfect, divinely ordained woman, and that he would talk to her again. He danced the Virginia reel. Instead of clumping sulkily through the steps, as at other parties, he heeded Adelaide Benner's lessons, and watched Gertie in the hope that she would see how well he was dancing. He shouted a demand that they play "Skip to Maloo," and cried down the shy girls who giggled that they were too old for the childish party-game. He howled, without prejudice in favor of any particular key, the ancient words:

"Rats in the sugar-bowl, two by two,Bats in the belfry, two by two,Rats in the sugar-bowl, two by two,Skip to Maloo, my darling."

In the nonchalant company of the smarter young bachelors up-stairs he smoked a cigarette. But he sneaked away. He paused at the bend in the stairs. Below him was Gertie, silver-gowned, wonderful. He wanted to go down to her. He would have given up his chance for a motor-car to be able to swagger down like an Eddie Klemm. For the Carl Ericson who sailed his ice-boat over inch-thick ice was timid now. He poked into the library, and in a nausea of discomfort he conversed with Mrs. Cowles, Mrs. Cowles doing the conversing.

"Are you going to be a Republican or a Democrat, Carl?" asked the forbidding lady.

"Yessum," mumbled Carl, peering over at Gertie's throne, where Ben Rusk was being cultured.

"I hope you are having a good time. We always wish our young friends to have an especially good time at Gertrude's parties," Mrs. Cowles sniffed, and bowed away.

Carl sat beside Adelaide Benner in the decorous and giggling circle that ringed the room, waiting for the "refreshments." He was healthily interested in devouring maple ice-cream and chocolate layer-cake. But all the while he was spying on the group gathering about Gertie—Ben Rusk, Howard Griffin, and Joe Jordan. He took the most strategic precautions lest some one think that he wanted to look at Gertie; made such ponderous efforts to prove he was care-free that every one knew something was the matter.

Ben Rusk was taking no part in the gaiety of Howard and Joe. The serious man of letters was not easily led into paths of frivolity. Carl swore to himself: "Ben 's the only guy I know that's got any delicate feelings. He appreciates how Gertie feels when she's sick, poor girl. He don't make a goat of himself, like Joe.... Or maybe he's got a stomach-ache."

"Post-office!" cried Howard Griffin to the room at large. "Come on! We're all of us going to be kids again, and play post-office. Who's the first girl wants to be kissed?"

"The idea!" giggled Adelaide Benner.

"Me for Adelaide!" bawled Joe Jordan.

"Oh, Jo-oe, bet I kiss Gertie!" from Irving Lamb.

"The idea!"

"Just as if we were children——"

"He must think we're kids again——"

"Shamey! Winnie wants to be kissed, and Carl won't——"

"I don't, either, so there——"

"I think it's awful."

"Bet I kiss Gertie——"

Carl was furious at all of them as they strained their shoulders forward from their chairs and laughed. He asked himself, "Haven't these galoots got any sense?"

To speak so lightly of kissing Gertie! He stared at the smooth rounding of her left cheek below the cheek-bone till it took a separate identity, and its white softness filled the room.

Ten minutes afterward, playing "post-office," he was facing Gertie in the semi-darkness of the sitting-room, authorized by the game to kiss her; shut in with his divinity.

She took his hand. Her voice was crooning, "Are you going to kiss me terribly hard?"

He tried to be gracefully mocking: "Oh yes! Sure! I'm going to eat you alive."

She was waiting.

He wished that she would not hold his hand. Within he groaned, "Gee whiz! I feel foolish!" He croaked: "Do you feel better, now? You'll catch more cold in here, won't you? There's kind of a draught. Lemme look at this window."

Crossing to the obviously tight window, he ran his finger along the edge of the sash with infinite care. He trembled. In a second, *now*, he had to turn and make light of the lips which he would fain have approached with ceremony pompous and lingering.

Gertie flopped into a chair, laughing: "I believe you're afraid to kiss me! 'Fraid cat! You'll never be a squire of dames, like those actors are! All right for you!"

"I am not afraid!" he piped.... Even his prized semi-bass voice had deserted him.... He rushed to the back of her chair and leaned over, confused, determined. Hastily he kissed her. The kiss landed on the tip of her cold nose.

And the whole party was tumbling in, crying:

"Time 's up! You can't hug her all evening!"

"Did you see? He kissed her on the nose!"

"Did he? Ohhhhh!"

"Time 's up. Can't try it again."

Joe Jordan, in the van, was dancing fantastically, scraping his forefinger at Carl, in token of disgrace.

The riotous crowd, Gertie and Carl among them, flooded out again. To show that he had not minded the incident of the misplaced kiss, Carl had to be very loud and merry in the library for a few minutes; but when the game of "post-office" was over and Mrs. Cowles asked Ray to turn down the lamp in the sitting-room, Carl insisted:

"I'll do it, Mrs. Cowles; I'm nearer 'n Ray," and bolted.

He knew that he was wicked in not staying in the library and continuing his duties to the party. He had to crowd into a minute all his agonizing and be back at once.

It was beautiful in the stilly sitting-room, away from the noisy crowd, to hear love's heart beating. He darted to the chair where Gertie had sat and guiltily kissed its arm. He tiptoed to the table, blew out the lamp, remembered that he should only have turned down the wick, tried to raise the chimney, burnt his fingers, snatched his handkerchief, dropped it, groaned, picked up the handkerchief, raised the chimney, put it on the table, searched his pockets for a match, found it, dropped it, picked it up from the floor, dropped his knife from his pocket as he stooped, felt itchy about the scalp, picked up the knife, relighted the lamp, exquisitely adjusted the chimney—and again blew out the flame. And swore.

As darkness whirled into the room again the vision of Gertie came nearer. Then he understood his illness, and gasped: "Great jumping Jupiter on a high mountain! I guess—I'm—in—love! *Me!*"

The party was breaking up. Each boy, as he accompanied a girl from the yellow lamplight into the below-zero cold, shouted and scuffled the snow, to indicate that there was nothing serious in his attentions, and immediately tried to manœuver his girl away from the others. Mrs. Cowles was standing in the hall—not hurrying the guests away, you understand, but perfectly resigned to accepting any farewells—when Gertie, moving gently among them with little sounds of pleasure, penned Carl in a corner and demanded:

"Are you going to see some one home? I suppose you'll forget poor me completely, now!"

"I will not!"

"I wanted to tell you what Ray and Mr. Griffin said about Plato and about being lawyers. Isn't it nice you'll know them when you go to Plato?"

"Yes, it 'll be great."

"Mr. Griffin 's going to be a lawyer and maybe Ray will, too, and why don't you think about being one? You can get to be a judge and know all the best people. It would be lovely.... Refining influences—they—that's——"

"I couldn't ever be a high-class lawyer like Griffin will," said Carl, his head on one side, much pleased.

"You silly boy, of course you could. I think you've got just as much brains as he has, and Ray says they all look up to him even in Plato. And I don't see why Plato isn't just as good—of course it isn't as large, but it's so select and the faculty can give you so much more individual attention, and I don't see why it isn't every bit as good as Yale and Michigan and all those Eastern colleges.... Howard—Mr. Griffin—he says that he wouldn't ever have thought of being a lawyer only a girl was such a good influence with him, and if you get to be a famous man, too, maybe I'll have been just a teeny-weeny bit of an influence, too, won't I?"

"Oh *yes!*"

"I must get back now and say good-by to my guests. Good night, Carl."

"I am going to study—you just watch me; and if I do get to go to Plato—— Oh, gee! you always have been a good influence——" He noticed that Doris

Carson was watching them. "Well, I gotta be going. I've had a peach of a time. Good night."

Doris Carson was expectantly waiting for one of the boys to "see her home," but Carl guiltily stole up to Ben Rusk and commanded:

"Le's hike, Fatty. Le's take a walk. Something big to tell you."

CHAPTER V

Carl kicked up the snow in moon-shot veils. The lake boomed. For all their woolen mittens, ribbed red-cotton wristlets, and plush caps with ear-laps, the cold seared them. Carl encouraged Ben to discourse of Gertie and the delights of a long and hopeless love. He discovered that, actually, Ben had suddenly fallen in love with Adelaide Benner. "Gee!" he exulted. "Maybe that gives me a chance with Gertie, then. But I won't let her know Ben ain't in love with her any more. Jiminy! ain't it lucky Gertie liked me just when Ben fell in love with somebody else! Funny the way things go; and her never knowing about Ben." He laid down his cards. While they plowed through the hard snow-drifts, swinging their arms against their chests like milkmen, he blurted out all his secret: that Gertie was the "slickest girl in town"; that no one appreciated her.

"Ho, ho!" jeered Ben.

"I thought you were crazy about her, and then you start kidding about her! A swell bunch of chivalry you got, you and your Galahad! You———"

"Don't you go jumping on Galahad, or I'll fight!"

"He was all right, but you ain't," said Carl. "You hadn't ought to ever sneer at love."

"Why, you said, just this afternoon———"

"You poor yahoo, I was only teasing you. No; about Gertie. It's like this: she was telling me a lot about how Griffin 's going to be a lawyer, about how much they make in cities, and I've about decided I'll be a lawyer."

"Thought you were going to be a mechanical engineer?"

"Well, can't a fellow change his mind? When you're an engineer you're always running around the country, and you never get shaved or anything, and there ain't any refining influences———"

The absorbing game of "what we're going to be" made them forget snow and cold-squeezed fingers. Ben, it was decided, was to own a newspaper and support C. Ericson, Attorney-at-Law, in his dramatic run for state senator.

Carl did not mention Gertie again. But it all meant Gertie.

Carl made his round trimming the arc-lights next day, apparently a rudely healthy young person, but really a dreamer love-lorn and misunderstood. He had found a good excuse for calling on Gertie, at noon, and had been informed that Miss Gertrude was taking a nap. He determined to go up the lake for rabbits. He doubted if he would ever return, and wondered if he would be missed. Who would care if he froze to death? He wouldn't! (Though he did seem to be taking certain precautions, by donning a mackinaw coat, two pairs of trousers, two pairs of woolen socks, and shoe-packs.)

He was graceful as an Indian when he swept, on skees he had made himself, across miles of snow covering the lake and dazzling in the diffused light of an even gray sky. The reeds by the marshy shore were frost-glittering and clattered faintly. Marshy islands were lost in snow. Hummocks and ice-jams and the weaving patterns of mink tracks were blended in one white immensity, on which Carl was like a fly on a plaster ceiling. The world was deserted. But Carl was not lonely. He forgot all about Gertie as he cached his skees by the shore and prowled through the woods, leaping on brush-piles and shooting quickly when a rabbit ran out.

When he had bagged three rabbits he was besieged by the melancholy of loneliness, the perfection of the silver-gowned Gertie. He wanted to talk. He thought of Bone Stillman.

It was very likely that Bone was, as usual in winter, up beyond Big Bend, fishing for pickerel with tip-ups. A never-stopping dot in the dusk, Carl headed for Big Bend, three miles away.

The tip-up fisher watches a dozen tip-ups—short, automatic fishing-rods, with lines running through the ice, the pivoted arm signaling the presence of a fish at the bait. Sometimes, for warmth, he has a tiny shanty, perhaps five feet by six in ground area, heated by a powder-can stove. Bone Stillman often spent the night in his movable shanty on the lake, which added to his reputation as village eccentric. But he was more popular, now, with the local sporting gentlemen, who found that he played a divine game of poker.

"Hello, son!" he greeted Carl. "Come in. Leave them long legs of yours up on shore if there ain't room."

"Say, Bone, do you think a fellow ever ought to join a church?"

"Depends. Why?"

"Well, suppose he was going to be a lawyer and go in for politics?"

"Look here. What 're you thinking of becoming a lawyer for?"

"Didn't say I was."

"Of course you're thinking of it. Look here. Don't you know you've got a chance of seeing the world? You're one of the lucky people that can have a touch of the wanderlust without being made useless by it—as I have. You may, you *may* wander in thought as well as on freight-trains, and discover something for the world. Whereas a lawyer——They're priests. They decide what's holy and punish you if you don't guess right. They set up codes that it takes lawyers to interpret, and so they perpetuate themselves. I don't mean to say you're extraordinary in having a chance to wander. Don't get the big-head over it. You're a pretty average young American. There's plenty of the same kind. Only, mostly they get tied up to something before they see what a big world there is to hike in, and I want to keep you from that. I'm not roasting lawyers——Yes, I am, too. They live in calf-bound books. Son, son, for God's sake live in life."

"Yes, but look here, Bone; I was just thinking about it, that's all. You're always drumming it into me about not taking anything for granted. Anyway, by the time I go to Plato I'll know——"

"D'you mean to say you're going to that back-creek nunnery? That Blackhaw University? Are you going to play checkers all through life?"

"Oh, I don't know, now, Bone. Plato ain't so bad. A fellow's got to go some place so he can mix with people that know what's the proper thing to do. Refining influences and like that."

"Proper! *Refining!* Son, son, are you going to get Joralemonized? If you want what the French folks call the grand manner, if you're going to be a tip-top, A Number 1, genuwine grand senyor, or however they pronounce it, why, all right, go to it; that's one way of playing a big game. But when it comes down to a short-bit, fresh-water sewing-circle like Plato College, where an imitation scholar teaches you imitation translations of useless classics, and amble-footed girls teach you imitation party manners that 'd make you just as plumb ridic'lous in a real *salon* as they would in a lumber-camp, why——Oh, sa-a-a-y! I've got it. Girls, eh? What girl 've you been falling in love with to get this Plato idea from, eh?"

"Aw, I ain't in love, Bone."

"No, I don't opine you are. At your age you got about as much chance of being in love as you have of being a grandfather. But somehow I seem to have a little old suspicion that you *think* you're in love. But it's none of my business, and I ain't going to ask questions about it." He patted Carl on the shoulder, moving his arm with difficulty in their small, dark space. "Son, I've learned this in my life—and I've done quite some hiking at that, even if I didn't have the book-l'arnin' and the git-up-and-git to make anything out of my experience. It's a thing I ain't big enough to follow up, but I know it's there. Life is just a little old checker game played by the alfalfa contingent at the country store unless you've got an ambition that's too big to ever quite lasso it. You want to know that there's something ahead that's bigger and more beautiful than anything you've ever seen, and never stop till—well, till you can't follow the road any more. And anything or anybody that doesn't pack any surprises—get that?—*surprises* for you, is dead, and you want to slough it like a snake does its skin. You want to keep on remembering that Chicago's beyond Joralemon, and Paris beyond Chicago, and beyond Paris—well, maybe there's some big peak of the Himalayas."

For hours they talked, Bone desperately striving to make his dreams articulate to Carl—and to himself. They ate fish fried on the powder-can stove, with half-warm coffee. They walked a few steps outside the shack in the ringing cold, to stretch stiff legs. Carl saw a world of unuttered freedom and beauty forthshadowed in Bone's cloudy speech. But he was melancholy. For he was going to give up his citizenship in wonderland for Gertie Cowles.

Gertie continued to enjoy ill health for another week. Every evening Carl walked past her house, hoping that he might see her at a window, longing to dare to call. Each night he pictured rescuing her from things—rescuing her from fire, from drowning, from evil men. He felt himself the more bound to her by the social recognition of having his name in the *Joralemon Dynamite*, the following Thursday:

One of the pleasantest affairs of the holiday season among the younger set was held last Friday evening, when Gertrude Cowles entertained a number of her young friends at a party at her mother's handsome residence on Maple Hill. Among those present were Mesdames Benner and Rusk, who came in for a brief time to assist in the jollities of the evening, Misses Benner, Carson, Wesselius, Madlund, Ripka, Smith, Lansing, and Brick; and Messrs. Ray Cowles, his classmate Howard Griffin, who is spending his vacation here from Plato College, Carl Ericson, Joseph Jordan, Irving Lamb, Benjamin Rusk, Nels Thorsten, Peter Schoenhof, and William T. Upham. After dancing and games, which were thoroughly enjoyed by all present, and a social hour spent in discussing the events of the season in J. H. S., a most delicious repast was served and the party adjourned, one and all voting that they had been royally entertained.

The glory was the greater because at least seven names had been omitted from the list of guests. Such social recognition satisfied Carl—for half an hour. Possibly it nerved him finally to call on Gertie.

Since for a week he had been dreading a chilly reception when he should call, he was immeasurably surprised when he did call and got what he expected. He had not expected the fates to be so treacherous as to treat him as he expected, after he had disarmed them by expecting it.

When he rang the bell he was an immensely grown-up lawyer (though he couldn't get his worn, navy-blue tie to hang exactly right). He turned into a crestfallen youth as Mrs. Cowles opened the door and waited—waited!—for him to speak, after a crisp:

"Well? What is it, Carl?"

"Why, uh, I just thought I'd come and see how Gertie is."

"Gertrude is much better, thank you. I presume she will return to school at the end of vacation."

The hall behind Mrs. Cowles seemed very stately, very long.

"I've heard a lot saying they hoped she was better."

"You may tell them that she is better."

Mrs. Cowles shivered. No one could possibly have looked more like a person closing a door without actually closing one. "Lena!" she shrieked, "close the kitchen door. There's a draught." She turned back to Carl.

The shy lover vanished. An angry young man challenged, "If Gertie 's up I think I'll come in a few minutes and see her."

"Why, uh——" hesitated Mrs. Cowles.

He merely walked in past her. His anger kept its own council, for he could depend upon Gertie's warm greeting—lonely Gertie, he would bring her the cheer of the great open.

The piano sounded in the library, and the voice of the one perfect girl mingled with a man's tenor in "Old Black Joe." Carl stalked into the library. Gertie was there, much corseted, well powdered, wearing a blue foulard frenziedly dotted with white, and being cultured in company with Dr. Doyle, the lively young dentist who had recently taken an office in the National Bank Block. He was a graduate of the University of Minnesota—dental department. He had oily black hair, and smiled with gold-filled teeth before one came to the real point of a joke. He sang in the Congregational church choir, and played tennis in a crimson-and-black blazer—the only one in Joralemon.

To Carl Dr. Doyle was dismayingly mature and smart. He horribly feared him as a rival. For the second time that evening he did not balk fate by fearing it. The dentist was a rival. After fluttering about the mature charms of Miss Dietz, the school drawing-teacher, and taking a tentative buggy-ride or two with the miller's daughter, Dr. Doyle was bringing all the charm of his professional position and professional teeth and patent-leather shoes to bear upon Gertie.

And Gertie was interested. Obviously. She was all of eighteen to-night. She frowned slightly as she turned on the piano-stool at Carl's entrance, and mechanically: "This is a pleasant surprise." Then, enthusiastically: "Isn't it too bad that Dr. Doyle was out of town, or I would have invited him to my party, and he would have given us some of his lovely songs.... Do try the second verse, doctor. The harmony is so lovely."

Carl sat at the other end of the library from Gertie and the piano, while Mrs. Cowles entertained him. He obediently said "Yessum" and "No, 'm" to the observations which she offered from the fullness of her lack of experience of life. He sat straight and still. Behind his fixed smile he was simultaneously longing to break into the musical fiesta, and envying the dentist's ability to get married without having to wait to grow up, and trying to follow what Mrs. Cowles was saying.

She droned, while crocheting with high-minded industry a useless piano-scarf, "Do you still go hunting, Carl?"

"Yessum. Quite a little rabbit-hunting. Oh, not very much."

(At the distant piano, across the shining acres of floor, the mystical woman and a dentist had ceased singing, and were examining a fresh sheet of music. The dentist coyly poked his finger at her coiffure, and she slapped the finger, gurgling.)

"I hope you don't neglect your school work, though, Carl." Mrs. Cowles held the scarf nearer the lamp and squinted at it, deliberately and solemnly, through the eye-glasses that lorded it atop her severe nose. A headachy scent of moth-balls was in the dull air. She forbiddingly moved the shade of the lamp about a tenth of an inch. She removed some non-existent dust from the wrought-iron standard. Her gestures said that the lamp was decidedly more chic than the pink-shaded hanging lamps, raised and lowered on squeaking chains, which characterized most Joralemon living-rooms. She glanced at the red lambrequin over the nearest window. The moth-ball smell grew more stupifying.

Carl felt stuffy in the top of his nose as he mumbled, "Oh, I work pretty hard at chemistry, but, gee! I can't see much to all this Latin."

"When you're a little *older*, Carl, you'll *learn* that the things you like now aren't necessarily the things that are *good* for you. I used to say to Gertrude—of course she is older than you, but she hasn't been a young lady for so very long, even yet—and I used to say to her, 'Gertrude, you will do exactly what I *tell* you to, and not what you *want* to do, and we shall make—no—more—words—*about* it!' And I think she *sees* now that her mother was right about some things! Dr. Doyle said to me, and of course you know, Carl, that he's a very fine scholar—our pastor told me that the doctor reads French better than *he* does, and the doctor's told me some things about modern French authors that I didn't know, and I used to read French almost as well as

English, when I was a girl, my teachers all told me—and he says that he thinks that Gertrude has a very fine mind, and he was *so* glad that she hasn't been taken in by all this wicked, hysterical way girls have to-day of thinking they know more than their mothers."

"Yes, she is—Gertie is——I think she's got a very fine mind," Carl commented.

(From the other end of the room Gertie could be overheard confiding to the dentist in tones of hushed and delicious adult scandal, "They say that when she was in St. Paul she——")

"So," Mrs. Cowles serenely sniffed on, while the bridge of Carl's nose felt broader and broader, stretching wider and wider, as that stuffy feeling increased and the intensive heat stung his eyelids, "you see you mustn't think because you'd rather play around with the boys than study Latin, Carl, that it's the fault of your Latin-teacher." She nodded at him with a condescending smile that was infinitely insulting.

He knew it and resented it, but he did not resent it actively, for he was busy marveling, "How the dickens is it I never heard Doc Doyle was stuck on Gertie? Everybody thought he was going with Bertha. Dang him, anyway! The way he snickers, you'd think she was his best girl."

Mrs. Cowles was loftily pursuing her pillared way: "Latin was *known* to be the best study for developing the mind a long, long time——" And her clicking crochet-needles impishly echoed, "A long, *long* time," and the odor of moth-balls got down into Carl's throat, while in the golden Olympian atmosphere at the other end of the room Gertie coyly pretended to slap the dentist's hand with a series of tittering taps. "A long, *long* time before either you or I were born, Carl, and we can't very well set ourselves up to be wiser than the wisest men that ever lived, now *can* we?" Again the patronizing smile. "That would scarcely——"

Carl resolved: "This 's got to stop. I got to do something." He felt her monologue as a blank steel wall which he could not pierce. Aloud: "Yes, that's so, I guess. Say, that's a fine dress Gertie 's got on to-night, ain't it.... Say, I been learning to play crokinole at Ben Rusk's. You got a board, haven't you? Would you like to play? Does the doctor play?"

"Indeed, I haven't the slightest idea, but I have very little doubt that he does—he plays tennis so beautifully. He is going to teach Gertrude, in the spring." She stopped, and again held the scarf up to the light. "I am so glad that my girly, that was so naughty once and ran away with you—I don't think I shall *ever* get over the awful fright I had that night!—I am so glad that, now she is growing up, clever people like Dr. Doyle appreciate her so much, so very much."

She dropped her crochet to her lap and stared squarely at Carl. Her warning that he would do exceedingly well to go home was more than plain. He stared back, agitated but not surrendering. Deliberately, almost suavely, with ten years of experience added to the sixteen years that he had brought into the room, he said:

"I'll see if they'd like to play." He sauntered to the other end of the room, abashed before the mystic woman, and ventured: "I saw Ray, to-day.... I got to be going, pretty quick, but I was wondering if you two felt like playing some crokinole?"

Gertie said, slowly: "I'd like to, Carl, but——Unless you'd like to play, doctor?"

"Why of course it's *comme il faut* to play, Miss Cowles, but I was just hoping to have the pleasure of hearing you make some more of your delectable music," bowed the dentist, and Gertie bowed back; and their smiles joined in a glittery bridge of social aplomb.

"Oh yes," from Carl, "that—yes, do——But you hadn't ought to play too much if you haven't been well."

"Oh, Carl!" shrieked Gertie. "'Ought not to,' not 'hadn't ought to'!"

"'Ought not to,'" repeated Mrs. Cowles, icily, while the dentist waved his hand in an amused manner and contributed:

"Ought not to say 'hadn't ought to,' as my preceptor used to tell me.... I'd like to hear you sing Longfellow's 'Psalm of Life,' Miss Cowles."

"Don't you think Longfellow's a bum poet?" growled Carl. "Bone Stillman says Longfellow's the grind-organ of poetry. Like this: 'Life is re-al, life is earnest, tum te diddle dydle dum!'"

"Carl," ordered Mrs. Cowles, "you will please to never mention that Stillman person in my house!"

"Oh, Carl!" rebuked Gertie. She rose from the piano-stool. Her essence of virginal femininity, its pure and cloistered and white-camisoled odor, bespelled Carl to fainting timidity. And while he was thus defenseless the dentist thrust:

"Why, they tell me Stillman doesn't even believe the Bible!"

Carl was not to retrieve his credit with Gertie, but he couldn't betray Bone Stillman. Hastily: "Yes, maybe, that way——Oh, say, doctor, Pete Jordan was telling me" (liar!) "that you were one of the best tennis-players at the U."

Gertie sat down again.

The dentist coyly fluffed his hair and deprecated, "Oh no, I wouldn't say that!"

Carl had won. Instantly they three became a country club of urban aristocrats, who laughed at the poor rustics of Joralemon for knowing nothing of golf and polo. Carl was winning their tolerance—though not their close attention—by relating certain interesting facts from the inside pages of the local paper as to how far the tennis-rackets sold in one year would extend, if laid end to end, when he saw Gertie and her mother glance at the hall. Gertie giggled. Mrs. Cowles frowned. He followed their glance.

Clumping through the hall was his second cousin, Lena, the Cowleses' "hired girl." Lena nodded and said, "Hallo, Carl!"

Gertie and the dentist raised their eyebrows at each other.

Carl talked for two minutes about something, he did not know what, and took his leave. In the intensity of his effort to be resentfully dignified he stumbled over the hall hat-rack. He heard Gertie yelp with laughter.

"I *got* to go to college—be worthy of her!" he groaned, all the way home. "And I can't afford to go to the U. of M. I'd like to be free, like Bone says, but I've got to go to Plato."

CHAPTER VI

Plato College, Minnesota, is as earnest and undistinguished, as provincially dull and pathetically human, as a spinster missionary. Its two hundred or two hundred and fifty students come from the furrows, asking for spiritual bread, and are given a Greek root. Red-brick buildings, designed by the architect of county jails, are grouped about that high, bare, cupola-crowned gray-stone barracks, the Academic Building, like red and faded blossoms about a tombstone. In the air is the scent of crab-apples and meadowy prairies, for a time, but soon settles down a winter bitter as the learning of the Rev. S. Alcott Wood, D.D., the president. The town and college of Plato disturb the expanse of prairie scarce more than a group of haystacks. In winter the walks blur into the general whiteness, and the trees shrink to chilly skeletons, and the college is like five blocks set on a frozen bed-sheet—no shelter for the warm and timid soul, yet no windy peak for the bold. The snow wipes out all the summer-time individuality of place, and the halls are lonelier at dusk than the prairie itself—far lonelier than the yellow-lighted jerry-built shops in the town. The students never lose, for good or bad, their touch with the fields. From droning class-rooms the victims of education see the rippling wheat in summer; and in winter the impenetrable wall of sky. Footsteps and quick laughter of men and girls, furtively flirting along the brick walls under the beautiful maples, do make Plato dear to remember. They do not make it brilliant. They do not explain the advantages of leaving the farm for another farm.

To the freshman, Carl Ericson, descending from the dusty smoking-car of the M. & D., in company with tumultuous youths in pin-head caps and enormous sweaters, the town of Plato was metropolitan. As he walked humbly up Main Street and beheld two four-story buildings and a marble bank and an interurban trolley-car, he had, at last, an idea of what Minneapolis and Chicago must be. Two men in sweaters adorned with a large "P," athletes, generals, heroes, walked the streets in the flesh, and he saw—it really was there, for him!—the "College Book Store," whose windows were filled with leather-backed treatises on Greek, logic, and trigonometry; and, finally, he was gaping through a sandstone gateway at four buildings, each of them nearly as big as the Joralemon High School, surrounding a vast stone castle.

He entered the campus. He passed an old man with white side-whiskers and a cord on his gold-rimmed eye-glasses; an aged old man who might easily be a professor. A blithe student with "Y. M. C. A. Receptn. Com." large on his hat-band, rushed up to Carl, shook his hand busily, and inquired:

"Freshman, old man? Got your room yet? There's a list of rooming-houses over at the Y. M. Come on, I'll show you the way."

He was received in Academe, in Arcadia, in Elysium; in fact, in Plato College.

He was directed to a large but decomposing house conducted by the widow of a college janitor, and advised to take a room at $1.75 a week for his share of the rent. That implied taking with the room a large, solemn room-mate, fresh from teaching country school, a heavy, slow-spoken, serious man of thirty-one, named Albert Smith, registered as A. Smith, and usually known as "Plain Smith." Plain Smith sat studying in his cotton socks, and never emptied the wash-basin. He remarked, during the first hour of their discourse in the groves of Academe: "I hope you ain't going to bother me by singing and skylarking around. I'm here to work, bub." Smith then returned to the large books which he was diligently scanning that he might find wisdom, while Carl sniffed at the brown-blotched wall-paper, the faded grass matting, the shallow, standing wardrobe.... He liked the house, however. It had a real bath-room! He could, for the first time in his life, splash in a tub. Perhaps it would not be regarded as modern to-day; perhaps effete souls would disdain its honest tin tub, smeared with a paint that peeled instantly; but it was elegance and the Hesperides compared with the sponge and two lard-pails of hot water from the Ericson kitchen reservoir, which had for years been his conception of luxurious means of bathing.

Also, there were choicer spirits in the house. One man, who pressed clothes for a living and carried a large line of cigarettes in his room, was second vice-president of the sophomore class. As smoking was dourly forbidden to all Platonians, the sophomore's room was a refuge. The sophomore encouraged Carl in his natural talent for cheerful noises, while Plain Smith objected even to singing while one dressed.

Like four of his classmates, Carl became a waiter at Mrs. Henkel's student boarding-house, for his board and two dollars a week. The two dollars constituted his pin-money—a really considerable sum for Plato, where the young men were pure and smoked not, neither did they drink; where evening clothes were snobbish and sweaters thought rather well of; where the only theatrical attractions were week-stand melodramas playing such attractions as "Poor but True," or the Rev. Sam J. Pitkins's celebrated lecture on "The Father of Lies," annually delivered at the I.O.O.F. Hall.

Carl's father assured him in every letter that he was extravagant. He ran through the two dollars in practically no time at all. He was a member in good and regular standing of the informal club that hung about the Corner Drug Store, to drink coffee soda and discuss athletics and stare at the passing girls. He loved to set off his clear skin and shining pale hair with linen collars, though soft roll-collar shirts were in vogue. And he was ready for any wild expedition, though it should cost fifty or sixty cents. With the sophomore second vice-president and John Terry of the freshman class (usually known as "the Turk") he often tramped to the large neighboring town of Jamaica Mills to play pool, smoke Turkish cigarettes, and drink beer. They always chorused Plato songs, in long-drawn close harmony. Once they had imported English ale, out of bottles, and carried the bottles back to decorate and distinguish their rooms.

Carl's work at the boarding-house introduced him to pretty girl students, and cost him no social discredit whatever. The little college had the virtue of genuine democracy so completely that it never prided itself on being democratic. Mrs. Henkel, proprietor of the boarding-house, occasionally grew sarcastic to her student waiters as she stooped, red-faced and loosened of hair, over the range; she did suggest that they "kindly wash up a few of the dishes now and then before they went gallivantin' off." But songs arose from the freshmen washing and wiping dishes; they chucklingly rehashed jokes; they discussed the value of the "classical course" *versus* the "scientific course." While they waited on table they shared the laughter and arguments that ran from student to student through Mrs. Henkel's dining-room—a sunny room bedecked with a canary, a pussy-cat, a gilded rope portière, a comfortable rocker with a Plato cushion, a Garland stove with nickel ornaments, two geraniums, and an oak-framed photograph of the champion Plato football team of 1899.

Carl was readily accepted by the men and girls who gathered about the piano in the evening. His graceful-seeming body, his puppyish awkwardness, his quietly belligerent dignity, his eternal quest of new things, won him respect; though he was too boyish to rouse admiration, except in the breast of fat, pretty, cheerful, fuzzy-haired, candy-eating Mae Thurston. Mae so influenced Carl that he learned to jest casually; and he practised a new dance, called the "Boston," which Mae had brought from Minneapolis, though as a rival to the waltz and two-step the new dance was ridiculed by every one. He mastered all the *savoir faire* of the boarding-house. But he was always hurrying away from it to practise football, to prowl about the Plato power-house, to skim through magazines in the Y. M. C. A. reading-room, even to study.

Beyond the dish-washing and furnace-tending set he had no probable social future, though everybody knew everybody at Plato. Those immaculate upper-classmen, Murray Cowles and Howard Griffin, never invited him to their room (in a house on Elm Street with a screened porch and piano sounds). He missed Ben Rusk, who had gone to Oberlin College, and Joe Jordan, who had gone to work for the Joralemon Specialty Manufacturing Company.

Life at Plato was suspicious, prejudiced, provincial, as it affected the ambitious students; and for the weaker brethren it was philandering and vague. The class work was largely pure rot—arbitrary mathematics, antiquated botany, hesitating German, and a veritable military drill in the conjunction of Greek verbs conducted by a man with a non-com. soul, a pompous, sandy-whiskered manikin with cold eyes and a perpetual cold in the nose, who had inflicted upon a patient world the four-millionth commentary on Xenophon. Few of the students realized the futility of it all; certainly not Carl, who slept well and believed in football.

The life habit justifies itself. One comes to take anything as a matter of course; to take one's neighbors seriously, whether one lives in Plato or Persia, in Mrs. Henkel's kitchen or a fo'c's'le. The Platonians raced toward their various goals of high-school teaching, or law, or marriage, or permanently escaping their parents; they made love, and were lazy, and ate, and swore off bad habits, and had religious emotions, all quite naturally; they were not much bored, rarely exhilarated, always ready to gossip about their acquaintances; precisely like a duke or a delicatessen-keeper. They played out their game. But it was so tiny a game, so played to the exclusion of all other games, that it tended to dwarf its victims—and the restless children, such as Carl, instinctively resent this dwarfing. They seek to associate themselves with other rebels. Carl's unconscious rebel band was the group of rowdyish freshmen who called themselves "the Gang," and loafed about the room of their unofficial captain, John Terry, nicknamed "the Turk," a swarthy, large-featured youth with a loud laugh, a habit of slapping people upon the shoulder, an ingenious mind for deviltry, and considerable promise as a football end.

Most small local colleges, and many good ones, have their "gangs" of boys, who presumably become honorable men and fathers, yet who in college days regard it as heroic to sneak out and break things, and as humorous to lead countryside girls astray in sordid amours. The more cloistered the seat of learning, the more vicious are the active boys, to keep up with the swiftness of life forces. The Turk's gang painted the statues of the Memorial Arch; they stole signs; they were the creators of noises unexpected and intolerable, during small, quiet hours of moonlight.

As the silkworm draws its exquisite stuff from dowdy leaves, so youth finds beauty and mystery in stupid days. Carl went out unreservedly to practise with the football squad; he had a joy of martyrdom in tackling the dummy and peeling his nose on the frozen ground. He knew a sacred aspiration when Mr. Bjorken, the coach, a former University of Minnesota star, told him that he might actually "make" the team in a year or two; that he had twice as much chance as Ray Cowles, who—while Carl was thinking only of helping the scrub team to win—was too engrossed in his own dignity as a high-school notable to get into the scrimmage.

At the games, among the Gang on the bleachers, Carl went mad with fervor. He kept shooting to his feet, and believed that he was saving his country every time he yelled in obedience to the St. Vitus gestures of the cheer-leader, or sang "On the Goal-line of Plato" to the tune of "On the Sidewalks of New York." Tears of a real patriotism came when, at the critical moment of a losing game against the Minnesota Military Institute, with sunset forlorn behind bare trees, the veteran cheer-leader flung the hoarse Plato rooters into another defiant yell. It was the never-say-die of men who rose, with clenched hands and arms outstretched, to the despairing need of their college, and then—Lord! They hurled up to their feet in frenzy as Pete Madlund got away with the ball for a long run and victory.... The next week, when the University of Keokuk whipped them, 40 to 10, Carl stood weeping and cheering the defeated Plato team till his throat burned.

He loved the laughter of the Turk, Mae Thurston's welcome, experiments in the physics laboratory. And he was sure that he was progressing toward the state of grace in which he might aspire to marry Gertie Cowles.

He did not think of her every day, but she was always somewhere in his thoughts, and the heroines of magazine stories recalled some of her virtues to his mind, invariably. The dentist who had loved her had moved away. She was bored. She occasionally wrote to Carl. But she was still superior—tried to "influence him for good" and advised him to "cultivate nice people."

He was convinced that he was going to become a lawyer, for her sake, but he knew that some day he would be tempted by the desire to become a civil or a mechanical engineer.

A January thaw. Carl was tramping miles out into the hilly country north of Plato. He hadn't been able to persuade any of the Gang to leave their smoky loafing-place in the Turk's room, but his own lungs demanded the open. With his heavy boots swashing through icy pools, calling to an imaginary dog and victoriously running Olympic races before millions of spectators, he defied the chill of the day and reached Hiawatha Mound, a hill eight miles north of Plato.

Toward the top a man was to be seen crouched in a pebbly, sunny arroyo, peering across the bleak prairie, a lone watcher. Ascending, Carl saw that it was Eugene Field Linderbeck, a Plato freshman. That amused him. He grinningly planned a conversation. Every one said that "Genie Linderbeck was queer." A precocious boy of fifteen, yet the head of his class in scholarship; reported to be interested in Greek books quite outside of the course, fond of drinking tea, and devoid of merit in the three manly arts—athletics, flirting, and breaking rules by smoking. Genie was small, anemic, and too well dressed. He stuttered slightly and was always peering doubtfully at you with large and childish eyes that were made more eerie by his pale, bulbous forehead and the penthouse of tangled mouse-brown hair over it.... The Gang often stopped him on the campus to ask mock-polite questions about his ambition, which was to be a teacher of English at Harvard or Yale. Not very consistently, but without ever wearying of the jest, they shadowed him to find out if he did not write poetry; and while no one had actually caught him, he was still suspect.

Genie said nothing when Carl called, "H'lo, son!" and sat on a neighboring rock.

"What's trouble, Genie? You look worried."

"Why don't any of you fellows like me?"

Carl felt like a bug inspected by a German professor. "W-why, how d'you mean, Genie?"

"None of you take me seriously. You simply let me hang around. And you think I'm a grind. I'm not. I like to read, that's all. Perhaps you think I shouldn't like to go out for athletics if I could! I wish I could run the way you can, Ericson. Darn it! I was happy out here by myself on the Mound, where every prospect pleases, and—'n' now here I am again, envying you."

"Why, son, I—I guess—I guess we admire you a whole lot more than we let on to. Cheer up, old man! When you're valedictorian and on the debating team and wallop Hamlin you'll laugh at the Gang, and we'll be proud to write home we know you." Carl was hating himself for ever having teased Genie Linderbeck. "You've helped me a thundering lot whenever I've asked you about that blame Greek syntax. I guess we're jealous of you. You—uh—you don't want to *let* 'em kid you——"

Carl was embarrassed before Genie's steady, youthful, trusting gaze. He stooped for a handful of pebbles, with which he pelted the landscape, maundering, "Say, why don't you come around to the Turk's room and get better acquainted with the Gang?"

"When shall I come?"

"When? Oh, why, thunder!—you know, Genie—just drop in any time."

"I'll be glad to."

Carl was perspiring at the thought of what the Gang would do to him when they discovered that he had invited Genie. But he was game. "Come up to my room whenever you can, and help me with my boning," he added. "You mustn't ever get the idea that we're conferring any blooming favor by having you around. It's you that help us. Our necks are pretty well sandpapered, I'm afraid.... Come up to my room any time.... I'll have to be hiking on if I'm going to get much of a walk. Come over and see me to-night."

"I wish you'd come up to Mr. Frazer's with me some Sunday afternoon for tea, Ericson."

Henry Frazer, M.A. (Yale), associate professor of English literature, was a college mystery. He was a thin-haired young man, with a consuming love of his work, which was the saving of souls by teaching Lycidas and Comus. This was his first year out of graduate school, his first year at Plato—and possibly his last. It was whispered about that he believed in socialism, and the president, the Rev. Dr. S. Alcott Wood, had no patience with such silly fads.

Carl marveled, "Do you go to Frazer's?"

"Why, yes!"

"Thought everybody was down on him. They say he's an anarchist, and I know he gives fierce assignments in English lit.; that's what all the fellows in his classes say."

"All the fools are down on him. That's why I go to his house."

"Don't the fellows—uh—kind of——"

"Yes," piped Genie in his most childish tone of anger, his tendency to stammer betraying him, "they k-kid me for liking Frazer. He's—he's the only t-teacher here that isn't p-p-p——"

"Spit!"

"——provincial!"

"What d'you mean by 'provincial'?"

"Narrow. Villagey. Do you know what Bernard Shaw says——?"

"Never read a word of him, my son. And let me tell you that my idea of no kind of conversation is to have a guy spring 'Have you read?' on me every few seconds, and me coming back with: 'No, I haven't. Ain't it interesting!' If that's the brand of converse at Prof Frazer's you can count me out."

Genie laughed. "Think how much more novelty you get out of roasting me like that than telling Terry he's got 'bats in his belfry' ten or twelve times a day."

"All right, my son; you win. Maybe I'll go to Frazer's with you. Sometime."

The Sunday following Carl went to tea at Professor Henry Frazer's.

The house was Platonian without, plain and dumpy, with gingerbread Gothic on the porch, blistered paint, and the general lines of a prairie barn, but the living-room was more nearly beautiful than any room Carl had seen. In accordance with the ideal of that era it had Mission furniture with large leather cushions, brown wood-work, and tan oatmeal paper scattered with German color prints, instead of the patent rockers and carbon prints of Roman monuments which adorned the houses of the other professors. While waiting with Genie Linderbeck for the Frazers to come down, Carl found in a rack on the oak table such books as he had never seen: exquisite books from England, bound in terra-cotta and olive-green cloth with intricate gold designs, heavy-looking, but astonishingly light to the hand; books about Celtic legends and Provençal jongleurs, and Japanese prints and other matters of which he had never heard; so different from the stained text-books and the shallow novels by brisk ladies which had constituted his experiences of literature that he suddenly believed in culture.

Professor Frazer appeared, walking into the room *after* his fragile wife and gracious sister-in-law, and Carl drank tea (with lemon instead of milk in it!) and listened to bewildering talk and to a few stanzas, heroic or hauntingly musical, by a new poet, W. B. Yeats, an Irishman associated with a thing called the Gaelic Movement. Professor Frazer had a funny, easy friendliness; his sister-in-law, a Diana in brown, respectfully asked Carl about the practicability of motor-cars, and all of them, including two newly come "high-brow" seniors, listened with nodding interest while Carl bashfully analyzed each of the nine cars owned in Plato and Jamaica Mills. At dusk the Diana in brown played MacDowell, and the light of the silken-shaded lamp was on a print of a fairy Swiss village.

That evening Carl wrestled with the Turk for one hour, catch-as-catch-can, on the Turk's bed and under it and nearly out of the window, to prove the value of Professor Frazer and culture. Next morning Carl and the Turk enrolled in Frazer's optional course in modern poetry, a desultory series of lectures which did not attempt Tennyson and Browning. So Carl discovered Shelley and Keats and Walt Whitman, Swinburne and Rossetti and Morris. He had to read by crawling from word to word as though they were ice-cakes in a cataract of emotion. The allusiveness was agonizing. But he pulled off his shoes, rested his feet on the foot-board of his bed, drummed with a pair of scissors on his knee, and persisted in his violent pursuit of the beautiful. Meanwhile his room-mate, Plain Smith, flapped the pages of a Latin lexicon or took a little recreation by reading the Rev. Mr. Todd's *Students' Manual*, that gem of the alarm-clock and water-bucket epoch in American colleges.

Carl never understood Genie Linderbeck's conviction that words are living things that dream and sing and battle. But he did learn that there was speech transcending the barking of the Gang.

In the spring of his freshman year Carl gave up waiting on table and drove a motor-car for a town banker. He learned every screw and spring in the car. He also made Genie go out with him for track athletics. Carl won his place on the college team as a half-miler, and viciously assaulted two freshmen and a junior for laughing at Genie's legs, which stuck out of his large running-pants like straws out of a lemonade-glass.

In the great meet with Hamlin University, though Plato lost most of the events, Carl won the half-mile race. He was elected to the exclusive fraternity of Ray Cowles and Howard Griffin, Omega Chi Delta, just before Commencement. That excited him less than the fact that the Turk and he were to spend the summer up north, in the hard-wheat country, stringing wire for the telephone company with a gang of Minneapolis wiremen.

Oh yes. And he would see Gertie in Joralemon.... She had written to him with so much enthusiasm when he had won the half-mile.

CHAPTER VII

He saw Gertie two hours after he had reached Joralemon for a week's stay before going north. They sat in rockers on the grass beside her stoop. They were embarrassed, and rocked profusely and chattily. Mrs. Cowles was surprised and not much pleased to find him, but Gertie murmured that she had been lonely, and Carl felt that he must be nobly patient under Mrs. Cowles's slight. He got so far as to sigh, "O Gertie!" but grew frightened, as though he were binding himself for life. He wished that Gertie were not wearing so many combs stuck all over her pompadoured hair. He noted that his rocker creaked at the joints, and thought out a method of strengthening it by braces. She bubbled that he was going to be the Big Man in his class. He said, "Aw, rats!" and felt that his collar was too tight.... He went home. His father remarked that Carl was late for supper, that he had been extravagant in Plato, and that he was unlikely to make money out of "all this runnin' races." But his mother stroked his hair and called him her big boy.... He tramped out to Bone Stillman's shack, impatient for the hand-clasp of the pioneer, and grew eloquent, for the first time since his home-coming, as he described Professor Frazer and the delights of poesy. A busy week Carl had in Joralemon. Adelaide Benner gave a porch-supper for him. They sat under the trees, laughing, while in the dimly lighted street bicycles whirred, and box-elders he had always known whispered that this guest of honor was Carl Ericson, come home a hero.

The cycling craze still existed in Joralemon. Carl rented a wheel for a week from the Blue Front Hardware Store. Once he rode with a party of boys and girls to Tamarack Lake. Once he rode to Wakamin with Ben Rusk, home from Oberlin College. The ride was not entirely enjoyable, because Oberlin had nearly two thousand students and Ben was amusedly superior about Plato. They did, however, enjoy the stylishness of buying bottles of strawberry pop at Wakamin.

Twice Carl rode to Tamarack Lake with Gertie. They sat on the shore, and while he shied flat skipping-stones across the water and flapped his old cap at the hovering horse-flies he babbled of the Turk's "stunts," and the banker's car, and the misty hinterlands of Professor Frazer's lectures. Gertie appeared interested, and smiled at regular intervals, but so soon as Carl fumbled at one of Frazer's abstract theories she interrupted him with highly concrete Joralemon gossip.... He suspected that she had not kept up with the times. True, she referred to New York, but as the reference was one she had been using these two years he still identified her with Joralemon.... He did not even hold her hand, though he wondered if it might not be possible; her hand lay so listlessly by her skirt, on the sand.... They rode back in twilight of early June. Carl was cheerful as their wheels crunched the dirt roads in a long, crisp hum. The stilly rhythm of frogs drowned the clank of their pedals, and the sky was vast and pale and wistful.

Gertie, however, seemed less cheerful.

On the last evening of his stay in Joralemon Gertie gave him a hay-ride party. They sang "Seeing Nelly Home," and "Merrily We Roll Along," and "Suwanee River," and "My Old Kentucky Home," and "My Bonnie Lies Over the Ocean," and "In the Good Old Summertime," under a delicate new moon in a sky of apple-green. Carl pressed Gertie's hand; she returned the pressure so quickly that he was embarrassed. He withdrew his hand as quickly as possible, ostensibly to help in the unpacking of the basket of ginger-ale and chicken sandwiches and three cakes (white-frosted, chocolate layer, and banana cake).

The same group said good-by to Carl at the M. & D. station. As the train started, Carl saw Gertie turn away disconsolately, her shoulders so drooping that her blouse was baggy in the back. He mourned that he had not been more tender with her that week. He pictured himself kissing Gertie on the shore of Tamarack Lake, enfolded by afternoon and the mystery of sex and a protecting reverence for Gertie's loneliness. He wanted to go back—back for one more day, one more ride with Gertie. But he picked up a mechanics magazine, glanced at an article on gliders, read in the first paragraph a prophecy about aviation, slid down in his seat with his head bent over the magazine—and the idyl of Gertie and afternoon was gone.

He was reading the article on gliders in June, 1905, so early in the history of air conquest that its suggestions were miraculous to him; for it was three years before Wilbur Wright was to startle the world by his flights at Le Mans; four years before Blériot was to cross the Channel—though, indeed, it was a year and a half after the Wrights' first secret ascent in a motor-driven aeroplane at Kittyhawk, and fourteen years after Lilienthal had begun that epochal series of glider-flights which was followed by the experiments of Pilcher and Chanute, Langley and Montgomery.

The article declared that if gasoline or alcohol engines could be made light enough we should all be aviating to the office in ten years; that now was the time for youngsters to practise gliding, as pioneers of the new age. Carl "guessed" that flying would be even better than automobiling. He made designs for three revolutionary new aeroplanes, drawing on the margins of the magazine with a tooth-mark-pitted pencil stub.

Gertie was miles back, concealed behind piles of triplanes and helicopters and following-surface monoplanes which the wizard inventor, C. Ericson, was creating and ruthlessly destroying.... A small boy was squalling in the seat opposite, and Carl took him from his tired mother and lured him into a game of tit-tat-toe.

He joined the Turk and the wire-stringers at a prairie hamlet—straggly rows of unpainted frame shanties, the stores with tin-corniced false fronts that pretended to be two stories high. There were pig-pens in the dooryards, and the single church had a square, low, white steeple like the paper cap which Labor wears in the posters. Farm-wagons were hitched before a gloomy saloon. Carl was exceeding glum. But the Turk introduced him to a University of Minnesota Pharmacy School student who was with the crew during vacation, and the three went tramping across breezy, flowered prairies. So began for Carl a galloping summer.

The crew strung telephone wire from pole to pole all day, playing the jokes of hardy men, and on Sunday loafed in haystacks, recalling experiences from Winnipeg to El Paso. Carl resolved to come back to this life of the open, with Gertie, after graduation. He would buy a ranch "on time." Or the Turk and Carl would go exploring in Alaska or the Orient. "Law?" he would ask himself in monologues, "law? Me in a stuffy office? Not a chance!"

The crew stayed for four weeks in a boom town of nine thousand, installing a complete telephone system. South-east of the town lay rolling hills. As Carl talked with the Turk and the Pharmacy School man on a hilltop, the first evening of their arrival, he told them the scientific magazine's prophecies about aviation, and noted that these hills were of the sort Lilienthal would probably have chosen for his glider-flights.

"Say! by the great Jim Hill, let's make us a glider!" he exulted, sitting up, his eyelids flipping rapidly.

"Sure!" said the Pharmacy man. "How would you make one?"

"Why—uh—I guess you could make a frame out of willow—have to; the willows along the creeks are the only kind of trees near here. You'd cover it with varnished cotton—that's what Lilienthal did, anyway. But darned if I know how you'd make the planes curved—cambered—like he did. You got to have it that way. I suppose you'd use curved stays. Like a quarter barrel-hoop.... I guess it would be better to try to make a Chanute glider—just a plain pair of sup'rimposed planes, instead of one all combobulated like a bat's wings, like Lilienthal's glider was.... Or we could try some experiments with paper models——Oh no! Thunder! Let's make a glider."

They did.

They studied with aching heads the dry-looking tables of lift and resistance for which Carl telegraphed to Chicago. Stripped to their undershirts, they worked all through the hot prairie evenings in the oil-smelling, greasy engine-room of the local power-house, in front of the dynamos, which kept evilly throwing out green sparks and rumbling the mystic syllable "Om-m-m-m," to greet their modern magic.

They hunted for three-quarter-inch willow rods, but discarded them for seasoned ash from the lumber-yard. They coated cotton with thin varnish. They stopped to dispute furiously over angles of incidence, bellowing, "Well, look here then, you mutton-head; I'll draw it for you."

On their last Sunday in the town they assembled the glider, single-surfaced, like a monoplane, twenty-two feet in span, with a tail, and with a double bar beneath the plane, by which the pilot was to hang, his hands holding cords attached to the entering edge of the plane, balancing the glider by movements of his body.

At dawn on Monday they loaded the glider upon a wagon and galloped with it out to a forty-foot hill. They stared down the easy slope, which grew in steepness and length every second, and thought about Lilienthal's death.

"W-w-well," shivered the Turk, "who tries it first?"

All three pretended to be adjusting the lashings, waiting for one another, till Carl snarled, "Oh, all *right!* I'll do it if I got to."

"Course it breaks my heart to see you swipe the honor," the Turk said, "but I'm unselfish. I'll let you do it. Brrrr! It's as bad as the first jump into the swimming-hole in spring."

Carl was smiling at the comparison as they lifted the glider, with him holding the bars beneath. The plane was instantly buoyed up like a cork on water as the fifteen-mile head-wind poured under it. He stopped smiling. This was a dangerous living thing he was going to guide. It jerked at him as he slipped his arms over the suspended bars. He wanted to stop and think this all over. "Get it done!" he snapped at himself, and began to run down-hill, against the wind.

The wind lifted the plane again. With a shock Carl knew that his feet had left the ground. He was actually flying! He kicked wildly in air. All his body strained to get balance in the air, to control itself, to keep from falling, of which he now felt the world-old instinctive horror.

The plane began to tip to one side, apparently irresistibly, like a sheet of paper turning over in the wind. Carl was sick with fear for a tenth of a second. Every cell in his body shrank before coming disaster. He flung his legs in the direction opposite to the tipping of the plane. With this counter-balancing weight, the glider righted. It was running on an even keel, twenty-five feet above the sloping ground, while Carl hung easily by the double bar beneath, like a circus performer with a trapeze under each arm. He ventured to glance down. The turf was flowing beneath him, a green and sunny blur. He exulted. Flying!

The glider dipped forward. Carl leaned back, his arms wide-spread. A gust struck the plane, head on. Overloaded at the back, it tilted back, then soared up to thirty-five or forty feet. Slow-seeming, inevitable, the whole structure turned vertically upward.

Carl dangled there against a flimsy sheet of wood and cotton, which for part of a second stuck straight up against the wind, like a paper on a screen-door.

The plane turned turtle, slithered sidewise through the air, and dropped, horizontal now, but upside down, Carl on top.

Thirty-five, forty feet down.

"I'm up against it," was his only thought while he was falling.

The left tip of the plane smashed against the ground, crashing, horribly jarring. But it broke the fall. Carl shot forward and landed on his shoulder.

He got up, rubbing his shoulder, wondering at the suspended life in the faces of the other two as they ran down-hill toward him.

"Jiminy," he said. "Glad the glider broke the fall. Wish we had time to make a new glider, with wing-warp. Say, we'll be late on the job. Better beat it P. D. Q."

The others stood gaping.

CHAPTER VIII

A pile of shoes and nose-guards and bicycle-pumps and broken hockey-sticks; a wall covered with such stolen signs as "East College Avenue," and "Pants Presser Ladys Garments Carefully Done," and "Dr. Sloats Liniment for Young and Old"; a broken-backed couch with a red-and-green afghan of mangy tassels; an ink-spattered wooden table, burnt in small black spots along the edges; a plaster bust of Martha Washington with a mustache added in ink; a few books; an inundation of sweaters and old hats; and a large, expensive mouth-organ—such were a few of the interesting characteristics of the room which Carl and the Turk were occupying as room-mates for sophomore year at Plato.

Most objectionable sounds came from the room constantly: the Gang's songs, suggestive laughter, imitations of cats and fowls and fog-horns. These noises were less ingenious, however, than the devices of the Gang for getting rid of tobacco-smoke, such as blowing the smoke up the stove.

Carl was happy. In this room he encouraged stammering Genie Linderbeck to become adaptable. Here he scribbled to Gertie and Ben Rusk little notes decorated with badly drawn caricatures of himself loafing. Here, with the Turk, he talked out half the night, planning future glory in engineering. Carl adored the Turk for his frankness, his lively speech, his interest in mechanics—and in Carl.

Carl was still out for football, but he was rather light for a team largely composed of one-hundred-and-eighty-pound Norwegians. He had a chance, however. He drove the banker's car two or three evenings a week and cared for the banker's lawn and furnace and cow. He still boarded at Mrs. Henkel's, as did jolly Mae Thurston, whom he took for surreptitious rides in the banker's car, after which he wrote extra-long and pleasant letters to Gertie. It was becoming harder and harder to write to Gertie, because he had, in freshman year, exhausted all the things one can say about the weather without being profane. When, in October, a new bank clerk stormed, meteor-like, the Joralemon social horizon, and became devoted to Gertie, as faithfully reported in letters from Joe Jordan, Carl was melancholy over the loss of a comrade. But he strictly confined his mourning to leisure hours—and with books, football, and chores for the banker, he was a busy young man.... After about ten days it was a relief not to have to plan letters to Gertie. The emotions that should have gone to her Carl devoted to Professor Frazer's new course in modern drama.

This course was officially announced as a study of Bernard Shaw, Ibsen, Strindberg, Pinero, Hauptmann, Sudermann, Maeterlinck, D'Annunzio, and Rostand; but unofficially announced by Professor Frazer as an attempt to follow the spirit of to-day wherever it should be found in contemporary literature. Carl and the Turk were bewildered but staunchly enthusiastic disciples of the course. They made every member of the Gang enroll in it, and discouraged inattention in the lecture-room by dexterous side-kicks.

Even to his ex-room-mate, Plain Smith, the grim and slovenly school-teacher who had called him "bub" and discouraged his confidences, Carl presented the attractions of Professor Frazer's lectures when he met him on the campus. Smith looked quizzical and "guessed" that plays and play-actin' were useless, if not actually immoral.

"Yes, but this isn't just plays, my young friend," said Carl, with a hauteur new but not exceedingly impressive to Plain Smith. "He takes up all these new stunts, all this new philosophy and stuff they have in London and Paris. There's something besides Shakespeare and the Bible!" he added, intending to be spiteful. It may be stated that he did not like Plain Smith.

"What new philosophy?"

"The spirit of brotherhood. I suppose you're too orthodox for that!"

"Oh no, sonny, not for that, not for that. And it ain't so *very* new. That's what Christ taught! No, sonny, I ain't so orthodox but what I'm willing to have 'em show me anything that tries to advance brotherhood. Not that I think it's very likely to be found in a lot of Noo York plays. But I'll look in at one lesson, anyway," and Plain Smith clumped away, humming "Greenland's Icy Mountains."

Professor Frazer's modern drama course began with Ibsen. The first five lectures were almost conventional; they were an attempt to place contemporary dramatists, with reflections on the box-office standpoint. But his sixth lecture began rather unusually.

There was an audience of sixty-four in Lecture-room A—earnest girl students bringing out note-books and spectacle-cases, frivolous girls feeling their back hair, and the men settling down with a "Come, let's get it over!" air, or glowing up worshipingly, like Eugene Field Linderbeck, or determined not to miss anything, like Carl—the captious college audience, credulous as to statements of fact and heavily unresponsive to the spirit. Professor Frazer, younger than half a dozen of the plow-trained undergraduates, thin of hair and sensitive of face, sitting before them, with one hand in his pocket and the other nervously tapping the small reading-table, spoke quietly:

"I'm not going to be a lecturer to-day. I'm not going to analyze the plays of Shaw which I assigned to you. You're supposed to have read them yourselves. I am going to imagine that I am at tea in New Haven, or down in New York, at dinner in the basement of the old Brevoort, talking with a bunch of men who are trying to find out where the world is going, and why and when and how, and asking who are the prophets who are going to show it the way. We'd be getting excited over Shaw and Wells. There's something really worth getting excited over.

"These men have perceived that this world is not a crazy-quilt of unrelated races, but a collection of human beings completely related, with all our interests—food and ambitions and the desire to play—absolutely in common; so that if we would take thought all together, and work together, as a football team does, we would start making a perfect world.

"That's what socialism—of which you're beginning to hear so much, and of which you're going to hear so much more—means. If you feel genuinely impelled to vote the Republican ticket, that's not my affair, of course. Indeed, the Socialist party of this country constitutes only one branch of international socialism. But I do demand of you that you try to think for yourselves, if you are going to have the nerve to vote at all—think of it—to vote how this whole nation is to be conducted! Doesn't that tremendous responsibility demand that you do something more than inherit your way of voting? that you really think, think hard, why you vote as you do?... Pardon me for getting away from the subject proper—yet am I, actually? For just what I have been saying is one of the messages of Shaw and Wells.

"The great vision of the glory that shall be, not in one sudden millennium, but slowly advancing toward joys of life which we can no more prevision than the aboriginal medicine-man could imagine the X-ray! I wish that this were the time and the place to rhapsodize about that vision, as William Morris has done, in *News from Nowhere*. You tell me that the various brands of socialists differ so much in their beliefs about this future that the bewildered layman can make nothing at all of their theories. Very well. They differ so much because there are so many different things we *can* do with this human race.... The defeat of death; the life period advancing to ten-score years all crowded with happy activity. The solution of labor's problem; increasing safety and decreasing hours of toil, and a way out for the unhappy consumer who is ground between labor and capital. A real democracy and the love of work that shall come when work is not relegated to wage-slaves, but joyously shared in a community inclusive of the living beings of all nations. France and Germany uniting precisely as Saxony and Prussia and Bavaria have united. And, most of all, a general realization that the fact that we cannot accomplish all these things at once does not indicate that they are hopeless; an understanding that one of the wonders of the future is the fact that we shall *always*, in all ages, have improvements to look forward to.

"Fellow-students, object as strongly as you wish to the petty narrowness and vituperation of certain street-corner ranters, but do not be petty and narrow and vituperative in doing it!

"Now, to relate all this to the plays of Bernard Shaw. When he says——"

Professor Frazer's utterances seem tamely conservative nowadays; but this was in 1905, in a small, intensely religious college among the furrows. Imagine a devout pastor when his son kicks the family Bible and you have the mental state of half the students of Plato upon hearing a defense of socialism. Carl, catching echoes of his own talks with Bone Stillman in the lecture, exultantly glanced about, and found the class staring at one another with frightened anxiety. He saw the grim Plain Smith, not so much angry as ill. He saw two class clowns snickering at the ecstasy in the eyes of Genie Linderbeck.

In the corner drug-store, popularly known as "The Club," where all the college bloods gather to drink lemon phosphate, an excited old man, whose tieless collar was almost concealed by his tobacco-stained beard, pushed back his black slouch-hat with the G. A. R. cord, and banged his fist on the prescription-counter, shouting, half at the clerk and half at the students matching pennies on the soda-counter, "I've lived in Plato, man and boy, for forty-seven years—ever since it wa'n't nothing but a frontier trading-post. I packed logs on my back and I tramped fifty-three miles to get me a yoke of oxen. I remember when the Indians went raiding during the war and the cavalry rode here from St. Paul. And this town has always stood for decency and law and order. But when things come to such a pass that this fellow Frazer or any of the rest of these infidels from one of these here Eastern colleges is allowed to stand up on his hind legs in a college building and bray about anarchism and tell us to trample on the old flag that we fought for, and none of these professors that call themselves 'reverends' step in and stop him, then let me tell you I'm about ready to pull up stakes and go out West, where there's patriotism and decency still, and where they'd hang one of these foreign anarchists to the nearest lamp-post, yes, sir, and this fellow Frazer, too, if he encouraged them in their crank notions. Got no right in the country, anyway. Better deport 'em if they ain't satisfied with the way we run things. I won't stand for preaching anarchism, and never knew any decent place that would, never since I was a baby in Canada. Yes, sir, I mean it; I'm an old man, but I'd pull up stakes and go plugging down the Santa Fe trail first, and I mean it."

"Here's your Bog Bitters, Mr. Goff," said the clerk, hastily, as a passer-by was drawn into the store by the old man's tirade.

Mr. Goff stalked out, muttering, and the college sports at the soda-counter grinned at one another. But Gus Osberg, of the junior class, remarked to Carl Ericson: "At that, though, there's a good deal to what old Goff says. Bet a hat Prexy won't stand for Prof Frazer's talking anarchy. Fellow in the class told me it was fierce stuff he was talking. Reg'lar anarchy."

"Rats! It wasn't anything of the kind," protested Carl. "I was there and I heard the whole thing. He just explained what this Bernard Shaw that writes plays meant by socialism."

"Well, even so, don't you think it's kind of unnecessary to talk publicly, right out in a college lecture-room, about socialism?" inquired a senior who was high up in the debating society.

"Well, thunder——!" was all Carl said, as the whole group stared at him. He felt ridiculous; he was afraid of seeming to be a "crank." He escaped from the drug-store.

When he arrived at Mrs. Henkel's boarding-house for supper the next evening he found the students passing from hand to hand a copy of the town paper, the *Plato Weekly Times*, which bore on the front page what the town regarded as a red-hot news story:

PLATO PROFESSOR

TALKS SEDITIOUSLY

As we go to press we learn that rumors are flying about the campus that the "powers that be" are highly incensed by the remarks of a well-known member of the local faculty praising Socialism and other form of anarchy. It is said that one of the older members of the faculty will demand from the erring teacher an explanation of his remarks which are alleged to have taken the form of a defense of the English anarchist Bernhard Shaw. Those on the que vive are expecting sensational developments and campus talk is so extensively occupied with discussions of the affair that the important coming game with St. John's college is almost forgotten.

While the TIMES has always supported Plato College as one of the chief glories in the proud crown of Minnesota learning, we can but illy stomach such news. It goes without saying that we cannot too strongly disapprove express our disapproval of such incendiary utterances and we shall fearlessly report the whole of this fair let the chips fall where they may.

"There, Mr. Ericson," said Mrs. Henkel, a plump, decent, disapproving person, who had known too many generations of great Platonians to be impressed by anything, "you see what the public thinks of your Professor Frazer. I told you people wouldn't stomach such news, and I wouldn't wonder if they strongly disapproved."

"This ain't anything but gossip," said Carl, feebly; but as he read the account in the *Weekly Times* he was sick and frightened, such was his youthful awe of print. He wanted to beat the mossy-whiskered editor of the *Times*, who always had white food-stains on his lapels. When he raised his eyes the coquette Mae Thurston tried to cheer him: "It 'll all come out in the wash, Eric; don't worry. These editors have to have something to write about or they couldn't fill up the paper."

He pressed her foot under the table. He was chatty, and helped to keep the general conversation away from the Frazer affair; but he was growing more and more angry, with a desire for effective action which expressed itself within him only by, "I'll show 'em! Makes me so *sore*!"

Everywhere they discussed and rediscussed Professor Frazer: in the dressing-room of the gymnasium, where the football squad dressed in the sweat-reeking air and shouted at one another, balancing each on one leg before small lockers, and rubbing themselves with brown, unclean Turkish towels; in the neat rooms of girl co-eds with their banners and cushions and pink comforters and chafing-dishes of nut fudge and photographic postal-cards showing the folks at home; in the close, horse-smelling, lap-robe and whip scattered office of the town livery-stable, where Mr. Goff droned with the editor of the *Times*.

Everywhere Carl heard the echoes, and resolved, "I've got to *do* something!"

CHAPTER IX

The day of Professor Frazer's next lecture, a rain-sodden day at the end of October, with the stubble-fields bleakly shelterless beyond the campus. The rain splashed up from pools on the worn brick walks and dripped from trees and whipped about buildings, soaking the legs and leaving them itchingly wet and the feet sloshily uncomfortable. Carl returned to his room at one; talked to the Turk, his feet thrust against the side of their rusty stove. He wanted to keep three o'clock, the hour of Frazer's lecture, from coming. "I feel as if I was in for a fight and scared to death about it. Listen to that rain outside. Gee! but the old dame keeps these windows dirty. I hope Frazer will give it to them good and hard. I wish we could applaud him. I do feel funny, like something tragic was going to happen."

"Oh, tie that dog outside," yawned the Turk, stanch adherent of Carl, and therefore of Professor Frazer, but not imaginative. "Come on, young Kerl; I'll play you a slick little piece on the mouth-organ. Heh?"

"Oh, thunder! I'm too restless to listen to anything except a cannon." Carl stumped to the window and pondered on the pool of water flooding the graying grass stems in the shabby yard.

When it was time to start for Professor Frazer's lecture the Turk blurted: "Why don't we stay away and forget about it? Get her off your nerves. Let's go down to the bowling-alley and work up a sweat."

"Not a chance, Turk. He'll want all the supporters he's got. And you'd hate to stay away as much as I would. I feel cheered up now; all ready for the scrap. Yip! Come on!"

"All right, governor. I like the scrap, all right, but I don't want to see you get all worked up."

Through the rain, across the campus, an unusual number of students in shining, cheap, black raincoats were hastening to the three o'clock classes, clattering up the stone steps of the Academic Building, talking excitedly, glancing up at the arched door as though they expected to see something startling. Dozens stared at Carl. He felt rather important. It was plain that he was known as a belligerent, a supporter of Professor Frazer. As he came to the door of Lecture-room A he found that many of the crowd were deserting their proper classes to attend the Frazer event. He bumped down into his own seat, gazing back superciliously at the outsiders who were edging into unclaimed seats at the back of the room or standing about the door— students from other classes, town girls, the young instructor in French, German, and music; a couple of town club-women in glasses and galoshes and woolen stockings bunchy at the ankles. Every one was rapidly whispering, watching every one else, peeping often at the platform and the small door beside it through which Professor Frazer would enter. Carl had a smile ready for him. But there was no chance that the smile would be seen. There must have been a hundred and fifty in the room, seated and standing, though there were but seventy in the course, and but two hundred and fifty-six students in the whole college that year.

Carl looked back. He clenched his fist and pounded the soft side of it on his thigh, drawing in his breath, puffing it out with a long exasperated "Hellll!" For the Greek professor, the comma-sized, sandy-whiskered martinet, to whom nothing that was new was moral and nothing that was old was to be questioned by any undergraduate, stalked into the room like indignant Napoleon posing before two guards and a penguin at St. Helena. A student in the back row thriftily gave the Greek god his seat. The god sat down, with a precise nod. Instantly a straggly man with a celluloid collar left the group by the door, whisked over to the Greek professor, and fawned upon him. It was the fearless editor and owner (also part-time type-setter) of the *Plato Weekly Times*, who dated back to the days of Washington flat-bed hand-presses and pure Jeffersonian politics, and feared neither man nor devil, though he was uneasy in the presence of his landlady. He ostentatiously flapped a wad of copy-paper in his left hand, and shook a spatter of ink-drops from a fountain-pen as he interviewed the Greek professor, who could be seen answering pompously. Carl was hating them both, fearing the Greek as a faculty spy on Frazer, picturing himself kicking the editor, when he was aware of a rustling all over the room, of a general turning of heads toward the platform.

He turned. He was smiling like a shy child in his hero-worship. Professor Frazer was inconspicuously walking through the low door beside the platform. Frazer's lips were together. He was obviously self-conscious. His motions were jerky. He elaborately did not look at the audience. He nearly stumbled on the steps up to the platform. His hand shook as he drew papers from a leather portfolio and arranged them on the small reading-table. One of the papers escaped and sailed off the platform, nearly to the front row. Nearly every one in the room snickered. Frazer flushed. A girl student in the front row nervously bounded out of her seat, picked up the paper, and handed it up to Frazer. They both fumbled it, and their heads nearly touched. Most of the crowd laughed audibly.

Professor Frazer sat down in his low chair, took out his watch with a twitching hand, and compared his time with the clock at the back of the room—and so closely were the amateur executioners observing their victim that every eye went back to the clock as well. Even Carl was guilty of that imitation. Consequently he saw the editor, standing at the back, make notes on his copy-paper and smirk like an ill-bred hound stealing a bone. And the

Greek professor stared at Frazer's gauche movements with a grim smugness that indicated, "Quite the sort of thing I expected." The Greek's elbows were on the arm of the seat, and he held up before his breast a small red-leather-covered note-book which he superciliously tapped with a thin pencil. He was waiting. Like a judge of the Inquisition....

"Old Greek 's going to take notes and make a report to the faculty about what Frazer says," reflected Carl. "If I could only get hold of his notes and destroy them!"

Carl turned again. It was just three. Professor Frazer had risen. Usually he sat while lecturing. Fifty whispers commented on that fact; fifty regular members of the course became self-important through knowing it. Frazer was leaning slightly against the table. It moved an inch or two with his weight, but by this time every one was too high-strung to laugh. He was pale. He re-arranged his papers. He had to clear his throat twice before he could speak, in the now silent, vulturishly attentive room, smelling of wet second-rate clothes.

The gusty rain could be heard. They all hitched in their seats.

"Oh, Frazer *can't* be going to retract," groaned Carl; "but he's scared."

Carl suddenly wished himself away from all this useless conflict; out tramping the wet roads with the Turk, or slashing through the puddles at thirty-five miles an hour in the banker's car. He noted stupidly that Genie Linderbeck's hair was scarcely combed. He found he was saying, "Frazer 'll flunk, flunk, flunk; he's going to flunk, flunk, flunk."

Then Frazer spoke. His voice sounded harsh and un-rhythmical, but soon swung into the natural periods of a public speaker as he got into his lecture:

"My friends," said he, "a part of you have come here legitimately, to hear a lecture; a part to satisfy the curiosity aroused by rumors to the effect that I am likely to make indecorous and indecent remarks, which your decorum and decency make you wish to hear, and of which you will carry away evil and twisted reports, to gain the reputation of being fearless defenders of the truth. It is a temptation to gratify your desire and shock you—a far greater temptation than to be repentant and reactionary. Only, it occurs to me that this place and time are supposed to be devoted to a lecture by Henry Frazer on his opinions about contemporary drama. It is in no sense to be given to the puling defense of a martyr, nor to the sensational self-advertisement of either myself or any of you. I have no intention of devoting any part of my lecture, aside from these introductory adumbrations, to the astonishing number of new friends whose bright and morning faces I see before me. I shall neither be so insincerely tactful as to welcome you, nor so frightened as to ignore you. Nor shall I invite you to come to me with any complaints you have about me. I am far too busy with my real work!

"I am not speaking patiently. I am not patient with you! I am not speaking politely. Truly, I do not think that I shall much longer be polite!

"Wait. That sounds now in my ears as rhetorical! Forgive me, and translate my indiscretions into more colloquial language.

"Though from rumors I have overheard, I fancy some of you will do that, anyway.... And now, I think, you see where I stand.

"Now then. For such of you as have a genuine interest in the brilliant work of Bernard Shaw I shall first continue the animadversions on the importance of his social thought, endeavor to link it with the great and growing vision of H. G. Wells (novelist and not dramatist though he is, because of the significance of his new books, *Kips* and *Mankind in the Making*), and point out the serious purpose that seems to me to underlie Shaw's sarcastic pictures of life's shams.

"In my last lecture I endeavored to present the destructive side of present social theories as little as possible; to dwell more on the keen desire of the modern thinkers for constructive imagination. But I judge that I was regarded as too destructive, which amuses me, and to which I shall apply the antidote of showing how destructive modern thought is and must be—whether running with sootily smoking torch of individuality in Bakunin, or hissing in Nietzsche, or laughing at Olympus in Bernard Shaw. My 'radicalism' has been spoken of. Radical! Do you realize that I am not suggesting that there might possibly some day be a revolution in America, but rather that now I am stating that there is, this minute, and for some years has been, an actual state of warfare between capital and labor? Do you know that daily more people are saying openly and violently that we starve our poor, we stuff our own children with useless bookishness, and work the children of others in mills and let them sell papers on the streets in red-light districts at night, and thereby prove our state nothing short of insane? If you tell me that there is no revolution because there are no barricades, I point to actual battles at Homestead, Pullman, and the rest. If you say that there has been no declaration of war, open war, I shall read you editorials from *The Appeal to Reason*.

"Mind you, I shall not say whether I am enlisted for or against the revolutionary army. But I demand that you look about you and understand the significance of the industrial disturbances and religious unrest of the time. Never till then will you understand anything—certainly not that Shaw is something more than an *enfant terrible*; Ibsen something more than an ill-natured old man with dyspepsia and a silly lack of interest in skating. Then you will realize that in the most extravagant utterances of a red-shirted strike-leader there may be more fervent faith and honor, oftentimes, than in the virgin prayers of a girl who devoutly attends Christian Endeavor, but presumes to call Emma Goldman 'that dreadful woman.' Follow the labor-leader. Or fight him, good and hard. But do not overlook him.

"But I must be more systematic. When John Tanner's independent chauffeur, of whom you have—I hope you have—read in *Man and Superman*——"

Carl looked about. Many were frowning; a few leaning sidewise to whisper to neighbors, with a perplexed head-shake that plainly meant, "I don't quite get that." Wet feet were shifted carefully; breaths caught quickly; hands nervously played with lower lips. The Greek professor was writing something. Carl's ex-room-mate, Plain Smith, was rigid, staring unyieldingly at the platform. Carl hated Smith's sinister stillness.

Professor Frazer was finishing his lecture:

"If it please you, flunk this course, don't read a single play I assign to you, be disrespectful, disbelieve all my contentions. And I shall still be content. But do not, as you are living souls, blind yourself to the fact that there is a world-wide movement to build a wider new world—and that the world needs it—and that in Jamaica Mills, on land owned by a director of Plato College, there are two particularly vile saloons which you must wipe out before you disprove me!" Silence for ten seconds. Then, "That is all."

The crowd began to move hesitatingly, while Professor Frazer hastily picked up his papers and raincoat and hurried out through the door beside the platform. Voices immediately rose in a web of talk, many-colored, hot-colored.

Carl babbled to the man next him, "He sure is broad. He doesn't care whether they're conservative or not. And some sensation at the end!"

"Heh? What? Him?" The sophomore was staring.

"Yes. Why, sure! Whadya mean?" demanded Carl.

"Well, and wha' do *you* mean by 'broad'? Sure! He's broad just like a razor edge."

"Heh?" echoed the next man down the row, a Y. M. C. A. senior. "Do you mean to say you liked it?"

"Why, sure! Why not? Didn't you?"

"Oh yes. Yes indeed! All he said was that scarlet women like Emma Goldman were better than a C. E. girl, and that he hoped his students would bluff the course and flunk it, and that we could find booze at Jamaica Mills, and a few little things like that. That's all. Sure! That's the sort of thing we came here to study." The senior was buttoning his raincoat with angry fingers. "That's——Why, the man was insane! And the way he denounced decency and——Oh, I can't talk about it!"

"W-w-w-well by gosh, of all the—the——" spluttered Carl. "You and your Y. M. C. A.—calling yourself religious, and misrepresenting like that—you and your——Why, you ain't worth arguing with. I don't believe you 'came to study' anything. You know it all already." Passionate but bewildered, trying not to injure the cause of Frazer by being nasty, he begged: "Straight, didn't you like his spiel? Didn't it give you some new ideas?"

The senior vouchsafed: "No, 'me and my Y. M.' didn't like it. Now don't let me keep you, Ericson. I suppose you'll be wanting to join dear Mr. Frazer in a highball; you're such a pet of his. Did he teach you to booze? I understand you're good at it."

"You apologize or I'll punch your face off," said Carl. "I don't understand Professor Frazer's principles like I ought to. I'm not fighting for them. Prob'ly would if I knew enough. But I don't like your face. It's too long. It's like a horse's face. It's an insult to Frazer to have a horse-faced guy listen to him. You apologize for having a horse face, see?"

"You're bluffing. You wouldn't start anything here, anyway."

"Apologize!" Carl's fist was clenched. People were staring.

"Cut it out, will you! I didn't mean anything."

"You wouldn't," snapped Carl, and rammed his way out, making wistful boyish plans to go to Frazer with devotion and offers of service in a fight whose causes grew more confused to him every moment. Beside him, as he hurried off to football practice, strode a big lineman of the junior class, cajoling:

"Calm down, son. You can't lick the whole college."

"But it makes me so sore——"

"Oh, I know, but it strikes me that no matter how much you like Frazer, he was going pretty far when he said that anarchists had more sense than decent folks."

"He didn't! You didn't get him. He meant——O Lord, what's the use!"

He did not say another word as they hastened to the gymnasium for indoor practice.

He was sure that they who knew of his partisanship would try to make him lose his temper. "Dear Lord, please just let me take out just one bonehead and beat him to a pulp, and then I'll be good and not open my head again," was his perfectly reverent prayer as he stripped before his locker.

Carl and most of the other substitutes had to wait, and most of them gossiped of the lecture. They all greedily discussed Frazer's charge that some member of the corporation owned saloon lots, and tried to decide who it was, but not one of them gave Frazer credit. Twenty times Carl wanted to deny; twenty times speech rose in him so hotly that he drew a breath and opened his mouth; but each time he muttered to himself: "Oh, shut up! You'll only make 'em worse." Students who had attended the lecture declared that Professor Frazer had advocated bomb-throwing and obscenity, and the others believed, marveling, "Well, well, well, well!" with unctuous appreciation of the scandal.

Still Carl sat aloof on a pair of horizontal bars, swinging his legs with agitated quickness, while the others covertly watched him—slim, wire-drawn, his china-blue eyes blurred with fury, his fair Norse skin glowing dull red, his chest strong under his tight football jersey; a clean-carved boy.

The rubber band of his nose-guard snapped harshly as he plucked at it, playing a song of hatred on that hard little harp.

An insignificant thing made him burst out. Tommy La Croix, the French Canuck, a quick, grinning, evil-spoken, tobacco-chewing, rather likeable young thug, stared directly at Carl and said, loudly: "'Nother thing I noticed was that Frazer didn't have his pants pressed. Funny, ain't it, that when even these dudes from Yale get to be cranks they're short on baths and tailors?"

Carl slid from the parallel bars. He walked up to the line of substitutes, glanced sneeringly along them, dramatized himself as a fighting rebel, remarked, "Half of you are too dumm to get Frazer, and the other half are old-woman gossips and ought to be drinking tea," and gloomed away to the dressing-room, while behind him the substitutes laughed, and some one called: "Sorry you don't like us, but we'll try to bear up. Going to lick the whole college, Ericson?"

His ears burned, in the dressing-room. He did not feel that they had been much impressed.

To tell the next day or two in detail would be to make many books about the mixed childishness and heroic fineness of Carl's partisanship; to repeat a thousand rumors running about the campus to the effect that the faculty would demand Frazer's resignation; to explain the reason why Frazer's charge that a Plato director owned land used by saloons was eagerly whispered for a little while, then quite forgotten, while Frazer's reputation as a "crank" was never forgotten, so much does muck resent the muck-raker; to describe Carl's brief call on Frazer and his confusing discovery that he had nothing to say; to repeat the local paper's courageous reports of the Frazer affair, Turk's great oath to support Frazer "through hell and high water," Turk's repeated defiance: "Well, by golly! we'll show the mutts, but I wish we could *do* something"; to chronicle dreary classes whose dullness was evident to Carl, now, after his interest in Frazer's lectures.

Returning from Genie Linderbeck's room, Carl found a letter from Gertie Cowles on the black-walnut hat-rack. Without reading it, but successfully befooling himself into the belief that he was glad to have it, he went whistling up to his room.

Ray Cowles and Howard Griffin, those great seniors, sat tilted back in wooden chairs, and between them was the lord of the world, Mr. Bjorken, the football coach, a large, amiable, rather religious young man, who believed in football, foreign missions, and the Democratic party.

"Hello! Waiting for me or the Turk?" faltered Carl, gravely shaking hands all round.

"Just dropped up to see you for a second," said Mr. Bjorken.

"Sorry the Turk wasn't here." Carl had an ill-defined feeling that he wanted to keep them from becoming serious as long as he could.

Ray Cowles cleared his throat. Never again would the black-haired Adonis, blossom of the flower of Joralemon, be so old and sadly sage as then. "We want to talk to you seriously about something—for your own sake. You know I've always been interested in you, and Howard, and course we're interested in you as frat brothers, too. For old Joralemon and Plato, eh? Mr. Bjorken believes—might as well tell him now, don't you think, Mr. Bjorken?"

The coach gave a regally gracious nod. Hitching about on the wood-box, Carl felt the bottom drop out of his anxious stomach.

"Well, Mr. Bjorken thinks you're practically certain to make the team next year, and maybe you may even get put in the Hamlin game for a few minutes this year, and get your P."

"Honest?"

"Yes, if you do something for old Plato, same 's you expect her to do something for you." Ray was quite sincere. "But not if you put the team discipline on the bum and disgrace Omega Chi. Of course I can't speak as an actual member of the team, but still, as a senior, I hear things———"

"How d'you mean 'disgrace'?"

"Don't you know that because you've been getting so savage about Frazer the whole team 's getting mad?" said the coach. "Cowles and Griffin and I have been talking over the whole proposition. Your boosting Frazer——"

"Look here," from Carl, "I won't crawl down on my opinion about Frazer. Folks haven't understood him."

"Lord love you, son," soothed Howard Griffin, "we aren't trying to change your opinion of Frazer. We're, your friends, you know. We're proud of you for standing up for him. Only thing is, now that he's practically fired, just tell me how it's going to help him or you or anybody else, now, to make everybody sore by roasting them because they can't agree with you. Boost; don't knock! Don't make everybody think you're a crank."

"To be frank," added Mr. Bjorken, "you're just as likely to hurt Frazer as to help him by stirring up all this bad blood. Look here. I suppose that if the faculty had already fired Frazer you'd still go ahead trying to buck them."

"Hadn't thought about it, but suppose I would."

"Afraid it might be that way. But haven't you seen by this time about how much good it does for one lone sophomore to try and run the faculty?" It was the coach talking again, but the gravely nodding mandarin-like heads of Howard and Ray accompanied him. "Mind you, I don't mean to disparage you personally, but you must admit that you can't hardly expect to boss everything. Just what good 'll it do to go on shouting for Frazer? Quite aside from the question of whether he is likely to get fired or not."

"Well," grunted Carl, nervously massaging his chin, "I don't know as it will do any direct good—except maybe waking this darn conservative college up a little; but it does make me so dog-gone sore——"

"Yes, yes, we understand, old man," the coach said, "but on the other hand here's the direct good of sitting tight and playing the game. I've heard you speak about Kipling. Well, you're like a young officer—a subaltern they call it, don't they?—in a Kipling story, a fellow that's under orders, and it's part of his game to play hard and keep his mouth shut and to not criticize his superior officers, ain't it?"

"Oh, I suppose so, but——"

"Well, it's just the same with you. Can't you see that? Think it over. What would you think of a lieutenant that tried to boss all the generals? Just same thing.... Besides, if you sit tight, you can make the team this year, I can practically promise you that. Do understand this now; it isn't a bribe; we want you to be able to play and *do* something for old Plato in a *real* way—in athletics. But you most certainly can't make the team if you're going to be a disorganizer."

"All we want you to do," put in Ray Cowles, "is not to make a public spectacle of yourself—as I'm afraid you've been doing. Admire Frazer all you want to, and talk about him to your own bunch, and don't back down on your own opinions, only don't think you've got to go round yelling about him. People get a false idea of you. I hate to have to tell you this, but several of the fellows, even in Omega Chi, have spoken about you, and wondered if you really were a regular crank. 'Of course he isn't, you poor cheese,' I tell 'em, but I can't be around to answer every one all the time, and you can't lick the whole college; that ain't the way the world does things. You don't know what a bad impression you make when you're too brash. See how I mean?"

As the council of seers rose, Carl timidly said to Ray, "Straight, now, have quite a lot of the fellows been saying I was a goat?"

"Good many, I'm afraid. All talking about you.... It's up to you. All you got to do is not think you know it all, and keep still. Keep still till you understand the faculty's difficulties just a little better. Savvy? Don't that sound fairly reasonable?"

CHAPTER X

They were gone. Carl was full of the nauseating shame which a matter-of-fact man, who supposes that he is never pilloried, knows when a conscientious friend informs him that he has been observed, criticized; that his enthusiasms have been regarded as eccentricities; his affectionate approaches toward friendship as impertinence.

There seemed to be hundreds of people in the room, nudging one another, waiting agape for him to do something idiotic; a well-advertised fool on parade. He stalked about, now shamefaced, now bursting out with a belligerent, "Aw, rats! I'll show 'em!" now plaintively beseeching, "I don't suppose I am helping Frazer, but it makes me so darn sore when nobody stands up for him—and he teaches stuff they need so much here. Gee! I'm coming to think this is a pretty rough-neck college. He's the first teacher I ever got anything out of—and——Oh, hang it! what 'd I have to get mixed up in all this for, when I was getting along so good? And if it isn't going to help him——"

His right hand became conscious of Gertie's letter crumpled in his pocket. As turning the letter over and over gave him surprisingly small knowledge of its contents, he opened it:

DEAR CARL,—You are just *silly* to tease me about any bank clerk. I don't like him any more at all and he can go with Linda all he likes, much I care!

We are enjoying good health, though it is getting quite cold now and we have the furnace running now and it feels pretty good to have it. We had *such* a good time at Adelaide's party she wore such a pretty dress. She flirted terribly with Joe Jordan though of course you'll call me a cat for telling you because you like her so much better than me & all.

Oh I haven't told you the news yet Joe has accepted a position at St. Hilary in the mill there.

I have some pretty new things for my room, a beautiful hand-painted picture. Before Joe goes there is going to be a party for him at Semina's. I wish you could come I suppose you have learned to dance well, of course you go to lots of parties at Plato with all the pretty girls & forget all about *me*.

I wish I was in Minneapolis it is pretty dull here, & such good talks you and me had *didn't* we!

Oh Carl dear Ray writes us you are sticking up for that crazy Professor Frazer. I know it must take lots of courage & I admire you *lots* for it even if Ray doesn't but oh Carl dear if you can't do any *good* by it I hope you won't get everybody talking about you without its doing any good, will you, Carl?

I do so expect you to succeed wonderfully & I hope you won't blast your career even to stand up for folks when it's too late & won't do any good.

We all expect so much of you—we are waiting! You are our knight & you aren't going to forget to keep your armor bright, nor forget,

Yours as ever,

GERTIE.

"Mmm!" remarked Carl. "Dun'no' about this knight-and-armor business. I'd look swell, I would, with a wash-boiler and a few more tons of junk on. Mmm! 'Expect you to succeed wonderfully——' Oh, I don't suppose I had ought to disappoint 'em. Don't see where I can help Frazer, anyway. Not a bit."

The Frazer affair seemed very far from him; very hysterical.

Two of the Gang ambled in with noisy proposals in regard to a game of poker, penny ante, but the thought of cards bored him. Leaving them in possession, one of them smoking the Turk's best pipe, which the Turk had been so careless as to leave in sight, he strolled out on the street and over to the campus.

There was a light in the faculty-room in the Academic Building, yet it was not a "first and third Thursday," dates on which the faculty regularly met. Therefore, it was a special meeting; therefore——

Promptly, without making any plans, Carl ran to the back of the building, shinned up a water-spout (humming "Just Before the Battle, Mother"), pried open a class-room window with his large jack-knife, of the variety technically known as a "toad-stabber" (changing his tune to "Onward, Christian Soldiers"), climbed in, tiptoed through the room, stopping often to listen, felt along the plaster walls to find the door, eased the door open, calmly sat down in the corridor, pulled off his shoes, said, "Ouch, it's cold on the feets!" slipped into another class-room in the front of the building, put on his shoes, crawled out of the window, walked along a limestone ledge one foot wide to a window of the faculty-room, and peeped in.

All of the eleven assistant professors and full professors, except Frazer, were assembled, with President S. Alcott Wood in the chair, and the Greek professor addressing them, referring often to a red-leather-covered note-book.

"Um! Making a report on Frazer's lecture," said Carl, clinging precariously to the rough faces of the stones. A gust swooped around the corner of the building. He swayed, gripped the stones more tightly, and looked down. He could not see the ground. It was thirty-five or forty feet down. "Almost fell," he observed. "Gosh! my hands are chilly!" As he peered in the window again he saw the Greek professor point directly at the window, while the whole gathering startled, turned, stared. A young assistant professor ran toward the door of the room.

"Going to cut me off. Dog-gone it," said Carl. "They'll wait for me at the math.-room window. Hooray! I've started something."

He carefully moved along the ledge to a point half-way between windows and waited, flat against the wall.

Again he glanced down from the high, windy, narrow ledge. "It 'd be a long drop.... My hands are cold.... I could slip. Funny, I ain't really much scared, though.... Say! Where'd I do just this before? Oh yes!" He saw himself as little Carl, lost with Gertie in the woods, caught by Bone Stillman at the window. He laughed out as he compared the bristly virile face of Bone with the pasty face of the young professor. "Seems almost as though I was back there doing the same thing right over. Funny. But I'm not quite as scared as I was then. Guess I'm growing up. Hel-lo! here's our cunning Spanish Inquisition rubbering out of the next window."

The window of the mathematics class-room, next to the faculty-room, had opened. The young professor who was pursuing Carl peppered the night with violent words delivered in a rather pedagogic voice. "Well, sir! We have you! You might as well come and give yourself up."

Carl was silent.

The voice said, conversationally: "He's staying out there. I'll see who it is." Carl half made out a head thrusting itself from the window, then heard, in *sotto voce*, "I can't see him." Loudly again, the pursuing professor yapped: "Ah, I see you. You're merely wasting time, sir. You might just as well come here now. I shall let you stay there till you do." Softly: "Hurry back into the faculty-room and see if you can get him from that side. Bet it's one of the sneaking Frazer faction."

Carl said nothing; did not budge. He peeped at the ledge above him. It was too far for him to reach it. He tried to discern the mass of the ground in the confusing darkness below. It seemed miles down. He did not know what to do. He was lone as a mateless hawk, there on the ledge, against the wall whose stones were pinchingly cold to the small of his back and his spread-eagled arms. He swayed slightly; realized with trembling nausea what would happen if he swayed too much.... He remembered that there was pavement below him. But he did not think about giving himself up.

From the mathematics-room window came: "Watch him. I'm going out after him."

The young professor's shoulders slid out of the window. Carl carefully turned his head and found that now a form was leaning from the faculty-room window as well.

"Got me on both sides. Darn it! Well, when they haul me up on the carpet I'll have the pleasure of telling them what I think of them."

The young professor had started to edge along the ledge. He was coming very slowly. He stopped and complained to some one back in the mathematics-room, "This beastly ledge is icy, I'm afraid."

Carl piped: "Look out! Y're slipping!"

In a panic the professor slid back into the window. As his heels disappeared through it, Carl dashed by the window, running sidewise along the ledge. While the professor was cautiously risking his head in the night air outside the window again, gazing to the left, where, he had reason to suppose, Carl would have the decency to remain, Carl was rapidly worming to the right. He reached the corner of the building, felt for the tin water-pipe, and slid down it, with his coat-tail protecting his hands. Half-way down, the cloth slipped and his hand was burnt against the corrugated tin. "Consid'able slide," he murmured as he struck the ground and blew softly on his raw palm.

He walked away—not at all like a melodramatic hero of a slide-by-night, but like a matter-of-fact young man going to see some one about business of no great importance. He abstractedly brushed his left sleeve or his waistcoat, now and then, as though he wanted to appear neat.

He tramped into the telephone-booth of the corner drug-store, called up Professor Frazer:

"Hello? Professor Frazer?... This is one of your students in modern drama. I've just learned—I happened to be up in the Academic Building and I happened to find out that Professor Drood is making a report to the faculty—special meeting!— about your last lecture. I've got a hunch he's going to slam you. I don't want to butt in, but I'm awfully worried; I thought perhaps you ought to know.... Who? Oh, I'm just one of your students.... You're welcome. Oh, say, Professor, g-good luck. G'-by."

Immediately, without even the excuse that some evil mind in the Gang had suggested it, he prowled out to the Greek professor's house and tied both the front and back gates. Now the fence of that yard was high and strong and provided with sharp pickets; and the professor was short and dignified. Carl regretted that he could not wait for the pleasure of seeing the professor fumble with the knots and climb the fence. But he had another errand.

He walked to the house of Professor Frazer. He stood on the walk before it. His shoulders straightened, his heels snapped together, and he raised his arm in a formal salute.

He had saluted the gentleness of Henry Frazer. He had saluted his own soul. He cried: "I will stick by him, as long as the Turk or any of 'em. I won't let Omega Chi and the coach scare me—not the whole caboodle of them. I——Oh, I don't *think* they can scare me...."

CHAPTER XI

The students of Plato were required to attend chapel every morning. President S. Alcott Wood earnestly gave out two hymns, and between them informed the Almighty of the more important news events of the past twenty-four hours, with a worried advisory manner which indicated that he felt something should be done about them at once.

President Wood was an honest, anxious body, something like a small, learned, Scotch linen-draper. He was given to being worried and advisory and to sitting up till midnight in his unventilated library, grinding at the task of putting new wrong meanings into perfectly obvious statements in the Bible. He was a series of circles—round head with smooth gray hair that hung in a bang over his round forehead; round face with round red cheeks; absurdly heavy gray mustache that almost made a circle about his puerile mouth; round button of a nose; round heavy shoulders; round little stomach in a gray sack-suit; round dumplings of feet in congress shoes that were never quite fresh-blacked or quite dusty. A harassed, honorable, studious, ignorant, humorless, joke-popping, genuinely conscientious thumb of a man. His prayers were long and intimate.

After the second hymn he would announce the coming social events—class prayer-meetings and lantern-slide lectures by missionaries. During the prayer and hymns most of the students hastily prepared for first-hour classes, with lists of dates inside their hymn-books; or they read tight-folded copies of the Minneapolis *Journal* or *Tribune*. But when the announcements began all Plato College sat up to attention, for Prexy Wood was very likely to comment with pedantic sarcasm on student peccadillos, on cards and V-neck gowns and the unforgivable crime of smoking.

As he crawled to the bare, unsympathetic chapel, the morning after spying on the faculty-room, Carl looked restlessly to the open fields, sniffed at the scent of burning leaves, watched a thin stream of blackbirds in the windy sky. He sat on the edge of a pew, nervously jiggling his crossed legs.

During the prayer and hymns a spontaneously born rumor that there would be something sensational in President Wood's announcements went through the student body. The president, as he gave out the hymns, did not look at the students, but sadly smoothed the neat green cloth on the reading-stand. His prayer, timid, sincere, was for guidance to comprehend the will of the Lord.

Carl felt sorry for him. "Poor man 's fussed. Ought to be! I'd be, too, if I tried to stop a ten-inch gun like Frazer.... He's singing hard.... Announcements, now.... What's he waiting for? Jiminy! I wish he'd spring it and get it over.... Suppose he said something about last night—me——"

President Wood stood silent. His glance drifted from row to row of students. They moved uneasily. Then his dry, precise voice declaimed:

"My friends, I have an unpleasant duty to perform this morning, but I have sought guidance in prayer, and I hope——"

Carl was agonizing: "He does know it's me! He'll ball me out and fire me publicly!... Sit tight, Ericson; hold y' nerve; think of good old Turk." Carl was not a hero. He was frightened. In a moment now all the eyes in the room would be unwinkingly focused on him. He hated this place of crowding, curious young people and drab text-hung walls. In the last row he noted the pew in which Professor Frazer sat (infrequently). He could fancy Frazer there, pale and stern. "I'm glad I spied on 'em. Might have been able to put Frazer wise to something definite if I could just have overheard 'em."

President Wood was mincing on:

"——and so, my friends, I hope that in devotion to the ideals of the Baptist Church we shall strive ever onward and upward in even our smallest daily concerns, *per aspera ad astra*, not in a spirit of materialism and modern unrest, but in a spirit of duty.

"I need not tell you that there has been a great deal of rumor about the so-called 'faculty dissensions.' But let me earnestly beseech you to give me your closest attention when I assure you that there have been *no* faculty dissensions. It is true that we have found certain teachings rather out of harmony with the ideals of Plato College. The Word of God in the Bible was good enough for our fathers who fought to defend this great land, and the Bible is still good enough for us, I guess—and I cannot find anything in the Bible about such doctrines as socialism and anarchism and evolution. Probably most of you have been fortunate enough to not have wasted any time on this theory called 'evolution.' If you don't know anything about it you have not lost anything. Absurd as it may seem, evolution says that we are all descended from monkeys! In spite of the fact that the Bible teaches us that we are the children of God. If you prefer to be the children of monkeys rather than of God, well, all I can say is, I don't! [Laughter.]

"But the old fellow Satan is always busy going to and fro even in colleges, and in the unrestrained, overgrown, secularized colleges of the East they have actually been teaching this doctrine openly for many years. Indeed, I am told that right at the University of Chicago, though it is a Baptist institution, they teach this same silly twaddle of evolution, and I cannot advise any of you to go there for graduate work. But these scientific fellows that are too wise for the Bible fall into the pits they themselves have digged, sooner or later, and they have been so smart in discovering new things about evolution that they have contradicted almost everything that Darwin, who was the high priest of this abominable cult, first taught, and they have turned the whole theory into a hodge-podge of contradictions from which even they themselves are now turning in disgust. Indeed, I am told that Darwin's own son has come out and admitted that there is nothing to this evolution. Well, we could have told him that all along, and told his father, and saved all their time, for now they are all coming right back to the Bible. We could have told them in the first place that the Word of God definitely explains the origin of man, and that anybody who tried to find out whether we were descended from monkeys was just about as wise as the man who tried to make a silk purse out of a sow's ear."

Carl was settled down in his pew, safe.

President Wood was in his stride. "All this evolutionary fad becomes ridiculous, of course, when a mind that is properly trained in clear thinking by the diligent perusal of the classics strips it of its pseudo-scientific rags and shows it straight out from the shoulder, in the fire of common sense and sound religion. And here is the point of my disquisition:

"On this selfsame evolution, this bombast of the self-pushing scientists, are founded *all* such un-Christian and un-American doctrines as socialism and anarchism and the lusts of feminism, with all their followers, such as Shaw and the fellow who tried to shoot Mr. Frick, and all the other atheists of the stripe that think so well of themselves that they are quite willing to overthrow the grand old institutions that our forefathers founded on the Constitution; and they want to set up instead—oh, they're quite willing to tell us how to run the government! They want to set up a state in which all of us who are honest enough to do a day's work shall support the lazy rascals who aren't. Yet they are very clever men. They can pull the wool over your eyes and persuade you—if you let them—that a universal willingness to let the other fellow do the work while you paint pictures of flowers and write novels about the abominations of Babylon is going to evolute a superior race! Well, when you think they are clever, this Shaw and this fellow Wells and all of them that copy Robert G. Ingersoll, just remember that the cleverest fellow of them all is the old Satan, and that he's been advocating just such lazy doctrines ever since he stirred up rebellion and discontent in the Garden of Eden!

"If these things are so, then the teachings of Professor Henry Frazer, however sincere he is, are not in accordance with the stand which we have taken here at Plato. My friends, I want you all to understand me. Certain young students of Plato appear to have felt that the faculty have not appreciated Professor Frazer. One of these students, I presume it was one of them, went so far as to attempt to spy on faculty meeting last night. Who that man is I have means of finding out at any time. But I do not wish to. For I cannot believe that he realized how dishonest was such sneaking.

"I wish to assure the malcontents that I yield to no one in my admiration of Professor Frazer's eloquence and learning in certain subjects. Only, we have not found his doctrines quite consistent with what we are trying to do. They may be a lot more smart and new-fangled than what we have out here in Minnesota, and we may be a lot of old fogies, but we are not narrow, and we wish to give him just as much right of free speech—we wish—there is—uh—no slightest—uh—desire, in fact, to impose any authority on any one. But against any perversive doctrine we must in all honesty take a firm stand.

"We carefully explained this to Professor Frazer, and permit me to inform those young men who have taken it upon themselves to be his champions, that they would do well to follow his example! For he quite agrees with us as to the need of keeping the Plato College doctrine consistent. In fact, he offered his resignation, which we reluctantly accepted, very, very reluctantly. It will take effect the first of the month, and, owing to illness in his family, he will not be giving any lectures before then. Students in his classes, by the way, are requested to report to the dean for other assignments.... And so you see how little there is to the cowardly rumors about 'faculty dissensions'!"

"Liar, liar! Dear God, they've smothered that kind, straight Frazer," Carl was groaning.

"Now, my friends, I trust you understand our position, and—uh——"

President Wood drew a breath, slapped the reading-stand, and piped, angrily:

"We have every desire to permit complete freedom of thought and speech among the students of Plato, but on my *word*, when it comes to a pass where a few students can cause this whole great institution to forget its real tasks and devote all its time to quarreling about a fad like socialism, then it's time to call a halt!

"If there are any students here who, now that I have explained that Professor Frazer leaves us of his own free will, still persist in their stubborn desire to create trouble, and still feel that the faculty have not treated Professor Frazer properly, or that we have endeavored to coerce him, then let them stand up, right here and now, in chapel. I mean it! Let them stop this cowardly running to and fro and secret gossip. Let them stand right up before us, in token of protest, here—and—now! or otherwise hold their peace!"

So well trained to the authority of schoolmasters were the students of Plato, including Carl Ericson, that they sat as uncomfortable as though they were individually accused by the plump pedant who was weakly glaring at them, his round, childish hand clutching the sloping edge of the oak reading-stand, his sack-coat wrinkled at the shoulders and sagging back from his low linen collar. Carl sighted back at Frazer's pew, hoping that he would miraculously be there to confront the dictator. The pew was empty as before. There was no one to protest against the ousting of Frazer for saying what he believed true.

Then Carl was agitated to find that Carl Ericson, a back-yard boy, was going to rise and disturb all these learned people. He was frightened again. But he stood up, faced the president, affectedly folded his arms, hastily unfolded them and put his hands in his pockets, one foot before the other, one shoulder humped a little higher than the other.

The whole audience was staring at him. He did not dare peep at them, but he could hear their murmur of amazement. Now that he was up he rather enjoyed defying them.

"Well, young man, so you are going to let us know how to run Plato," teetered the president. "I'm sure everybody will feel much obliged to you."

Carl did not move. He was aware of Genie Linderbeck rising, to his left. No one else was up, but, with Genie's frail adherence, Carl suddenly desired to rouse every one to stand for Frazer and freedom. He glanced over at the one man whom he could always trust to follow him—the Turk. A tiny movement of Carl's lips, a covert up-toss of his head, warned the Turk to rise now.

The Turk moved, started to rise, slowly, as though under force. He looked rather shamefaced. He uncrossed his legs and put his hands on the pew, on either side of his legs.

"Shame!" trembled a girl's voice in the junior section.

"Sit down!" two or three voices of men softly snarled, with a rustle of mob-muttering.

The Turk hastily crossed his legs and slumped down in his seat. Carl frowned at him imploringly, then angrily. He felt spiritually naked to ask support so publicly, but he *had* to get the Turk up. The Turk shook his head beseechingly. Carl could fancy him grunting, "Aw, thunder! I'd like to stand up, but I don't want to be a goat."

Another man rose. "I'll be darned!" thought Carl. It was the one man who would be expected not to support the heretic Frazer—it was Carl's rustic ex-room-mate, Plain Smith. Genie was leaning against the pew in front of him, but Plain Smith bulked more immovable than Carl.

No one joined the three. All through the chapel was an undertone of amazed comment and a constant low hissing of, "Sssssit down!"

The president, facing them, looked strained. It occurred to Carl that S. Alcott Wood had his side of the question. He argued about the matter, feeling detached from his stolidly defiant body. Then he cursed the president for keeping them there. He wanted to sit down. He wanted to cry out....

President Wood was speaking. "Is there any one else? Stand up, if there is. No one else? Very well, young men, I trust that you are now satisfied with your heroism, which we have all greatly appreciated, I am sure. [Laughter.] Chapel dismissed."

Instantly a swirl of men surrounded Carl, questioning: "What j' do it for? Why didn't you keep still?"

He pushed out through them. He sat blind through the first-hour quiz in physics, with the whole class watching him. The thought of the Turk's failure to rise kept unhappy vigil in his mind. The same sequence of reflections ran around like midnight mice in the wall:

"Just when I needed him.... After all his talk.... And us so chummy, sitting up all hours last night. And then the Turk throws me down.... When he'd said so many times he just wanted the chance to show how strong he was for Frazer.... Damn coward! I'll go room with Genie. By gosh——Oh, I got to be fair to the Turk. I don't suppose he could have done much real good standing up. Course it does make you feel kind of a poor nut, doing it. Genie looked——Yes, by the Jim Hill! there you are. Poor little scrawny Genie— oh yes, sure, it was up to *him* to stand up. He wasn't afraid. And the Turk, the big stiff, he was afraid to.... Just when I needed him. After all our talk about Frazer, sitting up all hours——"

Through the black whirlpool in his head pierced an irritated, "Mr. Ericson, I said! Have you gone to sleep? I understood you were excellent at standing up! What is your explanation of the phenomenon?" The professor of physics and mathematics—the same who had pursued Carl on the ledge—was speaking to him.

Carl mumbled, sullenly, "Not prepared." The class sniggered. He devoted a moment to hating them, as pariahs hate, then through his mind went whirling again, "Just wait till I see the Turk!"

- 86 -

CHAPTER XII

A notice from the president's office, commanding Carl's instant presence, was in his post-office box. He slouched into the waiting-room of the offices of the president and dean. He was an incarnate desire to say exactly what he thought to the round, woolly President Wood.

Plain Albert Smith was leaving the waiting-room. He seized Carl's hand with his plowman's paw, and, "Good-by, boy," he growled. There was nothing gallant about his appearance—his blue-flannel shirt dusty with white fuzz, his wrinkled brick-red neck, the oyster-like ear at which he kept fumbling with a seamy finger-nail of his left hand. But Carl's salute was a salute to the new king.

"How d'you mean 'good-by,' Al?"

"I've just resigned from Plato, Carl."

"How'd you happen to do that? Did they summon you here?"

"No. Just resigned," said Plain Smith. "One time when I was school-teaching I had a set-to with a school committee of farmers about teaching the kids a little botany. They said the three R's were enough. I won out, but I swore I'd stand up for any teacher that tried to be honest the way he seen it. I don't agree with Frazer about these socialists and all—fellow that's worked at the plow like I have knows a man wants to get ahead for his woman and himself, first of all, and let the walking-delegates go to work, too. But I think he's honest, all right, and, well, I stood up, and that means losing my scholarship. They won't try to fire me. Guess I'll mosey on to the U. of M. Can't probably live there as cheap as here, but a cousin of mine owns a big shoe-store and maybe I can get a job with him.... Boy, you were plucky to get up.... Glad we've got each other, finally. I feel as though you'd freed me from something. God bless you."

To the dean's assistant, in the waiting-room, Carl grandly stated: "Ericson, 1908. I'm to see the president."

"It's been arranged you're to see the dean instead. Sit down. Dean's engaged just now."

Carl was kept waiting for a half-hour. He did not like the transference to the dean, who was no anxious old lamb like S. Alcott Wood, but a young collegiate climber, with a clipped mustache, a gold eye-glass chain over one ear, a curt voice, many facts, a spurious appreciation of music, and no mellowness. He was a graduate of the University of Chicago, and aggressively proud of it. He had "earned his way through college," which all tradition and all fiction pronounce the perfect manner of acquiring a noble independence and financial ability. Indeed, the blessing of early poverty is in general praised as the perfect training for acquiring enough wealth to save one's own children from the curse of early poverty. It would be safer to malign George Washington and the Boy Scouts, professional baseball and the Y. M. C. A., than to suggest that working one's way through college is not necessarily manlier than playing and dreaming and reading one's way through.

Diffidently, without generalizing, the historian reports this fact about the dean; he had lost the graciousness of his rustic clergyman father and developed an itchingly bustling manner, a tremendous readiness for taking charge of everything in sight, by acquiring during his undergraduate days a mastery of all the petty ways of earning money, such as charging meek and stupid wealthy students too much for private tutoring, and bullying his classmates into patronizing the laundry whose agent he was.... The dean stuck his little finger far out into the air when drinking from a cup, and liked to be taken for a well-dressed man of the world.

The half-hour of waiting gave Carl a feeling of the power of the authorities. And he kept seeing Plain Smith in his cousin's shoe-store, trying to "fit" women's shoes with his large red hands. When he was ordered to "step into the dean's office, now," he stumbled in, pulling at his soft felt hat.

With his back to Carl, the dean was writing at a roll-top desk. The burnished top of his narrow, slightly bald head seemed efficient and formidable. Not glancing up, the dean snapped, "Sit down, young man."

Carl sat down. He crumpled his hat again. He stared at a framed photograph, and moved his feet about, trying to keep them quiet.

More waiting.

The dean inspected Carl, over his shoulder. He still held his pen. The fingers of his left hand tapped his desk-tablet. He turned in his swivel-chair deliberately, as though he was now ready to settle everything permanently.

"Well, young man, are you prepared to apologize to the president and faculty?"

"Apologize? What for? The president said those that wanted to protest——"

"Now we won't have any blustering, if you please, Ericson. I haven't the slightest doubt that you are prepared to give an exhibition of martyrdom. That is why I asked the privilege of taking care of you, instead of permitting you to distress President Wood any further. We will drop all this posing, if you don't mind. I assure you that it doesn't make——"

"I——"

"——the slightest impression on me, Ericson. Let's get right down to business. You know perfectly well that you have stirred up all the trouble you——"

"I——"

"——could in regard to Mr. Frazer. And I think, I really think, that we shall either have to have your written apology and your promise to think a little more before you talk, hereafter, or else we shall have to request your resignation from college. I am sorry that we apparently can't run this college to suit you, Ericson, but as we can't, why, I'm afraid we shall have to ask you not to increase our inefficiency by making all the trouble you can. Wait now; let's not have any melodrama! You may as well pick up that hat again. It doesn't seem to impress me much when you throw it down, though doubtless it was ver-ee dramatically done, oh yes, indeed, ver-ee dramatic. See here. I know you, and I know your type, my young friend, and I haven't——"

"Look here. Why do I get picked out as the goat, the one to apologize? Because I stood up first? When Prexy said to?"

"Oh, not at all. Say it's because you quite shamelessly made motions at others while you stood there, and did your best to disaffect men who hadn't the least desire to join in your trouble-making.... Now I'm very busy, young man, and I think this is all the time I shall waste on you. I shall expect to find your written——"

"Say, honest, dean," Carl suddenly laughed, "may I say just one thing before I get thrown out?"

"Certainly. We have every desire to deal justly with you, and to always give—always to give you every opportunity——"

"Well, I just wanted to say, in case I resign and don't see you again, that I admire you for your nerve. I wish I could get over feeling like a sophomore talking to a dean, and then I could tell you I hadn't supposed there was anybody could talk to me the way you have and get away with it. I'd always thought I'd punch their head off, and here you've had me completely buffaloed. It's wonderful! Honestly, it never struck me till just this second that there isn't any law that compels me to sit here and take all this. You had me completely hypnotized."

"You know I might retort truthfully and say I am not accustomed to have students address me in quite this manner. I'm glad, however, to find that you are sensible enough not to make an amusing show of yourself by imagining that you are making a noble fight for freedom. By decision of the president and myself I am compelled to give you this one chance only. Unless I find your apology in my letter-box here by five this evening I shall have to suspend you or bring you up before the faculty for dismissal. But, my boy, I feel that perhaps, for all your mistaken notions, you do have a certain amount of courage, and I want to say a word——"

The dean did say a word; in fact he said a large number of admirable words, regarding the effect of Carl's possible dismissal on his friends, his family, and, with an almost tearful climax, on his mother.

"Now go and think it over; pray over it, unselfishly, my boy, and let me hear from you before five."

Only——

The reason why Carl *did* visualize his mother, the reason why the Ericson kitchen became so clear to him that he saw his tired-faced mother reaching up to wind the alarm-clock that stood beside the ball of odd string on the shelf above the water-pail, the reason why he felt caved-in at the stomach, was that he knew he was going to leave Plato, and did not know where in the world he was going.

A time of quick action; of bursting the bonds even of friendship. He walked quietly into Genie Linderbeck's neat room, with its rose-hued comforter on a narrow brass bed, passe-partouted Copley prints, and a small oak table with immaculate green desk-blotter, and said good-by.... His hidden apprehension, the cold, empty feeling of his stomach, the nervous intensity of his motions, told him that he was already on the long trail that leads to fortune and Bowery lodging-houses and death and happiness. Even while he was warning himself that he must not go, that he owed it to his "folks" to apologize and stay, he was stumbling into the bank and drawing out his ninety-two dollars. It seemed a great sum. While waiting for it he did sums on the back of a deposit-slip:

	92.00	out of bank	
	2.27	in pocket	
	about .10	at room	
	———————		
	tot. 94.37		
	Owe Tailor	1.45	
	" Turk	.25	
	To Mpls.	3.05	

	To Chi. probably 15 to	18.00	
.	To N. Y 20 to	30.00	
	To Europe (steerage)	40.00	
	————	————	
	Total (about)	92.75	————would take me to Europe!

"Golly! I could go to Europe, to Europe! now, if I wanted to, and have maybe two plunks over, for grub on the railroad. But I'd have to allow something for tips, I guess. Maybe it wouldn't be as much as forty dollars for steerage. Ought to allow———Oh, thunder! I've got enough to make a mighty good start seeing the world, anyway."

On the street a boy was selling extras of the *Plato Weekly Times*, with the heading:

PRESIDENT CRUSHES STUDENT
REBELLION

Plato Demonstration for Anarchist Handled
Without Gloves

Carl read that he and two other students, "who are alleged to have been concerned in several student pranks," had attempted to break up a chapel meeting, but had been put to shame by the famous administrator, S. Alcott Wood. He had never seen his name in the press, except some three times in the local items of the *Joralemon Dynamite*. It looked so intimidatingly public that he tried to forget it was there. He chuckled when he thought of Plain Smith and Genie Linderbeck as "concerned in student pranks." But he was growing angry. He considered staying and fighting his opponents to the end. Then he told himself that he must leave Plato, after having announced to Genie that he was going.... He had made all of his decision except the actual deciding.

He omitted his noonday dinner and tramped into the country, trying to plan how and where he would go. As evening came, cloudy and chill in a low wooded tract miles north of Plato, with dead boughs keening and the uneasy air threatening a rain that never quite came, the loneliness of the land seemed to befog all the possibilities of the future.... He wanted the lamp-lit security of his room, with the Turk and the Gang in red sweaters, singing ragtime; with the Frazer affair a bad dream that was forgotten. The world outside Plato would all be like these lowering woods and dreary swamps.

He turned. He could find solace only in making his mind a blank. Sullen, dull, he watched the sunset, watched the bellying cumulus clouds mimic the Grand Cañon. He had to see the Grand Cañon! He would!... He had turned the corner. His clammy heart was warming. He was slowly coming to understand that he was actually free to take youth's freedom.

He saw the vision of the America through which he might follow the trail like the pioneers whose spiritual descendant he was. How noble was the panorama that thrilled this one-generation American can be understood only by those who have smelled our brown soil; not by the condescending gods from abroad who come hither to gather money by lecturing on our evil habit of money-gathering, and return to Europe to report that America is a land of Irish politicians, Jewish theatrical managers, and mining millionaires who invariably say, "I swan to calculate"; all of them huddled in unfriendly hotels or in hovels set on hopeless prairie. Not such the America that lifted Carl's chin in wonder——

Cities of tall towers; tawny deserts of the Southwest and the flawless sky of cornflower blue over sage-brush and painted butte; silent forests of the Northwest; golden China dragons of San Francisco; old orchards of New England; the oily Gulf of Mexico where tramp steamers puff down to Rio; a snow-piled cabin among somber pines of northern mountains. Elsewhere, elsewhere, elsewhere, beyond the sky-line, under larger stars, where men ride jesting and women smile. Names alluring to the American he repeated— Shenandoah, Santa Ynez, the Little Big Horn, Baton Rouge, the Great Smokies, Rappahannock, Arizona, Cheyenne, Monongahela, Androscoggin; cañon and bayou; sycamore and mesquite; Broadway and El Camino Real....

He hurled along into Plato. He went to Mrs. Henkel's for supper. He smiled at the questions dumped upon him, and evaded answering. He took Mae Thurston aside and told her that he was leaving Plato. He wanted to call on Professor Frazer. He did not dare. From a pleasant gentleman drinking tea Frazer had changed to a prophet whom he revered.

Carl darted into his room. The Turk was waiting for him. Carl cut short the Turk's apologies for not having supported Frazer, with the dreadful curt pleasantness of an alienated friend, and, as he began packing his clothes in two old suit-cases, insisted, "It's all right—was your biz whether you stood up in chapel or not." He hunted diligently through the back of the closet for a non-existent shoe, in order to get away from the shamefaced melancholy which covered the Turk when Carl presented him with all his books, his skees, and his pet hockey-stick. He prolonged the search because it had occurred to him that, as it was now eleven o'clock, and the train north left at midnight, the Minneapolis train at 2 A.M., it might be well to decide where he was going when he went away. Well, Minneapolis and Chicago. Beyond that—he'd wait and see. Anywhere—he could go anywhere in all the world, now....

He popped out of the closet cheerfully.

While the Turk mooned, Carl wrote short honest notes to Gertie, to his banker employer, to Bennie Rusk, whom he addressed as "Friend Ben." He found himself writing a long and spirited letter to Bone Stillman, who came out of the backwater of ineffectuality as a man who had dared. Frankly he wrote to his mother—his mammy he wistfully called her. To his father he could not write. With quick thumps of his fist he stamped the letters, then glanced at the Turk. He was gay, mature, business-like, ready for anything. "I'll pull out in half an hour now," he chuckled.

"Gosh!" sighed the Turk. "I feel as if I was responsible for everything. Oh, say, here's a letter I forgot to give you. Came this afternoon."

The letter was from Gertie.

DEAR CARL,—I hear that you *are* standing for that Frazer just as much as ever and really Carl I think you might consider other people's feelings a little and not be so selfish——

Without finishing it, Carl tore up the letter in a fury. Then, "Poor kid; guess she means well," he thought, and made an imaginary bow to her in farewell.

There was a certain amount of the milk of human-kindness in the frozen husk he had for a time become. But he must be blamed for icily rejecting the Turk's blundering attempts to make peace. He courteously—courtesy, between these two!—declined the Turk's offer to help him carry his suit-cases to the station. That was like a slap.

"Good-by. Hang on tight," he said, as he stooped to the heavy suit-cases and marched out of the door without looking back.

By some providence he was saved from the crime of chilly self-righteousness. On the darkness of the stairs he felt all at once how responsive a chum the Turk had been. He dropped the suit-cases, not caring how they fell, rushed back into the room, and found the Turk still staring at the door. He cried:

"Old man, I was——Say, you yahoo, are you going to make me carry both my valises to the depot?"

They rushed off together, laughing, promising to write to each other.

The Minneapolis train pulled out, with Carl trying to appear commonplace. None of the sleepy passengers saw that the Golden Fleece was draped about him or that under his arm he bore the harp of Ulysses. He was merely a young man taking a train at a way-station.

PART II
THE ADVENTURE OF ADVENTURING

CHAPTER XIII

There are to-day in the mind of Carl Ericson many confused recollections of the purposeless wanderings which followed his leaving Plato College. For more than a year he went down, down in the social scale, down to dirt and poverty and association with the utterly tough and reckless. But day by day his young joy of wandering matured into an ease in dealing with whatever man or situation he might meet. He had missed the opportunity of becoming a respectable citizen which Plato offered. Now he did all the grubby things which Plato obviated that her sons might rise to a place in society, to eighteen hundred dollars a year and the possession of evening clothes and a knowledge of Greek. But the light danced more perversely in his eyes every day of his roving.

The following are the several jobs for which Carl first applied in Chicago, all the while frightened by the roar and creeping shadows of the city:

Tutoring the children of a millionaire brewer; keeping time on the Italian and Polack washers of a window-cleaning company; reporting on an Evanston newspaper; driving a taxicab, a motor-truck; keeping books for a suburban real-estate firm. He had it ground into him, as grit is ground into your face when you fall from a bicycle, that every one in a city of millions is too busy to talk to a stranger unless he sees a sound reason for talking. He changed the *Joralemon Dynamite's* phrase, "accept a position" to "get a job"—and he got a job, as packer in a department store big as the whole of Joralemon. Since the street throngs had already come to seem no more personal and separable than the bricks in the buildings, he was not so much impressed by the crowds in the store as by the number of things for women to hang upon themselves. He would ramble in at lunch-time to stare at them and marvel, "You can't beat it!"

From eight till twelve-thirty and from one till six or seven, during nearly two months, Carl stood in a long, brick-walled, stuffy room, inundated by floods of things to pack, wondering why he had ever left Plato to become the slave of a Swede foreman. The Great World, as he saw it through a tiny hole in one of the opaque wire-glass windows, consisted of three bars of a rusty fire-escape-landing against a yellow brick wall, with a smudge of black on the wall below the landing.

Within two days he was calling the packing-room a prison. The ceaseless rattle of speckled gray wrapping-paper, the stamp of feet on the gray cement floor, the greasy gray hair of the packer next to him, the yellow-stained, cracked, gray wash-bowl that served for thirty men, such was his food for dreams.

Because his muscles were made of country earth and air he distanced the packers from the slums, however. He became incredibly swift at nailing boxes and crates and smashing the heavy wrapping-paper into shape about odd bundles. The foreman promised to make Carl his assistant. But on the cold December Saturday when his elevation was due he glanced out of a window, and farewell all ambition as a packer.

The window belonged to the Florida Bakery and Lunch Room, where Carl was chastely lunching. There was dirty sawdust on the floor, six pine tables painted red and adorned with catsup-bottles whose mouths were clotted with dried catsup, and a long counter scattered with bread and white cakes and petrified rolls. Behind the counter a snuffling, ill-natured fat woman in slippers handed bags of crullers to shrill-voiced children who came in with pennies. The tables were packed with over-worked and underpaid men, to whom lunch was merely a means of keeping themselves from feeling inconveniently empty—a state to which the leadlike viands of the Florida Lunch Room were a certain prevention.

Carl was gulping down salty beef stew and bitter coffee served in handleless cups half an inch thick. Beside him, elbow jogging elbow, was a surly-faced man in overalls. The old German waiters shuffled about and bawled, "*Zwei* bif stew, *ein* cheese-cake." Dishes clattered incessantly. The sicky-sweet scent of old pastry, of coffee-rings with stony raisins and buns smeared with dried cocoanut fibers, seemed to permeate even the bitter coffee.

Carl got down most of his beef stew, attacked and gave up a chunk of hard boiled potato, and lighted a cheap Virginia cigarette. He glanced out of the dirty window. Before it, making inquiries of a big, leisurely policeman, was a slim, exquisite girl of twenty, rosy-cheeked, smart of hat, impeccable of gloves, with fluffy white furs beneath her chin, which cuddled into the furs with a hint of a life bright and spacious. She laughed as she talked to the policeman, she shrugged her shoulders with the exhilaration of winter, and skipped away.

"Bet she'd be a peach to know.... Fat chance I'd have to meet her, wrapping up baby-carriages for the North Shore commuters all day! All day!... Well, guess I'm going to honorably discharge myself!"

He left the job that afternoon.

His satiny Norse cheeks shone as he raced home through a rising blizzard, after dinner at the Florida Lunch Room, where he had allowed himself a ten-cent dessert for celebration.

But when he lolled in his hall bedroom, with his eyes attracted, as usual, to the three cracks in the blue-painted ceiling which made a rough map of Africa, when he visioned lands where there were lions and desert instead of department-store packages, his happiness wilted in face of the fact that he had only $10.42, with $8.00 due him from the store the following Tuesday. Several times he subtracted the $3.00 he owed the landlady from $18.42, but the result persisted in being only $15.42. He could not make $15.42 appear a reasonable sum with which to start life anew.

He had to search for a new job that evening. Only—he was so tired; it was so pleasant to lie there with his sore feet cooling against the wall, picturing a hunt in Africa, with native servants bringing him things to eat: juicy steaks and French-fried potatoes and gallons of ale (a repast which he may have been ignorant in assigning to the African jungles, but which seemed peculiarly well chosen, after a lunch-room dinner of watery corned-beef hash, burnt German-fried potatoes, and indigestible hot mince-pie). His thoughts drifted off to Plato. But Carl had a certain resoluteness even in these loose days. He considered the manœuvers for a new job. He desired one which would permit him to go to theaters with the girl in white furs whom he had seen that noon—the unknown fairy of his discontent.

It may be noted that he took this life quite seriously. Though he did not suppose that he was going to continue dwelling in a hall bedroom, yet never did he regard himself as a collegian Haroun-al-Raschid on an amusing masquerade, pretending to be no better than the men with whom he worked. Carl was no romantic hero incog. He was a workman, and he knew it. Was not his father a carpenter? his father's best friend a tailor? Had he not been a waiter at Plato?

But not always a workman. Carl had no conception of world-wide class-consciousness; he had no pride in being a proletarian. Though from Bone's musings and Frazer's lectures he had drawn a vague optimism about a world-syndicate of nations, he took it for granted that he was going to be rich as soon as he could.

Job. He had to have a job. He got stiffly up from the iron bed, painfully drew on his shoes, after inspecting the hole in the sole of the left shoe and the ripped seam at the back of the right. He pulled tight the paper-thin overcoat which he had bought at a second-hand dealer's shop, and dared a Chicago blizzard, with needles of snow thundering by on a sixty-mile gale. Through a street of unutterably drab stores and saloons he plowed to the Unallied Taxicab Company's garage. He felt lonely, cold, but he observed with ceaseless interest the new people, different people, who sloped by him in the dun web of the blizzard. The American marveled at a recently immigrated Slav's astrachan cap.

He had hung about the Unallied garage on evenings when he was too poor to go to vaudeville. He had become decidedly friendly with the night washer, a youngster from Minneapolis. Trotting up to the washer, who was digging caked snow from the shoes of a car, he blurted:

"Say, Coogan, I've beat my job at ——'s. How's chances for getting a taxi to drive? You know I know the game."

"You? Driving a taxi?" stammered the washer. "Why, say, there was a guy that was a road-tester for the Blix Company and he's got a cousin that knows Bathhouse John, and that guy with all his pull has been trying to get on drivin' here for the last six months and ain't landed it, so you see about how much chance you got!"

"Gosh! it don't look much like I had much chance, for a fact."

"Tell you what I'll do, though. Why don't you get on at some automobile factory, and then you could ring in as a chauffeur, soon 's you got some recommends you could take to the Y. M. C. A. employment bureau." The washer gouged at a clot of ice with his heel, swore profusely, and went on: "Here. You go over to the Lodestar Motor Company's office, over on La Salle, Monday, and ask for Bill Coogan, on the sales end. He's me cousin, and you tell him to give you a card to the foreman out at the works, and I guess maybe you'll get a job, all right."

Tuesday morning, after a severe questioning by the foreman, Carl was given a week's try-out without pay at the Lodestar factory. He proved to be one of those much-sought freaks in the world of mechanics, a natural filer. The uninspired filer, unaware of the niceties of the art, saws up and down, whereas the instinctive filer, like Carl, draws his file evenly across the metal, and the result fits its socket truly. So he was given welcome, paid twenty-five cents an hour, and made full member of exactly such a gang as he had known at Plato, after he had laughed away the straw boss who tried to make him go ask for a left-handed monkey-wrench. He roomed at a machinists' boarding-house, and enjoyed the furious discussions over religion and the question of air *versus* water cooling far more than he had ever enjoyed the polite jesting at Mrs. Henkel's.

He became friendly with the foreman of the repair-shop, and was promised a "chance." While the driver who made the road-tests of the cars was ill Carl was called on as a substitute. The older workmen warned him that no one could begin road-testing so early and hold the job. But Carl happened to drive the vice-president of the firm. He discussed bass-fishing in Minnesota with the vice-president, and he was retained as road-tester, getting his chauffeur's license. Two months later, when he was helping in the overhauling of a car in the repair-shop, he heard a full-bodied man with a smart English overcoat and a supercilious red face ask curtly of the shop foreman where he could get a "crack shuffer, right away, one that can give the traffic cops something to do for their money."

The foreman always stopped to scratch his chin when he had to think. This process gave Carl time to look up from his repairs and blandly remark: "That's me. Want to try me?"

Half an hour later Carl was engaged at twenty-five dollars a week as the Ruddy One's driver. Before Monday noon he had convinced the Ruddy One that he was no servant, but a mechanical expert. He drove the Ruddy One to his Investments and Securities office in the morning, and back at five; to restaurants in the evening. Not infrequently, with the wind whooping about corners, he slept peacefully in the car till two in the morning, outside a café. And he was perfectly happy. He was at last seeing the Great World. As he manœuvered along State Street he rejoiced in the complications of the traffic and tooted his horn unnecessarily. As he waited before tall buildings, at noon, he gazed up at them with a superior air of boredom—because he was so boyishly proud of being a part of all this titanic life that he was afraid he might show it. He gloried in every new road, in driving along the Lake Shore, where the horizon was bounded not by unimaginative land, but by restless water.

Then the Ruddy One's favorite roads began to be familiar to Carl, too familiar, and he so hated his sot of an employer that he caught himself muttering, while driving, "Thank the Lord I sit in front and don't have to see that chunk of raw beefsteak he calls a neck."

While he waited for the fifth time before a certain expensive but not exclusive roadhouse, with the bouncing giggles of girls inside spoiling the spring night, he studied the background as once he had studied his father's woodshed. He was not, unfortunately, shocked by wine and women. But he was bored by box-trees. There was a smugly clipped box-tree on either side of the carriage entrance, the leaves like cheap green lacquer in the glare of the arc-light, which brought out all the artificiality of the gray-and-black cinder drive. He felt that five pilgrimages to even the best of box-trees were enough. It would be perfectly unreasonable for a free man to come here to stare at box-trees a sixth time. "All right," he growled. "I guess my-wandering-boy-to-night is going to beat it again."

While he drove to the garage he pondered: "Is it worth twenty-five plunks to me to be able to beat it to-night instead of waiting four days till pay-day? Nope. I'm a poor man."

But at 5 A.M. he was hanging about the railroad-yards at Hammond, recalling the lessons of youth in "flipping trains"; and at seven he was standing on the bumpers between two freight-cars, clinging to the brake-rod, looking out to the open meadows of Indiana, laughing to see farm-houses ringed with apple-blossoms and sweet with April morning. The cinders stormed by him. As he swung with the cars, on curves, he saw the treacherous wheels grinding beneath him. But to the chuck-a-chuck, chuck-a-chuck, chuck-a-chuck of the trucks he hummed, "Never turn back, never tur' back, never tur' back."

CHAPTER XIV

A young hobo named Carl Ericson crawled from the rods of an N. & W. freight-car at Roanoke, Virginia, on a May day, with spring at full tide and the Judas-trees a singing pink on the slopes of the Blue Ridge.

"Hm!" grunted the young hobo. "I like these mountains. Guess I'll stay here awhile.... Virginia! Plantations and Civil War history and Richmond and everything, and me here!"

A frowzy old hobo poked a somnolent head up from a pile of lumber near the tracks and yawned welcome to the recruit. "Hello, Slim. How's tricks?"

"Pretty good. What's the best section to batter for a poke-out, Billy?"

"To the right, over that way, and straight out."

"Much 'bliged," said Slim—erstwhile Ericson. "Say, j' know of any jobs in this——"

"Any *whats*?"

"Jobs."

"Jobs? You looking for——Say, you beat it. Gwan. Chase yourself. Gwan now; don't stand there. You ain't no decent 'bo. You're another of those Unfortunate Workmen that's spoiling the profesh." The veteran stared at Carl reprovingly, yet with a little sadness, too, at the thought of how bitterly he had been deceived in this young comrade, and his uncombed head slowly vanished amid the lumber.

Carl grinned and started up-town. He walked into four restaurants. At noon, in white jacket, he was bustling about as waiter in the dining-room of the Waskahominie Hotel, which had "white service" as a feature.

Within two days he was boon companion of a guest of the Waskahominie— Parker Heye, an actor famous from Cape Charles to Shockeysville, now playing heavies at Roanoke in the Great Riley Tent Show, Presenting a Popular Repertoire of Famous Melodramas under Canvas, Rain or Shine, Admittance Twenty-five Cents, Section Reserved for Colored People, the Best Show under Canvas, This Week Only.

When Parker Heye returned from the theater Carl sat with him in a room which had calico-like wall-paper, a sunken bed with a comforter out of which oozed a bit of its soiled cotton entrails, a cracked water-pitcher on a staggering wash-stand, and a beautiful new cuspidor of white china hand-painted with pink moss-roses tied with narrow blue ribbon.

Carl listened credulously to Heye's confidences as to how jealous was Riley, the actor-manager, of Heye's art, how Heye had "knocked them all down" in a stock company at Newport News, and what E. H. Sothern had said to him when they met in Richmond as guests of the Seven Pines Club.

"Say," rasped Heye, "you're a smart young fellow, good-looking, ejucated. Why don't you try to get an engagement? I'll knock you down to Riley. The second juvenile 's going to leave on Saturday, and there ain't hardly time to get anybody from Norfolk."

"Golly! that 'd be great!" cried Carl, who, like every human being since Eden, with the possible exceptions of Calvin and Richard Mansfield, had a secret belief that he could be a powerful actor.

"Well, I'll see what I can do for you," said Heye, at parting, alternately snapping his suspenders and scratching his head. Though he was in his stocking-feet and coat-less, though the back of his neck was a scraggle of hair, Parker Heye was preferable to the three Swiss waiters snoring in the hot room under the eaves, with its door half open, opposite the half-open door of the room where negro chambermaids tumbled and snorted in uncouth slumber. Carl's nose wrinkled with bitter fastidiousness as he pulled off his clothes, sticky with heat, and glared at the swathed forms of the waiters. He was the aristocrat among proletarians, going back to His Own People—of the Great Riley Tent Show.

As second juvenile of the Tent Show, Carl received only twelve dollars a week, but Mr. Riley made him promises rich as the Orient beryl, and permitted him to follow the example of two of the bandsmen and pitch a cot on the trampled hay flooring of the dressing-room tent, behind the stage. There also Carl prepared breakfast on an alcohol-stove. The canvas creaked all night; negroes and small boys stuck inquisitive heads under the edge of the canvas. But it was worth it—to travel on again; to have his mornings free except for an hour's rehearsal; to climb to upland meadows of Virginia and Kentucky, among the pines and laurel and rhododendron; tramping up past the log cabins plastered with mud, where pickaninnies stared shyly, past glens shining with dogwood, and friendly streams. Once he sat for an hour on Easter Knob, gazing through a distant pass whose misty blue he pretended was the ocean. Once he heard there were moonshiners back in the hills. He talked to bearded Dunkards and their sunbonneted wives; and when he found a Confederate veteran he listened to the tale of the defense of Richmond, delighted to find that the Boys in Gray were not merely names in the history-books.

Of all these discoveries he wrote to his mother, wishing that her weary snow-bleached life might know the Southern sun. And the first five dollars he saved he sent to her.

But as soon as Carl became an actor Parker Heye grew jealous of him, and was gratingly contemptuous when he showed him how to make up, among the cheap actors jammed in the men's dressing-room, before a pine board set on two saw-horses, under the light of a flaring kerosene-torch. Carl came to hate Heye and his splotched face, his pale, large eyes and yellow teeth and the bang on his forehead, his black string tie that was invariably askew, his slovenly blue suit, his foppishly shaped tan button shoes with "bulldog" toes. Heye invariably jeered: "Don't make up so heavy.... Well, put a *little* rouge on your lips. What d'you think you are? A blooming red-lipped Venus?... Try to learn to walk across the stage as if you had *one* leg that wasn't wood, anyway.... It's customary to go to sleep when you're playing a listening rôle, but don't snore!... Oh, you're a swell actor! Think of me swallering your story about having been t' college!... Don't make up your eyebrows so heavy, you fool.... Why you ever wanted to be an actor——!"

The Great Riley agreed with all that Heye said, and marveled with Heye that he had ever tried an amateur. Carl found the dressing-room a hay-dusty hell. But he enjoyed acting in "The Widow's Penny," "Alabama Nell," "The Moonshiner's Daughter," and "The Crook's Revenge" far more than he had enjoyed picking phrases out of Shakespeare at a vaguely remembered Plato. Since, in Joralemon and Plato, he had been brought up on melodrama, he believed as much as did the audience in the plays. It was a real mountain cabin from which he fired wonderfully loud guns in "The Moonshiner's Daughter"; and when the old mountaineer cried, "They ain't going to steal mah gal!" Carl was damp at the eyes, and swore with real fervor the oath to protect the girl, sure that in the ravine behind the back-drop his bearded foe-men were lurking.

"The Crook's Revenge" was his favorite, for he was cast as a young millionaire and wore evening clothes (second-hand). He held off a mob of shrieking gangsters, crouched behind an overturned table in a gambling-den. He coolly stroked the lovely hair of the ingénue, Miss Evelyn L'Ewysse, with one hand, leveled a revolver with the other, and made fearless jests the while, to the infinite excitement of the audience, especially of the hyah-hyah-hyahing negroes, whose faces, under the flicker of lowered calcium-carbide lights, made a segregated strip of yellow-black polka-dotted with white eye-balls.

When the people were before him, respectful to art under canvas, Carl could love them; but even the tiniest ragged-breeched darky was bold in his curiosity about the strolling players when they appeared outside, and Carl was self-conscious about the giggles and stares that surrounded him when he stopped on the street or went into a drug-store for the comfortable solace of a banana split. He was in a rage whenever a well-dressed girl peeped at him amusedly from a one-lunged runabout. The staring so flustered him that even the pride of coming from Chicago and knowing about motors did not prevent his feeling feeble at the knees as he tried to stalk by the grinning motored aristocracy. He would return to the show-tent, to hate the few tawdry drops and flats—the patch of green spattered with dirty white which variously simulated a daisy-field, a mountainside, and that part of Central Park directly opposite the Fifth Avenue residence of the millionaire counterfeiter, who, you remember, always comes out into the street to plot with his confederates. Carl hated with peculiar heartiness the anemic, palely varnished, folding garden bench, which figured now as a seat in the moonshiner's den, and now, with a cotton leopard-skin draped over it, as a fauteuil in the luxurious drawing-room of Mrs. Van Antwerp. The garden bench was, however, associated with his learning to make stage love to Miss Evelyn L'Ewysse.

It was difficult to appear unconscious of fifty small boys all smacking their lips in unison, while he kissed the air one centimeter in front of Miss L'Ewysse's lips. But he learned the art. Indeed, he began to lessen that centimeter of safety.

Miss Evelyn L'Ewysse (christened Lena Ludwig, and heir presumptive to one of the best delicatessens in Newport News) reveled in love-making on and off. Carl was attracted by her constantly, uncomfortably. She smiled at him in the wings, smoothed her fluffy blond hair at him, and told him in confidence that she was a high-school graduate, that she was used to much, oh, *much* better companies, and was playing under canvas for a lark. She bubbled: "*Ach*, Louie, say, ain't it hot! Honest, Mr. Ericson, I don't see how you stand it like you do.... Say, honest, that was swell business you pulled in the third act last night.... Say, I know what let's do—let's get up a swell act and get on the Peanut Circuit. We'd hit Broadway with a noise like seventeen marine bands.... Say, honest, Mr. Ericson, you do awful well for——I bet you ain't no amachoor. I bet you been on before."

He devoured it.

One night, finding that Miss Evelyn made no comment on his holding her hand, he lured her out of the tent during a long wait, trembled, and kissed her. Her fingers gripped his shoulders agitatedly, plucked at his sleeve as she kissed him back. She murmured, "Oh, you hadn't ought to do that." But afterward she would kiss him every time they were alone, and she told him with confidential giggles of Parker Heye's awkward attempts to win her. Heye's most secret notes she read, till Carl seriously informed her that she was violating a trust. Miss Evelyn immediately saw the light and promised she would "never, never, never do anythin' like that again, and, honest, she hadn't realized she was doing anythin' dishon'able, but Heye is such an old pest"; which was an excuse for her weeping on his shoulder and his kissing the tears away.

All day he looked forward to their meetings. Yet constantly the law of the adventurer, which means the instinct of practical decency, warned him that this was no amour for him; that he must not make love where he did not love; that this good-hearted vulgarian was too kindly to tamper with and too absurd to love. Only——And again his breath would draw in with swift exultation as he recalled how elastic were her shoulders to stroke.

It was summer now, and they were back in Virginia, touring the Eastern Shore. Carl, the prairie-born, had been within five miles of the open Atlantic, though he had not seen it. Along the endless flat potato-fields, broken by pine-groves under whose sultry shadow negro cabins sweltered, the heat clung persistently. The show-tent was always filled with a stale scent of people.

At the town of Nankiwoc the hotel was not all it might have been. Evelyn L'Ewysse announced that she was "good and sick of eating a vaudeville dinner with the grub acts stuck around your plate in a lot of birds' bath-tubs—little mess of turnips and a dab of spinach and a fried cockroach. And when it comes to sleeping another night on a bed like a gridiron, no—thank—*you*! And believe me, if I see that old rube hotel-keeper comb his whiskers at the hall hat-rack again—he keeps a baby comb in his vest pocket with a lead-pencil and a cigar some drummer gave him—if I have to watch him comb that alfalfa again I'll bite his ears off and get pinched by the S. P. C. A.!"

With Mrs. Lubley, the old lady and complacent unofficial chaperon of the show, Eve was going to imitate Carl and the two bandsmen, and sleep in the dressing-room tent, over half of which was devoted to the women of the company.

Every day Carl warned himself that he must go no farther, but every night as Eve and he parted, to sleep with only a canvas partition between them, he cursed the presence of the show chaperon, and of the two bandsmen, always distressingly awake and talking till after midnight.

A hot June night. The whole company had been invited to a dance at the U. C. V. Hall; the two bandsmen were going; the chaperon—lively old lady with experience on the burlesque circuit—was gaily going. Carl and Eve were not. It had taken but one glance between them to decide that.

They sat outside the silent tent, on a wardrobe trunk. What manner of night it was, whether starlit or sullen, Carl did not know; he was aware only that it was oppressive, and that Eve was in his arms in the darkness. He kissed her moist, hot neck. He babbled incoherently of the show people, but every word he said meant that he was palpitating because her soft body was against his. He knew—and he was sure that she knew—that when they discussed Heye's string tie and pretended to laugh, they were agitatedly voicing their intoxication.

His voice unsteady, Carl said: "Jiminy! it's so hot, Eve! I'm going to take off this darn shirt and collar and put on a soft shirt. S-say, w-why don't you put on a kimono or something? Be so much cooler."

"Oh, I don't know as I ought to——" She was frightened, awed at Bacchic madness. "D-do you think it would be all right?"

"Why not? Guess anybody's got a right to get cool—night like this. Besides, they won't be back till 4 P.M. And you got to get cool. Come on."

And he knew—and he was sure that she knew—that all he said was pretense. But she rose and said, nebulously, as she stood before him, ruffling his hair: "Well, I would like to get cool. If you think it's all right——I'll put on something cooler, anyway."

She went. Carl could hear a rustling in the women's end of the dressing-room tent. Fevered, he listened to it. Fevered, he changed to an outing-shirt, open at the throat. He ran out, not to miss a moment with her.... She had not yet come. He was too overwrought to heed a small voice in him, a voice born of snow-fields colored with sunset and trained in the quietudes of Henry Frazer's house, which insisted: "Go slow! Stop!" A louder voice throbbed like the pulsing of the artery in his neck, "She's coming!"

Through the darkness her light garment swished against the long grass. He sprang up. Then he was holding her, bending her head back. He exulted to find that his gripping hand was barred from the smoothness of her side only by thin silk that glided and warmed under his fingers. She sat on his knees and snuggled her loosened hair tinglingly against his bare chest. He felt that she was waiting for him to go on.

Suddenly he could not, would not, go on.

"Dearest, we mustn't!" he mourned.

"O Carl!" she sobbed, and stopped his words with clinging lips.

He found himself waiting till she should finish the kiss that he might put an end to this.

Perhaps he was checked by provincial prejudices about chivalry. But perhaps he had learned a little self-control. In any case, he had stopped for a second to think, and the wine of love was gone flat. He wished she would release him. Also, her hair was tickling his ear. He waited, patiently, till she should finish the kiss.

Her lips drew violently from his, and she accused, "You don't want to kiss me!"

"Look here; I want to kiss you, all right—Lord——" For a second his arms tightened; then he went on, cold: "But we'll both be good and sorry if we go too far. It isn't just a cowardly caution. It's——Oh, you know."

"Oh yes, yes, yes, we mustn't go too far, Carl. But can't we just sit like this? O sweetheart, I am so tired! I want somebody to care for me a little. That isn't wicked, is it? I want you to take me in your arms and hold me close, close, and comfort me. I want so much to be comforted. We needn't go any further, need we?"

"Oh now, good Lord! Eve, look here: don't you know we can't go on and not go farther? I'm having a hard enough time——" He sprang up, shakily lighting a cigarette. He stroked her hair and begged: "Please go, Eve. I guess I haven't got very good control over myself. Please. You make me——"

"Oh yes, yes, sure! Blame it on me! Sure! I made you let me put on a kimono! I'm leading your pure white shriveled peanut of a soul into temptation!... Don't you ever dare speak to me again! Oh, you—you——"

She flounced away.

Carl caught her, in two steps. "See here, child," he said, gravely, "if you go off like this we'll both be miserable.... You remember how happy we were driving out to the old plantation at Powhasset?"

"O Gawd! won't you men never say anything original? Remember it? Of course I remember it! What do you suppose I wore that little branch of laurel you picked for me, wore it here, here, at my breast, and I thought you'd *care* if I hid it here where there wasn't any grease paint, and you don't—you don't care—and we picnicked, and I sang all the time I put up those sandwiches and hid the grape-fruit in the basket to surprise you——"

"O darling Eve, I don't know how to say how sorry I am, so terribly sorry I've started things going! It is my fault. But can't you see I've got to stop it before it's too late, just for that reason? Let's be chums again."

She shook her head. Her hand crept to his, slid over it, drew it up to her breast. She was swaying nearer to him. He pulled his hand free and fled to his tent.

Perhaps his fiercest gibe at himself was that he had had to play the rôle of virgin Galahad rejecting love, which is praised in books and ridiculed in clubs. He mocked at his sincere desire to be fair to Eve. And between mockeries he strained to hear her moving beyond the canvas partition. He was glad when the bandsmen came larruping home from the dance.

Next day she went out of her way to be chilly to him. He did not woo her friendship. He had resigned from the Great Riley Show, and he was going—going anywhere, so long as he kept going.

CHAPTER XV

He had been a jolly mechanic again, in denim overalls and jumper and a defiant black skull-cap with long, shiny vizor; the tender of the motor-boat fleet at an Ontario summer hotel. One day he had looked up, sweating and greasy, to see Howard Griffin, of Plato, parading past in white flannels. He had muttered: "I don't want Them to know I've just been bumming around. I'll go some place else. And I'll do something worth while." Now he was on the train for New York, meditating impersonally on his uselessness, considering how free of moss his rolling had kept him. He could think of no particularly masterful plan for accumulating moss. If he had not bought a ticket through to New York he would have turned back, to seek a position in one of the great automobile factories that now, this early autumn of 1906, were beginning to distinguish Detroit. Well, he had enough money to last for one week in New York. He would work in an automobile agency there; later he would go to Detroit, and within a few years be president of a motor company, rich enough to experiment with motor-boats and to laugh at Howard Griffin or any other Platonian.

So he sketched his conquering entrance into New York. Unfortunately it was in the evening, and, having fallen asleep at Poughkeepsie, he did not awake till a brakeman shook his shoulder at the Grand Central Station. He had heard of the old Grand Union Hotel, and drowsily, with the stuffy nose and sandy eyes and unclean feeling about the teeth that overpower one who sleeps in a smoking-car, he staggered across to the hotel and spent his first conquering night in filling a dollar room with vulgar sounds of over-weary slumber.

But in the morning, when he stared along Forty-second Street; when he breakfasted at a Childs' restaurant, like a gigantic tiled bath-room, and realized that the buckwheat cakes were New York buckwheats; when he sighted the noble *Times* Building and struck out for Broadway (the magic name that promised marble palaces, even if it provided two-story shacks); when he bustled into a carburetor agency and demanded a job—then he found the gateway of wonder.

But he did not find a job.

Eight nights after his arrival he quietly paid his bill at the hotel; tipped a curly-headed bell-boy; checked his baggage, which consisted of a shirt, a razor, and an illustrated catalogue of automobile accessories; put his tooth-brush in his pocket; bought an evening paper in order to feel luxurious; and walked down to the Charity Organization Society, with ten cents in his pocket.

In the Joint Application Bureau, filled with desks and filing-cabinets, where poor men cease to be men and become Cases, Carl waited on a long bench till it was his turn to tell his troubles to a keen, kindly, gray-bearded man behind a roll-top desk. He asked for work. Work was, it seemed, the one thing the society could not give. He received a ticket to the Municipal Lodging House.

This was not the hygienic hostelry of to-day, but a barracks on First Avenue. Carl had a chunk of bread with too much soda in it, and coffee with too little coffee in it, from a contemptuous personage in a white jacket, who, though his cuffs were grimy, showed plainly that he was too good to wait on bums. Carl leaned his elbows on the long scrubbed table and chewed the bread of charity sullenly, resolving to catch a freight next day and get out of town.

He slept in a narrow bunk near a man with consumption. The room reeked of disinfectants and charity.

The East Side of New York. A whirlwind of noise and smell and hovering shadows. The jargon of Jewish matrons in brown shawls and orthodox wigs, chaffering for cabbages and black cotton stockings and gray woolen undershirts with excitable push-cart proprietors who had beards so prophetic that it was startling to see a frivolous cigarette amid the reverend mane. The scent of fried fish and decaying bits of kosher meat, and hallways as damnably rotten of floor as they were profitable to New York's nicest circles. The tall gloom of six-story tenements that made a prison wall of dulled yellow, bristling with bedding-piled fire-escapes and the curious heads of frowzy women. A potpourri of Russian signs, Yiddish newspapers, synagogues with six-pointed gilt stars, bakeries with piles of rye bread crawling with caraway-seeds, shops for renting wedding finery that looked as if it could never fit any one, second-hand furniture-shops with folding iron beds, a filthy baby holding a baby slightly younger and filthier, mangy cats slinking from pile to pile of rubbish, and a withered geranium in a tin can whose label was hanging loose and showed rust-stains amid the dry paste on its back. Everywhere crowds of voluble Jews in dark clothes, and noisily playing children that catapulted into your legs. The lunger-blocks in which we train the victims of Russian tyranny to appreciate our freedom. A whirlwind of alien ugliness and foul smells and incessant roar and the deathless ambition of young Jews to know Ibsen and syndicalism. It swamped the courage of hungry Carl as he roamed through Rivington Street and Essex and Hester, vainly seeking jobs from shopkeepers too poor to be able to bathe.

He felt that he, not these matter-of-fact crowds, was alien. He was hungry and tired. There was nothing heroic to do—just go hungry. There was no place where he could sit down. The benches of the tiny hard-trodden parks were full.... If he could sit down, if he could rest one little hour, he would be able to go and find freight-yards, where there would be the clean clang of bells and rattle of trucks instead of gabbled Yiddish. Then he would ride out into the country, away from the brooding shadows of this town, where there were no separable faces, but only a fog of ceaselessly moving crowds....

Late that night he stood aimlessly talking to a hobo on a dirty corner of the Bowery, where the early September rain drizzled through the gaunt structure of the Elevated. He did not feel the hunger so much now, but he was meekly glad to learn from his new friend, the hobo, that in one more hour he could get food in the bread-line. He felt very boyish, and would have confided the fact that he was starving to any woman, to any one but this transcontinental hobo, the tramp royal, trained to scorn hunger. Because he was one of them he watched incuriously the procession of vagrants, in coats whose collars were turned up and fastened with safety-pins against the rain. The vagrants shuffled rapidly by, their shoulders hunched, their hands always in their trousers pockets, their shoe-heels always ground down and muddy.

And incuriously he watched a saloon-keeper, whose face was plastered over with a huge mustache, come out and hang a sign, "Porter wanted in A.M.," on the saloon door.

As he slouched away to join the bread-line, a black deuce in the world's discard, Carl was wondering how he could get that imperial appointment as porter in a Bowery saloon. He almost forgot it while waiting in the bread-line, so occupied was he in hating two collegians who watched the line with that open curiosity which nice, clean, respectable young men suppose the poor never notice. He restrained his desire to go over and quote Greek at them, because they were ignorant and not to blame for being sure that they were of clay superior to any one in a bread-line. And partly because he had forgotten his Greek.

He came back to the Bowery briskly, alone, with the manhood of a loaf of bread in him. He was going to get that job as porter. He planned his campaign as a politician plans to become a statesman. He slipped the sign, "Porter wanted in A.M.," from its nail and hid it beneath his coat. He tramped the block all night and, as suspicious characters always do to avoid seeming suspicious, he begged a match from a policeman who was keeping an eye on him. The policeman chatted with him about baseball and advised him to keep away from liquor and missions.

At 5 A.M. Carl was standing at the saloon door. When the bartender opened it Carl bounced in, slightly dizzy, conscious of the slime of mud on his fraying trouser-ends.

The saloon had an air of cheap crime and a floor covered with clotted sawdust. The bar was a slab of dark-brown wood, so worn that semicircles of slivers were showing. The nasty gutter was still filled with cigar-ends and puddles of beer and bits of free-lunch cheese.

"I want that job as porter," said Carl.

"Oh, you do, do you? Well, you wait and see who else comes to get it."

"Nobody else is going to come."

"How do you know they ain't?"

Carl drew the sign from beneath his coat and carefully laid it on the bar. "That's why."

"Well, you got nerve. You got the nerve of a Republican on Fourteenth Street, like the fellow says. You must want it. Well, all right, I guess you can have it if the boss don't kick."

Carl was accepted by the "boss," who gave him a quarter and told him to go out and get a "regular feed." He hummed over breakfast. He had been accepted again by all men when he had been accepted by the proprietor of a Bowery saloon. He was going to hold this job, no matter what happened. The rolling stone was going to gather moss.

For three months Carl took seriously the dirtiest things in the world. He worked sixteen hours a day for eight dollars a week, cleaning cuspidors, scrubbing the floor, scattering clean sawdust, cutting the more rotten portions off the free-lunch meat. As he slopped about with half-frozen, brittle rags, hoboes pushed him aside and spat on the floor he had just cleaned.

Of his eight dollars a week he saved four. He rented an airshaft bedroom in the flat of a Jewish sweatshop worker for one dollar and seventy-five cents a week. It was occupied daytimes by a cook in an all-night restaurant, who had taken a bath in 1900 when at Coney Island on excursion of the Pip O'Gilligan Association. The room was unheated, and every night during January Carl debated whether to go to bed with his shoes on or off.

The sub-landlord's daughter was a dwarfish, blotched-faced, passionate child of fifteen, with moist eyes and very low-cut waists of coarse voile (which she pronounced "voyle"). She would stop Carl in the dark "railroad" hallway and, chewing gum rapidly, chatter about the aisleman at Wanamacy's, and what a swell time there would be at the coming ball of the Thomas J. Monahan Literary and Social Club, tickets twenty-five cents for lady and gent, including hat-check. She let Carl know that she considered him close-fisted for never taking her to the movies on Sunday afternoons, but he patted her head and talked to her like a big brother and kept himself from noticing that she had clinging hands and would be rather pretty, and he bought her a wholesome woman's magazine to read—not an entirely complete solution to the problem of what to do with the girl whom organized society is too busy to nourish, but the best he could contrive just then.

Sundays, when he was free for part of the day, he took his book of recipes for mixed drinks to the reading-room of the Tompkins Square library and gravely studied them, for he was going to be a bartender.

Every night when he staggered from the comparatively clean air of the street into the fetid chill of his room he asked himself why he—son of Northern tamaracks and quiet books—went on with this horrible imitation of living; and each time answered himself that, whether there was any real reason or not, he was going to make good on one job at least, and that the one he held. And admonished himself that he was very well paid for a saloon porter.

If Carl had never stood in the bread-line, if he had never been compelled to clean a saloon gutter artistically, in order to keep from standing in that bread-line, he would surely have gone back to the commonplaceness for which every one except Bone Stillman and Henry Frazer had been assiduously training him all his life. They who know how naturally life runs on in any sphere will understand that Carl did not at the time feel that he was debased. He lived twenty-four hours a day and kept busy, with no more wonder at himself than is displayed by the professional burglar or the man who devotes all his youth to learning Greek or soldiering. Nevertheless, the work itself was so much less desirable than driving a car or wandering through the moonlight with Eve L'Ewysse in days wonderful and lost that, to endure it, to conquer it, he had to develop a control over temper and speech and body which was to stay with him in windy mornings of daring.

Within three months Carl had become assistant bar-keeper, and now he could save eight dollars a week. He bought a couple of motor magazines and went to one vaudeville show and kept his sub-landlord's daughter from running off with a cadet, wondering how soon she would do it in any case, and receiving a depressing insight into the efficiency of society for keeping in the mire most of the people born there.

Three months later, at the end of winter, he was ready to start for Panama.

He was going to Panama because he had read in a Sunday newspaper of the Canal's marvels of engineering and jungle.

He had avoided making friends. There was no one to give him farewell when he emerged from the muck. But he had one task to perform—to settle with the Saloon Snob.

Petey McGuff was the name of this creature. He was an oldish and wicked man, born on the Bowery. He had been a heavy-weight prize-fighter in the days of John L. Sullivan; then he had met John, and been, ever since, an honest crook who made an excellent living by conducting a boxing-school in which the real work was done by assistants. He resembled a hound with a neat black bow tie, and he drooled tobacco-juice down his big, raw-looking, moist, bristly, too-masculine chin. Every evening from eleven to midnight Petey McGuff sat at the round table in the mildewed corner at the end of the bar, drinking old-fashioned whisky cocktails made with Bourbon, playing Canfield, staring at the nude models pasted on the milky surface of an old mirror, and teasing Carl.

"Here, boy, come 'ere an' wipe off de whisky you spilled.... Come on, you tissy-cat. Get on de job.... You look like Sunday-school Harry. Mamma's little rosy-cheeked boy.... Some day I'm going to bust your beezer. Gawd! it makes me sick to sit here and look at dose goily-goily cheeks.... Come 'ere, Lizzie, an' wipe dis table again. On de jump, daughter."

Carl held himself in. Hundreds of times he snarled to himself: "I *won't* hit him! I will make good on *this* job, anyway." He created a grin which he could affix easily.

Now he was leaving. He had proven that he could hold a job; had answered the unspoken criticisms from Plato, from Chicago garages, from the Great Riley Show. For the first time since he had deserted college he had been able to write to his father, to answer the grim carpenter's unspoken criticisms of the son who had given up his chance for an "education." And proudly he had sent to his father a little check. He had a beautiful new fifteen-dollar suit of blue serge at home. In his pocket was his ticket—steerage by the P. R. R. line to Colon—and he would be off for bluewater next noon. His feet danced behind the bar as he filled schooners of beer and scraped off their foam with a celluloid ruler. He saw himself in Panama, with a clean man's job, talking to cosmopolitan engineers against a background of green-and-scarlet jungle. And, oh yes, he was going to beat Petey McGuff that evening, and get back much of the belligerent self-respect which he had been drawing off into schooners with the beer.

Old Petey rolled in at two minutes past eleven, warmed his hands at the gas-stove, poked disapprovingly at the pretzels on the free-lunch counter, and bawled at Carl: "Hey, keep away from dat cash-register! Wipe dem goilish tears away, will yuh, Agnes, and bring us a little health-destroyer and a couple matches."

Carl brought a whisky cocktail.

"Where's de matches, you tissy-cat?"

Carl wiped his hands on his apron and beamed: "Well, so the old soak is getting too fat and lazy to reach over on the bar and get his own! You'll last quick now!"

"Aw, is dat so!... For de love of Mike, d'yuh mean to tell me Lizzie is talking back? Whadda yuh know about dat! Whadda yuh know about dat! You'll get sick on us here, foist t'ing we know. Where was yuh hoited?"

Petey McGuff's smile was absolutely friendly. It made Carl hesitate, but it had become one of the principles of cosmic ethics that he had to thump Petey, and he growled: "I'll give you all the talking back you want, you big stiff. I'm getting through to-night. I'm going to Panama."

"No, straight, is dat straight?"

"That's what I said."

"Well, dat's fine, boy. I been watching yuh, and I sees y' wasn't cut out to be no saloon porter. I made a little bet with meself you was ejucated. Why, y'r cuffs ain't even doity—not very doity. Course you kinda need a shave, but dem little blond hairs don't show much. I seen you was a gentleman, even if de bums didn't. You're too good t' be a rum-peddler. Glad y're going, boy, mighty glad. Sit down. Tell us about it. We'll miss yuh here. I was just saying th' other night to Mike here dere ain't one feller in a hundred could 'a' stood de kiddin' from an old he-one like me and kep' his mout' shut and grinned and said nawthin' to nobody. Dat's w'at wins fights. But, say, boy, I'll miss yuh, I sure will. I get to be kind of lonely as de boys drop off—like boozers always does. Oh, hell, I won't spill me troubles like an old tissy-cat.... So you're going to Panama? I want yuh to sit down and tell me about it. Whachu taking, boy?"

"Just a cigar.... I'll miss you, too, Petey. Tell you what I'll do. I'll send you some post-cards from Panama."

Next noon as the S.S. *Panama* pulled out of her ice-lined dock Carl saw an old man shivering on the wharf and frantically waving good-by—Petey McGuff.

CHAPTER XVI

The S.S. *Panama* had passed Watling's Island and steamed into story-land. On the white-scrubbed deck aft of the wheel-house Carl sat with his friends of the steerage—sturdy men all, used to open places; old Ed, the rock-driller, long, Irish, huge-handed, irate, kindly; Harry, the young mechanic from Cleveland. Ed and an oiler were furiously debating about the food aboard:

"Aw, it's rotten, all of it."

"Look here, Ed, how about the chicken they give the steerage on Sunday?"

"Chicken? I didn't see no chicken. I see some sea-gull, though. No wonder they ain't no more sea-gulls following us. They shot 'em and cooked 'em on us."

"Say," mused Harry, "makes me think of when I was ship-building in Philly— no, it was when I was broke in K. C.—and a guy——"

Carl smiled in content, exulting in the talk of the men of the road, exulting in his new blue serge suit, his new silver-gray tie with no smell of the saloon about it, finger-nails that were growing pink again—and the sunset that made glorious his petty prides. A vast plane of unrippling plum-colored sea was set with mirror-like pools where floated tree-branches so suffused with light that the glad heart blessed them. His first flying-fish leaped silvery from silver sea, and Carl cried, almost aloud, "This is what I've been wanting all my life!"

Aloud, to Harry: "Say, what's it like in Kansas? I'm going down through there some day." He spoke harshly. But the real Carl was robed in light and the murmurous wake of evening, with the tropics down the sky-line.

Lying in his hot steerage bunk, stripped to his under-shirt, Carl peered through the "state-room" window to the swishing night sea, conscious of the rolling of the boat, of the engines shaking her, of bolts studding the white iron wall, of life-preservers over his head, of stokers singing in the gangway as they dumped the clinkers overboard. The *Panama* was pounding on, on, on, and he rejoiced, "This is just what I've wanted, always."

They are creeping in toward the wharf at Colon. He is seeing Panama! First a point of palms, then the hospital, the red roofs of the I. C. C. quarters at Cristobal, and negroes on the sun-blistered wharf.

At last he is free to go ashore in wonderland—a medley of Colon and Cristobal, Panama and the Canal Zone of 1907; Spiggoty policemen like monkeys chattering bad Spanish, and big, smiling Canal Zone policemen in khaki, with the air of soldiers; Jamaica negroes with conical heads and brown Barbados negroes with Cockney accents; English engineers in lordly pugrees, and tourists from New England who seem servants of their own tortoise-shell spectacles; comfortable ebon mammies with silver bangles and kerchiefs of stabbing scarlet, dressed in starched pink-and-blue gingham, vending guavas and green Toboga Island pineapples. Carl gapes at Panamanian nuns and Chilean consuls, French peasant laborers and indignant Irish foremen and German concessionaries with dueling scars and high collars. Gold Spanish signs and Spiggoty money and hotels with American cuspidors and job-hunters; tin roofs and arcades; shops open to the street in front, but mysterious within, giving glimpses of the canny Chinese proprietors smoking tiny pipes. Trains from towns along the Canal, and sometimes the black funeral-car, bound for Monkey Hill Cemetery. Gambling-houses where it is considered humorous to play "Where Is My Wandering Boy To-night?" on the phonograph while wandering boys sit at poker; and less cleanly places, named after the various states. Negro wenches in yellow calico dancing to fiddled tunes older than voodoo; Indian planters coming sullenly in with pale-green bananas; memories of the Spanish Main and Morgan's raid, of pieces of eight and cutlasses ho! Capes of cocoanut palms running into a welter of surf; huts on piles streaked with moss, round whose bases land-crabs scuttle with a dry rattling that carries far in the hot, moist, still air, and suggests the corpses of disappeared men found half devoured.

Then, for contrast, the transplanted North, with its seriousness about the Service; the American avenues and cool breezes of Cristobal, where fat, bald chiefs of the I. C. C. drive pompously with political guests who, in 1907, are still incredulous about the success of the military socialism of the Canal, and where wives from Oklahoma or Boston, seated in Grand Rapids golden-oak rockers on the screened porches of bungalows, talk of hats, and children, and mail-orders, and cards, and The Colonel, and malarial fever, and Chautauqua, and the Culebra slide.

Colon! A kaleidoscope of crimson and green and dazzling white, warm-hued peoples and sizzling roofs, with echoes from the high endeavor of the Canal and whispers from the unknown Bush; drenched with sudden rain like escaping steam, or languid under the desert glare of the sky, where hangs a gyre of buzzards whose slow circles are stiller than death and calmer than wisdom.

"Lord!" sighs Carl Ericson from Joralemon, "this is what I've wanted ever since I was a kid."

At Pedro Miguel, which the Canal employees always called "Peter McGill," he found work, first as an unofficial time-keeper; presently, after examinations, as a stationery engineer on the roll of the I. C. C. Within a month he showed no signs of his Bowery experiences beyond a shallow hollow in his smooth cheeks. He lived in quarters like a college dormitory, communistic and jolly, littered with shoes and cube-cut tobacco and college banners; clean youngsters dropping in for an easy chat—and behind it all, the mystery of the Bush. His room-mate, a conductor on the P. R. R., was a globe-trotter, and through him Carl met the Adventurers, whom he had been questing ever since he had run away from Oscar Ericson's woodshed. There was a young engineer from Boston Tech., who swore every morning at 7.07 (when it rained boiling water as enthusiastically as though it had never done such a thing before) that he was going to Chihuahua, mining. There was Cock-eye Corbett, an ex-sailor, who was immoral and a Lancashireman, and knew more about blackbirding and copra and Kanakas, and the rum-holes from Nagasaki to Mombasa, than it is healthy for a civil servant to know.

Every Sunday a sad-faced man with ash-colored hair and bony fingers, who had been a lieutenant in the Peruvian navy, a teacher in St. John's College, China, and a sub-contractor for railroad construction in Montana, and who was now a minor clerk in the cool, lofty offices of the Materials and Supplies Department, came over from Colon, relaxed in a tilted-back chair, and fingered the Masonic charm on his horsehair watch-guard, while he talked with the P. R. R. conductor and the others about ruby-hunting and the Relief of Peking, and Where is Hector Macdonald? and Is John Orth dead? and Shall we try to climb Chimborazo? and Creussot guns and pig-sticking and Swahili tribal lore. These were a few of the topics regarding which he had inside information. The others drawled about various strange things which make a man discontented and bring him no good.

Carl was full member of the circle because of his tales of the Bowery and the Great Riley Show, and because he pretended to be rather an authority on motors for dirigibles, about which he read in *Aeronautics* at the Y. M. C. A. reading-room. It is true that at this time, early 1907, the Wrights were still working in obscurity, unknown even in their own Dayton, though they had a completely successful machine stowed away; and as yet Glenn Curtiss had merely developed a motor for Captain Baldwin's military dirigible. But Langley and Maxim had endeavored to launch power-driven, heavier-than-air machines; lively Santos Dumont had flipped about the Eiffel Tower in his dirigible, and actually raised himself from the ground in a ponderous aeroplane; and in May, 1907, a sculptor named Delagrange flew over six hundred feet in France. Various crank inventors were "solving the problem of flight" every day. Man was fluttering on the edge of his earthy nest, ready to plunge into the air. Carl was able to make technical-sounding predictions which caught the imaginations of the restless children.

The adventurers kept moving. The beach-combing ex-sailor said that he was starting for Valparaiso, started for San Domingo, and landed in Tahiti, whence he sent Carl one post-card, worded, "What price T. T.?" The engineer from Boston Tech. kept his oath about mining in Chihuahua. He got the appointment as assistant superintendent of the Tres Reyes mine—and he took Carl with him.

Carl reached Mexico and breathed the air of high-lying desert and hill. He found rare days, purposeless and wonderful as the voyages of ancient Norse Ericsens; days of learning Spanish and sitting quietly balancing a .32-20 Marlin, waiting for bandits to attack; the joy of repairing machinery and helping to erect a new crusher, nursing peons with broken legs, and riding cow-ponies down black mountain trails at night under an exhilarating splendor of stars. It never seemed to him that the machinery desecrated the mountains' stern grandeur.

Stolen hours he gave to the building of box-kites with cambered wings, after rapturously learning, in the autumn of 1908, that in August a lanky American mechanic named Wilbur Wright had startled the world by flying an aeroplane many miles publicly in France; that before this, on July 4, 1908, another Yankee mechanic, Glenn Curtiss, had covered nearly a mile, for the *Scientific American* trophy, after a series of trials made in company with Alexander Graham Bell, J. A. D. McCurdy, "Casey" Baldwin, and Augustus Post.

He might have gone on until death, dealing with excitable greasers and hysterical machinery, but for the coming of a new mine superintendent—one of those Englishmen, stolid, red-mustached, pipe-smoking, eye-brow-lifting, who at first seem beefily dull, but prove to have known every one from George Moore to Marconi. He inspected Carl hundreds of times, then told him that the period had come when he ought to attack a city, conquer it, build up a reputation cumulatively; that he needed a contrast to Platonians and Bowery bums and tropical tramps, and even to his beloved engineers.

"You can do everything but order a *petit dîner à deux*, but you must learn to do that, too. Go make ten thousand pounds and study Pall Mall and the boulevards, and then come back to us in Mexico. I'll be sorry to have you go—with your damned old silky hair like a woman's and your wink when Guittrez comes up here to threaten us—but don't let the hinterland enslave you too early."

A month later, in January, 1909, aged twenty-three and a half, Carl was steaming out of El Paso for California, with one thousand dollars in savings, a beautiful new Stetson hat, and an ambition to build up a motor business in San Francisco. As the desert sky swam with orange light and a white-browed woman in the seat behind him hummed Musetta's song from "La Bohème" he was homesick for the outlanders, whom he was deserting that he might stick for twenty years in one street and grub out a hundred thousand dollars.

CHAPTER XVII

On a grassy side-street of Oakland, California, was "Jones & Ericson's Garage: Gasoline and Repairs: Motor Cycles and Bicycles for Rent: Oakland Agents for Bristow Magnetos."

It was perhaps the cleverest garage in Oakland and Berkeley for the quick repairing of motor-cycles; and newly wed owners of family runabouts swore that Carl Ericson could make a carburetor out of a tomato-can, and even be agreeable when called on for repairs at 2 A.M. He had doubled old Jones's business during the nine months—February to November, 1909—that they had been associated.

Carl believed that he thought of nothing but work and the restaurants and theaters of civilization. No more rolling for him until he had gathered moss! He played that he was a confirmed business man. The game had hypnotized him for nearly a year. He whistled as he cleaned plugs, and glanced out at the eucalyptus-trees and the sunny road, without wanting to run away. But just to-day, just this glorious rain-cleansed November day, with high blue skies and sunlight on the feathery pepper-trees, he was going to sneak away from work and have a celebration all by himself.

He was going down to San Mateo to see his first flying-machine!

November, 1909. Blériot had crossed the English Channel; McCurdy had, in March, 1909, calmly pegged off sixteen miles in the "Silver Dart" biplane; Paulhan had gone eighty-one miles, and had risen to the incredible height of five hundred feet, to be overshadowed by Orville Wright's sixteen hundred feet; Glenn Curtiss had won the Gordon Bennett cup at Rheims.

California was promising to be in the van of aviation. She was remembering that her own Montgomery had been one of the pioneers. Los Angeles was planning a giant meet for January. A dozen cow-pasture aviators were taking credulous young reporters aside and confiding that next day, or next week, or at latest next month, they would startle the world by ascending in machines "on entirely new and revolutionary principles, on which they had been working for ten years." Sometimes it was for eight years they had been working. But always they remarked that "the model from which the machine will be built has flown perfectly in the presence of some of the most prominent men in the locality." These machines had a great deal to do with the mysterious qualities of gyroscopes and helicopters.

Now, Dr. Josiah Bagby, the San Francisco physician and oil-burning-marine-engine magnate, had really brought three genuine Blériot monoplanes from France, with Carmeau, graduate of the Blériot school and licensed French aviator, for working pilot; and was experimenting with them at San Mateo, near San Francisco, where the grandsons of the Forty-niners play polo. It had been rumored that he would open a school for pilots and build Blériot-type monoplanes for the American market.

Carl had lain awake for an hour the night before, picturing the wonder of flight that he hoped to see. He rose early, put on his politest garments, and informed grumpy old Jones that he was off for a frolic—he wasn't sure, he said, whether he would get drunk or get married. He crossed the bay, glad of the sea-gulls, the glory of Mt. Tamalpais, and San Francisco's hill behind fairy hill. He consumed a Pacific sundæ, with a feeling of holiday, and hummed "Mandalay." On the trolley to San Mateo he read over and over the newspaper accounts of Bagby's monoplanes.

Walking through San Mateo, Carl swung his cocky green hat and scanned the sky for aircraft. He saw none. But as he tramped out on the flying-field he began to run at the sight of two wide, cambered wings, rounded at the ends like the end of one's thumb, attached to a fragile long body of open framework. Men were gathered about it. A man with a short, crisp beard and a tight woolen toboggan-cap was seated in the body, the wings stretching on either side of him. He scratched his beard and gesticulated. A mechanic revolved the propeller, and the unmuffled motor burst out with a trrrrrrr whose music rocked Carl's heart. Black smoke hurled back along the machine. The draught tore at the hair of two men crouched on the ground holding the tail. They let go. The monoplane ran forward along the ground, and suddenly was off it, a foot up, ten feet up—really flying. Carl could see the aviator calmly staring ahead, working his arms, as the machine turned and slipped away over distant trees.

His first impression of an aeroplane in the air had nothing to do with birds or dragon-flies or the miracle of it, because he was completely absorbed in an impression of Carl Ericson, which he expressed after this wise:

"I—am—going—to—be—an—aviator!"

And later, "Yes, *that's* what I've always wanted."

He joined the group in front of the hangar-tent. Workmen were hammering on wooden sheds back of it. He recognized the owner, Dr. Bagby, from his pictures: a lean man of sixty with a sallow complexion, a gray mustache like a rat-tail, a broad, black countrified slouch-hat on the back of his head, a gray sack-suit which would have been respectable but unfashionable at any period whatsoever. He looked like a country lawyer who had served two terms in the state legislature. His shoes were black, but not blackened, and had no toe-caps—the comfortable shoes of an oldish man. He was tapping his teeth with a thin corded forefinger and remarking in a monotonous voice to a Mexican youth plump and polite and well dressed, "Wel-l-l-l, Tony, I guess those plugs were better; I guess those plugs were better. Heh?" Bagby turned to the others, marveled at them as if trying to remember who they were, and said, slowly, "I guess those plugs were all right. Heh?"

The monoplane was returning, for a time apparently not moving, like a black mark painted on the great blue sky; then soaring overhead, the sharply cut outlines clear as a pen-and-ink drawing; then landing, bouncing on the slightly uneven ground.

As the French aviator climbed out, Dr. Bagby's sad face brightened and he suggested: "Those plugs went better, Munseer. Heh? I've been thinking. Maybe you been giving her too rich a mixture."

While they were wiping the Gnôme engine Carl shyly approached Dr. Bagby. He felt frightfully an outsider; wondered if he could ever be intimate with the magician as was the plump Mexican youth they called "Tony." He said "Uh" once or twice, and blurted, "I want to be an aviator."

"Yes, yes," said Dr. Bagby, gently, glancing away from Carl to the machine. He went over, twanged a supporting-wire, and seemed to remember that some one had spoken to him. He returned to the fevered Carl, walking sidewise, staring all the while at the resting monoplane, so efficient, yet so quiet now and slender and feminine. "Yes, yes. So you'd like to be an aviator. So you'd like—like——(Hey, boy, don't touch that!)——to be an aviator. Yes, yes. They all would, m' boy. They all would. Well, maybe you can be, some day. Maybe you can be.... Some day."

"I mean now. Right away. Heard you were going t' start a school. Want to join."

"Hm, hm," sighed Dr. Bagby, tapping his teeth, jingling his heavy gold watch-chain, brushing a trail of cigar-ashes from a lapel, then staring abstractedly at Carl, who was turning his hat swiftly round and round, so flushed of cheek, so excited of eye, that he seemed twenty instead of twenty-four. "Yes, yes, so you'd like to join. Tst. But that would cost you five hundred dollars, you know."

"Right!"

"Well, you go talk to Munseer about it; Munseer Carmeau. He is a very good aviator. He is a licensed aviator. He knows Henry Farman. He studied under Blériot. He is the boss here. I'm just the poor old fellow that stands around. Sometimes Munseer takes me up for a little ride in our machine; sometimes he takes me up; but he is the boss. He is the boss, my friend; you'll have to see him." And Dr. Bagby walked away, apparently much discouraged about life.

Carl was not discouraged about life. He swore that now he would be an aviator even if he had to go to Dayton or Hammondsport or France.

He returned to Oakland. He sold his share in the garage for $1,150.

Before the end of January he was enrolled as a student in the Bagby School of Aviation and Monoplane Building.

On an impulse he wrote of his wondrous happiness to Gertie Cowles, but he tore up the letter. Then proudly he wrote to his father that the lost boy had found himself. For the first time in all his desultory writing of home-letters he did not feel impelled to defend himself.

CHAPTER XVIII

Crude were the surroundings where Carmeau turned out some of the best monoplane pilots America will ever see. There were two rude shed-hangars in which they kept the three imported Blériots—a single-seat racer of the latest type, a Blériot XII. passenger-carrying machine with the seat under the plane, and "P'tite Marie," the school machine, which they usually kept throttled down to four hundred or five hundred, but in which Carmeau made such spirited flights as the one Carl had first witnessed. Back of the hangars was the workshop, which had little architecture, but much machinery. Here the pupils were building two Blériot-type machines, and trying to build an eight-cylinder V motor. All these things had Bagby given for the good of the game, expecting no profit in return. He was one of the real martyrs of aviation, this sapless, oldish man, never knowing the joy of the air, yet devoting a lifetime of ability to helping man sprout wings and become superman.

His generosity did not extend to living-quarters. Most of the students lived at the hangars and dined on Hamburg sandwiches, fried eggs, and Mexican *enchiladas*, served at a lunch-wagon anchored near the field. That lunch-wagon was their club. Here, squatted on high stools, treating one another to ginger-ale, they argued over torque and angles of incidence and monoplanes *vs.* biplanes. Except for two unpopular aristocrats who found boarding-houses in San Mateo, they slept in the hangars, in their overalls, sprawled on mattresses covered with horse-blankets. It was bed at eight-thirty. At four or five Carmeau would crawl out, scratch his beard, start a motor, and set every neighborhood dog howling. The students would gloomily clump over to the lunch-wagon for a ham-and-egg breakfast. The first flights began at dawn, if the day was clear. At eight, when the wind was coming up, they would be heard in the workshop, adjusting and readjusting, machining down bearings, testing wing strength, humming and laughing and busy; a life of gasoline and hammers and straining attempts to get balance exactly right; a happy life of good fellows and the achievements of machinery and preparation for daring the upper air; a life of very ordinary mechanics and of sheer romance!

It is a grievous heresy that aviation is most romantic when the aviator is portrayed as a young god of noble rank and a collar high and spotless, carelessly driving a transatlantic machine of perfect efficiency. The real romance is that a perfectly ordinary young man, the sort of young man who cleans your car at the garage, a prosaically real young man wearing overalls faded to a thin blue, splitting his infinitives, and frequently having for idol a bouncing ingénue, should, in a rickety structure of wood and percale, be able to soar miles in the air and fulfil the dream of all the creeping ages.

In English and American fiction there are now nearly as many aeroplanes as rapiers or roses. The fictional aviators are society amateurs, wearers of evening clothes, frequenters of The Club, journalists and civil engineers and lordlings and international agents and gentlemen detectives, who drawl, "Oh yes, I fly a bit—new sensation, y' know—tired of polo"; and immediately thereafter use the aeroplane to raid arsenals, rescue a maiden from robbers or a large ruby from its lawful but heathenish possessors, or prevent a Zeppelin from raiding the coast. But they never by any chance fly these machines before gum-chewing thousands for hire. In England they absolutely must motor from The Club to the flying-field in a "powerful Rolls-Royce car." The British aviators of fiction are usually from Oxford and Eton. They are splendidly languid and modest and smartly dressed in society, but when they condescend to an adventure or to a coincidence, they are very devils, six feet of steel and sinew, boys of the bulldog breed with a strong trace of humming-bird. Like their English kindred, the Americans take up aviation only for gentlemanly sport. And they do go about rescuing things. Nothing is safe from their rescuing. But they do not have Rolls-Royce cars.

Carl and his class at Bagby's were not of this gilded race. Carl's flying was as sordidly real as laying brick for a one-story laundry in a mill-town. Therefore, being real, it was romantic and miraculous.

Among Carl's class was Hank Odell, the senior student, tall, thin, hopelessly plain of face; a drawling, rough-haired, eagle-nosed Yankee, who grinned shyly and whose Adam's apple worked slowly up and down when you spoke to him; an unimaginative lover of dogs and machinery; the descendant of Lexington and Gettysburg and a flinty Vermont farm; an ex-fireman, ex-sergeant of the army, and ex-teamster. He always wore a khaki shirt—the wrinkles of which caught the grease in black lines, like veins—with black trousers, blunt-toed shoes, and a pipe, the most important part of his costume.

There was the round, anxious, polite Mexican, Tony Beanno, called "Tony Bean"—wealthy, simple, fond of the violin and of fast motoring. There was the "school grouch," surly Jack Ryan, the chunky ex-chauffeur. There were seven nondescripts—a clever Jew from Seattle, two college youngsters, an apricot-rancher's son, a circus acrobat who wanted a new line of tricks, a dull ensign detailed by the navy, and an earnest student of aerodynamics, aged forty, who had written marvelously dull books on air-currents and had shrinkingly made himself a fair balloon pilot. The navy ensign and the student were the snobs who lived away from the hangars, in boarding-houses.

There was Lieutenant Forrest Haviland, detailed by the army—Haviland the perfect gentle knight, the well-beloved, the nearest approach to the gracious fiction aviator of them all, yet never drawling in affected modesty, never afraid of grease; smiling and industrious and reticent; smooth of hair and cameo of face; wearing khaki riding-breeches and tan puttees instead of overalls; always a gentleman, even when he tried to appear a workman. He pretended to be enthusiastic about the lunch-wagon, and never referred to his three generations of army officers. But most of the others were shy of him, and Jack Ryan, the "school grouch," was always trying to get him into a fight.

Finally, there was Carl Ericson, who slowly emerged as star of them all. He knew less of aerodynamics than the timid specialist, less of practical mechanics than Hank Odell; but he loved the fun of daring more. He was less ferocious in competition than was Jack Ryan, but he wasted less of his nerve. He was less agile than the circus acrobat, but knew more of motors. He was less compactly easy than Lieutenant Haviland, but he took better to overalls and sleeping in hangars and mucking in grease—he whistled ragtime while Forrest Haviland hummed MacDowell.

Carl's earliest flights were in the school machine, "P'tite Marie," behind Carmeau, the instructor. Reporters were always about, talking of "impressions," and Carl felt that he ought to note his impressions on his first ascent, but all that he actually did notice was that it was hard to tell at what instant they left the ground; that when they were up, the wind threatened to crush his ribs and burst his nostrils; that there must be something perilously wrong, because the machine climbed so swiftly; and, when they were down, that it had been worth waiting a whole lifetime for the flight.

For days he merely flew with the instructor, till he was himself managing the controls. At last, his first flight by himself.

He had been ordered to try a flight three times about the aerodrome at a height of sixty feet, and to land carefully, without pancaking—"and be sure, Monsieur, be veree sure you do not cut off too high from the ground," said Carmeau.

It was a day when five reporters had gathered, and Carl felt very much in the limelight, waiting in the nacelle of the machine for the time to start. The propeller was revolved, Carl drew a long breath and stuck up his hand—and the engine stopped. He was relieved. It had seemed a terrific responsibility to go up alone. He wouldn't, now, not for a minute or two. He knew that he had been afraid. The engine was turned over once more—and once more stopped. Carl raged, and never again, in all his flying, did real fear return to him. "What the deuce is the matter?" he snarled. Again the propeller was revolved, and this time the engine hummed sweet. The monoplane ran along the ground, its tail lifting in the blast, till the whole machine seemed delicately poised on its tiptoes. He was off the ground, his rage leaving him as his fear had left him.

He exulted at the swiftness with which a distant group of trees shot at him, under him. He turned, and the machine mounted a little on the turn, which was against the rules. But he brought her to even keel so easily that he felt all the mastery of the man who has finally learned to be natural on a bicycle. He tilted up the elevator slightly and shot across a series of fields, climbing. It was perfectly easy. He would go up—up. It was all automatic now—cloche toward him for climbing; away from him for descent; toward the wing that tipped up, in order to bring it down to level. The machine obeyed perfectly. And the foot-bar, for steering to right and left, responded to such light motions of his foot. He grinned exultantly. He wanted to shout.

He glanced at the barometer and discovered that he was up to two hundred feet. Why not go on?

He sailed out across San Mateo, and the sense of people below, running and waving their hands, increased his exultation. He curved about at the end, somewhat afraid of his ability to turn, but having all the air there was to make the turn in, and headed back toward the aerodrome. Already he had flown five miles.

Half a mile from the aerodrome he realized that his motor was slackening, missing fire; that he did not know what was the matter; that his knowledge had left him stranded there, two hundred feet above ground; that he had to come down at once, with no chance to choose a landing-place and no experience in gliding. The motor stopped altogether.

The ground was coming up at him too quickly.

He tilted the elevator, and rose. But, as he was volplaning, this cut down the speed, and from a height of ten feet above a field the machine dropped to the ground with a flat plop. Something gave way—but Carl sat safe, with the machine canted to one side.

He climbed out, cold about the spine, and discovered that he had broken one wheel of the landing-chassis.

All the crowd from the flying-field were running toward him, yelling. He grinned at the foolish sight they made with their legs and arms strewn about in the air as they galloped over the rough ground. Lieutenant Haviland came up, panting: "All right, o' man? Good!" He seized Carl's hand and wrung it. Carl knew that he had a new friend.

Three reporters poured questions on him. How far had he flown? Was this really his first ascent by himself? What were his sensations? How had his motor stopped? Was it true he was a mining engineer, a wealthy motorist?

Hank Odell, the shy, eagle-nosed Yankee, running up as jerkily as a cow in a plowed field, silently patted Carl on the shoulder and began to examine the fractured landing-wheel. At last the instructor, M. Carmeau.

Carl had awaited M. Carmeau's praise as the crown of his long flight. But Carmeau pulled his beard, opened his mouth once or twice, then shrieked: "What the davil you t'ink you are? A millionaire that we build machines for you to smash them? I tole you to fly t'ree time around—you fly to Algiers an' back—you t'ink you are another Farman brother—you are a damn fool! Suppose your motor he stop while you fly over San Mateo? Where you land? In a well? In a chimney? *Hein?* You know naut'ing yet. Next time you do what I tal' you. *Zut!* That was a flight, a flight, you make a flight, that was fine, fine, you make the heart to swell. But nex' time you break the chassis and keel yourself, *nom d'un tonnerre*, I scol' you!"

Carl was humble. But the *Courier* reporter spread upon the front page the story of "Marvelous first flight by Bagby student," and predicted that a new Curtiss was coming out of California. Under a half-tone ran the caption, "Ericson, the New Hawk of the Birdmen."

The camp promptly nicknamed him "Hawk." They used it for plaguing him at first, but it survived as an expression of fondness—Hawk Ericson, the cheeriest man in the school, and the coolest flier.

CHAPTER XIX

Not all their days were spent in work. There were mornings when the wind would not permit an ascent and when there was nothing to do in the workshop. They sat about the lunch-wagon wrangling endlessly, or, like Carl and Forrest Haviland, wandered through fields which were all one flame with poppies.

Lieutenant Haviland had given up trying to feel comfortable with the naval ensign student, who was one of the solemn worthies who clear their throats before speaking, and then speak in measured terms of brands of cigars and weather. Gradually, working side by side with Carl, Haviland seemed to find him a friend in whom to confide. Once or twice they went by trolley to San Francisco, to explore Chinatown or drop in on soldier friends of Haviland at the Presidio.

From the porch of a studio on Telegraph Hill, in San Francisco, they were looking down on the islands of the bay, waiting for the return of an artist whom Haviland knew. Inarticulate dreamers both, they expressed in monosyllables the glory of bluewater before them, the tradition of R. L. S. and Frank Norris, the future of aviation. They gave up the attempt to explain the magic of San Francisco—that city-personality which transcends the opal hills and rare amber sunlight, festivals, and the transplanted Italian hill-town of Telegraph Hill, liners sailing out for Japan, and memories of the Forty-niners. It was too subtle a spirit, too much of it lay in human life with the passion of the Riviera linked to the strength of the North, for them to be able to comprehend its spell.... But regarding their own ambitions to do, they became eloquent.

"I say," hesitated Haviland, "why is it I can't get in with most of the fellows at the camp the way you can? I've always been chummy enough with the fellows at the Point and at posts."

"Because you've been brought up to be afraid to be anything but a gentleman."

"Oh, I don't think it's that. I can get fond as the deuce of some of the commonest common soldiers—and, Lord! some of them come from the Bowery and all sorts of impossible places."

"Yes, but you always think of them as 'common.' They don't think of each other that way. Suppose I'd worked——Well, just suppose I'd been a Bowery bartender. Could you be loafing around here with me? Could you go off on a bat with Jack Ryan?"

"Well, maybe not. Maybe working with Jack Ryan is a good thing for me. I'm getting now so I can almost stand his stories! I envy you, knocking around with all sorts of people. Oh, I *wish* I could call Ryan 'Jack' and feel easy about it. I can't. Perhaps I've got a little of the subaltern snob some place in me."

"You? You're a prince."

"If you've elevated me to a princedom, the least I can do is to invite you down home for a week-end—down to the San Spirito Presidio. My father's commandant there."

"Oh, I'd like to, but——I haven't got a dress-suit."

"Buy one."

"Yes, I could do that, but——Oh, rats! Forrest, I've been knocking around so long I feel shy about my table manners and everything. I'd probably eat pie with my fingers."

"You make me so darn tired, Hawk. You talk about my having to learn to chum with people in overalls. You've got to learn not to let people in evening clothes put anything over on you. That's your difficulty from having lived in the back-country these last two or three years. You have an instinct for manners. But I did notice that as soon as you found out I was in the army you spent half the time disliking me as a militarist, and the other half expecting me to be haughty—Lord knows what over. It took you two weeks to think of me as Forrest Haviland. I'm ashamed of you! If you're a socialist you ought to think that anything you like belongs to you."

"That's a new kind of socialism."

"So much the better. Me and Karl Marx, the economic inventors.... But I was saying: if you act as though things belong to you people will apologize to you for having borrowed them from you. And you've *got* to do that, Hawk. You're going to be one of the best-known fliers in the country, and you'll have to meet all sorts of big guns—generals and Senators and female climbers that work the peace societies for social position, and so on, and you've got to know how to meet them.... Anyway, I want you to come to San Spirito."

To San Spirito they went. During the three days preceding, Carl was agonized at the thought of having to be polite in the presence of ladies. No matter how brusquely he told himself, "I'm as good as anybody," he was uneasy about forks and slang and finger-nails, and looked forward to the ordeal with as much pleasure as a man about to be hanged, hanged in a good cause, but thoroughly.

Yet when Colonel Haviland met them at San Spirito station, and Carl heard the kindly salutation of the gracious, fat, old Indian-fighter, he knew that he had at last come home to his own people—an impression that was the stronger because the house of Oscar Ericson had been so much house and so little home. The colonel was a widower, and for his only son he showed a proud affection which included Carl. The three of them sat in state, after dinner, on the porch of Quarters No. 1, smoking cigars and looking down to a spur of the Santa Lucia Mountains, where it plunged into the foam of the Pacific. They talked of aviation and eugenics and the Benét-Mercier gun, of the post doctor's sister who had come from the East on a visit, and of a riding-test, but their hearts spoke of affection.... Usually it is a man and a woman that make home; but three men, a stranger one of them, talking of motors on a porch in the enveloping dusk, made for one another a home to remember always.

They stayed over Monday night, for a hop, and Carl found that the officers and their wives were as approachable as Hank Odell. They did not seem to be waiting for young Ericson to make social errors. When he confessed that he had forgotten what little dancing he knew, the sister of the post doctor took him in hand, retaught him the waltz, and asked with patent admiration: "How does it feel to fly? Don't you get frightened? I'm terribly in awe of you and Mr. Haviland. I know I should be frightened to death, because it always makes me dizzy just to look down from a high building."

Carl slipped away, to be happy by himself, and hid in the shadow of palms on the porch, lapped in the flutter of pepper-trees. The orchestra began a waltz that set his heart singing. He heard a girl cry: "Oh, goody! the 'Blue Danube'! We must go in and dance that."

"The Blue Danube." The name brought back the novels of General Charles King, as he had read them in high-school days; flashed the picture of a lonely post, yellow-lighted, like a topaz on the night-swathed desert; a rude ball-room, a young officer dancing to the "Blue Danube's" intoxication; a hot-riding, dusty courier, hurling in with news of an Apache outbreak; a few minutes later a troop of cavalry slanting out through the gate on horseback, with a farewell burning the young officer's lips.... He was in just such an army story, now!

The scent of royal climbing-roses enveloped Carl as that picture changed into others. San Spirito Presidio became a vast military encampment over which Hawk Ericson was flying.... From his monoplane he saw a fairy town, with red roofs rising to a tower of fantastic turrets. (That was doubtless the memory of a magazine-cover painted by Maxfield Parrish.)... He was wandering through a poppy-field with a girl dusky of eyes, soft black of hair, ready for any jaunt.... Pictures bright and various as tropic shells, born of music and peace and his affection for the Havilands; pictures which promised him the world. For the first time Hawk Ericson realized that he might be a

Personage instead of a back-yard boy.... The girl with twilight eyes was smiling.

The Bagby camp broke up on the first of May, with all of them, except one of the nondescript collegians and the air-current student, more or less trained aviators. Carl was going out to tour small cities, for the George Flying Corporation. Lieutenant Haviland was detailed to the army flying-camp.

Parting with Haviland and kindly Hank Odell, with Carmeau and anxiously polite Tony Bean, was as wistful as the last night of senior year. Till the old moon rose, sad behind tulip-trees, they sat on packing-boxes by the larger hangar, singing in close harmony "Sweet Adeline," "Teasing," "I've Been Working on the Railroad."... "Hay-ride classics, with barber-shop chords," the songs are called, but tears were in Carl's eyes as the minors sobbed from the group of comrades who made fun of one another and were prosaic and pounded their heels on the packing-boxes—and knew that they were parting to face death. Carl felt Forrest Haviland's hand on one shoulder, then an awkward pat from tough Jack Ryan's paw, as Tony Bean's violin turned the plaintive half-light into music, and broke its heart in the "Moonlight Sonata."

CHAPTER XX

"Yuh, piston-ring burnt off and put the exhaust-valve on the blink. That means one cylinder out of business," growled Hawk Ericson. "I could fly, maybe, but I don't like to risk it in this wind. It was bad enough this morning when I tried it."

"Oh, this hick town 's going to be the death of us, all right—and Riverport to-morrow, with a contract nice as pie, if we can only get there," groaned his manager, Dick George, a fat man with much muscle and more diamonds. "Listen to that crowd. Yelling for blood. Sounds like a bunch of lumber-jacks with the circus slow in starting."

The head-line feature of the Onamwaska County spring fair was "Hawk Ericson, showing the most marvelous aerial feats of the ages with the scientific marvels of aviation, in his famous French Blériot flying-machine, the first flying-machine ever seen in this state, no balloon or fake, come to Onamwaska by the St. L. & N." The spring fair was usually a small gathering of farmers to witness races and new agricultural implements, but this time every road for thirty-five miles was dust-fogged with buggies and democrat wagons and small motor-cars. Ten thousand people were packed about the race-track.

It was Carl's third aviation event. A neat, though not imposing figure, in a snug blue flannel suit, with his cap turned round on his head, he went to the flap of the rickety tent which served as his hangar. A fierce cry of "Fly! Fly! Why don't he fly?" was coming from the long black lines edging the track, and from the mound of people on the small grand stand; the pink blur of their faces turned toward him—him, Carl Ericson; all of them demanding *him*! The five meek police of Onamwaska were trotting back and forth, keeping them behind the barriers. Carl was apprehensive lest this ten-thousandfold demand drag him out, make him fly, despite a wind that was blowing the flags out straight, and whisking up the litter of newspapers and cracker-jack boxes and pink programs. While he stared out, an official crossing the track fairly leaned up against the wind, which seized his hat and sailed it to the end of the track.

"Some wind!" Carl grunted, stolidly, and went to the back of the silent tent, to reread the local papers' accounts of his arrival at Onamwaska. It was a picturesque narrative of the cheering mob following him down the street ("Gee! that was *me* they followed!"), crowding into the office of the Astor House and making him autograph hundreds of cards; of girls throwing roses ("Humph! geraniums is more like it!") from the windows.

"A young man," wrote an enthusiastic female reporter, "handsome as a Greek god, but honestly I believe he is still in his twenties; and he is as slim and straight as a soldier, flaxen-haired and rosy-cheeked—the birdman, the god of the air."

"Handsome as a Greek——" Carl commented. "I look like a Minnesota Norwegian, and that ain't so bad, but handsome——Urrrrg!... Sure they love me, all right. Hear 'em yell. Oh, they love me like a dog does a bone.... Saint Jemima! talk about football rooting.... Come on, Greek god, buck up."

He glanced wearily about the tent, its flooring of long, dry grass stained with ugly dark-blue lubricating-oil, under the tan light coming through the canvas. His manager was sitting on a suit-case, pretending to read a newspaper, but pinching his lower lip and consulting his watch, jogging his foot ceaselessly. Their temporary mechanic, who had given up trying to repair the lame valve, squatted with bent head, biting his lip, harkening to the blood-hungry mob. Carl's own nerves grew tauter and tauter as he saw the manager's restless foot and the mechanic's tension. He strolled to the monoplane, his back to the tent-opening.

He started as the manager exclaimed: "Here they come! After us!"

Outside the tent a sound of running.

The secretary of the fair, a German hardware-dealer with an automobile-cap like a yachting-cap, panted in, gasping: "Come quick! They won't wait any longer! I been trying to calm 'em down, but they say you got to fly. They're breaking over the barriers into the track. The p'lice can't keep 'em back."

Behind the secretary came the chairman of the entertainment committee, a popular dairyman, who was pale as he demanded: "You got to play ball, Mr. Ericson. I won't guarantee what 'll happen if you don't play ball, Mr. Ericson. You got to make him fly, Mr. George. The crowd 's breaking——"

Behind him charged a black press of people. They packed before the tent, trying to peer in through the half-closed tent-opening, like a crowd about a house where a policeman is making an arrest. Furiously:

"Where's the coward? Fake! Bring 'im out! Why don't he fly? He's a fake! His flying-machine's never been off the ground! He's a four-flusher! Run 'im out of town! Fake! Fake! Fake!"

The secretary and chairman stuck out deprecatory heads and coaxed the mob. Carl's manager was an old circus-man. He had removed his collar, tie, and flashy diamond pin, and was diligently wrapping the thong of a black-jack about his wrist. Their mechanic was crawling under the side of the tent. Carl caught him by the seat of his overalls and jerked him back.

As Carl turned to face the tent door again the manager ranged up beside him, trying to conceal the black-jack in his hand, and casually murmuring, "Scared, Hawk?"

"Nope. Too mad to be scared."

The tent-flap was pulled back. Tossing hands came through. The secretary and chairman were brushed aside. The mob-leader, a red-faced, loud-voiced town sport, very drunk, shouted, "Come out and fly or we'll tar and feather you!"

"Yuh, come on, you fake, you four-flusher!" echoed the voices.

The secretary and chairman were edging back into the tent, beside Carl's cowering mechanic.

Something broke in Carl's hold on himself. With his arm drawn back, his fist aimed at the point of the mob-leader's jaw, he snarled: "You can't make me fly. You stick that ugly mug of yours any farther in and I'll bust it. I'll fly when the wind goes down——You would, would you?"

As the mob-leader started to advance, Carl jabbed at him. It was not a very good jab. But the leader stopped. The manager, black-jack in hand, caught Carl's arm, and ordered: "Don't start anything! They can lick us. Just look ready. Don't say anything. We'll hold 'em till the cops come. But nix on the punch."

"Right, Cap'n," said Carl.

It was a strain to stand motionless, facing the crowd, not answering their taunts, but he held himself in, and in two minutes the yell came: "Cheese it! The cops!" The mob unwillingly swayed back as Onamwaska's heroic little band of five policemen wriggled through it, requesting their neighbors to desist.... They entered the tent and, after accepting cigars from Carl's manager, coldly told him that Carl was a fake, and lucky to escape; that Carl would better "jump right out and fly if he knew what was good for him." Also, they nearly arrested the manager for possessing a black-jack, and warned him that he'd better not assault any of the peaceable citizens of beautiful Onamwaska....

When they had coaxed the mob behind the barriers, by announcing that Ericson would now go up, Carl swore: "I won't move! They can't make me!"

The secretary of the fair, who had regained most of his courage, spoke up, pertly, "Then you better return the five hundred advance, pretty quick sudden, or I'll get an attachment on your fake flying-machine!"

"You go——Nix, nix, Hawk, don't hit him; he ain't worth it. You go to hell, brother," said the manager, mechanically. But he took Carl aside, and groaned: "Gosh! we got to do something! It's worth two thousand dollars to us, you know. Besides, we haven't got enough cash in our jeans to get out of town, and we'll miss the big Riverport purse.... Still, suit yourself, old man. Maybe I can get some money by wiring to Chicago."

"Oh, let's get it over!" Carl sighed. "I'd love to disappoint Onamwaska. We'll make fifteen thousand dollars this month and next, anyway, and we can afford to spit 'em in the eye. But I don't want to leave you in a hole.... Here you, mechanic, open up that tent-flap. All the way across.... No, not like *that*, you boob!... So.... Come on, now, help me push out the machine. Here you, Mr. Secretary, hustle me a couple of men to hold her tail."

The crowd rose, the fickle crowd, scenting the promised blood, and applauded as the monoplane was wheeled upon the track and turned to face the wind. The mechanic and two assistants had to hold it as a dust-filled gust caught it beneath the wings. As Carl climbed into the seat and the mechanic went forward to start the engine, another squall hit the machine and she almost turned over sidewise.

As the machine righted, the manager ran up and begged: "You never in the world can make it in this wind, Hawk. Better not try it. I'll wire for some money to get out of town with, and Onamwaska can go soak its head."

"Nope. I'm gettin' sore now, Dick.... Hey you, mechanic: hurt that wing when she tipped?... All right. Start her. Quick. While it's calm."

The engine whirred. The assistants let go the tail. The machine labored forward, but once it left the ground it shot up quickly. The head-wind came in a terrific gust. The machine hung poised in air for a moment, driven back by the gale nearly as fast as it was urged forward by its frantically revolving propeller.

Carl was as yet too doubtful of his skill to try to climb above the worst of the wind. If he could only keep a level course——

He fought his way up one side of the race-track. He crouched in his seat, meeting the sandy blast with bent head. The parted lips which permitted him to catch his breath were stubborn and hard about his teeth. His hands played swiftly, incessantly, over the control as he brought her back to even keel. He warped the wings so quickly that he balanced like an acrobat sitting rockingly on a tight-wire. He was too busy to be afraid or to remember that there was a throng of people below him. But he was conscious that the grand stand, at the side of the track, half-way down, was creeping toward him.

More every instant did he hate the clamor of the gale and the stream of minute drops of oil, blown back from the engine, that spattered his face. His ears strained for misfire of the engine, if it stopped he would be hurled to earth. And one cylinder was not working. He forgot that; kept the cloche moving; fought the wind with his will as with his body.

Now, he was aware of the grand stand below him. Now, of the people at the end of the track. He flew beyond the track, and turned. The whole force of the gale was thrown behind him, and he shot back along the other side of the race-track at eighty or ninety miles an hour. Instantly he was at the end; then a quarter of a mile beyond the track, over plowed fields, where upward currents of warm air increased the pitching of the machine as he struggled to turn her again and face the wind.

The following breeze was suddenly retarded and he dropped forty feet, tail down.

He was only forty feet from the ground, falling straight, when he got back to even keel and shot ahead. How safe the nest of the nacelle where he sat seemed then! Almost gaily he swung her in a great wavering circle—and the wind was again in his face, hating him, pounding him, trying to get under the wings and turn the machine turtle.

Twice more he worked his way about the track. The conscience of the beginner made him perform a diffident Dutch roll before the grand stand, but he was growling, "And that's all they're going to get. See?"

As he soared to earth he looked at the crowd for the first time. His vision was so blurred with oil and wind-soreness that he saw the people only as a mass and he fancied that the stretch of slouch-hats and derbies was a field of mushrooms swaying and tilted back. He was curiously unconscious of the presence of women; he felt all the spectators as men who had bawled for his death and whom he wanted to hammer as he had hammered the wind.

He was almost down. He cut off his motor, glided horizontally three feet above the ground, and landed, while the cheers cloaked even the honking of the parked automobiles.

Carl's manager, fatly galloping up, shrilled, "How was it, old man?"

"Oh, it was pretty windy," said Carl, crawling down and rubbing the kinks out of his arms. "But I think the wind 's going down. Tell the announcer to tell our dear neighbors that I'll fly again at five."

"But weren't you scared when she dropped? You went down so far that the fence plumb hid you. Couldn't see you at all. Ugh! Sure thought the wind had you. Weren't you scared then? You don't look it."

"Then? Oh! Then. Oh yes, sure, I guess I was scared, all right!... Say, we got that seat padded so she's darn comfortable now."

The crowd was collecting. Carl's manager chuckled to the president of the fair association, "Well, that was some flight, eh?"

"Oh, he went down the opposite side of the track pretty fast, but why the dickens was he so slow going up my side? My eyes ain't so good now that it does me any good if a fellow speeds up when he's a thousand miles away. And where's all these tricks in the air———"

"That," murmured Carl to his manager, "is the i-den-ti-cal man that stole the blind cripple's crutch to make himself a toothpick."

CHAPTER XXI

The great Belmont Park Aero Meet, which woke New York to aviation, in October, 1910, was coming to an end. That clever new American flier, Hawk Ericson, had won only sixth place in speed, but he had won first prize in duration, by a flight of nearly six hours, driving round and round and round the pylons, hour on hour, safe and steady as a train, never taking the risk of sensational banking, nor spiraling like Johnstone, but amusing himself and breaking the tedium by keeping an eye out on each circuit for a fat woman in a bright lavender top-coat, who stood out in the dark line of people that flowed beneath. When he had descended—acclaimed the winner—thousands of heads turned his way as though on one lever; the pink faces flashing in such October sunshine as had filled the back yard of Oscar Ericson, in Joralemon, when a lonely Carl had performed duration feats for a sparrow. That same shy Carl wanted to escape from the newspaper-men who came running toward him. He hated their incessant questions—always the same: "Were you cold? Could you have stayed up longer?"

Yet he had seen all New York go mad over aviation—rather, over news about aviation. The newspapers had spread over front pages his name and the names of the other fliers. Carl chuckled to himself, with bashful awe, "Gee! can you beat it?—that's *me!*" when he beheld himself referred to in editorial and interview and picture-caption as a superman, a god. He heard crowds rustle, "Look, there's Hawk Ericson!" as he walked along the barriers. He heard cautious predictions from fellow-fliers, and loud declarations from outsiders, that he was the coming cross-country champion. He was introduced to the mayor of New York, two Cabinet members, an assortment of Senators, authors, bank presidents, generals, and society rail-birds. He regularly escaped from them—and their questions—to help the brick-necked Hank Odell, from the Bagby School, who had entered for the meet, but smashed up on the first day, and ever since had been whistling and working over his machine and encouraging Carl, "Good work, bud; you've got 'em all going."

With vast secrecy and a perception that this was twice as stirring as steadily buzzing about in his Blériot, he went down to the Bowery and, in front of the saloon where he had worked as a porter four years before, he bought a copy of the *Evening World* because he knew that on the third page of it was a large picture of him and a signed interview by a special-writer. He peered into the saloon windows to see if Petey McGuff was there, but did not find him. He went to the street on which he had boarded in the hope that he might do something for the girl who had been going wrong. The tenement had been torn down, with blocks of others, to make way for a bridge-terminal, and he saw the vision of the city's pitiless progress. This quest of old acquaintances made him think of Joralemon. He informed Gertie Cowles that he was now "in the aviation game, and everything is going very well." He sent his mother a check for five hundred dollars, with awkward words of affection.

A greater spiritual adventure was talking for hours, over a small table in the basement of the Brevoort, to Lieutenant Forrest Haviland, who was attending the Belmont Park Meet as spectator. Theirs was the talk of tried friends; droning on for a time in amused comment, rising to sudden table-pounding enthusiasms over aviators or explorers, with exclamations of, "Is that the way it struck you, too? I'm awfully glad to hear you say that, because that's just the way I felt about it." They leaned back in their chairs and played with spoons and reflectively broke up matches and volubly sketched plans of controls, drawing on the table-cloth.

Carl took the sophisticated atmosphere of the Brevoort quite for granted. Why *shouldn't* he be there! And after the interest in him at the meet it did not hugely abash him to hear a group at a table behind him ejaculate: "I think that's Hawk Ericson, the aviator! Yes, sir, that's—who—it—is!"

Finally the gods gave to Carl a new mechanic, a prince of mechanics, Martin Dockerill. Martin was a tall, thin, hatchet-faced, tousle-headed, slow-spoken, irreverent Irish-Yankee from Fall River; the perfect type of American aviators; for while England sends out its stately soldiers of the air, and France its short, excitable geniuses, practically all American aviators and aviation mechanics are either long-faced and lanky, like Martin Dockerill and Hank Odell, or slim, good-looking youngsters of the college track-team type, like Carl and Forrest Haviland.

Martin Dockerill ate pun'kin pie with his fingers, played "Marching through Georgia" on the mouth-organ, admired burlesque-show women in sausage-shaped pink tights, and wore balbriggan socks that always reposed in wrinkles over the tops of his black shoes with frayed laces. But he probably could build a very decent motor in the dark, out of four tin cans and a crowbar. In A.D. 1910 he still believed in hell and plush albums. But he dreamed of wireless power-transmission. He was a Free and Independent American Citizen who called the Count de Lesseps, "Hey, Lessup." But he would have gone with Carl aeroplaning to the South Pole upon five minutes' notice—four minutes to devote to the motor, and one minute to write, with purple indelible pencil, a post-card to his aunt in Fall River. He was precise about only two things—motor-timing and calling himself a "mechanician," not a "mechanic." He became very friendly with Hank Odell; helped him repair his broken machine, went with him to vaudeville, or stood with him before the hangar, watching the automobile parties of pretty girls with lordly chaperons that came to call on Grahame-White and Drexel. "Some heart-winners, them guys, but I back my boss against them and ev'body else, Hank," Martin would say.

The meet was over; the aviators were leaving. Carl had said farewell to his new and well-loved friends, the pioneers of aviation—Latham, Moisant, Leblanc, McCurdy, Ely, de Lesseps, Mars, Willard, Drexel, Grahame-White, Hoxsey, and the rest. He was in the afterglow of the meet, for with Titherington, the Englishman, and Tad Warren, the Wright flier, he was going to race from Belmont Park to New Haven for a ten-thousand-dollar prize jointly offered by a New Haven millionaire and a New York newspaper. At New Haven the three competitors were to join with Tony Bean (of the Bagby School) and Walter MacMonnies (flying a Curtiss) in an exhibition meet.

Enveloped in baggy overalls over the blue flannel suit which he still wore when flying, Carl was directing Martin Dockerill in changing his spark-plugs, which were fouled. About him, the aviators were having their machines packed, laughing, playing tricks on one another—boys who were virile men; mechanics in denim who stammered to the reporters, "Oh, well, I don't know——" yet who were for the time more celebrated than Roosevelt or Harry Thaw or Bernard Shaw or Champion Jack Johnson.

Before 9.45 A.M., when the race to New Haven was scheduled to start, the newspaper-men gathered; but there were not many outsiders. Carl felt the lack of the stimulus of thronging devotees. He worked silently and sullenly. It was "the morning after." He missed Forrest Haviland.

He began to be anxious. Could he get off on time?

Exactly at 9.45 Titherington made a magnificent start in his Henry Farman biplane. Carl stared till the machine was a dot in the clouds, then worked feverishly. Tad Warren, the second contestant, was testing out his motor, ready to go. At that moment Martin Dockerill suggested that the carburetor was dirty.

"I'll fly with her the way she is," Carl snapped, shivering with the race-fever.

A cub reporter from the City News Association piped, like a fox-terrier, "What time 'll you get off, Hawk?"

"Ten sharp."

"No, I mean what time will you really get off!"

Carl did not answer. He understood that the reporters were doubtful about him, the youngster from the West who had been flying for only six months. At last came the inevitable pest, the familiarly suggestive outsider. A well-dressed, well-meaning old bore he was; a complete stranger. He put his podgy hand on Carl's arm and puffed: "Well, Hawk, my boy, give us a good flight to-day; not but what you're going to have trouble. There's something I want to suggest to you. If you'd use a gyroscope——"

"Oh, beat it!" snarled Carl. He was ashamed of himself—but more angry than ashamed. He demanded of Martin, aside: "All right, heh? Can I fly with the carburetor as she is? Heh?"

"All right, boss. Calm down, boss, calm down."

"What do you mean?"

"Look here, Hawk, I don't want to butt in. You can have old Martin for a chopping-block any time you want to cut wood. But if you don't calm down you'll get so screwed up mit nerves that you won't have any control. Aw, come on, boss, speak pretty! Just keep your shirt on and I'll hustle like a steam-engine."

"Well, maybe you're right. But these assistant aviators in the crowd get me wild.... All right? Hoorray. Here goes.... Say, don't stop for anything after I get off. Leave the boys to pack up, and you hustle over to Sea Cliff for the speed-boat. You ought to be in New Haven almost as soon as I am."

Calmer now, he peeled off his overalls, drew a wool-lined leather jacket over his coat, climbed into the cockpit, and inspected the indicators. As he was testing the spark Tad Warren got away.

Third and last was Carl. The race-fever shook him.

He would try to save time. Like the others, he had planned to fly from Belmont Park across Long Island to Great Neck, and cross Long Island Sound where it was very narrow. He studied his map. By flying across to the vicinity of Hempstead Harbor and making a long diagonal flight over water, straight over to Stamford, he would increase the factor of danger, but save many miles; and the specifications of the race permitted him to choose any course to New Haven. Thinking only of the new route, taking time only to nod good-by to Martin Dockerill and Hank Odell, he was off, into the air.

As the ground dropped beneath him and the green clean spaces and innumerous towns of Long Island spread themselves out he listened to the motor. Its music was clear and strong. Here, at least, the wind was light.

He would risk the long over-water flight—very long they thought it in 1910.

In a few minutes he sighted the hills about Roslyn and began to climb, up to three thousand feet. It was very cold. His hands were almost numb on the control. He descended to a thousand feet, but the machine jerked like a canoe shooting rapids, in the gust that swept up from among the hills. The landscape rose swiftly at him over the ends of the wings, now on one side, now on the other, as the machine rolled.

His arms were tired with the quick, incessant wing-warping. He rose again. Then he looked at the Sound, and came down to three hundred feet, lest he lose his way. For the Sound was white with fog.... No wind out there!... Water and cloud blurred together, and the sky-line was lost in a mass of somber mist, which ranged from filmy white to the cold dead gray of old cigar-ashes. He wanted to hold back, not dash out into that danger-filled twilight. But already he was roaring over gray-green marshes, then was above fishing-boats that were slowly rocking in water dully opaque as a dim old mirror. He noted two men on a sloop, staring up at him with foolish, gaping, mist-wet faces. Instantly they were left behind him. He rose, to get above the fog. Even the milky, sulky water was lost to sight.

He was horribly lonely, abominably lonely.

At five hundred feet altitude he was not yet entirely above the fog. Land was blotted out. Above him, gray sky and thin writhing filaments of vapor. Beneath him, only the fog-bank, erupting here and there like the unfolding of great white flowers as warm currents of air burst up through the mist-blanket.

Completely solitary. All his friends were somewhere far distant, in a place of solid earth and sun-warmed hangars. The whole knowable earth had ceased to exist. There was only slatey void, through which he was going on for ever. Or perhaps he was not moving. Always the same coil of mist about him. He was horribly lonely.

He feared that the fog was growing thicker. He studied his compass with straining eyes. He was startled by a gull's plunging up through the mist ahead of him, and disappearing. He was the more lonely when it was gone. His eyebrows and cheeks were wet with the steam. Drops of moisture shone desolately on the planes. It was an unhealthy shine. He was horribly lonely.

He pictured what would happen if the motor should stop and he should plunge down through that flimsy vapor. His pontoonless frail monoplane would sink almost at once.... It would be cold, swimming. How long could he keep up? What chance of being found? He didn't want to fall. The cockpit seemed so safe, with its familiar watch and map-stand and supporting-wires. It was home. The wings stretching out on either side of him seemed comfortingly solid, adequate to hold him up. But the body of the machine behind him was only a framework, not even inclosed. And cut in the bottom of the cockpit was a small hole for observing the earth. He could see fog through it, in unpleasant contrast to the dull yellow of the cloth sides and bottom. Not before had it daunted him to look down through that hole.

Now, however, he kept his eyes away from it, and, while he watched the compass and oil-gauge, and kept a straight course, he was thinking of how nasty it would be to drop, drop down *there*, and have to swim. It would be horribly lonely, swimming about a wrecked monoplane, hearing steamers' fog-horns, hopeless and afar.

As he thought that, he actually did hear a steamer hoarsely whistling, and swept above it, irresistibly. He started; his shoulders drooped.

More than once he wished that he could have seen Forrest Haviland again before he started. He wished with all the poignancy of man's affection for a real man that he had told Forrest, when they were dining at the Brevoort, how happy he was to be with him. He was horribly lonely.

He cursed himself for letting his thoughts become thin and damp as the vapor about him. He shrugged his shoulders. He listened thankfully to the steady purr of the engine and the whir of the propeller. He *would* get across! He ascended, hoping for a glimpse of the shore. The fog-smothered horizon stretched farther and farther away. He was unspeakably lonely.

Through a tear in the mist he saw sunshine reflected from houses on a hill, directly before him, perhaps one mile distant. He shouted. He was nearly across. Safe. And the sun was coming out.

Two minutes later he was turning north, between the water and a town which his map indicated as Stamford. The houses beneath him seemed companionable; friendly were the hand-waving crowds, and factory-whistles gave him raucous greeting.

Instantly, now that he knew where he was, the race-fever caught him again. Despite the strain of crossing the Sound, he would not for anything have come down to rest. He began to wonder how afar ahead of him were Titherington and Tad Warren.

He spied a train running north out of Stamford, swung over above it, and raced with it. The passengers leaned out of the windows, trainmen hung perilously from the opened doors of vestibuled platforms, the engineer tooted his frantic greetings to a fellow-mechanic who, above him in the glorious bird, sent telepathic greetings which the engineer probably never got. The engineer speeded up; the engine puffed out vast feathery plumes of dull black smoke. But he drew away from the train as he neared South Norwalk.

He was ascending again when he noted something that seemed to be a biplane standing in a field a mile away. He came down and circled the field. It was Titherington's Farman biplane. He hoped that the kindly Englishman had not been injured. He made out Titherington, talking to a group about the machine. Relieved, he rose again, amused by the ant-hill appearance as hundreds of people, like black bugs, ran toward the stalled biplane, from neighboring farms and from a trolley-car standing in the road.

He should not have been amused just then. He was too low. Directly before him was a hillside crowned with trees. He shot above the trees, cold in the stomach, muttering, "Gee! that was careless!"

He sped forward. The race-fever again. Could he pass Tad Warren as he had passed Titherington? He whirled over the towns, shivering but happy in the mellow, cool October air, far enough from the water to be out of what fog the brightening sun had left. The fields rolled beneath him, so far down that they were turned into continuous and wonderful masses of brown and gold. He sang to himself. He liked Titherington; he was glad that the Englishman had not been injured; but it was good to be second in the race; to have a chance to win a contest which the whole country was watching; to be dashing into a rosy dawn of fame. But while he sang he was keeping a tense lookout for Tad Warren. He had to pass him!

With the caution of the Scotchlike Norwegian, he had the cloche constantly on the jiggle, with ceaseless adjustments to the wind, which varied constantly as he passed over different sorts of terrain. Once the breeze dropped him sidewise. He shot down to gain momentum, brought her to even keel, and, as he set her nose up again, laughed boisterously.

Never again would he be so splendidly young, never again so splendidly sure of himself and of his medium of expression. He was to gain wisdom, but never to have more joy of the race.

He was sure now that he was destined to pass Tad Warren.

The sun was ever brighter; the horizon ever wider, rimming the saucer-shaped earth. When he flew near the Sound he saw that the fog had almost passed. The water was gentle and colored like pearl, lapping the sands, smoking toward the radiant sky. He passed over summer cottages, vacant and asleep, with fantastic holiday roofs of red and green. Gulls soared like flying sickles of silver over the opal sea. Even for the racer there was peace.

He made out a mass of rock covered with autumn-hued trees to the left, then a like rock to the right. "West and East Rock—New Haven!" he cried.

The city mapped itself before him like square building-blocks on a dark carpet, with railroad and trolley tracks like flashing spider-webs under the October noon.

So he had arrived, then—and he had not caught Tad Warren. He was furious.

He circled the city, looking for the Green, where (in this day before the Aero Club of America battled against over-city flying) he was to land. He saw the

Yale campus, lazy beneath its elms, its towers and turrets dreaming of Oxford. His anger left him.

He plunged down toward the Green—and his heart nearly stopped. The spectators were scattered everywhere. How could he land without crushing some one? With trees to each side and a church in front, he was too far down to rise again. His back pressed against the back of the little seat, and seemed automatically to be trying to restrain him from this tragic landing.

The people were fleeing. In front there was a tiny space. But there was no room to sail horizontally and come down lightly. He shut off his motor and turned the monoplane's nose directly at the earth. She struck hard, bounced a second. Her tail rose, and she started, with dreadful deliberateness, to turn turtle. With a vault Carl was out of the cockpit and clear of the machine as she turned over.

Oblivious of the clamorous crowd which was pressing in about him, cutting off the light, replacing the clean smell of gasoline and the upper air by the hot odor of many bodies, he examined the monoplane and found that she had merely fractured the propeller and smashed the rudder.

Some one was fighting through the crowd to his side—Tony Bean—Tony the round, polite Mexican from the Bagby School. He was crying: "*Hombre*, what a landing! You have saved lives.... Get out of the way, all you people!"

Carl grinned and said: "Good to see you, Tony. What time did Tad Warren get here? Where's——"

"He ees not here yet."

"What? Huh? How's that? Do I win? That——Say, gosh! I hope he hasn't been hurt."

"Yes, you win."

A newspaper-man standing beside Tony said: "Warren had to come down at Great Neck. He sprained his shoulder, but that's all."

"That's good."

"But you," insisted Tony, "aren't you badly jarred, Hawk?"

"Not a bit."

The gaping crowd, hanging its large collective ear toward the two aviators, was shouting: "Hoorray! He's all right!"—As their voices rose Carl became aware that all over the city hundreds of factory-whistles and bells were howling their welcome to him—the victor.

The police were clearing a way for him. As a police captain touched a gold-flashing cap to him, Carl remembered how afraid of the police that hobo Slim Ericson had been.

Tony and he completed examination of the machine, with Tony's mechanician, and sent it off to a shop, to await Martin Dockerill's arrival by speed-boat and racing-automobile. Carl went to receive congratulations—and a check—from the prize-giver, and a reception by Yale officials on the campus. Before him, along his lane of passage, was a kaleidoscope of hands sticking out from the wall of people—hands that reached out and shook his own till they were sore, hands that held out pencil and paper to beg for an autograph, hands of girls with golden flowers of autumn, hands of dirty, eager, small boys—weaving, interminable hands. Dizzy with a world peopled only by writhing hands, yet moved by their greeting, he made his way across the Green, through Phelps Gateway, and upon the campus. Twisting his cap and wishing that he had taken off his leather flying-coat, he stood upon a platform and heard officials congratulating him.

The reception was over. But the people did not move. And he was very tired. He whispered to a professor: "Is that a dormitory, there behind us? Can I get into it and get away?"

The professor beckoned to one of the collegians, and replied, "I think, Mr. Ericson, if you will step down they will pass you into Vanderbilt Courtyard—by the gate back of us—and you will be able to escape."

Carl trusted himself to the bunch of boys forming behind him, and found himself rushed into the comparative quiet of a Tudor courtyard. A charming youngster, hatless and sleek of hair, cried, "Right this way, Mr. Ericson—up this staircase in the tower—and we'll give 'em the slip."

From the roar of voices to the dusky quietude of the hallway was a joyous escape. Suddenly Carl was a youngster, permitted to see Yale, a university so great that, from Plato College, it had seemed an imperial myth. He stared at the list of room-occupants framed and hung on the first floor. He peeped reverently through an open door at a suite of rooms.

He was taken to a room with a large collection of pillows, fire-irons, Morris chairs, sets of books in crushed levant, tobacco-jars and pipes—a restless and boyish room, but a real haven. He stared out upon the campus, and saw the crowd stolidly waiting for him. He glanced round at his host and waved his hand deprecatingly, then tried to seem really grown up, really like the famous Hawk Ericson. But he wished that Forrest Haviland were there so that he might marvel: "Look at 'em, will you! Waiting for *me!* Can you beat it? Some start for my Yale course!"

In a big chair, with a pipe supplied by the youngster, he shyly tried to talk to a senior in the great world of Yale (he himself had not been able to climb to seniorhood even in Plato), while the awed youngster shyly tried to talk to the great aviator.

He had picked up a Yale catalogue and he vaguely ruffled its pages, thinking of the difference between its range of courses and the petty inflexible curriculum of Plato. Out of the pages leaped the name "Frazer." He hastily turned back. There it was: "Henry Frazer, A.M., Ph.D., Assistant Professor in English Literature."

Carl rejoiced boyishly that, after his defeat at Plato, Professor Frazer had won to victory. He forgot his own triumph. For a second he longed to call on Frazer and pay his respects. "No," he growled to himself, "I've been so busy hiking that I've forgotten what little book-learnin' I ever had. I'd like to see him, but——By gum! I'm going to begin studying again."

Hidden away in the youngster's bedroom for a nap, he dreamed uncomfortably of Frazer and books. That did not keep him from making a good altitude flight at the New Haven Meet that afternoon, with his hastily repaired machine and a new propeller. But he thought of new roads for wandering in the land of books, as he sat, tired and sleepy, but trying to appear bright and appreciative, at the big dinner in his honor—the first sacrificial banquet to which he had been subjected—with earnest gentlemen in evening clothes, glad for an excuse to drink just a little too much champagne; with mayors and councilmen and bankers; with the inevitable stories about the man who was accused of stealing umbrellas and about the two skunks on a fence enviously watching a motor-car.

Equally inevitable were the speeches praising Carl's flight as a "remarkable achievement, destined to live forever in the annals of sport and heroism, and to bring one more glory to the name of our fair city."

Carl tried to appear honored, but he was thinking: "Rats! I'll live in the annals of nothin'! Curtiss and Brookins and Hoxsey have all made longer flights than mine, in this country alone, and they're aviators I'm not worthy to fill the gas-tanks of.... Gee! I'm sleepy! Got to look polite, but I wish I could beat it.... Let's see. Now look here, young Carl; starting in to-morrow, you begin to read oodles of books. Let's see. I'll start out with Forrest's favorites. There's *David Copperfield*, and that book by Wells, *Tono-Bungay*, that's got aerial experiments in it, and *Jude the Ob—*, *Obscure*, I guess it is, and *The Damnation of Theron Ware* (wonder what he damned), and *McTeague*, and *Walden*, and *War and Peace*, and *Madame Bovary*, and some Turgenev and some Balzac. And something more serious. Guess I'll try William James's book on psychology."

He bought them all next morning. His other belongings had been suited to rapid transportation, and Martin Dockerill grumbled, "That's a swell line of baggage, all right—one tooth-brush, a change of socks, and ninety-seven thousand books."

Two nights later, in a hotel at Portland, Maine, Carl was plowing through the Psychology. He hated study. He flipped the pages angrily, and ran his fingers through his corn-colored hair. But he sped on, concentrated, stopping only to picture a day when the people who honored him publicly would also know him in private. Somewhere among them, he believed, was the girl with whom he could play. He would meet her at some aero race, and she would welcome him as eagerly as he welcomed her.... Had he, perhaps, already met her? He walked over to the writing-table and scrawled a note to Gertie Cowles—regarding the beauty of the Yale campus.

CHAPTER XXII

(*Editor's Note*: The following pages are extracts from a diary kept by Mr. C. O. Ericson in a desultory fashion from January, 1911, to the end of April, 1912. They are reprinted quite literally. Apparently Mr. Ericson had no very precise purpose in keeping his journal. At times it seems intended as *materia* for future literary use; at others, as comments for his own future amusement; at still others, as a sort of long letter to be later sent to his friend, Lieut. Forrest Haviland, U.S.A. I have already referred to them in my *Psycho-Analysis of the Subconscious with Reference to Active Temperaments*, but here reprint them less for their appeal to us as a scientific study of reactions than as possessing, doubtless, for those interested in pure narrative, a certain curt expression of somewhat unusual exploits, however inferior is their style to a more critical thesis on the adventurous.)

May 9, (1911). Arrived at Mineola flying field, N. Y. to try out new Bagby monoplane I have bought. Not much accomodation here yet. Many of us housed in tents. Not enough hangars. We sit around and tell lies in the long grass at night, like a bunch of kids out camping. Went over and had a beer at Peter McLoughlin's today, that's where Glenn Curtiss started out from to make his first flight for Sci. Amer. cup.

Like my new Bagby machine better than Blériot in many respects, has non-lifting tail, as should all modern machines. Rudder and elevator a good deal like the Nieuport. One passenger. Roomy cockpit and enclosed fuselage. Blériot control. Nearer streamline than any American plane yet. Span, 33.6 ft., length 24, chord of wing at fuselage 6′ 5″. Chauviere propeller, 6′ 6″, pitch 4′ 5″. Dandy new Gnôme engine, 70 h.p., should develop 60 to 80 m.p.h.

Martin Dockerill my mechanician is pretty cute. He said to me to-day when we were getting work-bench up, "I bet a hat the spectators all flock here, now. Not that you're any better flier than some of the other boys, but you got the newest plane for them to write their names on."

Certainly a scad of people butting in. Come in autos and motor cycles and on foot, and stand around watching everything you do till you want to fire a monkey wrench at them.

Hank Odell has joined the Associated Order of the Pyramid and just now he is sitting out in front of his tent talking to some of the Grand Worthy High Mighties of it I guess—fat old boy with a yachting cap and a big brass watch chain and an Order of Pyramid charm big as your thumb, and a tough young fellow with a black sateen shirt and his hat on sideways with a cigarette hanging out of one corner of his mouth.

Since I wrote the above a party of sports, the women in fade-away gowns made to show their streamline forms came butting in, poking their fingers at everything, while the slob that owned their car explained everything wrong. "This is a biplane," he says, "you can see there's a plane sticking out on each side of the place where the aviator sits, it's a new areoplane (that's the way he pronounced it), and that dingus in front is a whirling motor." I was sitting here at the work-bench, writing, hot as hell and sweaty and in khaki pants and soft shirt and black sneakers, and the Big Boss comes over to me and says, "Where is Hawk Ericson, my man." "How do I know," I says. "When will he be back," says he, as though he was thinking of getting me fired p. d. q. for being fresh. "Next week. He ain't come yet."

He gets sore and says, "See here, my man, I read in the papers to-day that he has just joined the flying colony. Permit me to inform you that he is a very good friend of mine. If you will ask him, I am quite sure that he will remember Mr. Porter Carruthers, who was introduced to him at the Belmont Park Meet. Now if you will be so good as to show the ladies and myself about——" Well, I asked Hawk, and Hawk seemed to be unable to remember his friend Mr. Carruthers, who was one of the thousand or so people recently introduced to him, but he told me to show them about, which I did, and told them the Gnôme was built radial to save room, and the wires overhead were a frame for a little roof for bad weather, and they gasped and nodded to every fool thing I said, swallowed it hook line and sinker till one of the females showed her interest by saying "How fascinating, let's go over to the Garden City Hotel, Porter, I'm dying for a drink." I hope she died for it.

May 10: Up at three, trying out machine. Smashed landing chassis in coming down, shook me up a little. Interesting how when I rose it was dark on the ground but once up was a little red in the east like smoke from a regular fairy city.

Another author out to-day bothering me for what he called "copy."

Must say I've met some darn decent people in this game though. To-day there was a girl came out with Billy Morrison of the N. Y. Courier, she is an artist but crazy about outdoor life, etc. Named Istra Nash, a red haired girl, slim as a match but the strangest face, pale but it lights up when she's talking to you. Took her up and she was not scared, most are.

May 11: Miss Istra Nash came out by herself. She's thinking quite seriously about learning to fly. She sat around and watched me work, and when nobody was looking smoked a cigarette. Has recently been in Europe, Paris, London, etc.

Somehow when I'm talking to a woman like her I realize how little I see of women with whom I can be really chummy, tho I meet so many people at receptions etc. sometimes just after I have been flying before thousands of people I beat it to my hotel and would be glad for a good chat with the night clerk, of course I can bank on Martin Dockerill to the limit but when I talk to a person like Miss Nash I realize I need some one who knows good art from bad. Though Miss Nash doesn't insist on talking like a high-brow, indeed is picking up aviation technologies very quickly. She talks German like a native.

Think Miss Nash is perhaps older than I am, perhaps couple of years, but doesn't make any difference.

Reading a little German to-night, almost forgot what I learned of it in Plato.

May 14, Sunday: Went into town this afternoon and went with Istra to dinner at the Lafayette. She told me all about her experiences in Paris and studying art. She is quite discontented here in N. Y. I don't blame her much, it must have been bully over in Paree. We sat talking till ten. Like to see Vedrines fly, and the Louvre and the gay grisettes too by heck! Istra ought not to drink so many cordials, nix on the booze you learn when you try to keep in shape for flying, though Tad Warren doesn't seem to learn it. After ten we went to studio where Istra is staying on Washington Sq. several of her friends there and usual excitement and fool questions about being an aviator, it always makes me feel like a boob. But they saw Istra and I wanted to be alone and they beat it.

This is really dawn but I'll date it May 14, which is yesterday. No sleep for me to-night, I'm afraid. Going to fly around NY in aerial derby this afternoon. Must get plenty sleep now.

May 15: Won derby, not much of an event though. Struck rotten currents over Harlem River, machine rolled like a whale-back.

Istra out here to-morrow. Glad. But after last night afraid I'll get so I depend on her, and the aviator that keeps his nerve has to be sort of a friendless cuss some ways.

May 16: Istra came out here. Seems very discontented. I'm afraid she's the kind to want novelty and attention incessantly, she seems to forget that I'm pretty busy.

May 17: Saw Istra in town, she forgot all her discontent and her everlasting dignity and danced for me then came over and kissed me, she is truly a wonder, can hum a French song so you think you're among the peasants, but she expects absolute devotion and constant amusing and I must stick to my last if a mechanic like me is to amount to anything.

May 18: Istra out here, she sat around and looked bored, wanted to make me sore, I think. When I told her I had to leave to-morrow morning for Rochester and couldn't come to town for dinner etc. she flounced home. I'm sorry, I'm mighty sorry; poor kid she's always going to be discontented wherever she is, and always getting some one and herself all wrought up. She always wants new sensations yet doesn't want to work, and the combination isn't very good. It'd be great if she really worked at her painting, but she usually stops her art just this side of the handle of a paint-brush.

Curious thing is that when she'd gone and I sat thinking about her I didn't miss her so much as Gertie Cowles. I hope I see Gertie again some day, she is a good pal.

Istra wanted me to name my new monoplane Babette, because she says it looks "cunning" which the Lord knows it don't, it may look efficient but not cunning. But I don't think I'll name it anything, tho she says that shows lack of imagination.

People especially reporters are always asking me this question, do aviators have imagination? I'm not sure I know what imagination is. It's like this stuff about "sense of humor." Both phrases are pretty bankrupt now. A few years ago when I was running a car I would make believe I was different people, like a king driving through his kingdom, but when I'm warping and banking I don't have time to think about making believe. Of course I do notice sunsets and so on a good deal but that is not imagination. And I do like to go different places; possibly I take the imagination out that way—I guess imagination is partly wanting to be places where you aren't—well, I go when I want to, and I like that better.

Anyway darned if I'll give my monoplane a name. Tad Warren has been married to a musical comedy soubrette with ringlets of red-brown hair (Istra's hair is quite bright red, but this woman has dark red hair, like the color of California redwood chips, no maybe darker) and she wears a slimpsy bright blue dress with the waist-line nearly down to her knees, and skirt pretty short, showing a lot of ankle, and a kind of hat I never noticed before, must be getting stylish now I guess, flops down so it almost hides her face like a basket. She's a typical wife for a 10 h.p. aviator with exhibition fever. She and Tad go joy riding almost every night with a bunch of gasoline and alcohol sports and all have about five cocktails and dance a new Calif. dance called the Turkey Trot. This bunch have named Tad's new Wright "Sammy," and they think it's quite funny to yell "Hello Sammy, how are you, come have a drink."

I guess I'll call mine a monoplane and let it go at that.

July 14: Quebec. Lost race Toronto to Quebec. Had fair chance to win but motor kept misfiring, couldn't seem to get plugs that would work, and smashed hell out of elevator coming down on tail when landing here. Glad Hank Odell won, since I lost. Hank has designed new rocker-arm for Severn motor valves. All of us invited to usual big dinner, never did see so many uniforms, also members of Canadian parliament. I don't like to lose a race, but thunder it doesn't bother me long. Good filet of sole at dinner. Sat near a young lieutenant, leftenant I suppose it is, who made me think of Forrest Haviland. I miss Forrest a lot. He's doing some good flying for the army, flying Curtiss hydro now, and trying out muffler for military scouting. What I like as much as anything about him is his ease, I hope I'm learning a little of it anyway. This stuff is all confused but must hustle off to reception at summer school of Royal College for Females. Must send all this to old Forrest to read some day—if you ever see this, Forrest, hello, dear old man, I thought about you when I flew over military post.

Later: Big reception, felt like an awful nut, so shy I didn't hardly dare look up off the ground. After the formal reception I was taken around the campus by the Lady President, nice old lady with white hair and diamond combs in it. What seemed more than a million pretty girls kept dodging out of doorways and making snapshots of me. Good thing I've been reading quite a little lately, as the Lady Principal (that was it, not Lady President) talked very high brow. She asked me what I thought of this "terrible lower class unrest." Told her I was a socialist and she never batted an eye—of course an aviator is permitted to be a nut. Wonder if I am a good socialist as a matter of fact, I do know that most governments, maybe all, permit most children to never have a chance, start them out by choking them with dirt and T.B. germs, but how can we make international solidarity seem practical to the dub average voters, *how*!

Letter from Gertie to-night, forwarded here. She seems sort of bored in Joralemon, but is working hard with Village Improvement Committee of woman's club for rest room for farmers' wives, also getting up P.E. Sunday school picnic. Be good for Istra if she did common nice things like that, since she won't really get busy with her painting, but how she'd hate me for suggesting that she be what she calls "burjoice." Guess Gertie is finding herself. Hope yours truly but sleepy is finding himself too. How I love my little bed!

CHAPTER XXIII

(THE DIARY OF MR. ERICSON, CONTINUED.—EDITOR)

AUGUST 20, (1911, as before): Big Chicago meet over. They sure did show us a good time. Never saw better meet. Won finals in duration to-day. Also am second in altitude, but nix on the altitude again, I'm pretty poor at it. I'm no Lincoln Beachey! Don't see how he breathes. His 11,578 ft. was *some* climb.

Tomorrow starts my biggest attempt, by far; biggest distance flight ever tried in America, and rather niftier than even the European Circuit and British Circuit that Beaumont has won.

To fly as follows: Chicago to St. Louis to Indianapolis to Columbus to Washington to Baltimore to Philadelphia to Atlantic City to New York. The New York Chronicle in company with papers along line gives prize of $40,000. Ought to help bank account if win, in spite of big expenses to undergo. Now have $30,000 stowed away, and have sent mother $3,000.

To fly against my good old teacher M. Carmeau, and Tony Bean, Walter MacMonnies, M. Beaufort the Frenchman, Tad Warren, Billy Witzer, Chick Bannard, Aaron Solomons and other good men. Special NY Chronicle reporter, fellow named Forbes, assigned to me, and he hangs around all the time, sort of embarrassing (hurray, spelled it right, I guess) but I'm getting used to the reporters.

Martin Dockerill has an ambition! He said to me to-day, "Say, Hawk, if you win the big race you got to give me five plunks for my share and then by gum I'm going to buy two razor-strops." "What for?" I said. "Oh I bet there ain't anybody else in the world that owns *two* razor-strops!"

Not much to say about banquet, lots of speeches, good grub.

What tickles me more than anything is my new flying garments—not clothes but *garments*, by heck! I'm going to be a regular little old aviator in a melodrama. I've been wearing plain suits and a cap, same good old cap, always squeegee on my head. But for the big race I've got riding breeches and puttees and a silk shirt and a tweed Norfolk jacket and new leather coat and French helmet with both felt and springs inside the leather—this last really valuable. The real stage aviator, that's me. Watch the photographers fall for it. I bet Tad Warren's Norfolk jacket is worth $10,000 a year to him!

I pretended to Martin that I was quite serious about the clothes, the garments I mean. I dolled myself all up last night and went swelling into my hangar and anxiously asked Martin if he didn't like the get-up, and he nearly threw a fit. "Good Lord," he groans, "you look like an aviator on a Ladies Home Journal cover, guaranteed not to curse, swear or chaw tobacco. What's become of that girl you was kissing, last time I seen you on the cover?"

August 25: Not much time to write diary on race like this, it's just saw wood all the time or lose.

Bad wind to-day. Sometimes the wind don't bother me when I am flying, and sometimes, like to-day, it seems as though the one thing in the whole confounded world is the confounded wind that roars in your ears and makes your eyes water and sneaks down your collar to chill your spine and goes scooting up your sleeves, unless you have gauntlets, and makes your ears sting. Roar, roar, roar, the wind's worse than the noisiest old cast-iron tin-can Vrenskoy motor. You want to duck your head and get down out of it, and Lord it tires you so—aviation isn't all "brilliant risks" and "daring dives" and that kind of blankety-blank circus business, not by a long shot it ain't, lots of it is just sticking there and bucking the wind like a taxi driver speeding for a train in a storm. Tired to-night and mad.

September 5: New York! I win! Plenty smashes but only got jarred. I beat out Beaufort by eight hours, and Aaron Solomons by nearly a day. Carmeau's machine hopelessly smashed in Columbus, but he was not hurt, but poor Tad Warren *killed* crossing Illinois.

September 8: Had no time to write about my reception here in New York till now.

I've been worrying about poor Tad Warren's wife, bunch of us got together and made up a purse for her. Nothing more pathetic than these poor little women that poke down the cocktails to keep excited and then go to pieces.

I don't believe I was very decent to Tad. Sitting here alone in a hotel room, it seems twice as lonely after the fuss and feathers these last few days, a fellow thinks of all the rotten things he ever did. Poor old Tad. Too late now to cheer him up. Too late. Wonder if they shouldn't have called off race when he was killed.

Wish Istra wouldn't keep calling me up. Have I *got* to be rude to her? I'd like to be decent to her, but I can't stand the cocktail life. Lord, that time she danced, though.

Poor Tad was [See Transcriber's note.]

Oh hell, to get back to the reception. It was pretty big. Parade of the Aero Club and Squadron A, me in an open-face hack, feeling like a boob while sixty leven billion people cheered. Then reception by mayor, me delivering letter from mayor of Chicago which I had cutely sneaked out in Chicago and mailed to myself here, N. Y. general delivery, so I wouldn't lose it on the way. Then biggest dinner I've ever seen, must have been a thousand there, at the

Astor, me very natty in a new dress suit (hey bo, I fooled them, it was ready-made and cost me just $37.50 and fitted like my skin.)

Mayor, presidents of boroughs of NY, district attorney, vice president of U.S., lieut. governor of NY, five or six senators, chief of ordnance, U.S.A., arctic explorers and hundreds like that, but most of all Forrest Haviland whom I got them to stick right up near me. Speeches mostly about me, I nearly rubbed the silver off my flossy new cigarette case keeping from looking foolish while they were telling about me and the future of aviation and all them interesting subjects.

Forrest and I sneaked off from the reporters next afternoon, had quiet dinner down in Chinatown.

We have a bully plan. If we can make it and if he can get leave we will explore the headwaters of the Amazon with a two-passenger Curtiss flying boat, maybe next year.

Now the reception fans have done their darndest and all the excitement is over including the shouting and I'm starting for Newport to hold a little private meet of my own, backed by Thomas J. Watersell, the steel magnate, and by to-morrow night NY will forget me. I realized that after the big dinner. I got on the subway at Times Square, jumped quick into the car just as the doors were closing, and the guard yapped at me, "What are you trying to do, Billy, kill yourself?" He wasn't spending much time thinking about famous Hawk Ericson, and I got to thinking how comfortable NY will manage to go on being when they no longer read in the morning paper whether I dined with the governor, or with Martin Dockerill at Bazoo Junction Depot Lunch Counter.

They forget us quick. And already there's a new generation of aviators. Some of the old giants are gone, poor Moisant and Hoxsey and Johnstone and the rest killed, and there's coming along a bunch of youngsters that can fly enough to grab the glory, and they spread out the glory pretty thin. They go us old fellows except Beachey a few better on aerial acrobatics, and that's what the dear pee-pul like. (For a socialist I certainly do despise the pee-pul's *taste!*) I won't do any flipflops in the air no matter what the county fair managers write me. Somehow I'd just as soon be alive and exploring the Amazon with old Forrest as dead after "brilliant feats of fearless daring." Go to it, kids, good luck, only test your supporting wires, and don't try to rival Lincoln Beachey, he's a genius.

Glad got a secretary for a couple days to handle all this mail. Hundreds of begging letters and mash notes from girls since I won the big prize. Makes me feel funny! One nice thing out of the mail—letter from the Turk, Jack Terry, that I haven't seen since Plato. He didn't graduate, his old man died and he is assistant manager of quite a good sized fisheries out in Oregon, glad to hear from him again. Funny, I haven't thought of him for a year.

I feel lonely and melancholy to-night in spite of all I do to cheer up. Let up after reception etc. I suppose. I feel like calling up Istra, after all, but mustn't. I ought to hit the hay, but I couldn't sleep. Poor Tad Warren.

(The following words appear at the bottom of a page, in a faint, fine handwriting unlike Mr. Ericson's usual scrawl.—The Editor):

Whatever spirits there be, of the present world or the future, take this prayer from a plain man who knows little of monism or trinity or logos, and give to Tad another chance, as a child who never grew up.

September 11: Off to Kokomo, to fly for Farmers' Alliance.

Easy meet here (Newport, R.I.) yesterday, just straight flying and passenger carrying. Dandy party given for me after it, by Thomas J. Watersell, the steel man. Have read of such parties. Bird party, in a garden, Watersell has many acres in his place and big house with a wonderful brick terrace and more darn convenient things than I ever saw before, breakfast room out on the terrace and swimming pool and little gardens one outside of each guest room, rooms all have private doors, house is mission style built around patio. All the Newport swells came to party dressed as birds, and I had to dress as a hawk, they had the costume all ready, wonder how they got my measurements. Girls in the dance of the birds. Much silk stockings, very pretty. At end of dance they were all surrounding me in semi-circle I stood out on lawn beside Mrs. Watersell, and they bowed low to me, fluttering their silk wings and flashing out many colored electric globes concealed in wings and looked like hundreds of rainbow colored fireflies in the darkness. Just then the big lights were turned on again and they let loose hundreds of all kinds of birds, and they flew up all around me, surprised me to death. Then for grub, best sandwiches I ever ate.

Felt much flattered by it all, somehow did not feel so foolish as at banquets with speeches.

After the party was all over, quite late, I went with Watersell for a swim in his private pool. Most remarkable thing I ever saw. He said everybody has Roman baths and Pompei baths and he was going to go them one better, so he has an Egyptian bath, the pool itself like the inside of an ancient temple, long vista of great big green columns and a big idol at the end, and the pool all in green marble with lights underneath the water and among the columns, and the water itself just heat of air, so you can't tell where the water leaves off and the air above it begins, hardly, and feel as though you were swimming in air through a green twilight. Darndest sensation I ever felt, and the idol and columns sort of awe you.

I enjoyed the swim and the room they gave me, but I had lost my tooth-brush and that kind of spoiled the end of the party.

I noticed Watersell only half introduced his pretty daughter to me, they like me as a lion but——And yet they seem to like me personally well enough, too. If I didn't have old Martin trailing along, smoking his corn-cob pipe and saying what he thinks, I'd die of loneliness sometimes on the hike from meet to meet. Other times have jolly parties, but I'd like to sit down with the Cowleses and play poker and not have to explain who I am.

Funny—never used to feel lonely when I was bumming around on freights and so on, not paying any special attention to anybody.

October 23: I wonder how far I'll ever get as an aviator? The newspapers all praise me as a hero. Hero, hell! I'm a pretty steady flier but so would plenty of chauffeurs be. This hero business is mostly bunk, it was mostly chance my starting to fly at all. Don't suppose it is all accident to become as great a flier as Garros or Vedrines or Beachey, but I'm never going to be a Garros, I guess. Like the man that can jump twelve feet but never can get himself to go any farther.

December 1: Carmeau killed yesterday, flying at San Antone. Motor backfire, machine caught fire, burned him to death in the air. He was the best teacher I could have had, patient and wise. I can't write about him. And I can't get this insane question out of my mind: Was his beard burned? I remember just how it looked, and think of that when all the time I ought to remember how clever and darn decent he was. Carmeau will never show me new stunts again.

And Ely killed in October, Cromwell Dixon gone—the plucky youngster, Professor Montgomery, Nieuport, Todd Shriver whom Martin Dockerill and Hank Odell liked so much, and many others, all dead, like Moisant. I don't think I take any undue risks, but it makes me stop and think. And Hank Odell with a busted shoulder. Captain Paul Beck once told me he believed it was mostly carelessness, these accidents, and he certainly is a good observer, but when I think of a careful constructor like Nieuport——

Punk money I'm making. Thank heaven there will be one more good year of the game, 1912, but I don't know about 1913. Looks like the exhibition game would blow up then—nearly everybody that wants to has seen an aeroplane fly once, now, and that's about all they want, so good bye aviation, except for military use and flying boats for sportsmen. At least good bye during a slump of several years.

Hope to thunder Forrest and I will be able to make our South American hike, even if it costs every cent I have. That will be something like it, seeing new country instead of scrapping with fair managers about money.

December 22: Hoorray! Christmas time at sea! Quite excite to smell the ocean again and go rolling down the narrow gangways between the white state-room doors. Off for a month's flying in Brazil and Argentine, with Tony Bean. Will look up data for coming exploration of Amazon headwaters. Martin Dockerill like a regular Beau Brummel in new white flannels, parading the deck, making eyes at pretty Greaser girls. It's good to be *going*.

Feb. 22, 1912: Geo. W's birthday. He'd have busted that no-lie proviso if he'd ever advertised an aero meet.

Start of flight New Orleans to St. Louis. Looks like really big times, old fashioned jubilee all along the road and lots of prizes, though take a chance. Only measly little $2,500 prize guaranteed, but vague promises of winnings at towns all along, where stop for short exhibitions. Each of contestants has to fly at scheduled towns for percentage of gate receipts.

Feb. 23: What a rotten flight to-day. Small crowd out to see me off. No sooner up than trouble with plugs. Wanted to land, but nothing but bayous, rice fields, cane breaks, and marshes. Farmer shot at my machine. Soon motor stopped on me and had to come down awhooping on a small plowed field. Smashed landing gear and got an awful jar. Nothing serious though. It was two hours before a local blacksmith and I repaired chassis and cleaned plugs. I started off after coaching three scared darkies to hold the tail, while the blacksmith spun the propeller. He would give it a couple of bats, then dodge out of the way too soon, while I sat there and tried not to look mad, which by gum I was plenty mad. Landed in this bum town, called ——, fourth in the race, and found sweet (?) refuge in this chills and fever hotel. Wish I was back in New Orleans. Cheer up, having others ahead of me in the race just adds a little zip to it. Watch me to-morrow. And I'm not the only hard luck artist. Aaron Solomons busted propeller and nearly got killed.

Later. Cable. Tony Bean is dead. Killed flying. My god, Tony, impossible to think of him as dead, just a few days ago we were flying together and calling on senoritas and he playing the fiddle and laughing, always so polite, like he used to fiddle us into good nature when we got discouraged at Bagby's school. Seems like it was just couple minutes ago we drove in his big car through Avenida de Mayo and everybody cheered him, he was hero of Buenos Aires, yet he treated me as the Big Chief. Cablegram forwarded from New Orleans, dated yesterday, "Beanno killed fell 200 feet."

And to-morrow I'll have to be out and jolly the rustic meet managers again. Want to go off some place and be quiet and think. Wish I could get away, be off to South America with Forrest.

February 24: Rotten luck continues. Back in same town again! Got up yesterday and motor misfired, had to make quick landing in a bayou and haul out machine myself aided by scared kids. Got back here and found gasoline pipe fouled, small piece of tin stuck in it.

Martin feels as bad as I do at Tony's death, tho he doesn't say much of anything. "Gosh, and Tony such a nice little cuss," was about all he said, but he looked white around the gills.

Feb. 25: Another man has dropped out, I am third but still last in the race. Race fever got me to-day, didn't care for anything but winning, got off to a good start, then took chances, machine wobbled like a board in the surf. Am having some funny kind of chicken creole I guess it is for lunch, writing this in hotel dining room.

Later. Passed Aaron Solomons, am now second in the race, landed here just three hours behind Walter MacMonnies. Three letters forwarded here, from Forrest, he is flying daily at army aviation camp, also from Gertie Cowles, she and her mother are in Minneapolis, attending a week of grand opera, also to my surprise short note from Jack Ryan, the grouch, saying he has given up flying and gone back into motor business.

There won't be much more than money to pay expenses on this trip.

Tomorrow I'll show them some real flying.

Later. Telegram from a St. L. newspaper. Sweet business. Says that promoters of race have not kept promise to remove time limit as they promised. Doubt if either Walter MacMonnies or I can finish in time set.

Feb. 26: Bad luck continues but made fast flight after two forced descents, one of them had to make difficult landing, plane down on railroad track, avoiding telegraph wires, and get machine off track as could hear train coming, awful job. Nerves not very good. Once when up at 200 ft. heighth from which Tony Bean fell, I saw his face right in air in front of me and jumped so I jerked the stuffings out of control wires.

March 15: Just out of hospital, after three weeks there, broken leg still in splints. Glad Walter MacM got thru in time limit, got prize. Too week and shaky write much, shoulder still hurts.

March 18: How I came to fall (fall that broke my leg, three weeks ago) Was flying over rough country when bad gust came thru hill defile. Wing crumpled. Up at 400 ft. Machine plunged forward then sideways. Gosh, I thought, I'm gone, but will live as long as I can, even a few seconds more, and kept working with elevator, trying to right her even a little. Ground coming up fast. Must have jumped, I think. Landed in marsh, that saved my life, but woke up at doctor's house, leg busted and shoulder bad, etc. Machine shot to pieces, but Martin Dockerill has it pretty well repaired. He and the doc and I play poker every day, Martin always wins with his dog-gone funeral face no matter tho he has an ace full.

March 24: Leg all right, pretty nearly. Rigged up steering bar so I can work it with one foot. Flew a mile to-day, went not badly. Hope to fly at Springfield, Ill. meet next week. Will be able to make Brazil trip with Forrest Haviland all right. The dear old boy has been writing to me every day while I've been on the bum. Newspapers have made a lot of my flying so soon again, several engagements and now things look bright again. Reading lots and chipper as can be.

March 25: Forrest Haviland is dead He was killed to-day.

March 27: Disposed of monoplane by telegraph. Got Martin job with Sunset Aviation Company.

March 28: Started for Europe.

May 8, Paris: Forrest and I would have met to-day in New York to perfect plans for Brazil trip.

May 10: Am still trying to answer letter from Forrest's father. Can't seem to make it go right. If I could have seen Forrest again. But maybe they were right, holding funeral before I could get there. Captain Faber says Forrest was terribly crushed, falling from 1700 ft. I wish I didn't keep on thinking of plans for our Brazil trip, then remembering we won't make it after all. I don't think I will fly till fall, anyway, though I feel stronger now after rest in England, Titherington has beautiful place in Devonshire. England seems to stick to biplane, can't make them see monoplane. Don't think I shall fly before fall. To-day I would have been with Forrest Haviland in New York, I think he could have got leave for Brazil trip. We would taken Martin. Tony promised to meet us in Rio. I like France but can't get used to language, keep starting to speak Spanish. Maybe I'll fly here in France but certainly not for some time, though massage has fixed me all O.K. Am studying French. Maybe shall bicycle thru France. Mem.: Write to Colonel Haviland when I can.

Must when I can.

PART III
THE ADVENTURE OF LOVE

CHAPTER XXIV

In October, 1912, a young man came with an enthusiastic letter from the president of the Aero Club to old Stephen VanZile, vice-president and general manager of the VanZile Motor Corporation of New York. The young man was quiet, self-possessed, an expert in regard to motors, used to meeting prominent men. He was immediately set to work at a tentative salary of $2,500 a year, to develop the plans of what he called the "Touricar"—an automobile with all camping accessories, which should enable motorists to travel independent of inns, add the joy of camping to the joy of touring, and—a feature of nearly all inventions—add money to the purse of the inventor.

The young man was Carl Ericson, whom Mr. VanZile had seen fly at New Orleans during the preceding February. Carl had got the idea of the Touricar while wandering by motor-cycle through Scandinavia and Russia.

He was, at this time, twenty-seven years old; not at all remarkable in appearance nor to be considered handsome, but so clean, so well bathed, so well set-up and evenly tanned, that one thought of the swimming, dancing, tennis-playing city men of good summer resorts, an impression enhanced by his sleek corn-silk hair and small, pale mustache. His clothes came from London, his watch-chain was a thin line of platinum and gold, his cigarette-case of silver engraved in inconspicuous bands—a modest and sophisticated cigarette-case, which he had possessed long enough to forget that he had it. He was apparently too much the easy, well-bred, rather inexperienced Yale or Princeton man (not Harvard; there was a tiny twang in his voice, and he sometimes murmured "Gee!") to know much about life or work, as yet, and his smooth, rosy cheeks made it absurdly evident that he had not been away from the college insulation for more than two years.

But when he got to work with draftsman and stenographers, when a curt kindliness filled his voice, he proved to be concentrated, unafraid of responsibility, able to keep many people busy; trained to something besides family tradition and the collegians' naïve belief that it matters who wins the Next Game.

His hands would have given away the fact that he had done things. They were large, broad; the knuckles heavy; the palms calloused by something rougher than oar and tennis-racket. The microscopic traces of black grease did not for months quite come out of the cracks in his skin. And two of his well-kept but thick nails had obviously been smashed.

The men of the same rank as himself in the office, captains and first lieutenants of business, said that he "simply ate up work." They fancied, with the eager old-womanishness of office gossip, that he had a "secret sorrow," for, though he was pleasant enough, he kept very much to himself. The cause of his retirement from aviation was the theme of many romantic legends. They did not know precisely what it was he had done in the pre-historic period of a year before, but they treated him with reverence instead of the amused aloofness with which an office usually waits to see whether a new man will prove to be a fool or a "grouch," a clown or a good fellow. The stenographers and filing-girls and telephone-girls followed with yearning eyes the hero's straight back. The girl who discovered, in an old *New York Chronicle* lining a bureau drawer, an interview with Carl, became very haughty over its possession and lent it only to her best lady friends. The older women, who knew that Carl had had a serious accident, whispered in cloak-room confidences, "Poor fellow, and so brave about it."

Yet all the while Carl's china-blue eyes showed no trace of pain nor sorrow nor that detestable appeal for sympathy called "being brave about his troubles."

There were many thoughtful features which fitted the Touricar for use in camping—extra-sized baggage-box whose triangular shape made the car more nearly streamline, special folding silk tents, folding aluminum cooking-utensils, electric stove run by current from the car, electric-battery light attached to a curtain-rod. But the distinctive feature, the one which Carl could patent, was the means by which a bed was made up inside the car as Pullman seats are turned into berths. The back of the front seat was hinged, and dropped back to horizontal. The upholstery back of the back seat could be taken out and also placed on the horizontal. With blankets spread on the level space thus provided, with the extra-heavy top and side curtains in place, and the electric light switched on, tourists had a refuge cleaner than a country hotel and safer than a tent....

The first Touricar was being built. Carl was circularizing a list of possible purchasers, and corresponding with makers of camping goods.

Because he was not office-broken he did not worry about the risks of the new enterprise. The stupid details of affairs had, for him, a soul—the Adventure of Business.

To be consulted by draftsmen and shop foremen; to feel that if he should not arrive at 8.30 A.M. to the second the most important part of all the world's business would be halted and stenographers loll in expensive idleness; to have the chief, old VanZile, politely anxious as to how things were going; to plan ways of making a million dollars and not have the plans seem fantastic—all these made it interesting to overwork, and hypnotized Carl into a feeling of responsibility which was less spectacular than flying before thousands, but more in accordance with the spirit of the time and place.

Inside the office—busy and reaching for success. Outside the office—frankly bored.

Carl was a dethroned prince. He had been accustomed to a more than royal court of admirers. Now he was a nobody the moment he went twenty feet from his desk. He was forgotten. He did not seek out the many people he had met when he was an aviator and a somebody. He believed, perhaps foolishly, that they liked him only as a personage, not as a person. He sat lonely at dinner, in cheap restaurants with stains on the table-cloths, for he had put much of his capital into the new Touricar Company, mothered by the VanZile Corporation; and aeroplanes, accessories, traveling-expenses, and the like had devoured much of his large earnings at aviation before he had left the game.

In his large, shabby, fairly expensive furnished room on Seventy-fifth Street he spent unwilling evenings, working on Touricar plans, or reading French— French technical motor literature, light novels, Balzac, anything.

He tried to keep in physical form, and, much though the routine and silly gestures of gymnasium exercises bored him, he took them three times a week. He could not explain the reason, but he kept his identity concealed at the gymnasium, giving his name as "O. Ericson."

Even at the Aero Club, where scores knew him by sight, he was a nobody. Aviation, like all pioneer arts, must look to the men who are doing new things or planning new things, not to heroes past. Carl was often alone at lunch at the club. Any group would have welcomed him, but he did not seek them out. For the first time he really saw the interior decorations of the club. In the old days he had been much too busy talking with active comrades to gaze about. But now he stared for five minutes together at the stamped-leather wall-covering of the dining-room. He noted, much too carefully for a happy man, the trophies of the lounging-room. But at one corner he never glanced. For here was a framed picture of the forgotten Hawk Ericson, landing on Governor's Island, winner of the flight from Chicago to New York.... Such a beautiful swoop!...

There is no doubt of the fact that he disliked the successful new aviators, and did so because he was jealous of them. He admitted the fact, but he could not put into his desire to be a good boy one-quarter of the force that inspired his resentment at being a lonely man and a nobody. But, since he knew he was envious, he was careful not to show it, not to inflict it upon others. He was gracious and added a wrinkle between his brows, and said "Gosh!" and "ain't" much less often.

He had few friends these days. Death had taken many; and he was wary of lion-hunters, who in dull seasons condescend to ex-lions and dethroned princes. But he was fond of a couple of Aero Club men, an automobile ex-racer who was a selling-agent for the VanZile Corporation, and Charley Forbes, the bright-eyed, curly-headed, busy, dissipated little reporter who had followed him from Chicago to New York for the *Chronicle*. Occasionally one of the men with whom he had flown—Hank Odell or Walter MacMonnies or Lieutenant Rutledge of the navy—came to town, and Carl felt natural again. As for women, the only girl whom he had known well in years, Istra Nash, the painter, had gone to California to keep house for her father till she should have an excuse to escape to New York or Europe again.

Inside the office—a hustling, optimistic young business man. For the rest of the time—a dethroned prince. Such was Carl Ericson in November, 1912, when a letter from Gertrude Cowles, which had pursued him all over America and Europe, finally caught him:

—— West 157th St.

NEW YORK.

CARL DEAR,—Oh such excitement, we have come to *New York* to live! Ray has such a good position with a big NY real estate co. & Mama & I are going to make a home for him even if it's only just a flat (but it's quite a big one & looks out on the duckiest old house that must have been adorning Harlem for heaven knows how long,) & our house has all modern conveniences, elevator & all.

Think, Carl, I'm going to study dancing at Madame Vashkowska's school— she was with the Russian ballet & really is almost as wonderful a dancer as Isadora Duncan or Pavlova. Perhaps I'll teach all these ducky new dances to children some day. I'm just terribly excited to be here, like the silliest gushiest little girl in the world. And I do hope so much you will be able to come to NY & honor us with your presence at dinner, famous aviator—our Carl & we are so *proud* of you—if you will still remember simple people like us do come *any time*. Wonder where you will be when this reaches you.

I read in the papers that your accident isn't serious but I am worried, oh Carl you must take care of yourself.

Yours as ever,

GERTIE.

P.S. Mama sends her best regards, so does Ray, he has a black mustache now, we tease him about it dreadfully.

G.

One minute after reading the letter, in his room, Carl was standing on the chaste black-and-white tiles of the highly respectable white-arched hall downstairs asking Information for the telephone number of —— West 157th Street, while his landlord, a dry-bearded goat of a physician who had failed in the practise of medicine and was now failing in the practise of rooming-houses, listened from the front of the hall.

Glad to escape from the funereally genteel house, Carl hastily changed his collar and tie and, like the little boy Carl whom Gertie had known, dog-trotted to the subway, which was going to take him Home.

CHAPTER XXV

Before the twelve-story Bendingo Apartments, Carl scanned the rows of windows which pierced the wall like bank-swallows' nests in a bold cliff.... One group of those windows was home—Joralemon and memories, Gertie's faith and understanding.... It was she who had always understood him.... In anticipation he loitered through the big, marble-and-stucco, rug and rubber-tree, negro hallboy and Jew tenant hallway.... What would the Cowleses be like, now?

Gertie met him in the coat-smelling private hall of the Cowles apartment, greeted him with both hands clasping his, and her voice catching in, "Oh, *Carl*, it's so good to see you!" Behind Gertie was a swishing, stiff-backed Mrs. Cowles, piping in a high, worn voice: "Mr. Ericson! A friend from home! And such a famous friend!"

Gertie drew him into the living-room. He looked at her.

He found, not a girl, but a woman of thirty, plump, solid, with the tiniest wrinkles of past unhappiness or ennui at the corners of her mouth; but her eyes radiant with sweetness, and her hair appealingly soft and brown above her wide, calm forehead. She was gowned in lavender crêpe de Chine, with panniers of satin elaborately sprinkled with little bunches of futurist flowers; long jet earrings; a low-cut neck that hinted of a comfortable bosom. Eyes shining, hands firm on his arm, voice ringing, she was unaffectedly glad to see him—her childhood playmate, whom she had not beheld for seven years.

Mrs. Cowles was waiting for them to finish their greetings. Carl was startled to find Mrs. Cowles smaller than he had remembered, her hair nearly white and not perfectly matched, her face crisscrossed with wrinkles deeper than her age justified. But her old disapproval of Carl, son of a carpenter and cousin of a "hired girl," was gone. She even laughed mildly, like a kitten sneezing. And from a room somewhere beyond Ray shouted:

"Be right there in a second, old man. Crazy to have a look at you."

Carl did not really see the living-room, their background. Indeed, he never really saw it. There was nothing to see—chairs and a table and pictures of meadows and roses. It was comfortable, however, and had conveniences—a folding card-table, a cribbage-board, score-pads for whist and five hundred; a humidor of cigars; a large Morris chair and an ugly but well-padded couch of green tufted velvetine.

They sat about in chairs, talking.

Ray came in, slapped Carl on the back, roared: "Well, here's the stranger! Holy Mike! have you got a mustache, too? Better shave it off before Gert starts kidding you about it. Have a cigar?"

Carl felt at home for the first time in a year; for the first time talked easily.

"Say, Gertie, tell me about my folks, and Bone Stillman."

"Why, I saw your father just before we left, Carl. You know he still does quite a little business. We got your mother to join the Nautilus Club—she doesn't go very often; but she had a nice paper about 'Java and Its Products,' and she helps us a lot with the rest-room. I haven't seen Mr. Stillman for a long, long time. Ray, what has——"

Ray: "Why, I think old Bone's off on some expedition 'r other. Fellow told me Bone was some kind of a forest ranger or mine inspector, or some darn thing, up in the Big Woods. He must be pretty well along toward seventy now, at that."

Carl: "So dad's getting along well. His letters aren't very committal.... Oh, say, Gertie, what ever became of Ben Rusk? I've lost track of him entirely."

Gertie: "Why, didn't you know? He went to Rush Medical College. They say he did splendidly there; he stood awfully well in his classes, and now he's in practise with his father, home."

Carl: "Rush?"

Gertie: "Yes, you know, in Chi——"

Carl: "Oh yes, sure; in Chicago; sure, I remember now; I saw it when I was there one time. Why! That's the school his father went to, wasn't it?"

Ray: "Yes, sure, that's the one."

The point seemed settled.

Carl: "Well, well, so Ben *did* study medicine, after——Oh, *say*, how's Adelaide Benner?"

Gertie: "Why, you'll see her! She's coming to New York in just a couple of weeks to stay with us till she gets settled. Just think, she's to have a whole year here, studying domestic science, and then she's to have a perfectly dandy position teaching in the Fargo High School. I'm not supposed to tell—you mustn't breathe a *word* of it——"

Mrs. Cowles (interrupting): "Adelaide is a good girl....Ray! Don't tilt your chair!"

Gertie: "Yes, *isn't* she, mamma.... Well, I was just saying: between you and me, Carl, she is to have the position in Fargo all ready and waiting for her, though of course they can't announce it publicly, with all the cats that would like to get it, and all. Isn't that fine?"

Carl: "Certainly is.... 'Member the time we had the May party at Adelaide's, and all I could get for my basket was rag babies and May flowers? Gee, but I felt out of it!"

Gertie: "We did have some good parties, *didn't* we!"

Ray: "Don't call that much of a good party for Carl! Ring off, Gert; you got the wrong number that time, all right!"

Gertie (flushing): "Oh, I *didn't* mean———But we did have some good times. Oh, Carl, will you *ever* forget the time you and I ran away when we were just babies?"

Carl: "I'll never forget———"

Mrs. Cowles: "I'll never forget that time! My lands! I thought I should die, I was so frightened."

Carl: "You've forgiven me now, though, haven't you?"

Mrs. Cowles: "My dear boy, of course I have!" (She wiped away a few tears with a gentlewoman handkerchief of lace and thin linen. Carl crossed the room and kissed her pale-veined, silvery old hand. Abashed, he subsided on the couch, and, trying to look as though he hadn't done it———)

Carl: "Ohhhhh *say*, whatever did become of———Oh, I can't think of his name———Oh, *you* know———I know his name well as I do my own, but it's slipped me, just for the moment———You know, he ran the billiard-parlor; the son of the———"

(From Mrs. Cowles, a small, disapproving sound; from Ray, a grin of knowing naughtiness and a violent head-shake.)

Gertie (gently): "Yes.... He—has left Joralemon.... Klemm, you mean."

Carl (hastily, wondering what Eddie Klemm had done): "Oh, I see.... Have there been many changes in Joralemon?"

Mrs. Cowles: "Do you write to your father and mother, Carl? You ought to."

Carl: "Oh yes, I write to them quite often, now, though for a time I didn't."

Mrs. Cowles: "I'm glad, my boy. It's pretty good, after all, to have home folks that you can depend on, isn't it? When I first went to Joralemon, I thought it was a little pokey, but now I'm older, and I've been there so long and all, that I'm almost afraid of New York, and I declare I do get real lonely for home sometimes. I'd be glad to see Dr. Rusk—Ben's father, I mean, the old doctor—driving by, though of course you know I lived in Minneapolis a great many years, and I do feel I ought to take advantage of the opportunities here, and I've thought quite seriously about taking up French again, it's so long since I've studied it——You ought to study it; you will find it cultivates the mind. And you must be sure to write often to your mother; there's nothing you can depend on like a mother's love, my boy."

Ray: "Say, look here, Carl, I want to hear something about all this aviation. How does it feel to fly, anyway? I'd be scared to death; it's funny, I can't look off the top of a sky-scraper without feeling as though I wanted to jump. Gosh! I——"

Gertie: "Now you just let Carl tell us when he gets ready, you big, bad brother! Carl wants to hear all about Home first.... All these years!... You were asking about the changes. There haven't been so very many. You know it's a little slow there. Oh, of course, I almost forgot; why, you haven't been in Joralemon since they built up what used to be Tubbs's pasture."

Carl: "Not the old pasture by the lake? Well, well! Is that a fact! Why, gee! I used to snare gophers there!"

Gertie: "Oh yes. Why, you simply wouldn't *know* it, Carl, it's so much changed. There must be a dozen houses on it, now. Why, there's cement walks and everything, and Mr. Upham has a house there, a real nice one, with a screened-in porch and everything.... Of course you know they've put in the sewer now, and there's lots of modern bath-rooms, and almost everybody has a Ford. We would have bought one, but planning to come away so soon——Oh yes, and they've added a fire-escape to the school-house."

Carl: "Well, well!... Oh, say, Ray, how is Howard Griffin getting along?"

Ray: "Why, Howard's graduated from Chicago Law School, and he's practising in Denver. Doing pretty well, I guess; settled down and got quite some real-estate holdings.... Have 'nother cigar, old man?... Say, speaking of Plato, of course you know they ousted old S. Alcott Woodski from the presidency, for heresy, something about baptism; and the dean succeeded him.... Poor old cuss, he wasn't as mean as the dean, anyway.... Say, Carl, I've always thought they gave you a pretty raw deal there——"

Gertie (interrupting): "Perfectly dreadful!... Ray, *don't* put your feet on that couch; I brushed it thoroughly, just this morning.... It was simply terrible, Carl; I've always said that if Plato couldn't appreciate her greatest son——"

Mrs. Cowles (sleepily): "Outrageous.... And don't put your feet on that chair, Ray."

Ray: "Oh, leave my feet alone!... Everybody knew you were dead right in standing up for Prof Frazer. You remember how I roasted all the fellows in

Omega Chi when they said you were nutty to boost him? And when you stood up in Chapel——Lord! that was nervy."

Gertie: "Indeed you were right, and now you've got so famous I guess——"

Carl: "Oh, I ain't so——"

Mrs. Cowles: "I was simply amazed.... Children, if you don't mind, I'm afraid I must leave you. Mr. Ericson, I'm so ashamed to be sleepy so early. When we lived in Minneapolis, before Mr. Cowles passed beyond, he was a regular night-hawk, and we used to sit—sit—" (a yawn)—"sit up till all hours. But to-night——"

Gertie: "Oh, must you go so soon? I was just going to make Carl a rarebit. Carl has never seen one of my rarebits."

Mrs. Cowles: "Make him one by all means, my dear, and you young people sit up and enjoy yourselves just as long as you like. Good night, all.... Ray, will you please be sure and see that that window is fastened before you go to bed? I get so nervous when——Mr. Ericson, I'm very proud to think that one of our Joralemon boys should have done so well. Sometimes I wonder if the Lord ever meant men to fly—what with so many accidents, and you know aviators often do get killed and all. I was reading the other day—such a large percentage——But we have been so proud that you should lead them all, I was saying to a lady on the train that we had a friend who was a famous aviator, and she was so interested to find that we knew you. Good night."

They had the Welsh rarebit, with beer, and Carl helped to make it. Gertie summoned him into the scoured kitchen, saying, with a beautiful casualness, as she tied an apron about him:

"We can't afford a hired girl (I suppose I should say a 'maid'), because mamma has put so much of our money into Ray's business, so you mustn't expect anything so very grand. But you'd like to help, wouldn't you? You're to chop the cheese. Cut it into weenty cubes."

Carl did like to help. He boasted that he was the "champion cheese-chopper of Harlem and the Bronx, one-thirty-three ringside," while Gertie was toasting crackers, and Ray was out buying bottles of beer in a newspaper. It all made Carl feel more than ever at home.... It was good to be with people of such divine understanding that they knew what he meant when he said, "I suppose there *have* been worse teachers than Prof Larsen——!"

When the rabbit lay pale in death, a saddening *débâcle* of hardened cheese, and they sat with their elbows on the Modified Mission dining-table, Gertie exclaimed:

"Oh, Ray, you *must* do that new stunt of yours for Carl. It's screamingly funny, Carl."

Ray rose, had his collar and tie off in two jocund jerks, buttoned his collar on backward, cheerily turned his waistcoat back side foremost, lengthened his face to an expression of unctuous sanctimoniousness, and turned about—transformed in one minute to a fair imitation of a stage curate. With his hands folded, Ray droned, "Naow, sistern, it behooveth us heuh in St. Timothee's Chutch," while Carl pounded the table in his delight at seeing old Ray, the broad-shouldered, the lady-killer, the capable business man, drop his eyes and yearn.

"Now you must do a stunt!" shrieked Ray and Gertie; and Carl hesitatingly sang what he remembered of Forrest Haviland's foolish song:

"I went up in a balloon so bigThe people on the earth they looked like a pig,Like a mice, like a katydid, like flieses and like fleasen."

Then, without solicitation, Gertie decided to dance "Gather the Golden Sheaves," which she had learned at the school of Mme. Vashkowska, late (though not very late) of the Russian ballet.

She explained her work; outlined the theory of sensuous and esthetic dancing; mentioned the backgrounds of Bakst and the glories of Nijinsky; told her ambition to teach the New Dancing to children. Carl listened with awe; and with awe did he gaze as Gertie gathered the Golden Sheaves—purely hypothetical sheaves in a field occupying most of the living-room.

After the stunts Ray delicately vanished. It was not so much that he statedly went off to bed as that, presently, he was not there. Gertie and Carl were snugly alone, and at last he talked—of Forrest Haviland and Tony Bean, of flying and falling, of excited crowds and the fog-filled air-lanes.

In turn she told of her ambition to do something modern and urban. She had hesitated between dancing and making exotic jewelry; she was glad she had chosen the former; it was so human; it put one in touch with People.... She had recently gone to dinner with real Bohemians, spirits of fire, splendidly in contrast with the dull plodders of Joralemon. The dinner had been at a marvelous place on West Tenth Street—very foreign, every one drinking wine and eating spaghetti and little red herrings, and the women fearlessly smoking cigarettes—some of them. She had gone with a girl from Mme. Vashkowska's school, a glorious creature from London, Nebraska, who lived with the most fascinating girls at the Three Arts Club. They had met an artist with black hair and languishing eyes, who had a Yankee name, but sang Italian songs divinely, upon the slightest pretext, so bubbling was he with *joie de vivre*.

Carl was alarmed. "Gosh!" he protested, "I hope you aren't going to have much to do with the long-haired bunch.... I've invented a name for them— 'the Hobohemians.'"

"Oh no-o! I don't take them seriously at all. I was just glad to go once."

"Of course some of them are clever."

"Oh yes, aren't they clever!"

"But I don't think they last very well."

"Oh no, I'm sure they don't last well. Oh no, Carl, I'm too old and fat to be a Bohemian—a Hobohemian, I mean, so——"

"Nonsense! You look so—oh, thunder! I don't know just how to express it— well, so *real!* It's wonderfully comfortable to be with you-all again. I don't mean you're just the 'so good to her mother' sort, you understand. But I mean you're dependable as well as artistic."

"Oh, indeed, I won't take them too seriously. Besides, I suppose lots of the people that go to Bohemian restaurants aren't really artists at all; they just go to see the artists; they're just as bromidic as can be——Don't you hate bromides? Of course I want to see some of that part of life, but I think—— Oh, don't you think those artists and all are dreadfully careless about morals?"

"Well——"

"Yes," she breathed, reflectively. "No, I keep up with my church and all— indeed I do. Oh, Carl, you must come to our church—St. Orgul's. It's too sweet for anything. It's just two blocks from here; and it isn't so far up here, you know, not with the subway—not like commuting. It has the *loveliest* chapel. And the most wonderful reredos. And the services are so inspiring and high-church; not like that horrid St. Timothy's at home. I do think a church service ought to be beautiful. Don't you? It isn't as though we were like a lot of poor people who have to have their souls saved in a mission.... What church do you attend? You *will* come to St. Orgul's some time, won't you?"

"Be glad to——Oh, say, Gertie, before I forget it, what is Semina doing now? Is she married?"

Apropos of this subject, Gertie let it be known that she herself was not betrothed.

Carl had not considered that question; but when he was back in his room he was glad to know that Gertie was free.

At the Omega Chi Delta Club, Carl lunched with Ray Cowles. Two nights later, Ray and Gertie took Carl and Gertie's friend, the glorious creature from London, Nebraska, to the opera. Carl did not know much about opera. In other words, being a normal young American who had been water-proofed with college culture, he knew absolutely nothing about it. But he gratefully listened to Gertie's clear explanation of why Mme. Vashkowska preferred Wagner to Verdi.

He had, in the mean time, received a formal invitation for a party to occur at Gertie's the coming Friday evening.

Thursday evening Gertie coached him in a new dance, the turkey trot. She also gave him a lesson in the Boston, with a new dip invented by Mme. Vashkowska, which was certain to sweep the country, because, of course, Vashkowska was the only genuinely qualified *maîtresse de danse* in America.

It was a beautiful evening. Home! Ray came in, and the three of them had coffee and thin sandwiches. At Gertie's suggestion, Ray again turned his collar round and performed his "clergyman stunt." While the impersonation did not, perhaps, seem so humorous as before, Carl was amused; and he consented to sing the "I went up in a balloon so big" song, so that Ray might learn it and sing it at the office.

It was captivating to have Gertie say, quietly, as he left: "I hope you'll be able to come to the party a little early to-morrow, Carl. You know we count on you to help us."

CHAPTER XXVI

The party was on at the Cowles flat.

People came. They all set to it, having a party, being lively and gay, whether they wanted to or not. They all talked at once, and had delicious shocks over the girl from London, Nebraska, who, having moved to Washington Place, just a block or two from ever so many artists, was now smoking a cigarette and, wearing a gown that was black and clinging. It was no news to her that men had a tendency to become interested in her ankles. But she still went to church and was accepted by quite the nicest of the St. Orgul's set, to whom Gertie had introduced her.

She and Gertie were the only thoroughly qualified representatives of Art, but Beauty and Gallantry and Wit were common. The conspirators in holding a party were, on the male side:

An insurance adjuster, who was a frat-brother to Carl and Ray, though he came from Melanchthon College. A young lawyer, ever so jolly, with a banjo. A bantling clergyman, who was spoken of with masculine approval because he smoked a pipe and said charmingly naughty things. Johnson of the Homes and Long Island Real Estate Company, and his brother, of the Martinhurst Development Company. Four older men, ranging from thin-haired to very bald, who had come with their wives and secretly looked at their watches while they talked brightly with one another's wives. Five young men whom Carl could not tell apart, as they all had smooth hair and eye-glasses and smart dress-shirts and obliging smiles and complimentary references to his aviating. He gave up trying to remember which was which.

It was equally hard to remember which of the women Gertie knew as a result of her girlhood visit to New York, which from their membership in St. Orgul's Church, which from their relation to Minnesota. They all sat in rows on couches and chairs and called him "You wicked man!" for reasons none too clear to him. He finally fled from them and joined the group of young men, who showed an ill-bred and disapproved tendency to sneak off into Ray's room for a smoke. He did not, however, escape one young woman who stood out from the *mêlée*—a young woman with a personality almost as remarkable as that of the glorious creature from London, Nebraska. This was the more or less married young woman named Dorothy, and affectionately called "Tottykins" by all the St. Orgul's group. She was of the kind who look at men appraisingly, and expect them to come up, be unduly familiar, and be crushed. She had seven distinct methods of getting men to say indiscreet things, and three variations of reply, of which the favorite was to remark with well-bred calmness: "I'm afraid you have made a slight error, Mr. Uh——— I didn't quite catch your name? Perhaps they failed to tell you that I attend St.

Orgul's evvvv'ry Sunday, and have a husband and child, and am not at all, really, you know. I hope that there has been nothing I said that has given you the idea that I have been looking for a flirtation."

A thin, small female with bobbed hair was Tottykins, who kept her large husband and her fat, white grub of an infant somewhere in the back blocks. She fingered a long, gold, religious chain with her square, stubby hand, while she gazed into men's eyes with what she privately termed "daring frankness."

Tottykins the fair; Tottykins the modern; Tottykins who had read *Three Weeks* and nearly all of a wicked novel in French, and wore a large gold cross; Tottykins who worked so hard in her little flat that she had to rest all of every afternoon and morning; Tottykins the advanced and liberal—yet without any of the extremes of socialists and artists and vegetarians and other ill-conditioned persons who do not attend St. Orgul's; Tottykins the firmly domestic, whose husband grew more worried every year; Tottykins the intensely cultured and inquisitive about life, the primitively free and pervasively original, who announced in public places that she wanted always to live like the spirit of the Dancing Bacchante statue, but had the assistant rector of St. Orgul's in for coffee, every fourth Monday evening.

Tottykins beckoned Carl to a corner and said, with her manner of amused condescension, "Now you sit right down here, Hawk Ericson, and tell me *all* about aviation."

Carl was not vastly sensitive. He had not disliked the nice young men with eye-glasses. Not till now did he realize how Tottykins's shrill references to the Dancing Bacchante and the Bacchanting of her mud-colored Dutch-fashioned hair had bored him. Ennui was not, of course, an excuse; but it was the explanation of why he answered in this wise (very sweetly, looking Tottykins in the eyes and patting her hand with a brother-like and altogether maddening condescension):

"No, no, that isn't the way, Dorothy. It's quite *passé* to ask me to tell you all about aviation. That isn't done, not in 1912. Oh Dor-o-thy! Oh no, no! No-o! No, no. First you should ask me if I'm afraid when I'm flying. Oh, always begin that way. Then you say that there's a curious fact about you—when you're on a high building and just look down once, then you get so dizzy that you want to jump. Then, after you've said that——Let's see. You're a church member, aren't you? Well then, next you'd say, 'Just how does it feel to be up in an aeroplane?' or if you don't say that then you've simply got to say, 'Just how does it feel to fly, anyway?' But if you're just *terribly* interested, Dorothy, you might ask about biplanes *versus* monoplanes, and 'Do I think there'll ever be a flight across the Atlantic?' But whatever you do, Dorothy, don't fail to ask me if I'll give you a free ride when I start flying again. And we'll fly and fly——Like birds. You know. Or like the Dancing Bacchante.... That's the way to talk about aviation.... And now you tell me *all* about babies!"

"Really, I'm afraid babies is rather a big subject to tell all about! At a party! Really, you *know*——"

That was the only time Carl was not bored at the party. And even then he had spiritual indigestion from having been rude.

For the rest of the time:

Every one knew everybody else, and took Carl aside to tell him that everybody was "the most conscientious man in our office, Ericson; why, the Boss would trust him with anything." It saddened Carl to hear the insurance adjuster boom, "Oh you Tottykins!" across the room, at ten-minute intervals, like a human fog-horn on the sea of ennui.

They were all so uniformly polite, so neat-minded and church-going and dull. Nearly all the girls did their hair and coquetries one exactly like another. Carl is not to be pitied. He had the pleasure of martyrdom when he heard the younger Johnson tell of Martinhurst, the Suburb Beautiful. He believed that he had reached the nadir of boredom. But he was mistaken.

After simple and pleasing refreshments of the wooden-plate and paper-napkin school, Gertie announced: "Now we're going to have some stunts, and you're each to give one. I know you all can, and if anybody tries to beg off—my, what will happen——! My brother has a new one——"

For the third time that month, Carl saw Ray turn his collar round and become clerical, while every one rustled with delight, including the jolly bantling clergyman.

And for the fourth time he saw Gertie dance "Gather the Golden Sheaves." She appeared, shy and serious, in bloomers and flat dancing-shoes, which made her ample calves bulge the more; she started at sight of the harvest moon (and well she may have been astonished, if she did, indeed, see a harvest moon there, above the gilded buffalo horns on the unit bookcase), rose to her toes, flapped her arms, and began to gather the sheaves to her breast, with enough plump and panting energy to enable her to gather at least a quarter-section of them before the whistle blew.

It was not only esthetic, but Close to the Soil.

Then, to banjo accompaniment, the insurance adjuster sighed for his old Kentucky home, which Carl judged to have been located in Brooklyn. The whole crowd joined in the chorus and——

Suddenly, with a shock that made him despise himself for the cynical superiority which he had been enjoying, Carl remembered that Forrest

Haviland, Tony Bean, Hank Odell, even surly Jack Ryan and the alien Carmeau, had sung "My Old Kentucky Home" on their last night at the Bagby School. He felt their beloved presences in the room. He had to fight against tears as he too joined in the chorus.... "Then weep no more, my lady."... He was beside a California poppy-field. The blossoms slumbered beneath the moon, and on his shoulder was the hand of Forrest Haviland....

He had repented. He became part of the group. He spoke kindly to Tottykins. But presently Tottykins postponed her well-advertised return to her husband and baby, and gave a ten-minute dramatic recital from Byron; and the younger Johnson sang a Swiss mountaineer song with yodels.

Gertie looked speculatively at Carl twice during this offering. He knew that the gods were plotting an abominable thing. She was going to call upon him for the "stunt" which had been inescapably identified with him, the song, "I went up in a balloon so big." He met the crisis heroically. He said loudly, as the shaky strains of the Swiss ballad died on the midnight mountain air of 157th Street (while the older men concealed yawns and applauded, and the family in the adjoining flat rapped on the radiator): "I'm sorry my throat 's so sore to-night. Otherwise I'd sing a song I learned from a fellow in California—balloon s' big."

Gertie stared at him doubtfully, but passed to a kitten-faced girl from Minnesota, who was quite ready to give an imitation of a child whose doll has been broken. Her "stunt" was greeted with, "Oh, how cun-ning! Please do it again!"

She prepared to do it again. Carl made hasty motions of departure, pathetically holding his throat.

He did not begin to get restless till he had reached Ninety-sixth Street and had given up his seat in the subway to a woman who resembled Tottykins. He wondered if he had not been at the Old Home long enough. At Seventy-second Street, on an inspiration that came as the train was entering the station, he changed to a local and went down to Fifty-ninth Street. He found an all-night garage, hired a racing-car, and at dawn he was driving furiously through Long Island, a hundred miles from New York, on a roadway perilously slippery with falling snow.

CHAPTER XXVII

Carl wished that Adelaide Benner had never come from Joralemon to study domestic science. He felt that he was a sullen brute, but he could not master his helpless irritation as he walked with Adelaide and Gertie Cowles through Central Park, on a snowy Sunday afternoon of December. Adelaide assumed that one remained in the state of mind called Joralemon all one's life; that, however famous he might be, the son of Oscar Ericson was not sufficiently refined for Miss Cowles of the Big House on the Hill, though he might improve under Cowles influences. He was still a person who had run away from Plato! But that assumption was far less irritating than one into which Adelaide threw all of her faded yearning—that Gertie and he were in love.

Adelaide kept repeating, with coy slyness: "Isn't it too bad you two have me in the way!" and: "Don't mind poor me. Auntie will turn her back any time you want her to."

And Gertie merely blushed, murmuring, "Don't be a silly."

At Eightieth Street Adelaide announced: "Now I must leave you children. I'm going over to the Metropolitan Museum of Art. I do love to see art pictures. I've always wanted to. Now be as good as you can, you two."

Gertie was mechanical about replying. "Oh, don't run away, Addy dear."

"Oh yes, you two will miss an old maid like me terribly!" And Adelaide was off, a small, sturdy, undistinguished figure, with an unyielding loyalty to Gertie and to the idea of marriage.

Carl looked at her bobbing back (with wrinkles in her cloth jacket over the shoulders) as she melted into the crowd of glossy fur-trimmed New-Yorkers. He comprehended her goodness, her devotion. He sighed, "If she'd only stop this hinting about Gertie and me——" He was repentant of his irritation, and said to Gertie, who was intimately cuddling her arm into his: "Adelaide's an awfully good kid. Sorry she had to go."

Gertie jerked her arm away, averted her profile, grated: "If you miss her so much, perhaps you'd better run after her. Really, I wouldn't interfere, not for *worlds*!"

"Why, hello, Gertie! What seems to be the matter? Don't I detect a chill in the atmosphere? So sorry you've gone and gotten refined on me. I was just going to suggest some low-brow amusement like tea at the Casino."

"Well, you ought to know a lady doesn't——"

"Oh, now, Gertie dear, not 'lady.'"

"I don't think you're a bit nice, Carl Ericson, I don't, to be making fun of me when I'm serious. And why haven't you been up to see us? Mamma and Ray have spoken of it, and you've only been up once since my party, and then you were——"

"Oh, please let's not start anything. Sorry I haven't been able to get up oftener, but I've been taking work home. You know how it is—you know when you get busy with your dancing-school——"

"Oh, I meant to tell you. I'm through, just *through* with Vashkowska and her horrid old school. She's a cat and I don't believe she ever had anything to do with the Russian ballet, either. What do you think she had the effrontery to tell me? She said that I wasn't practising and really trying to learn anything. And I've been working myself into——Really, my nerves were in such a shape, I would have been in danger of a nervous breakdown if I had kept on. Tottykins told me how she had a nervous breakdown, and had me see her doctor, such a dear, Dr. St. Claire, so refined and sympathetic, and he told me I was right in suspecting that nobody takes Vashkowska seriously any more, and, besides, I don't think much of all this symbolistic dancing, anyway, and at last I've found out what I really want to do. Oh, Carl, it's so wonderful! I'm studying ceramics with Miss Deitz, she's so wonderful and temperamental and she has the dearest studio on Gramercy Park. Of course I haven't made anything yet, but I know I'm going to like it so much, and Miss Deitz says I have a natural taste for vahzes and——"

"Huh? Oh yes, vases. I get you."

"(Don't be vulgar.)——I'm going to go down to her studio and work every other day, and she doesn't think you have to work like a scrubwoman to succeed, like that horrid Vashkowska did. Miss Deitz has a temperament herself. And, oh, Carl, she says that 'Gertrude' isn't suited to me (and 'Gertie' certainly isn't!) and she calls me 'Eltruda.' Don't you think that's a sweet name? Would you like to call me 'Eltruda,' sometimes?"

"Look here, Gertie, I don't want to butt in, and I'm guessing at it, but looks to me as though one of these artistic grafters was working you. What do you know about this Deitz person? Has she done anything worth while? And honestly, Gertie——By the way, I don't want to be brutal, but I don't think I could stand 'Eltruda.' It sounds like 'Tottykins.'"

"Now really, Carl——"

"Wait a second. How do you know you've got what you call a temperament? Go to it, and good luck, if you can get away with it. But how do you know it isn't simply living in a flat and not having any work to do *except* developing a temperament? Why don't you try working with Ray in his office? He's a mighty good business man. This is just a sugges——"

"Now really, this is——"

"Look here, Gertie, the thing I've always admired about you is your wholesomeness and——"

"'Wholesome!' Oh, that word! As Miss Deitz was saying just the other day, it's as bad——"

"But you are wholesome, Gertie. That is, if you don't let New York turn your head; and if you'd use your ability on a real job, like helping Ray, or teaching—yes, or really sticking to your ceramics or dancing, and leave the temperament business to those who can get away with it. No, wait. I know I'm butting in; I know that people won't go and change their natures because I ask them to; but you see you—and Ray and Adelaide—you are the friends I depend on, and so I hate to see——"

"Now, Carl dear, you might let me talk," said Gertie, in tones of maddening sweetness. "As I think it over, I don't seem to recall that you've been an authority on temperament for so very long. I seem to remember that you weren't so terribly wonderful in Joralemon! I'm glad to be the first to honor what you've done in aviation, but I don't know that that gives you the right to——"

"Never said it did!" Carl insisted, with fictitious good humor.

"——assume that you are an authority on temperament and art. I'm afraid that your head has been just a little turned by——"

"Oh, hell.... Oh, I'm sorry. That just slipped."

"It *shouldn't* have slipped, you know. I'm *afraid* it can't be passed over so *easily*." Gertie might have been a bustling Joralemon school-teacher pleasantly bidding the dirty Ericson boy, "Now go and wash the little hands."

Carl said nothing. He was bored. He wished that he had not become entangled in their vague discussion of "temperament."

Even more brightly Gertie announced: "I'm afraid you're not in a very good humor this afternoon. I'm sorry that my plans don't interest you. Of course, I should be very temperamental if I expected you to apologize for cursing and swearing, so I think I'll just leave you here, and when you feel better——" She was infuriatingly cheerful. "——I should be pleased to have you call me up. Good-by, Carl, and I hope that your walk will do you good."

She turned into a footpath; left him muttering in tones of youthful injury, "Jiminy! I've done it now!"

He was in Joralemon.

A victoria drove by with a dowager who did not seem to be humbly courting the best set in Joralemon. A grin lightened Carl's face. He chuckled: "By golly! Gertie handled it splendidly! I'm to call up and be humble, and then—bing!—the least I can do is to propose and be led to the altar and teach a Sunday-school class at St. Orgul's for the rest of my life! Come hither, Hawk Ericson, let us hold council. Here's the way Gertie will dope it out, I guess. ('Eltruda!') I'll dine in solitary regret for saying 'hell'——No. First I'm to walk down-town, alone and busy repenting, and then I'll feed alone, and by eight o'clock I'll be so tired of myself that I'll call up and beg pretty. Rats! It's rotten mean to dope it out like that, but just the same——Me that have done what I've done—worried to death over one accidental 'hell'!... Hey there, you taxi!"

Grandly he rode through the Park, and in an unrepentant manner bowed to every pretty woman he saw, to the disapproval of their silk-hatted escorts.

He forgot the existence of Gertie Cowles and the Old Home Folks.

But he really could not afford a taxicab, and he had to make up for it by economy. At seven-thirty he gloomily entered Miggleton's Restaurant, on Forty-second Street, the least unbearable of the "Popular Prices—Tables for Ladies" dens, and slumped down at a table near the window. There were few diners. Carl was as much a stranger as on the morning when he had first invaded New York, to find work with an automobile company, and had passed this same restaurant; still was he a segregated stranger, despite the fact that, two blocks away, in the Aero Club, two famous aviators were agreeing that there had never been a more consistently excellent flight in America than Hawk Ericson's race from Chicago to New York.

Carl considered the delights of the Cowles flat, Ray's stories about Plato and business, and the sentimental things Gertie played on the guitar. He suddenly determined to go off some place and fly an aeroplane; as suddenly knew that he was not yet ready to return to the game. He read the *Evening Telegram* and cheerlessly peered out of the window at the gray snow-veil which shrouded Forty-second Street.

As he finished his dessert and stirred his coffee he stared into a street-car stalled in a line of traffic outside. Within the car, seen through the snow-mist, was a girl of twenty-two or three, with satiny slim features and ash-blond hair. She was radiant in white-fox furs. Carl craned to watch. He thought of the girl who, asking a direction before the Florida Lunch Room in Chicago, had inspired him to become a chauffeur.

The girl in the street-car was listening to her companion, who was a dark-haired girl with humor and excitement about life in her face, well set-up, not tall, in a smartly tailored coat of brown pony-skin and a small hat that was all lines and no trimming. Both of them seemed amused, possibly by the lofty melancholy of a traffic policeman beside the car, who raised his hand as though he had high ideals and a slight stomach-ache. The dark-haired girl tapped her round knees with the joy of being alive.

The street-car started. Carl was already losing in the city jungle the two acquaintances whom he had just made. The car stopped again, still blocked. Carl seized his coat, dropped a fifty-cent piece on the cashier's desk, did not wait for his ten cents change, ran across the street (barely escaping a taxicab), galloped around the end of the car, swung up on the platform.

As he took a seat opposite the two girls he asked himself just what he expected to do now. The girls were unaware of his existence. And why had he hurried? The car had not started again. But he studied his unconscious conquests from behind his newspaper, vastly content.

In the unnatural quiet of the stalled car the girls were irreverently discussing "George." He heard enough to know that they were of the rather smart, rather cultured class known as "New-Yorkers"—they might be Russian-American princesses or social workers or ill-paid governesses or actresses or merely persons with one motor-car and a useful papa in the family.

But in any case they were not of the kind he could pick up.

The tall girl of the ash-blond hair seemed to be named Olive, being quite unolive in tint, while her livelier companion was apparently christened Ruth. Carl wearied of Olive's changeless beauty as quickly as he did of her silver-handled umbrella. She merely knew how to listen. But the less spectacular, less beautiful, less languorous, dark-haired Ruth was born a good comrade. Her laughter marked her as one of the women whom earth-quake and flood and child-bearing cannot rob of a sense of humor; she would have the inside view, the sophisticated understanding of everything.

The car was at last free of the traffic. It turned a corner and started northward. Carl studied the girls.

Ruth was twenty-four, perhaps, or twenty-five. Not tall, slight enough to nestle, but strong and self-reliant. She had quantities of dark-brown hair, crisp and glinty, though not sleek, with eyebrows noticeably dark and heavy. Her smile was made irresistible by her splendidly shining teeth, fairly large but close-set and white; and not only the corners of her eyes joined in her smile, but even her nose, her delicate yet piquant nose, which could quiver like a deer's. When she laughed, Carl noted, Ruth had a trick of lifting her heavy lids quickly, and surprising one with a glint of blue eyes where brown were expected. Her smooth, healthy, cream-colored skin was rosy with winter, and looked as though in summer it would tan evenly, without freckles. Her chin was soft, but without a dimple, and her jaws had a clean, boyish leanness. Her smooth neck and delicious shoulders were curved, not fatly, but with youth and happiness. They were square, capable shoulders, with no mid-Victorian droop about them. Her waist was slender naturally, not from stays. Her short but not fat fingers were the ideal instruments for the piano. Slim were her crossed feet, and her unwrinkled pumps (foolish footgear for a snowy evening) seemed eager to dance.

There was no hint of the coquette about her. Physical appeal this Ruth had, but it was the allure of sunlight and meadows, of tennis and a boat with bright, canted sails, not of boudoir nor garden dizzy-scented with jasmine. She was young and clean, sweet without being sprinkled with pink sugar; too young to know much about the world's furious struggle; too happy to have realized its inevitable sordidness; yet born a woman who would not always wish to be "protected," and round whom all her circle of life would center....

So Carl inarticulately mused, with the intentness which one gives to strangers in a quiet car, till he laughed, "I feel as if I knew her like a book." The century's greatest problem was whether he would finally prefer her to Olive, if he knew them. If he could speak to them——But that was, in New York, more difficult than beating a policeman or getting acquainted with the mayor. He would lose them.

Already they were rising, going out.

He couldn't let them be lost. He glanced out of the window, sprang up with an elaborate pretense that he had come to his own street. He followed them out, still conning head-lines in his paper. His grave absorption said, plain that all might behold, that he was a respectable citizen to whom it would never occur to pursue strange young women.

His new friends had been close to him in the illuminated car, but they were alien, unapproachable, when they stood on an unfamiliar street-crossing snow-dimmed and silent with night. He stared at a street-sign and found that he was on Madison Avenue, up in the Fifties. As they turned east on Fifty-blankth Street he stopped under the street-light, took an envelope from his pocket, and found on it the address of that dear old friend, living on Fifty-blankth, on whom he was going to call. This was to convince the policeman of the perfect purity of his intentions. The fact that there was no policeman nearer than the man on fixed post a block away did not lessen Carl's pleasure in the make-believe. He industriously inspected the house-numbers as he followed the quickly moving girls, and frequently took out his watch. Nothing should make him late in calling on that dear old friend.

Not since Adam glowered at the intruder Eve has a man been so darkly uninterested in two charmers. He stared clear through them; he looked over their heads; he observed objects on the other side of the street. He indignantly told the imaginary policemen who stopped him that he hadn't even seen the girls till this moment; that he was the victim of a plot.

The block through which the cavalcade was passing was lined with shabby-genteel brownstone houses, with high stoops and haughty dark doors, and dressmakers' placards or doctors' cards in the windows. Carl was puzzled. The girls seemed rather too cheerful to belong in this decayed and gloomy block, which, in the days when horsehair furniture and bankers had mattered, had seemed imposing. But the girls ascended the steps of a house which was typical of the row, except that five motor-cars stood before it. Carl, passing, went up the steps of the next house and rang the bell.

"What a funny place!" he heard one of the girls—he judged that it was Ruth—remark from the neighboring stoop. "It looks exactly like Aunt Emma when she wears an Alexandra bang. Do we go right up? Oughtn't we to ring? It ought to be the craziest party—anarchists——"

"A party, eh?" thought Carl.

"——ought to ring, I suppose, but——Yes, there's sure to be all sorts of strange people at Mrs. Hallet's——" said the voice of the other girl, then the door closed upon both of them.

And an abashed Carl realized that a maid had opened the door of the house at which he himself had rung, and was glaring at him as he craned over to view the next-door stoop.

"W-where——Does Dr. Brown live here?" he stuttered.

"No, 'e don't," the maid snapped, closing the door.

Carl groaned: "He don't? Dear old Brown? Not live here? Huh? What shall I do?"

In remarkably good spirits he moved over in front of the house into which Ruth and Olive had gone. People were coming to the party in twos and threes. Yes. The men were in evening clothes. He had his information.

Swinging his stick up to a level with his shoulder at each stride, he raced to Fifty-ninth Street and the nearest taxi-stand. He was whirled to his room. He literally threw his clothes off. He shaved hastily, singing, "Will You Come to the Ball," from "The Quaker Girl," and slipped into evening clothes and his suavest dress-shirt. Seizing things all at once—top-hat, muffler, gloves, pocketbook, handkerchief, cigarette-case, keys—and hanging them about him as he fled down the decorous stairs, he skipped to the taxicab and started again for Fifty-blankth Street.

At the house of the party he stopped to find on the letter-box in the entry the name "Mrs. Hallet," mentioned by Olive. There was no such name. He tried the inner door. It opened. He cheerily began to mount steep stairs, which kept on for miles, climbing among slate-colored walls, past empty wall-niches with toeless plaster statues. The hallways, dim and high and snobbish, and the dark old double doors, scowled at him. He boldly returned the scowl. He could hear the increasing din of a talk-party coming from above. When he reached the top floor he found a door open on a big room crowded with shrilly chattering people in florid clothes. There was a hint of brassware and paintings and silken Turkish rugs.

But no sight of Ruth or Olive.

A maid was bobbing to him and breathing, "That way, please, at the end of the hall." He went meekly. He did not dare to search the clamorous crowd for the girls, as yet.

He obediently added his hat and coat and stick to an uncomfortable-looking pile of wraps writhing on a bed in a small room that had a Copley print of Sargent's "Prophets," a calendar, and an unimportant white rocker.

It was time to go out and face the party, but he had stage-fright. While climbing the stairs he had believed that he was in touch with the two girls, but now he was separated from them by a crowd, farther from them than when he had followed them down the unfriendly street. And not till now did he quite grasp the fact that the hostess might not welcome him. His glowing game was becoming very dull-toned. He lighted a cigarette and listened to the beating surf of the talk in the other room.

Another man came in. Like all the rest, he gave up the brilliant idea of trying to find an unpreëmpted place for his precious newly ironed silk hat, and resignedly dumped it on the bed. He was a passable man, with a gentlemanly mustache and good pumps. Carl knew that fact because he was comparing his own clothes and deciding that he had none the worst of it. But he was relieved when the waxed mustache moved a couple of times, and its owner said, in a friendly way: "Beastly jam!... May I trouble you for a match?"

Carl followed him out to the hostess, a small, busy woman who made a business of being vivacious and letting the light catch the fringes of her gold hair as she nodded. Carl nonchalantly shook hands with her, bubbling: "So afraid couldn't get here. My play——But at last——"

He was in a panic. But the hostess, instead of calling for the police, gushed, "*So* glad you *could* come!" combining a kittenish mechanical smile for him with a glance over his shoulder at the temporary butler. "I want you to meet Miss Moeller, Mr.—uh—Mr——"

"I knew you'd forget it!" Carl was brotherly and protecting in his manner. "Ericson, Oscar Ericson."

"Oh, of course. How stupid of me! Miss Moeller, want you to meet Mr. Oscar Ericson—you know——"

"S' happy meet you, Miss Mmmmmmm," said Carl, tremendously well-bred in manner. "Can we possibly go over and be clever in a corner, do you think?"

He had heard Colonel Haviland say that, but his manner gave it no quotation-marks.

Presumably he talked to Miss Moeller about something usual—the snow or the party or Owen Johnson's novels. Presumably Miss Moeller had eyes to look into and banalities to look away from. Presumably there was something in the room besides people and talk and rugs hung over the bookcases. But Carl never knew. He was looking for Ruth. He did not see her.

Within ten minutes he had manœuvered himself free of Miss Moeller and was searching for Ruth, his nerves quivering amazingly with the fear that she might already have gone.

How would he ever find her? He could scarce ask the hostess, "Say, where's Ruth?"

She was nowhere in the fog of people in the big room.... If he could find even Olive....

Strolling, nodding to perfectly strange people who agreeably nodded back under the mistaken impression that they were glad to see him, he systematically checked up all the groups. Ruth was not among the punch-table devotees, who were being humorous and amorous over cigarettes; not among the Caustic Wits exclusively assembled in a corner; not among the shy sisters aligned on the davenport and wondering why they had come; not in the general maelstrom in the center of the room.

He stopped calmly to greet the hostess again, remarking, "You look so beautifully sophisticated to-night," and listened suavely to her fluttering remarks. He was the picture of the cynical cityman who has to be nowhere at no especial time. But he was not cynical. He had to find Ruth!

He escaped and, between the main room and the dining-room, penetrated a small den filled with witty young men, old stories, cigarette-smoke, and siphons. Then he charged into the dining-room, where there were candles and plate much like silver—and Ruth and Olive at the farther end.

CHAPTER XXVIII

He wanted to run forward, take their hands, cry, "At last!" He seemed to hear his voice wording it. But, not glancing at them again, he established himself on a chair by the doorway between the two rooms.

It was safe to watch the two girls in this Babel, where words swarmed and battled everywhere in the air. Ruth was in a brown velvet frock whose golden tones harmonized with her brown hair. She was being enthusiastically talked at by a man to whom she listened with a courteously amused curiosity. Carl could fancy her nudging Olive, who sat beside her on the Jacobean settee and was attended by another talking-man. Carl told Ruth (though she did not know that he was telling her) that she had no right to be "so blasted New-Yorkishly superior and condescending," but he admitted that she was scarcely to blame, for the man made kindergarten gestures and emitted conversation like air from an exploded tire.

The important thing was that he heard the man call her "Miss Winslow."

"Great! Got her name—Ruth Winslow!"

Watching the man's lips (occasionally trying to find an excuse for eavesdropping, and giving up the quest because there was no excuse), he discovered that Ruth was being honored with a thrilling account of aviation. The talking-man, it appeared, knew a great deal about the subject. Carl heard through a rift in the cloud of words that the man had once actually flown, as a passenger with Henry Odell! For five minutes on end, judging by the motions with which he steered a monoplane through perilous abysses, the reckless spirit kept flying (as a passenger). Ruth Winslow was obviously getting bored, and the man showed no signs of volplaning as yet. Olive's man departed, and Olive was also listening to the parlor aviator, who was unable to see that a terrific fight was being waged by the hands of the two girls in the space down between them. It was won by Ruth's hand, which got a death-grip on Olive's thumb, and held it, to Olive's agony, while both girls sat up straight and beamed propriety.

Carl walked over and, smoothly ignoring the pocket entertainer, said: "So glad to see you, Miss Winslow. I think this is my dance?"

"Y-yes?" from Miss Winslow, while the entertainer drifted off into the flotsam of the party. Olive went to join a group about the hostess, who had just come in to stir up mirth and jocund merriment in the dining-room, as it had settled down into a lower state of exhilaration than the canons of talk-parties require.

Said Carl to Ruth, "Not that there's any dancing, but I felt you'd get dizzy if you climbed any higher in that aeroplane."

Ruth tried to look haughty, but her dark lashes went up and her unexpected blue eyes grinned at him boyishly.

"Gee! she's clever!" Carl was thinking. Since, to date, her only remark had been "Y-yes?" he may have been premature.

"That was a bully strangle hold you got on Miss Olive's hand, Miss Winslow."

"You saw our hands?"

"Perhaps.... Tell me a good way to express how superior you and I are to this fool party and its noise. Isn't it a fool party?"

"I'm afraid it really is."

"What's the purpose of it, anyway? Do the people have to come here and breathe this air, I wonder? I asked several people that, and I'm afraid they think I'm crazy."

"But you are here? Do you come to Mrs. Salisbury's often?"

"Never been before. Never seen a person here in my life before—except you and Miss Olive. Came on a bet. Chap bet I wouldn't dare come without being invited. I came. Bowed to the hostess and told her I was so sorry my play-rehearsals made me late, and she was *so* glad I could come, *after all*—you know. She's never seen me in her life."

"Oh? Are you a dramatist?"

"I was—in the other room. But I was a doctor out in the hall and a sculptor on the stairs, so I'm getting sort of confused myself—as confused as you are, trying to remember who I am, Miss Winslow. You really don't remember me at all? Tea at—wasn't it at the Vanderbilt? or the Plaza?"

"Oh yes, that must have been——I was trying to remember——"

Carl grinned. "The chap who introduced me to you called me 'Mr. Um-m-m,' because he didn't remember my name, either. So you've never heard it. It happens to be Ericson.... I'm on a mission. Serious one. I'm planning to go out and buy a medium-sized bomb and blow up this bunch. I suspect there's poets around."

"I do too," sighed Ruth. "I understand that Mrs. Salisbury always has seven lawyers and nineteen advertising men and a dentist and a poet and an explorer at her affairs. Are you the poet or the explorer?"

"I'm the dentist. I think——You don't happen to have done any authoring, do you?"

"Well, nothing except an epic poyem on Jonah and the Whale, which I wrote at the age of seven. Most of it consisted of a conversation between them, while Jonah was in the Whale's stomach, which I think showed agility on the part of the Whale."

"Then maybe it's safe to say what I think of authors—and more or less of poets and painters and so on. One time I was in charge of some mechanical investigations, and a lot of writers used to come around looking for what they called 'copy.' That's where I first got my grouch on them, and I've never really got over it; and coming here to-night and hearing the littery talk I've been thinking how these authors have a sort of an admiration trust. They make authors the heroes of their stories and so on, and so they make people think that writing is sacred. I'm so sick of reading novels about how young Bill, as had a pure white soul, came to New York and had an 'orrible time till his great novel was accepted. Authors seem to think they're the only ones that have ideals. Now I'm in the automobile business, and I help to make people get out into the country—bet a lot more of them get out because of motoring than because of reading poetry about spring. But if I claimed a temperament because I introduce the motorist's soul to the daisy, every one would die laughing."

"But don't you think that art is the—oh, the object of civilization and that sort of thing?"

"I do *not*! Honestly, Miss Winslow, I think it would be a good stunt to get along without any art at all for a generation, and see what we miss. We probably need dance music, but I doubt if we need opera. Funny how the world always praises its opera-singers so much and pays 'em so well and then starves its shoemakers, and yet it needs good shoes so much more than it needs opera—or war or fiction. I'd like to see all the shoemakers get together and refuse to make any more shoes till people promised to write reviews about them, like all these book-reviews. Then just as soon as people's shoes began to wear out they'd come right around, and you'd read about the new masterpieces of Mr. Regal and Mr. Walkover and Mr. Stetson."

"Yes! I can imagine it. 'This laced boot is one of the most vital and gripping and wholesome shoes of the season.' And probably all the young shoemakers would sit around cafés, looking quizzical and artistic. But don't you think your theory is dangerous, Mr. Ericson? You give me an excuse for being content with being a commonplace Upper-West-Sider. And aren't authors better than commonplaceness? You're so serious that I almost suspect you of having started to be an author yourself."

"Really not. As a matter of fact, I'm the kiddy in patched overalls you used to play with when you kept house in the willows."

"Oh, of course! In the Forest of Arden! And you had a toad that you traded for my hair-ribbon."

"And we ate bread and milk out of blue bowls!"

"Oh yes!" she agreed, "blue bowls with bunny-rabbits painted on them."

"And giants and a six-cylinder castle, with warders and a donjon keep. And Jack the Giant-killer. But certainly bunnies."

"Do you really like bunnies?" Her voice caressed the word.

"I like them so much that when I think of them I know that there's one thing worse than having a cut-rate literary salon, and that's to be too respectable——"

"Too Upper-West-Side!"

"——to dare to eat bread and milk out of blue bowls."

"Yes, I think I shall have to admit you to the Blue Bowl League, Mr. Ericson. Speaking of which——Tell me, who did introduce us, you and me? I feel so apologetic for not remembering."

"Mayn't I be a mystery, Miss Winslow? At least as long as I have this new shirt, which you observed with some approval while I was drooling on about authors? It makes me look like a count, you must admit. Or maybe like a Knight of the Order of the Bunny Rabbit. Please let me be a mystery still."

"Yes, you may. Life has no mysteries left except Olive's coiffure and your beautiful shirt.... Does one talk about shirts at a second meeting?"

"Apparently one does."

"Yes.... To-night, I *must* have a mystery.... Do you swear, as a man of honor, that you are at this party dishonorably, uninvited?"

"I do, princess."

"Well, so am I! Olive was invited to come, with a man, but he was called away and she dragged me here, promising me I should see——"

"Anarchists?"

"Yes! And the only nice lovable crank I've found—except you, with your vulgar prejudice against the whole race of authors—is a dark-eyed female who sits on a couch out in the big room, like a Mrs. St. Simeon Stylites in a tight skirt, and drags you in by her glittering eye, looking as though she was going to speak about theosophy, and then asks you if you think a highball would help her cold."

"I think I know the one you mean. When I saw her she was talking to a man whose beating whiskers dashed high on a stern and rock-bound face.... Thank you, I like that fairly well, too, but unfortunately I stole it from a chap named

Haviland. My own idea of witty conversation: is 'Some car you got. What's your magneto?'"

"Look. Olive Dunleavy seems distressed. The number of questions I shall have to answer about you!... Well, Olive and I felt very low in our minds to-day. We decided that we were tired of select associations, and that we would seek the Primitive, and maybe even Life in the Raw. Olive knows a woman mountain-climber who always says she longs to go back to the wilds, so we went down to her flat. We expected to have raw-meat sandwiches, at the very least, but the Savage Woman gave us Suchong and deviled-chicken sandwiches and pink cakes and Nabiscos, and told us how well her son was doing in his Old French course at Columbia. So we got lower and lower in our minds, and we decided we had to go down to Chinatown for dinner. We went, too! I've done a little settlement work——Dear me, I'm telling you too much about myself, O Man of Mystery! It isn't quite done, I'm afraid."

"Please, Miss Winslow! In the name of the—what was it—Order of the Blue Bowl?" He was making a mental note that Olive's last name was Dunleavy.

"Well, I've done some settlement work——Did you ever do any, by any chance?"

"I once converted a Chinaman to Lutheranism; I think that was my nearest approach," said Carl.

"My work was the kind where you go in and look at three dirty children and teach them that they'll be happy if they're good, when you know perfectly well that their only chance to be happy is to be bad as anything and sneak off to go swimming in the East River. But it kept me from being very much afraid of the Bowery (we went down on the surface cars), but Olive was scared beautifully. There was the dearest, most inoffensive old man in the most perfect state of intoxication sitting next to us in the car, and when Olive moved away from him he winked over at me and said, 'Honor your shruples, ma'am, ver' good form.' I think Olive thought he was going to murder us— she was sure he was the wild, dying remnant of a noble race or something. But even she was disappointed in Chinatown.

"We had expected opium-fiends, like the melodramas they used to have on Fourteenth Street, before the movies came. But we had a disgustingly clean table, with a mad, reckless picture worked in silk, showing two doves and a boiled lotos flower, hanging near us, to intimidate us. The waiter was a Harvard graduate, I know—perhaps Oxford—and he said, 'May I sugges' ladies velly nize China dinner?' He suggested chow-main—we thought it would be either birds' nests or rats' tails, and it was simply crisp noodles with the most innocuous sauce.... And the people! They were all stupid tourists like ourselves, except for a Jap, with his cunnin' Sunday tie, and his little trousers all so politely pressed, and his clean pocket-hanky. And he was reading *The Presbyterian*!... Then we came up here, and it doesn't seem so very primitive here, either. It's most aggravating.... It seems to me I've been telling you an incredible lot about our silly adventures—you're probably the man who won the Indianapolis motor-race or discovered electricity or something."

Through her narrative, her eyes had held his, but now she glanced about, noted Olive, and seemed uneasy.

"I'm afraid I'm nothing so interesting," he said; "but I have wanted to see new places and new things—and I've more or less seen 'em. When I've got tired of one town, I've simply up and beat it, and when I got there—wherever there was—I've looked for a job. And——Well, I haven't lost anything by it."

"Have you really? That's the most wonderful thing to do in the world. My travels have been Cook's tours, with our own little Thomas Cook *and* Son right in the family—I've never even had the mad freedom of choosing between a tour of the Irish bogs and an educational pilgrimage to the shrines of celebrated brewers. My people have always chosen for me. But I've wanted——One doesn't merely *go* without having an objective, or an excuse for going, I suppose."

"I do," declared Carl. "But——May I be honest?"

"Yes."

Intimacy was about them. They were two travelers from a far land, come together in the midst of strangers.

"I speak of myself as globe-trotting," said Carl. "I have been. But for a good many weeks I've been here in New York, knowing scarcely any one, and restless, yet I haven't felt like hiking off, because I was sick for a time, and because a chap that was going to Brazil with me died suddenly."

"To Brazil? Exploring?"

"Yes—just a stab at it, pure amateur.... I'm not at all sure I'm just making-believe when I speak of blue bowls and so on. Tell me. In the West, one would speak of 'seeing the girls home.' How would one say that gracefully in New-Yorkese, so that I might have the chance to beguile Miss Olive Dunleavy and Miss Ruth Winslow into letting me see them home?"

"Really, we're not a bit afraid to go home alone."

"I won't tease, but——May I come to your house for tea, some time?"

She hesitated. It came out with a rush. "Yes. Do come up. N-next Sunday, if you'd like."

She bobbed her head to Olive and rose.

"And the address?" he insisted.

"—— West Ninety-second Street.... Good night. I have enjoyed the blue bowl."

Carl made his decent devoirs to his hostess and tramped up-town through the flying snow, swinging his stick like an orchestra conductor, and whistling a waltz.

As he reached home he thought again of his sordid parting with Gertie in the Park—years ago, that afternoon. But the thought had to wait in the anteroom of his mind while he rejoiced over the fact that he was to see his new playmate the coming Sunday.

CHAPTER XXIX

Like a country small boy waiting for the coming of his city cousin, who will surely have new ways of playing Indians, Carl prepared to see Ruth Winslow and her background. What was she? Who? Where? He pictured her as dwelling in everything from a millionaire's imitation château, with footmen and automatic elevators, to a bachelor girl's flat in an old-fashioned red-brick Harlem tenement. But more than that: What would she herself be like against that background?

Monday he could think of nothing but the joy of having discovered a playmate. The secret popped out from behind everything he did. Tuesday he was worried by finding himself unable to remember whether Ruth's hair was black or dark brown. Yet he could visualize Olive's ash-blond. Why? Wednesday afternoon, when he was sleepy in the office after eating too much beefsteak and kidney pie, drinking too much coffee, and smoking too many cigarettes, at lunch with Mr. VanZile, when he was tortured by the desire to lay his head on his arms and yield to drowsiness, he was suddenly invaded by a fear that Ruth was snobbish. It seemed to him that he ought to do something about it immediately.

The rest of the week he merely waited to see what sort of person the totally unknown Miss Ruth Winslow might be. His most active occupation outside the office was feeling guilty over not telephoning to Gertie.

At 3.30 P.M., Sunday, he was already incased in funereal morning-clothes and warning himself that he must not arrive at Miss Winslow's before five. His clothes were new, stiff as though they belonged to a wax dummy. Their lines were straight and without individuality. He hitched his shoulders about and kept going to the mirror to inspect the fit of the collar. He repeatedly re brushed his hair, regarding the unclean state of his military brushes with disgust. About six times he went to the window to see if it had started to snow.

At ten minutes to four he sternly jerked on his coat and walked far north of Ninety-second Street, then back.

He arrived at a quarter to five, but persuaded himself that this was a smarter hour of arrival than five.

Ruth Winslow's home proved to be a rather ordinary three-story-and-basement gray stone dwelling, with heavy Russian net curtains at the broad, clear-glassed windows of the first floor, and an attempt to escape from the stern drabness of the older type of New York houses by introducing a box-stoop and steps with a carved stone balustrade, at the top of which perched a meek old lion of 1890, with battered ears and a truly sensitive stone nose.

A typical house of the very well-to-do yet not wealthy "upper middle class"; a house predicating one motor-car, three not expensive maids, brief European tours, and the best preparatory schools and colleges for the sons.

A maid answered the door and took his card—a maid in a frilly apron and black uniform—neither a butler nor a slatternly Biddy. In the hall, as the maid disappeared up-stairs, Carl had an impression of furnace heat and respectability. Rather shy, uncomfortable, anxious to be acceptable, warning himself that as a famous aviator he need not be in awe of any one, but finding that the warning did not completely take, he drew off his coat and gloves and, after a swift inspection of his tie, gazed about with more curiosity than he had ever given to any other house.

For all the stone lion in front, this was quite the old-line English-basement house, with the inevitable front and back parlors—though here they were modified into drawing-room and dining-room. The walls of the hall were decked with elaborate, meaningless scrolls in plaster bas-relief, echoed by raised circles on the ceiling just above the hanging chandelier, which was expensive and hideous, a clutter of brass and knobby red-and-blue glass. The floor was of hardwood in squares, dark and richly polished, highly self-respecting—a floor that assumed civic responsibility from a republican point of view, and a sound conservative business established since 1875 or 1880. By the door was a huge Japanese vase, convenient either for depositing umbrellas or falling over in the dark. Then, a long mirror in a dull-red mahogany frame, and a table of mahogany so refined that no one would ever dream of using it for anything more useful than calling-cards. It might have been the table by the king's bed, on which he leaves his crown on a little purple cushion at night. Solid and ostentatious.

The drawing-room, to the left, was dark and still and unsympathetic and expensive; a vista of brocade-covered French-gilt chairs and a marquetry table and a table of onyx top, on which was one book bound in ooze calf, and one vase; cream-colored heavy carpet and a crystal chandelier; fairly meretricious paintings of rocks, and thatched cottages, and ragged newsboys with faces like Daniel Webster, all of them in large gilt frames protected by shadow-boxes. In a corner was a cabinet of gilt and glass, filled with Dresden-china figurines and toy tables and a carven Swiss musical powder-box. The fireplace was of smooth, chilly white marble, with an ormolu clock on the mantelpiece, and a fire-screen painted with Watteau shepherds and shepherdesses, making silken unreal love and scandalously neglecting silky unreal sheep. By the hearth were shiny fire-irons which looked as though they had never been used. The whole room looked as though it had never been used—except during the formal calls of overdressed matrons with card-cases and prejudices. The one human piece of furniture in the room, a couch soft and slightly worn, on which lovers might have sat and small boys bounced, was trying to appear useless, too, under its row of stiff satin cushions with gold cords.... Well-dusted chairs on which no one wished to sit; expensive fireplace that never shone; prized pictures with less imagination than the engravings on a bond—that drawing-room had the soul of a banker with side-whiskers.

Carl by no means catalogued all the details, but he did get the effect of ingrowing propriety. It is not certain that he thought the room in bad taste. It is not certain that he had any artistic taste whatever; or that his attack upon the pretensions of authors had been based on anything more fundamental than a personal irritation due to having met blatant camp-followers of the arts. And it is certain that one of his reactions as he surveyed the abject respectability of that room was a slight awe of the solidity of social position which it represented, and which he consciously lacked. But, whether from artistic instinct or from ignorance, he was sure that into the room ought to blow a sudden great wind, with the scent of forest and snow. He shook his head when the maid returned, and he followed her up-stairs. Surely a girl reared here would never run away and play with him.

He heard lively voices from the library above. He entered a room to be lived in and be happy in, with a jolly fire on the hearth and friendly people on a big, brown davenport. Ruth Winslow smiled at him from behind the Colonial silver and thin cups on the tea-table, and as he saw her light-filled eyes, saw her cock her head gaily in welcome, he was again convinced that he had found a playmate.

A sensation of being pleasantly accepted warmed him as she cried, "So glad——" and introduced him, gave him tea and a cake with nuts in it. From a wing-chair Carl searched the room and the people. There were two paintings—a pale night sea and an arching Japanese bridge under slanting rain, both imaginative and well-done. There was a mahogany escritoire, which might have been stiff but was made human by scattered papers on the great blotter and books crammed into the shelves. Other books were heaped on a table as though people had been reading them. Later he found how amazingly they were assorted—the latest novel of Robert Chambers beside H. G. Wells's *First and Last Things*; a dusty expensive book on Italian sculpture near a cheap reprint of *Dodo*.

The chairs were capacious, the piano a workmanlike upright, not dominating the room, but ready for music; and in front of the fire was an English setter, an aristocrat of a dog, with the light glittering in his slowly waving tail. The people fitted into the easy life of the room. They were New-Yorkers and, unlike over half of the population, born there, considering New York a village where one knows everybody and remembers when Fourteenth Street was the shopping-center. Olive Dunleavy was shinily present, her ash-blond hair in a new coiffure. She was arguing with a man of tight morning-clothes and a high-bred face about the merits of "Parsifal," which, Olive declared, no one ever attended except as a matter of conscience.

"Now, Georgie," she said, "issa Georgie, you shall have your opera—and you shall jolly well have it alone, too!" Olive was vivid about it all, but Carl saw that she was watching him, and he was shy as he wondered what Ruth had told her.

Olive's brother, Philip Dunleavy, a clear-faced, slender, well-bathed boy of twenty-six, with too high a forehead, with discontent in his face and in his thin voice, carelessly well-dressed in a soft-gray suit and an impressionistic tie, was also inspecting Carl, while talking to a pretty, commonplace, finishing-school-finished girl. Carl instantly disliked Philip Dunleavy, and was afraid of his latent sarcasm.

Indeed, Carl felt more and more that beneath the friendliness with which he was greeted there was no real welcome as yet, save possibly on the part of Ruth. He was taken on trial. He was a Mr. Ericson, not any Mr. Ericson in particular.

Ruth, while she poured tea, was laughing with a man and a girl. Carl himself was part of a hash-group—an older woman who seemed to know Rome and Paris better than New York, and might be anything from a milliner to a mondaine; a keen-looking youngster with tortoise-shell spectacles; finally, Ruth's elder brother, Mason J. Winslow, Jr., a tall, thin, solemn, intensely well-intentioned man of thirty-seven, with a long, clean-shaven face, and a long, narrow head whose growing baldness was always spoken of as a result of his hard work. Mason J. Winslow, Jr., spoke hesitatingly, worried over everything, and stood for morality and good business. He was rather dull in conversation, rather kind in manner, and accomplished solid things by unimaginatively sticking at them. He didn't understand people who did not belong to a good club.

Carl contributed a few careful platitudes to a frivolous discussion of whether it would not be advisable to solve the woman-suffrage question by taking the vote away from men and women both and conferring it on children. Mason Winslow ambled to the big table for a cigarette, and Carl pursued him. While they stood talking about "the times are bad," Carl was spying upon Ruth, and the minute her current group wandered off to the davenport he made a dash at the tea-table and got there before Olive's brother, Philip Dunleavy, who was obviously manœuvering like himself. Philip gave him a covert "Who are you, fellow?" glance, took a cake, and retired.

From his wicker chair facing Ruth's, Carl said, gloomily, "It isn't done."

"Yes," said Ruth, "I know it, but still some very smart people are doing it this season."

"But do you think the woman that writes 'What the man will wear' in the theater programs would stand for it?"

"Not," gravely considered Ruth, "if there were black stitching on the dress-glove. Yet there is some authority for frilled shirts."

"You think it might be considered then?"

"I will not come between you and your haberdasher, Mr. Ericson."

"This is a foolish conversation. But since you think the better classes do it—gee! it's getting hard for me to keep up this kind of 'Dolly Dialogue.' What I wanted to do was to request you to give me concisely but fully a sketch of 'Who is Miss Ruth Winslow?' and save me from making any pet particular breaks. And hereafter, I warn you, I'm going to talk like my cousin, the carpet-slipper model."

"Name, Ruth Winslow. Age, between twenty and thirty. Father, Mason Winslow, manufacturing contractor for concrete. Brothers, Mason Winslow, Jr., whose poor dear head is getting somewhat bald, as you observe, and Bobby Winslow, ne'er-do-weel, who is engaged in subverting discipline at medical school, and who dances divinely. My mother died three years ago. I do nothing useful, but I play a good game of bridge and possess a voice that those as know pronounce passable. I have a speaking knowledge of French, a reading knowledge of German, and a singing knowledge of Italian. I am wearing an imported gown, for which the House of Winslow will probably never pay. I live in this house, and am Episcopalian—not so much High Church as highly infrequent church. I regard the drawing-room down-stairs as the worst example of late-Victorian abominations in my knowledge, but I shall probably never persuade father to change it because Mason thinks it is sacred to the past. My ambition in life is to be catty to the Newport set after I've married an English diplomat with a divine mustache. Never having met such a personage outside of *Tatler* and *Vogue*, I can't give you very many details regarding him. Oh yes, of course, he'll have to play a marvelous game of polo and have a château in Provence and also a ranch in Texas, where I shall wear riding-breeches and live next to Nature and have a Chinese cook in blue silk. I think that's my whole history. Oh, I forgot. I play at the piano and am very ignorant, and completely immersed in the worst traditions of the wealthy Micks of the Upper West Side, and I always pretend that I live here instead of on the Upper East Side because 'the air is better.'"

"What is this Upper West Side? Is it a state of mind?"

"Indeed it is not. It's a state of pocketbook. The Upper West Side is composed entirely of people born in New York who want to be in society, whatever that is, and can't afford to live on Fifth Avenue. You know everybody and went to school with everybody and played in the Park with everybody, and mostly your papa is in wholesale trade and haughty about people in retail. You go to Europe one summer and to the Jersey coast the next. All your clothes and parties and weddings and funerals might be described as 'elegant.' That's the Upper West Side. Now the dread truth about you.... Do you know, after the unscrupulous way in which you followed up a mere chance introduction at a tea somewhere, I suspect you to be a well-behaved young man who leads an entirely blameless life. Or else you'd never dare to jump the fence and come and play in my back yard when all the other boys politely knock at the front door and get sent home."

"Me—well, I'm a wage-slave of the VanZile Motor people, in charge of the Touricar department. Age, twenty-eight—almost. Habits, all bad.... No, I'll tell you. I'm one of those stern, silent men of granite you read about, and only my man knows the human side of me, because all the guys on Wall Street tremble in me presence."

"Yes, but then how can you belong to the Blue Bowl Sodality?"

"Um, Yes——I've got it. You must have read novels in which the stern, silent man of granite has a secret tenderness in his heart, and he keeps the band of the first cigar he ever smoked in a little safe in the wall, and the first dollar he ever made in a frame—that's me."

"Of course! The cigar was given him by his flaxen-haired sweetheart back in Jenkins Corners, and in the last chapter he goes back and marries her."

"Not always, I hope!" Of what Carl was thinking is not recorded. "Well, as a matter of fact, I've been a fairly industrious young man of granite the last few months, getting out the Touricar."

"What is a Touricar? It sounds like an island inhabited by cannibals, exports hemp and cocoanut, see pink dot on the map, nor' by nor'east of Mogador."

Carl explained.

"I'm terribly interested," said Ruth. (But she made it sound as though she really was.) "I think it's so wonderful.... I want to go off tramping through the Berkshires. I'm so tired of going to the same old places."

"Some time, when you're quite sure I'm an estimable young Y. M. C. A. man, I'm going to try to persuade you to come out for a real tramp."

She seemed to be considering the idea, not seriously, but——

Philip Dunleavy eventuated.

For some time Philip had been showing signs of interest in Ruth and Carl. Now he sauntered to the table, begged for another cup of tea, said agreeable things in regard to putting orange marmalade in tea, and calmly established himself. Ruth turned toward him.

Carl had fancied that there was, for himself, in Ruth's voice, something more friendly, in her infectious smile something more intimate than she had given the others, but when she turned precisely the same cheery expression upon Philip, Carl seemed to have lost something which he had trustingly treasured for years. He was the more forlorn as Olive Dunleavy joined them, and Ruth, Philip, and Olive discussed the engagement of one Mary Meldon. Olive recalled Miss Meldon as she had been in school days at the Convent of the Sacred Heart. Philip told of her flirtations at the old Long Beach Hotel.

The names of New York people whom they had always known; the names of country clubs—Baltusrol and Meadow Brook and Peace Waters; the names of streets, with a sharp differentiation between Seventy-fourth Street and Seventy-fifth Street; Durland's Riding Academy, the Rink of a Monday morning, and other souvenirs of a New York childhood; the score of the last American polo team and the coming dances—these things shut Carl out as definitely as though he were a foreigner. He was lonely. He disliked Phil Dunleavy's sarcastic references. He wanted to run away.

Ruth seemed to realize that Carl was shut out. Said she to Phil Dunleavy: "I wish you could have seen Mr. Ericson save my life last Sunday. I had an experience."

"What was that?" asked the man whom Olive called "Georgie," joining the tea-table set.

The whole room listened as Ruth recounted the trip to Chinatown, Mrs. Salisbury's party, and the hero who had once been a passenger in an aeroplane.

Throughout she kept turning toward Carl. It seemed to reunite him to the company. As she closed, he said:

"The thing that amused me about the parlor aviator was his laying down the law that the Atlantic will be crossed before the end of 1913, and his assumption that we'll all have aeroplanes in five years. I know from my own business, the automobile business, about how much such prophecies are worth."

"Don't you think the Atlantic will be crossed soon?" asked the keen-looking man with the tortoise-shell spectacles.

Phil Dunleavy broke in with an air of amused sophistication: "I think the parlor aviator was right. Really, you know, aviation is too difficult a subject for the layman to make any predictions about—either what it can or can't do."

"Oh yes," admitted Carl; and the whole room breathed. "Oh yes."

Dunleavy went on in his thin, overbred, insolent voice, "Now I have it on good authority, from a man who's a member of the Aero Club, that next year will be the greatest year aviation has ever known, and that the Wrights have an aeroplane up their sleeve with which they'll cross the Atlantic without a stop, during the spring of 1914 at the very latest."

"That's unfortunate, because the aviation game has gone up completely in this country, except for hydro-aeroplaning and military aviation, and possibly it never will come back," said Carl, a hint of pique in his voice.

"What is your authority for that?" Phil turned a large, bizarre ring round on his slender left little finger and the whole room waited, testing this positive-spoken outsider.

"Well," drawled Carl, "I have fairly good authority. Walter MacMonnies, for instance, and he is probably the best flier in the country to-day, except for Lincoln Beachey."

"Oh yes, he's a good flier," said Phil, contemptuously, with a shadowy smile for Ruth. "Still, he's no better than Aaron Solomons, and he isn't half so great a flier as that chap with the same surname as your own, Hawk Ericson, whom I myself saw coming up the Jersey coast when he won that big race to New York.... You see, I've been following this aviation pretty closely."

Carl saw Ruth's head drop an inch, and her eyes close to a slit as she inspected him with sudden surprise. He knew that it had just occurred to her who he was. Their eyes exchanged understanding. "She does get things," he thought, and said, lightly:

"Well, I honestly hate to take the money, Mr. Dunleavy, but I'm in a position to know that MacMonnies is a better flier to-day than Ericson is, be——"

"But see here——"

"——because I happen to *be* Hawk Ericson."

"What a chump I am!" groaned the man in tortoise-shell spectacles. "Of course! I remember your picture, now."

Phil was open-mouthed. Ruth laughed. The rest of the room gasped. Mason Winslow, long and bald, was worrying over the question of How to Receive Aviators at Tea.

And Carl was shy as a small boy caught stealing the jam.

CHAPTER XXX

At home, early that evening, Carl's doctor-landlord gave him the message that a Miss Gertrude Cowles had called him up, but had declined to leave a number. The landlord's look indicated that it was no fault of his if Carl had friends who were such fools that they didn't leave their numbers. Carl got even with him by going out to the corner drug-store to telephone Gertie, instead of giving him a chance to listen.

"Hello?" said Gertie over the telephone. "Oh, hello, Carl; I just called up to tell you Adelaide is going to be here this evening, and I thought perhaps you might like to come up if you haven't anything better to do."

Carl did have something better to do. He might have used the whole evening in being psychological about Ruth and Phil Dunleavy and English-basement houses with cream-colored drawing-rooms. But he went up to Gertie's.

They were all there—Gertie and Adelaide, Ray and his mother, and Miss Greene, an unidentified girl from Minneapolis; all playing parcheesi, explaining that they thought it not quite proper to play cards on Sunday, but that parcheesi was "different." Ray winked at Carl as they said it.

The general atmosphere was easy and livable. Carl found himself at home again. Adelaide told funny anecdotes about her school of domestic science, and the chief teacher, who wore her hair in a walnut on top of her head and interrupted a lecture on dietetics to chase a cockroach with a ruler.

As the others began to disappear, Gertie said to Carl: "Don't go till I read you a letter from Ben Rusk I got yesterday. Lots of news from home. Joe Jordan is engaged!"

They were left alone. Gertie glanced at him intimately. He stiffened. He knew that Gertie was honest, kindly, with enough sense of display to catch the tricks of a new environment. But to her, matrimony would be the inevitable sequence of a friendship which Ruth or Olive could take easily, pleasantly, for its own sake. And Carl, the young man just starting in business, was un-heroically afraid of matrimony.

Yet his stiffness of attitude disappeared when Gertie had read the letter from Joralemon and mused, chin on hand, dreamily melancholy: "I can just see them out sleighing. Sometimes I wish I was out there. Honest, Carl, for all the sea and the hills here, don't you wish sometimes it were August, and you were out home camping on a wooded bluff over a lake?"

"Yes!" he cried. "I've been away so long now that I don't ever feel homesick for any particular part of the country; but just the same I would like to see the lakes. And I do miss the prairies sometimes. Oh, I was reading something the other day—fellow was trying to define the different sorts of terrain—here it is, cut it out of the paper." He produced from among a bunch of pocket-worn envelopes and memorandums a clipping hacked from a newspaper with a nail-file, and read:

"'The combat and mystery of the sea; the uplift of the hills and their promise of wonder beyond; the kindliness of late afternoon nestling in small fields, or on ample barns where red clover-tops and long grasses shine against the gray foundation stones and small boys seek for hidden entrances to this castle of the farm; the deep holiness of the forest, whose leaves are the stained glass of a cathedral to grave saints of the open; all these I love, but nowhere do I find content save on the mid-western prairie, where the light of sky and plain drugs the senses, where the sound of meadow-larks at dawn fulfils my desire for companionship, and the easy creak of the buggy, as we top rise after rise, bespells me into an afternoon slumber which the nervous town shall never know.'

"I cut the thing out because I was thinking that the prairies, stretching out the way they do, make me want to go on and on, in an aeroplane or any old thing. Lord, Lord! I guess before long I'll have to be beating it again—like the guy in Kipling that always got sick of reading the same page too long."

"Oh, but Carl, you don't mean to say you're going to give up your business, when you're doing so well? And aviation shows what you can do if you stick to a thing, Carl, and not just wander around like you used to do. We do want to see you succeed."

His reply was rather weak: "Well, gee! I guess I'll succeed, all right, but I don't see much use of succeeding if you have to be stuck down in a greasy city street all your life."

"That's very true, Carl, but do you appreciate the city? Have you ever been in the Metropolitan Museum of Art, or gone to a single symphony concert at Carnegie Hall?"

Carl was convinced that Gertie was a highly superior person; that she was getting far more of the good of New York than he.... He would take her to a concert, have her explain the significance of the music.

It was never to occur sharply to him that, though Gertie referred frequently to concerts and pictures, she showed no vast amount of knowledge about them. She was a fixed fact in his mind; had been for twenty years. He could have a surface quarrel with her because he knew the fundamental things in her, and with these, he was sure, no one could quarrel. His thoughts of Ruth and Olive were delightful surprises; his impression of Gertie was stable as the Rockies.

Carl wasn't sure whether Upper West Side young ladies could be persuaded to attend a theater party upon short acquaintance, but he tried, and arranged a party of Ruth and Olive and himself, Walter MacMonnies (in town on his way from Africa to San Diego), Charley Forbes of the *Chronicle* and, for chaperon, the cosmopolitan woman whom he had met at Ruth's, and who proved to be a Mrs. Tirrell, a dismayingly smart dressmaker.

When he called for Ruth he expected such a gay girl as had poured tea. He was awed to find her a *grande dame* in black velvet, more dignified, apparently inches taller, and in a vice-regally bad temper. As they drove off she declared:

"Sorry I'm in such a villainous temper. I hadn't a single pair of decent white gloves, and I tore some old black Spanish lace on the gown I was going to wear, and my entire family, whom God unquestionably sent to be a trial to test me, clustered about my door while I was dressing and bawled in queries about laundry and other horribly vulgar things."

Carl did not see much of the play. He was watching Ruth's eyes, listening to her whispered comments. She declared that she was awed by the presence of two aviators and a newspaper man. Actually, she was working, working at bringing out MacMonnies, a shy, broad-shouldered, inarticulate youth who supposed that he never had to talk.

Carl had planned to go to the Ritz for after-theater supper, but Ruth and Olive persuaded him to take them to the café of the Rector's of that time; for, they said, they had never been in a Broadway café, and they wanted to see the famous actors with their make-ups off.

At the table Carl carried Ruth off in talk, like a young Lochinvar out of the Middle West. Around them was the storm of highballs and brandy and club soda, theatrical talk, and a confused mass of cigar-smoke, shirt-fronts, white shoulders, and drab waiters; yet here was a quiet refuge for the eternal force of life....

Carl was asking: "Would you rather be a perfect lady and have blue bowls with bunnies on them for your very worst dissipation, or be like your mountain-climbing woman and have anarchists for friends one day and be off hiking through the clouds the next?"

"Oh, I don't know. I know I'm terribly susceptible to the 'nice things of life,' but I do get tired of being nice. Especially when I have a bad temper, as I had to-night. I'm not at all imprisoned in a harem, and as for social aspirations, I'm a nobody. But still I have been brought up to look at things that aren't 'like the home life of our dear Queen' as impossible, and I'm quite sure that father believes that poor people are poor because they are silly and don't try to be rich. But I've been reading; and I've made—to you it may seem silly to call it a discovery, but to me it's the greatest discovery I've ever made: that people are just people, all of them—that the little mousey clerk may be a hero, and the hero may be a nobody—that the motorman that lets his beastly car spatter mud on my nice new velvet skirt may be exactly the same sort of person as the swain who commiserates with me in his cunnin' Harvard accent. Do you think that?"

"I know it. Most of my life I've been working with men with dirty finger-nails, and the only difference between them and the men with clean nails is a nail-cleaner, and that costs just ten cents at the corner drug-store. Seriously— I remember a cook I used to talk to on my way down to Panama once——"

("Panama! How I'd like to go there!")

"——and he had as much culture as anybody I've ever met."

"Yes, but generally do you find very much—oh, courtesy and that sort of thing among mechanics, as much as among what calls itself 'the better class'?"

"No, I don't."

"You don't? Why, I thought—the way you spoke——"

"Why, blessed, what in the world would be the use of their trying to climb if they already had all the rich have? You can't be as gracious as the man that's got nothing else to do, when you're about one jump ahead of the steam-roller every second. That's why they ought to *take* things. If I were a union man, I wouldn't trust all these writers and college men and so on, that try to be sympathetic. Not for one minute. They mean well, but they can't get what it means to a real workman to have to be up at five every winter morning, with no heat in the furnished housekeeping room; or to have to see his Woman sick because he can't afford a doctor."

So they talked, boy and girl, wondering together what the world really is like.

"I want to find out what we can do with life!" she said. "Surely it's something more than working to get tired, and then resting to go back to work. But I'm confused about things." She sighed. "My settlement work—I went into it because I was bored. But it did make me realize how many people are hungry. And yet we just talk and talk and talk—Olive and I sit up half the night when she comes to my house, and when we're not talking about the new negligées we're making and the gorgeous tea-gowns we're going to have when we're married, we rescue the poor and think we're dreadfully advanced, but does it do any good to just talk?—Dear me, I split that poor infinitive right down his middle."

"I don't know. But I do know I don't want to be just stupidly satisfied, and talking does keep me from that, anyway. See here, Miss Winslow, suppose some time I suggested that we become nice and earnest and take up socialism and single tax and this—what is it?—oh, syndicalism—and really studied them, would you do it? Make each other study?"

"Love to."

"Does Dunleavy think much?"

She raised her eyebrows a bit, but hesitated. "Oh yes—no, I don't suppose he does. Or anyway, mostly about the violin. He played a lot when he was in Yale."

Thus was Carl encouraged to be fatuous, and he said, in a manner which quite dismissed Phil Dunleavy: "I don't believe he's very deep. Ra-ther light, I'd say."

Her eyebrows had ascended farther. "Do you think so? I'm sorry."

"Why sorry?"

"Oh, he's always been rather a friend of mine. Olive and Phil and I roller-skated together at the age of eight."

"But——"

"And I shall probably—marry—Phil—some day before long." She turned abruptly to Charley Forbes with a question.

Lost, already lost, was the playmate; a loss that disgusted him with life. He beat his spirit, cursed himself as a clumsy mechanic. He listened to Olive only by self-compulsion. It was minutes before he had the ability and the chance to say to Ruth:

"Forgive me—in the name of the Blue Bowl. Mr. Dunleavy was rather rude to me, and I've been just as rude—and to you! And without his excuse. For he naturally would want to protect you from a wild aviator coming from Lord knows where."

"You are forgiven. And Phil *was* rude. And you're not a Lord-knows-where, I'm sure."

Almost brusquely Carl demanded: "Come for a long tramp with me, on the Palisades. Next Saturday, if you can and if it's a decent day.... You said you liked to run away.... And we can be back before dinner, if you like."

"Why—let me think it over. Oh, I *would* like to. I've always wanted to do just that—think of it, the Palisades just opposite, and I never see them except for a walk of half a mile or so when I stay with a friend of mine, Laura Needham, at Winklehurst, up on the Palisades. My mother never approved of a wilder wilderness than Central Park and the habit——I've never been able to get Olive to explore. But it isn't conventional to go on long tramps with even the nicest new Johnnies, is it?"

"No, but——"

"I know. You'll say, 'Who makes the convention?' and of course there's no answer but 'They.' But They are so all-present. They——Oh yes, yes, yes, I will go! But you will let me get back by dinner-time, won't you? Will you call for me about two?... And can you——I wonder if a hawk out of the windy skies can understand how daring a dove out of Ninety-second Street feels at going walking on the Palisades?"

CHAPTER XXXI

The iron Hudson flowed sullenly, far below the ice-enameled rock on the Palisades, where stood Ruth and Carl, shivering in the abrupt wind that cut down the defile. The scowling, slatey river was filled with ice-floes and chunks of floating, water-drenched snow that broke up into bobbing sheets of slush. The sky was solid cold gray, with no arch and no hint of the lost sun. Crows winging above them stood out against the sky like pencil-marks on clean paper. The estates in upper New York City, across the river, were snow-cloaked, the trees chilly and naked, the houses standing out as though they were freezing and longing for their summer wrap of ivy. And naked were the rattling trees on their side of the river, on the Palisades. But the cold breeze enlivened them, the sternness of the swift, cruel river and miles of brown shore made them gravely happy. As they tramped briskly off, atop the cliffs, toward the ferry to New York, five miles away, they talked with a quiet, quick seriousness which discovered them to each other. It was too cold for conversational fencing. It was too splendidly open for them not to rejoice in the freedom from New York streets and feel like heroes conquering the miles.

Carl was telling of Joralemon, of Plato, of his first flights before country fairs; something of what it meant to be a newspaper hero, and of his loneliness as a Dethroned Prince. Ruth dropped her defenses of a chaperoned young woman; confessed that now that she had no mother to keep her mobilized and in the campaign to get nearer to "Society" and a "decent marriage," she did not know exactly what she wanted to do with life. She spoke tentatively of her vague settlement work; in all she said she revealed an honesty as forthright as though she were a gaunt-eyed fanatic instead of a lively-voiced girl in a blue corduroy jacket with collar and cuffs of civet and buttons from Venice.

Then Carl spoke of his religion—the memory of Forrest Haviland. He had never really talked of him to any one save Colonel Haviland and Titherington, the English aviator; but now this girl, who had never seen Forrest, seemed to have known him for life. Carl made vivid by his earnestness the golden hours of work together in California; the confidences in New York restaurants; his long passion for their Brazilian trip. Ruth's eyes looked up at him with swift comprehension, and there was a tear in them as he told in ten words of the message that Forrest was dead.

They turned gay, Ruth's sturdy, charming shoulders shrugging like a Frenchman's with the exhilaration of fast walking and keen air, while her voice, light and cheerful, with graceful modulations and the singer's freedom from twang, rejoiced:

"I'm so glad we came! I'm so glad we came! But I'm afraid of the wild beasts I see in the woods there. They have no right to have twilight so early. I know a big newspaper man who lives at Pompton, N. J., and I'm going to ask him to write to the governor about it. The legislature ought to pass a law that dusk sha'n't come till seven, Saturday afternoons. Do you know how glad I am that you made me come?... And how honored I am to have you tell me— Lieutenant Haviland—and the very bad Carl that lived in Joralemon?"

"It's——I'm glad——Say, gee! we'll have to hurry like the dickens if we're going to catch a ferry in time to get you home for dinner."

"I have an idea. I wonder if we dare——I have a friend, sort of a distant cousin, who married her a husband at Winklehurst, on the Palisades, not very far from the ferry. I wonder if we couldn't make her invite us both for dinner? Of course, she'll want to know all about you; but we'll be mysterious, and that will make it all the more fun, don't you think? I do want to prolong our jaunt, you see."

"I can't think of anything I'd rather do. But do you dare impose a perfectly strange man on her?"

"Oh yes, I know her so well that she's told me what kind of a tie her husband had on when he proposed."

"Let's do it!"

"A telephone! There's some shops ahead there, in that settlement. Ought to be a telephone there.... I'll make her give us a good dinner! If Laura thinks she'll get away with hash and a custard with a red cherry in it, she'd better undeceive herself."

They entered a tiny wayside shop for the sale of candy and padlocks and mittens. While Ruth telephoned to her friend, Mrs. Laura Needham, Carl bought red-and-blue and lemon-colored all-day suckers, and a sugar mouse, and a candy kitten with green ears and real whiskers. He could not but hear Ruth telephoning, and they grinned at each other like conspirators, her eyelids in little wrinkles as she tried to look wicked, her voice amazingly innocent as she talked, Carl carefully arraying his purchases before her, making the candy kitten pursue the sugar mouse round and round the telephone.

"Hello, hello! Is Mrs. Needham there?... Hello!... Oh, hel-*lo*, Laura dear. This is Ruth. I.... Fine. I feel fine. But chillery. Listen, Laura; I've been taking a tramp along the Palisades. Am I invited to dinner with a swain?... What?... Oh yes, I am; certainly I'm invited to dinner.... Well, my dear, go in town by all means, with my blessing; but that sha'n't prevent you from having the opportunity to enjoy being hospitable.... I don't know. What ferry do you catch?... The 7.20?... N-no, I don't think we can get there till after that, so you can go right ahead and have the Biddy get ready for us.... All right; that *is* good of you, dear, to force the invitation on me." She flushed as her eyes met Carl's. She continued: "But seriously, will it be too much of a tax on the Biddy if we do come? We're drefful cold, and it's a long crool way to town.... Thank you, dear. It shall be returned unto you—after not too many days.... What?... Who?... Oh, a man.... Why, yes, it might be, but I'd be twice as likely to go tramping with Olive as with Phil.... No, it isn't.... Oh, as usual. He's getting to be quite a dancing-man.... Well, if you must know—oh, I can't give you his name. He's——" She glanced at Carl appraisingly, "——he's about five feet tall, and he has a long French shovel beard and a lovely red nose, and he's listening to me describe him!"

Carl made the kitten chase the mouse furiously.

"Perhaps I'll tell you about him some time.... Good-by, Laura dear."

She turned to Carl, rubbing her cold ear where the telephone-receiver had pressed against it, and caroled: "Her husband is held late at the office, and Laura is going to meet him in town, and they're going to the theater. So we'll have the house all to ourselves. Exciting!" She swung round to telephone home that she would not be there for dinner.

As they left the shop, went over a couple of blocks for the Winklehurst trolley, and boarded it, Carl did some swift thinking. He was not above flirting or, if the opportunity offered, carrying the flirtation to the most delicious, exciting, uncertain lengths he could. Here, with "dinner in their own house," with a girl interesting yet unknown, there was a feeling of sudden intimacy which might mean anything. Only—when their joined eyes had pledged mischief while she telephoned, she had been so quiet, so frank, so evidently free from a shamefaced erotic curiosity, that now he instantly dismissed the query, "How far could I go? What does she expect?" which, outside of pure-minded romances, really does come to men. It was a wonderful relief to dismiss the query; a simplification to live in the joy each moment gave of itself. The hour was like a poem. Yet he was no extraordinary person; he had, in the lonely hours of a dead room, been tortured with the unmoral longings which, good or bad, men do feel.

As they took their seats in the car, and Ruth beat on her knees with her fur-lined gloves, he laughed back, altogether happy, not pretending, as he had pretended with Eve L'Ewysse.

Happy. But hungry!

Mrs. Needham should have been graciously absent by the time they reached her house—a suburban residence with a large porch. But, as they approached, Ruth cried:

"'Shhhh! There seems to be somebody moving around in the living room. I don't believe Laura 's gone yet. That would spoil it. Come on. Let's peep. Let's be Indian scouts!"

Cautioning each other with warning pats, they tiptoed guiltily to the side of the house and peered in at the dining-room window, where the shade was raised a couple of inches above the sill. A noise at the back of the house made them start and flatten against the wall.

"Big chief," whispered Carl, "the redskins are upon us! But old Brown Barrel shall make many an one bite the dust!"

"Hush, silly.... Oh, it's just the maid. See, she's looking at the clock and wondering why we don't get here."

"But maybe Mrs. Needham 's in the other room."

"No. Because the maid's sniffing around—there, she's reading a post-card some one left on the side-table. Oh yes, and she's chewing gum. Laura has certainly departed. Probably Laura is chewing gum herself at the present moment, now that she's out from under the eye of her maid. Laura always was ree-fined, but I wouldn't trust her to be proof against the feeling of wild dissipation you can get out of chewing gum, if you live in Winklehurst."

They had rung the door-bell on the porch by now.

"I'm so glad," said Ruth, "that Laura is gone. She is very literal-minded. She might not understand that we could be hastily married and even lease a house, this way, and still be only tea acquaintances."

The maid had not yet answered. Waiting in the still porch, winter everywhere beyond it, Carl was all excited anticipation. He hastily pressed her hand, and she lightly returned the pressure, laughing, breathing quickly. They started like convicted lovers as the maid opened the door. The consciousness of their starting made them the more embarrassed, and they stammered before the maid. Ruth fled up-stairs, while Carl tried to walk up gravely, though he was tingling with the game.

When he had washed (discovering, as every one newly discovers after every long, chilly walk, that water from the cold tap feels amazingly warm on hands congealed by the tramp), and was loitering in the upper hall, Ruth called to him from Mrs. Needham's room:

"I think you'll find hair-brushes and things in Jack's room, to the right. Oh, I am very stupid; I forgot this was our house; I mean in your room, of course."

He had a glimpse of her, twisting up a strand of naturally wavy brown hair, a silver-backed hair-brush bright against it, her cheeks flushed to an even crimson, her blue corduroy jacket off, and, warmly intimate in its stead, a blouse of blue satin, opening in a shallow triangle at her throat. With a tender big-brotherliness he sought the room that was his, not Jack's. No longer was this the house of Other People, but one in which he belonged.

"No," he heard himself explain, "she isn't beautiful. Istra Nash was nearer that. But, golly! she is such a good pal, and she is beautiful if an English lane is. Oh, stop rambling.... If I could kiss that little honey place at the base of her throat...."

"Yes, Miss Winslow. Coming. *Am* I ready for dinner? Watch me!"

She confided as he came out into the hall, "Isn't it terribly confusing to have our home and even three toby-children all ready-made for us, this way!"

Her glance—eyes that always startled him with blue where dark-brown was expected; even teeth showing; head cocked sidelong; cheeks burning with fire of December snow—her glance and all her manner trusted him, the outlaw. It was not as an outsider, but as her comrade that he answered:

"Golly! have we a family, too? I always forget. So sorry. But you know—get so busy at the office———"

"Why, I *think* we have one. I'll go look in the nursery and make sure, but I'm almost positive———"

"No, I'll take your word for it. You're around the house more than I am.... But, oh, say, speaking of that, that reminds me: Woman, if you think that I'm going to buy you a washing-machine this year, when I've already bought you a napkin-ring and a portrait of Martha Washington———"

"*Oh weh!* I knew I should have a cruel husband who———Joy! I think the maid is prowling about and trying to listen. 'Shhh! The story Laura will get out of her!"

While the maid served dinner, there could scarce have been a more severely correct pair, though Carl did step on her toe when she was saying to the maid, in her best offhand manner, "Oh, Leah, will you please tell Mrs. Needham that I stole a handkerchief from my—I mean from her room?"

But when the maid had been unable to find any more imaginary crumbs to brush off the table, and had left them alone with their hearts and the dessert, a most rowdy young "married couple" quarreled violently over the washing-machine he still refused to buy for her.

Carl insisted that, as suburbanites, they had to play cards, and he taught her pinochle, which he had learned from the bartender of the Bowery saloon. But the cards dropped from their fingers, and they sat before the gas-log in the living-room, in a lazy, perfect happiness, when she said:

"All the while we've been playing cards—and playing the still more dangerous game of being married—I've been thinking how glad I am to know about your life. Somehow——I wonder if you have told so very many?"

"Practically no one."

"I do——I'm really not fishing for compliments, but I do want to be found understanding——"

"There's never been any one so understanding."

Silent then. Carl glanced about the modern room. Ruth's eyes followed. She nodded as he said:

"But it's really an old farm-house out in the hills where the snow is deep; and there's logs in the fireplace."

"Yes, and rag carpets."

"And, oh, Ruth, listen, a bob-sled with——Golly! I suppose it is a little premature to call you 'Ruth,' but after our being married all evening I don't see how I can call you 'Miss Winslow.'"

"No, I'm afraid it would scarcely be proper, under the circumstances. Then I must be 'Mrs. Ericson.' Ooh! It makes me think of Norse galleys and northern seas. Of course—your galley was the aeroplane.... 'Mrs. Eric——'" Her voice ran down; she flushed and said, defensively: "What time is it? I think we must be starting. I telephoned I would be home by ten." Her tone was conventional as her words.

But as they stood waiting for a trolley-car to the New York ferry, on a street corner transformed by an arc-light that swung in the wind and cast wavering films of radiance among the vague wintry trees of a wood-lot, Ruth tucked her arm under his, small beside his great ulster, and sighed like a child:

"I am ver-ee cold!"

He rubbed her hand protectingly, her mouselike hand in its fur-lined glove. His canny, self-defensive, Scotchlike Norse soul opened its gates. He knew a longing to give, a passion to protect her, a whelming desire to have shy secrets with this slim girl. All the poetry in the world sounded its silver harps within him because his eyes were opened and it was given to him to see her face. Gently he said:

"Yes, it's cold, and there's big gray ghosts hiding there in the trees, with their leathery wings, that were made out of sea-fog by the witches, folded in front of them, and they're glumming at us over the bony, knobly joints on top their wings, with big, round platter eyes. And the wind is calling us—it's trying to snatch us out on the arctic snow-fields, to freeze us. But I'll fight them all off. I won't let them take you, Ruth."

"I'm sure you won't, Carl."

"And—oh—you won't let Phil Dunleavy keep you from running away, not for a while yet?"

"M-maybe not."

The sky had cleared. She tilted up her chin and adored the stars—stars like the hard, cold, fighting sparks that fly from a trolley-wire. Carl looked down fondly, noting how fair-skinned was her forehead in contrast to her thick, dark brows, as the arc-light's brilliance rested on her worshiping face—her lips a-tremble and slightly parted. She raised her arms, her fingers wide-spread, praising the star-gods. She cried only, "Oh, all this———" but it was a prayer to a greater god Pan, shaking his snow-incrusted beard to the roar of northern music. To Carl her cry seemed to pledge faith in the starred sky and the long trail and a glorious restlessness that by a dead fireplace of white, smooth marble would never find content.

"Like sword-points, those stars are," he said, then———

Then they heard the trolley-car's flat wheels grinding on a curve. Its search-light changed the shadow-haunted woodland to a sad group of scanty trees, huddling in front of an old bill-board, with its top broken and the tattered posters flapping. The wanderers stepped from the mystical romance of the open night into the exceeding realism of the car—highly realistic wooden floor with small, muddy pools from lumps of dirty melting snow, hot air, a smell of Italian workmen, a German conductor with the sniffles, a row of shoes mostly wet and all wrinkled. They had to stand. Most realistic of all, they read the glossy car-signs advertising soap and little cigars, and the enterprising local advertisement of "Wm. P. Smith & Sons, All Northern New Jersey Real Estate, Cheaper Than Rent." So, instantly, the children of the night turned into two sophisticated young New-Yorkers who, apologizing for fresh-air yawns, talked of the theatrical season.

But for a moment a strange look of distance dwelt in Ruth's eyes, and she said: "I wonder what I can do with the winter stars we've found? Will Ninety-second Street be big enough for them?"

CHAPTER XXXII

For a week—the week before Christmas—Carl had seen neither Ruth nor Gertie; but of the office he had seen too much. They were "rushing work" on the Touricar to have it on the market early in 1913. Every afternoon or evening he left the office with his tongue scaly from too much nervous smoking; poked dully about the streets, not much desiring to go any place, nor to watch the crowds, after all the curiosity had been drawn out of him by hours of work. Several times he went to a super-movie, a cinema palace on Broadway above Seventy-second Street, with an entrance in New York Colonial architecture, and crowds of well-to-do Jewish girls in opera-cloaks.

On the two bright mornings of the week he wanted to play truant from the office, to be off with Ruth over the hills and far away. Both mornings there came to him a picture of Gertie, wanting to slip out and play like Ruth, but having no chance. He felt guilty because he had never bidden Gertie come tramping, and guiltily he recalled that it was with her that the boy Carl had gone to seek-our-fortunes. He told himself that he had been depending upon Gertie for the bread-and-butter of friendship, and begging for the opportunity to give the stranger, Ruth Winslow, dainties of which she already had too much.

When he called, Sunday evening, he found Gertie alone, reading a love-story in a woman's magazine.

"I'm so glad you came," she said. "I was getting quite lonely." She was as gratefully casual as ever.

"Say, Gertie, I've got a plan. Wouldn't you like to go for some good long hikes in the country?"

"Oh yes; that would be fine when spring comes."

"No; I mean now, in the winter."

She looked at him heavily. "Why, isn't it pretty cold, don't you think?"

He prepared to argue, but he did not think of her as looking heavily. He did not draw swift comparisons between Gertie's immobility and Ruth's lightness. He was used to Gertie; was in her presence comfortably understanding and understood; could find whatever he expected in her as easily as one finds the editorial page—or the sporting page—in a familiar newspaper. He merely became mildly contentious and made questioning noises in his throat as she went on:

"You know it is pretty cold here. They can say all they want to about the cold and all that out in Minnesota, but, really, the humidity——"

"Rats; it isn't so very cold, not if you walk fast."

"Well, maybe; anyway, I guess it would be nice to explore some."

"All right; let's."

"I do think people are so conventional. Don't you?" said Gertie, while Carl discerningly stole one of Ray's best cigars out of the humidor. "Awfully conventional. Not going out for good long walks. Dorothy Gibbons and I did find the nicest place to walk, up in Bronx Park, and there's such a dear little restaurant, right on the water; of course the water was frozen, but it seemed quite wild, you know, for New York. We might take that walk, whenever you'd like to."

"Oh—Bronx Park—gee! Gertie, I can't get up much excitement over that. I want to get away from this tame city, and forget all about offices and parks and people and everything like that."

"N-n-n-now!" she clucked in a patronizing way. "We mustn't ask New York to give us wilderness, you know! I'm afraid that would be a little too much to ask of it! Don't you think so yourself!"

Carl groaned to himself, "I won't be mothered!"

He was silent. His silence was positively noisy. He wanted her to hear it. But it is difficult to be sulky with a bland, plump woman of thirty who remembers your childhood trick of biting your nails, and glances up at you from her embroidery, occasionally patting her brown silk hair or smoothing her brown silk waist in a way which implies a good digestion, a perfect memory of the morning's lesson of her Sunday-school class, and a mild disbelief in men as anything except relatives, providers, card-players, and nurslings. Carl gave up the silence-cure.

He hummed about the room, running over the advertising pages of magazines, discussing Plato fraternities, and waiting till it should be time to go home. Their conversation kept returning to the fraternities. There wasn't much else to talk about. Before to-night they had done complete justice to all other topics—Joralemon, Bennie Rusk, Joe Jordan's engagement, Adelaide Benner, and symphony concerts. Gertie embroidered, patted her hair, smoothed her waist, looked cheerful, rocked, and spoke; embroidered, patted her hair, smoothed her sleeve, looked amiable, rocked, and spoke— embroidered, pat——

At a quarter to ten Carl gave himself permission to go. Said he: "I'll have to get on the job pretty early to-morrow. Not much taking it easy here in New York, the way you can in Joralemon, eh? So I guess I'd better——"

"I'm sorry you have to go so early." Gertie carefully stuck her embroidery needle into her doily, rolled up the doily meticulously, laid it down on the center-table, straightened the pile of magazines which Carl had deranged, and rose. "But I'm glad you could drop up this evening. Come up any time you haven't anything better to do. Oh—what about our tramp? If you know some place that is better than Bronx Park, we might try it."

"Why—uh—yes—why, sure; we'll have to, some time."

"And, Carl, you're coming up to have your Christmas turkey with us, aren't you?"

"I'd like to, a lot, but darn it, I've accepted 'nother invitation."

That was absolutely untrue, and Carl was wondering why he had lied, when the storm broke.

Gertie's right arm, affectedly held out from the elbow, the hand drooping, in the attitude of a refined hostess saying good-by, dropped stiffly to her side. Slowly she thrust out both arms, shoulder-high on either side, with her fists clenched; her head back and slightly on one side; her lips open in agony— the position of crucifixion. Her eyes looked up, unseeing; then closed tight. She drew a long breath, like a sigh that was too weary for sound, and her plump, placid left hand clutched her panting breast, while her right arm dropped again. All the passion of tragedy seemed to shriek in her hopeless gesture, and her silence was a wail muffled and despairing.

Carl stared, twisting his watch-chain with nervous fingers, wanting to flee.

It was raw woman, with all the proprieties of Joralemon and St. Orgul's cut away, who spoke, her voice constantly rising:

"Oh, Carl—Carl! Oh, why, why, why! Oh, why don't you want me to go walking with you, now? Why don't you want to go anywhere with me any more? Have I displeased you? Oh, I didn't mean to! Why do I bore you so?"

"Oh—Gertie—oh—gee!—thunder!" whimpered a dismayed youth. A more mature Hawk Ericson struggled to life and soothed her: "Gertie, honey, I didn't mean——Listen——"

But she moaned on, standing rigid, her left hand on her breast, her eyes red, moist, frightened, fixed: "We always played together, and I thought here in the city we could be such good friends, with all the different new things to do together—why, I wanted us to go to Chinatown and theaters, and I would have been so glad to pay my share. I've just been waiting and hoping you would ask me, and I wanted us to play and see—oh! so many different new things together—it would have been so sweet, so sweet——We were good friends at first, and then you—you didn't want to come here any more and—

—Oh, I couldn't help seeing it; more and more and more and *more* I've been seeing it; but I didn't want to see it; but now I can't fool myself any more. I was so lonely till you came to-night, and when you spoke about tramping——And then it seemed like you just went away from me again."

"Why, Gertie, you didn't seem——"

"——and long ago I really saw it, the day we walked in the Park and I was wicked about trying to make you call me 'Eltruda'—oh, Carl dear, indeed you needn't call me that or anything you don't like—and I tried to make you say I had a temperament. And about Adelaide and all. And you went away and I thought you would come back to me that evening—oh, I wanted you to come, so much, and you didn't even 'phone—and I waited up till after midnight, hoping you would 'phone, I kept thinking surely you would, and you never did, you never did; and I listened and listened for the 'phone to ring, and every time there was a noise——But it never was you. It never rang at all...."

She dropped back in the Morris chair, her eyes against the cushion, her hair disordered, both her hands gripping the left arm of the chair, her sobs throat-catching and long—throb-throb-throb in the death-still air.

Carl stared at her, praying for a chance to escape. Then he felt an instinct prompting him to sob with her. Pity, embarrassment, disgust, mingled with his alarm. He became amazed that Gertie, easy-going Gertie Cowles, had any passion at all; and indignant that it was visited upon himself.

But he had to help. He moved to her chair and, squatting boyishly on its arm, stroked her hair, begging: "Gertie, Gertie, I did mean to come up, that night. Indeed I did, honey. I would have come up, but I met some friends—couldn't break away from them all evening." A chill ran between his shoulder-blades. It was a shock to the pride he took in Ruth's existence. The evening in question had found Ruth for him! It seemed as though Gertie had dared with shrewish shrillness to intrude upon his beautiful hour. But pity came to him again. Stroking her hair, he went urgently on: "Don't you see? Why, blessed, I wouldn't hurt you for anything! Just to-night—why, you remember, first thing, I wanted us to plan for some walks; reason I didn't say more about it was, I didn't know as you'd want to, much. Why, Gertie, *anybody* would be proud to play with you. You know so much about concerts and all sorts of stuff. Anybody'd be proud to!" He wound up with a fictitious cheerfulness. "We'll have some good long hikes together, heh?... It's better now, isn't it, kiddy? You're just tired to-night. Has something been worrying you? Tell old Carl all about——"

She wiped her tears away with the adorable gesture of a child trying to be good, and like a child's was her glance, bewildered, hurt, yet trusting, as she said in a small, shy voice: "Would folks really be proud to play with me?... We did use to have some dear times, didn't we! Do you remember how we found some fool's gold, and we thought it was gold and hid it on the shore of the lake, and we were going to buy a ship? Do you remember? You haven't forgotten all our good times, while you've been so famous, have you?"

"Oh no, no!"

"But why don't—Carl, why don't you—why can't you care more now?"

"Why, I do care! You're one of the bulliest pals I have, you and Ray."

"And Ray!"

She flung his hand away and sat bolt up, angry.

Carl retired to a chair beside the Morris chair, fidgeting. "Can you beat it! Is this Gertie and me?" he inquired in a parenthesis in his heart. For a second, as she stared haughtily at him, he spitefully recalled the fact that Gertie had once discarded him for a glee-club dentist. But he submerged the thought and listened with a rather forced big-brother air as she repented of her anger and went on:

"Carl, don't you understand how hard it is for a woman to forget her pride this way?" The hauteur of being one of the élite of Joralemon again flashed out. "Maybe if you'll think real hard you'll remember I used to could get you to be so kind and talk to me without having to beg you so hard. Why, I'd been to New York and known the *nicest* people before you'd ever stirred a foot out of Joralemon! You were——Oh, please forgive me, Carl; I didn't mean to be snippy; I just don't know what to think of myself—and I did used to think I was a lady, and here I am practically up and telling you and——"

She leaned from her chair toward his, and took his hand, touching it, finding its hard, bony places and the delicate white hollows of flesh between his coarsened yet shapely fingers; tracing a scarce-seen vein on the back; exploring a well-beloved yet ill-known country. Carl was unspeakably disconcerted. He was thinking that, to him, Gertie was set aside from the number of women who could appeal physically, quite as positively as though she were some old aunt who had for twenty years seemed to be the same adult, plump, uninteresting age. Gertie's solid flesh, the monotony of her voice, the unimaginative fixity of her round cheeks, a certain increasing slackness about her waist, even the faint, stuffy domestic scent of her—they all expressed to him her lack of humor and fancy and venturesomeness. She was crystallized in his mind as a good friend with a plain soul and sisterly tendencies. Awkwardly he said:

"You mustn't talk like that.... Gee! Gertie, we'll be in a regular 'scene,' if you don't watch out!... We're just good friends, and you can always bank on me, same as I would on you."

"But why must we be just friends?"

He wanted to be rude, but he was patient. Mechanically stroking her hair again, leaning forward most uncomfortably from his chair, he stammered: "Oh, I've been——Oh, you know; I've wandered around so much that it's kind of put me out of touch with even my best friends, and I don't know where I'm at. I couldn't make any alliances——Gee! that sounds affected. I mean: I've got to sort of start in now all over, finding where I'm at."

"But why must we be just friends, then?"

"Listen, child. It's hard to tell; I guess I didn't know till now what it does mean, but there's a girl——Wait; listen. There's a girl—at first I simply thought it was good fun to know her, but now, Lord! Gertie, you'd think I was pretty sentimental if I told you what I think of her. God! I want to see her so much! Right now! I haven't let myself know how much I wanted her. She's everything. She's sister and chum and wife and everything."

"It's——But I am glad for you. Will you believe that? And perhaps you understand how I felt, now. I'm very sorry I let myself go. I hope you will——Oh, please go now."

He sprang up, only too ready to go. But first he kissed her hand with a courtly reverence, and said, with a sweetness new to him: "Dear, will you forgive me if I've ever hurt you? And will you believe how very, very much I honor you? And when I see you again there won't be—we'll both forget all about to-night, won't we? We'll just be the old Carl and Gertie again. Tell me to come when——"

"Yes. I will. Goodnight."

"Good night, Gertie. God bless you."

He never remembered where he walked that night when he had left Gertie. The exercise, the chill of the night, gradually set his numbed mind working again. But it dwelt with Ruth, not with Gertie. Now that he had given words to his longing for Ruth, to his pride in her, he understood that he had passed the hidden border of that misty land called "being in love," which cartographers have variously described as a fruitful tract of comfortable harvests, as a labyrinth with walls of rose and silver, and as a tenebrous realm of unhappy ghosts.

He stopped at a street corner where, above a saloon with a large beer-sign, stretched dim tenement windows toward a dirty sky; and on that drab corner glowed for a moment the mystic light of the Rose of All the World—before a Tammany saloon! Chin high, yearning toward a girl somewhere off to the south, Carl poignantly recalled how Ruth had worshiped the stars. His soul soared, lark and hawk in one, triumphant over the matter-of-factness of daily life. Carl Ericson the mechanic, standing in front of a saloon, with a laundry to one side and a cigars-and-stationery shop round the corner, was one with the young priest saying mass, one with the suffragist woman defying a jeering mob, one with Ruth Winslow listening to the ringing stars.

"God—help—me—to—be—worthy—of—her!"

Nothing more did he say, in words, yet he was changed for ever.

Changed. True that when he got home, half an hour later, and in the dark ran his nose against an opened door, he said, "Damn it!" very naturally. True that on Monday, back in the office that awaits its victims equally after Sundays golden or dreary, he forgot Ruth's existence for hours at a time. True that at lunch with two VanZile automobile salesmen he ate *Wiener Schnitzel* and shot dice for cigars, with no signs of a mystic change. It is even true that, dining at the Brevoort with Charley Forbes, he though of Istra Nash, and for a minute was lonely for Istra's artistic dissipation. Yet the change was there.

CHAPTER XXXIII

From Titherington, the aviator, in his Devonshire home, from a millionaire amateur flier among the orange-groves at Pasadena, from his carpenter father in Joralemon, and from Gertie in New York, Carl had invitations for Christmas, but none that he could accept. VanZile had said, pleasantly, "Going out to the country for Christmas?"

"Yes," Cal had lied.

Again he saw himself as the Dethroned Prince, and remembered that one year ago, sailing for South America to fly with Tony Bean, he had been the lion at a Christmas party on shipboard, while Martin Dockerill, his mechanic, had been a friendly slave.

He spent most of Christmas Eve alone in his room, turning over old letters, and aviation magazines with pictures of Hawk Ericson, wondering whether he might not go back to that lost world. Josiah Bagby, Jr., son of the eccentric doctor at whose school Carl had learned to fly, was experimenting with hydroaeroplanes and with bomb-dropping devices at Palm Beach, and imploring Carl, as the steadiest pilot in America, to join him. The dully noiseless room echoed the music of a steady motor carrying him out over a blue bay. Carl's own answer to the tempter vision was: "Rats! I can't very well leave the Touricar now, and I don't know as I've got my flying nerve back yet. Besides, Ruth——"

Always he thought of Ruth, uneasy with the desire to be out dancing, laughing, playing with her. He was tormented by a question he had been threshing out for days: Might he permissibly have sent her a Christmas present?

He went to bed at ten o'clock—on Christmas Eve, when the streets were surging with voices and gay steps, when rollicking piano-tunes from across the street penetrated even closed windows, and a German voice as rich as milk chocolate was caressing, "*Oh Tannenbaum, oh Tannenbaum, wie grün sind deine Blätter.*"... Then slept for nine hours, woke with rapturous remembrance that he didn't have to go to the office, and sang "The Banks of the Saskatchewan" in his bath. When he returned to the house, after breakfast, he found a letter from Ruth:

The Day before Xmas & all thru the MansionThe Maids with Turkey are Stirring—Please Pardon the Scansion.

DEAR PLAYMATE,—You said on our tramp that I would make a good playmate, but I'm sure that I should be a very poor one if I did not wish you a gloriously merry Xmas & a New Year that will bring you all the dear things you want. I shall be glad if you do not get this letter on Xmas day itself if that means that you are off at some charming country house having a most katische (is that the way it is spelled, probably not) time. But if by any chance you *are* in town, won't you make your playmate's shout to you from her back yard a part of your Xmas? She feels shy about sending this effusive greeting with all its characteristic sloppiness of writing, but she does want you to have a welcome to Xmas fun, & won't you please give the Touricar a pair of warm little slippers from

RUTH GAYLORD WINSLOW.

P.S. Mrs. Tirrell has sent me an angel miniature Jap garden, with a tiny pergola & real dwarf trees & a bridge that you expect an Alfred Noyes lantern on, & Oh Carl, an issa goldfish in a pool!

MISS R. WINSLOW.

"'——all the dear things I want'!" Carl repeated, standing tranced in the hall, oblivious of the doctor-landlord snooping at the back. "Ruth blessed, do you know the thing I want most?... Say! Great! I'll hustle out and send her all the flowers in the world. Or, no. I've got it." He was already out of the house, hastening toward the subway. "I'll send her one of these lingerie tea-baskets with all kinds of baby pots of preserves and tea-balls and stuff.... Wonder what Dunleavy sent her?... Rats! I don't care. Jiminy! I'm happy! Me to Palm Beach to fly? Not a chance!"

He had Christmas dinner in state, with the California Exiles Club. He was craftily careless about the manner in which he touched a letter in his pocket for gloves, which tailors have been inspired to put on the left side of dress-clothes.

Twice Carl called at Ruth's in the two weeks after Christmas. Once she declared that she was tired of modern life, that socialism and agnosticism shocked her, that the world needed the courtly stiffness of mid-Victorian days, as so ably depicted in the works of Mrs. Florence Barclay—needed hair-cloth as a scourge for white tango-dancing backs. As for her, Ruth announced, she was going to be mid-Victorian just as soon as she could find a hair-locket, silk mitts, and an elderly female tortoise-shell cat with an instinctive sense of delicacy. She sat bolt-upright on the front of the most impersonal French-gilt chair in the drawing-room and asserted that Phil Dunleavy, with his safe ancestry of two generations of wholesalers and strong probabilities about the respectability of still another generation, was her ideal of a Christian gentleman. She wore a full white muslin gown with a blue sash, her hair primly parted in the middle, her right hand laid flat over her left in her lap. Her vocabulary was choice. For a second, when she referred to winter sports at Lake Placid, she forgot herself and tucked one smooth, silk-clad, un-mid-Victorian leg under her, but instantly she recovered her poise of a vicarage, remarking, "I have been subject to very careless influences lately." She called him neither "Carl" nor "Mr. Ericson" nor anything else, and he dared not venture on Ruth.

He went home in bewilderment. As he crossed Broadway he loitered insolently, as though challenging the flying squadron of taxicabs to run him down. "What do I care if they hit me?" he inquired, savagely, of his sympathetic and applauding self. Every word she had said he examined, finding double and triple meanings, warning himself not to regard her mood seriously, but unable to make the warning take.

On his next call there was a lively Ruth who invited him up to the library, read extracts from Stephen Leacock's *Nonsense Novels*; turned companionably serious, and told him how divided were her sympathies between her father— the conscientiously worried employer—and a group of strikers in his factory. She made coffee in a fantastic percolator, and played Débussy and ragtime. At ten-thirty, the hour at which he had vehemently resolved to go, they were curled in two big chairs eating chocolate peppermints and talking of themselves apropos of astronomy and the Touricar and Lincoln Beachey's daring and Mason Winslow and patriotism and Joralemon. Ruth's father drifted in from his club at a quarter to eleven. Carl now met him for the first time. He was a large-stomached, bald, sober, friendly man, with a Gladstone collar, a huge watch-chain, kindly trousers and painfully smart tan boots, a father of the kind who gives cigars and non-committal encouragement to daughter's suitors.

It takes a voice with personality and modulations to make a fifteen-minute telephone conversation tolerable, and youth to make it possible. Ruth had both. For fifteen minutes she discussed with Carl the question of whether she should go to Marion Browne's dinner-dance at Delmonico's, as Phil wished, or go skeeing in the Westchester Hills, as Carl wished, the coming Saturday—the first Saturday in February, 1913. Carl won.

They arrived at a station in the Bedford Hills, bearing long, carved-prowed Norwegian skees, which seemed to hypnotize the other passengers. To Carl's joy (for he associated that suit with the Palisades and their discovery of each other), Ruth was in her blue corduroy, with high-lace boots and a gray sweater jacket of silky wool. Carl displayed a tweed Norfolk jacket, a great sweater, and mittens unabashed. He had a mysterious pack which, he informed the excited Ruth, contained Roland's sword and the magic rug of Bagdad. Together they were apple-cheeked, chattering children of outdoors.

For all the horizon's weight of dark clouds, clear sunshine lay on clear snow as they left the train and trotted along the road, carrying their skees beyond the outskirts of the town. Country sleigh-bells chinkled down a hill; children shouted and made snow houses; elders stamped their feet and clucked, "Fine day!" New York was far off and ridiculously unimportant. Carl and Ruth reached an open sloping field, where the snow that partly covered a large rock was melting at its lacy, crystaled edges, staining the black rock to a shiny wetness that was infinitely cheerful in its tiny reflection of the blue sky at the zenith. On a tree whose bleak bark the sun had warmed, vagrant sparrows in hand-me-down feathers discussed rumors of the establishment of a bread-crumb line and the better day that was coming for all proletarian sparrows. A rounded drift of snow stood out against a red barn. The litter of corn-stalks and straw in a barn-yard was transformed from disordered muck to a tessellation of warm silver and old gold. Not the delicate red and browns and grays alone, but everywhere the light, as well, caressed the senses. A distant dog barked good-natured greeting to all the world. The thawing land stirred with a promise that spring might in time return to lovers.

"Oh, to-day is beautiful as—as—it's beautiful as frosting on a birthday-cake!" cried Ruth, as she slipped her feet into the straps of her skees, preparing for her first lesson. "These skees seem so dreadfully long and unmanageable, now I get them on. Like seven-foot table-knives, and my silly feet like orange seeds in the middle of the knives!"

The skees *were* unmanageable.

One climbed up on the other, and Ruth tried to lift her own weight. When she was sliding down a hillock they spread apart, eager to chase things lying in entirely different directions. Ruth came down between them, her pretty nose plowing the wet snow-crust. Carl, speeding beside her, his obedient skees exactly parallel, lifted her and brushed the snow from her furs and her nose. She was laughing.

Falling, getting up, learning at last the zest of coasting and of handling those gigantic skates on level stretches, she accompanied him from hill to hill, through fences, skirting thickets, till they reached a hollow at the heart of a farm where a brooklet led into deeper woods. The afternoon was passing; the swarthy clouds marched grimly from the east; but the low sun red-lettered the day. The country-bred Carl showed her how thin sheets of ice formed on the bank of the stream and jutted out like shelves in an elfin cupboard, delicate and curious-edged as Venetian glass; and how, through an opening in the ice, she could spy upon a secret world of clear water, not dead from winter, but alive with piratical black bugs over sand of exquisitely pale gray, like Lilliputian submarines in a fairy sea.

A rabbit hopped away among the trees beyond them, and Carl, following its trail, read to her the forest hieroglyphics—tracks of rabbit and chipmunk and crow, of field-mouse and house-cat, in the snow-paved city of night animals with its edifices of twiggy underbrush.

The setting sun was overclouded, now; the air sharp; the grove uneasily quiet. Branches, contracting in the returning cold, ticked like a solemn clock of the woodland; and about them slunk the homeless mysteries that, at twilight, revisit even the tiniest forest, to wail of the perished wilderness.

"I know there's Indians sneaking along in there," she whispered, "and wolves and outlaws; and maybe a Hudson Bay factor coming, in a red Mackinaw coat."

"And maybe a mounted policeman and a lost girl."

"Saying which," remarked Ruth, "the brave young man undid his pack and disclosed to the admiring eyes of the hungry lass—meaning me, especially the 'hungry'—the wonders of his pack, which she had been covertly eying amid all the perils of the afternoon."

Carl did not know it, but all his life he had been seeking a girl who would, without apologetic explanation, begin a story with herself and him for its characters. He instantly continued her tale:

"And from the pack the brave young hero, whose new Norfolk jacket she admired such a lot—as I said, from the pack he pulled two clammy, blue, hard-boiled eggs and a thermos bottle filled with tea into which I've probably forgotten to put any sugar."

"And then she stabbed him and went swiftly home!" Ruth concluded the narration.... "Don't be frivolous about food. Just one hard-boiled egg and you perish! None of these gentle 'convenient' shoe-box picnics for me. Of course I ought to pretend that I have a bird-like appetite, but as a matter of fact I could devour an English mutton-chop, four kidneys, and two hot sausages, and then some plum-pudding and a box of chocolates, assorted."

"If this were a story," said Carl, knocking the crusted snow from dead branches and dragging them toward the center of a small clearing, "the young hero from Joralemon would now remind the city gal that 'tis only among God's free hills that you can get an appetite, and then the author would say, 'Nothing had ever tasted so good as those trout, yanked from the brook and cooked to a turn on the sizzling coals. She looked at the stalwart young man, so skilfully frying the flapjacks, and contrasted him with the effeminate fops she had met on Fifth Avenue.'... But meanwhile, squaw, you'd better tear some good dry twigs off this bush for kindling."

Gathering twigs while Carl scrabbled among the roots for dry leaves, Ruth went on again with their story: "'Yes,' said the fair maid o' the wilds, obediently, bending her poor, patient back at the cruel behest of the stern man of granite.... May I put something into the story which will politely indicate how much the unfortunate lady appreciates this heavenly snow-place in contrast to the beastly city, even though she is so abominably treated?"

"Yes, but as I warned you, nothing about the effect of out-o'-doors on the appetite. All you've got to do is to watch a city broker eat fourteen pounds of steak, three pots of coffee, and four black cigars at a Broadway restaurant to realize that the effeminate city man occasionally gets up quite some appetite, too!"

"My dear," she wailed, "aside from the vulgarity of the thing—you know that no one ever admits to a real interest in food—I am so hungry that if there is any more mention of eating I shall go off in a corner and howl. You know how those adorable German Christmas stories always begin: '*Es war Weinachtsabend. Tiefer Schnee lag am Boden. Durch das Wald kam ein armes Mädchen das weinte bitterlich.*' The reason why she weinted bitterlich was because her soul was hurt at being kept out of the secret of the beautiful, beautiful food that was hidden in the hero's pack. Now let's have no more imaginary menus. Let's discuss Nijinsky and the musical asses till you are ready———"

"All ready now!" he proclaimed, kneeling by the pyramid of leaves, twigs, and sticks he had been erecting. He lit a match and kindled a leaf. Fire ran through the mass and rosy light brightened the darkened snow. "By the way," he said, as with cold fingers he pulled at the straps of his pack, "I'm beginning to be afraid that we'll be a lot later getting home than we expected."

"Well, I suppose I'll go to sleep on the train, and wake up at every station and wail and make you uncomfortable, and Mason will be grieved and disapproving when I get home late, but just now I don't care. I don't! It's *la belle aventure!* Carl, do you realize that never in my twenty-four (almost twenty-five now!) never in all these years have I been out like this in the wilds, in the dark, not even with Phil? And yet I don't feel afraid—just terribly happy."

"You do trust me, don't you?"

"You know I do.... Yet when I realize that I really don't know you at all———!"

He had brought out, from the pack, granite-ware plates and cups, a stew-pan and a coffee-pot, a ruddied paper of meat and a can of peas, rolls, Johnny-cake, maple syrup, a screw-top bottle of cream, pasteboard boxes of salt and pepper and sugar. Lamb chops, coiled in the covered stew-pan, loudly broiled in their own fat, and to them the peas, heated in their can, were added when the coffee began to foam. He dragged a large log to the side of the fire, and Ruth, there sitting, gorged shamelessly. Carl himself did not eat reticently.

Light snow was falling now, driven by them on the rising wind. The fire, where hot coals had piled higher and higher, was a refuge in the midst of the darkness. Carl rolled up another log, for protection from the weather, and placed it at right angles to the first.

"You were saying, at Mrs. Needham's, that we ought to have an old farm-house," he remarked, while she snuggled before the fire, her back against a log, her round knees up under her chin, her arms clasping her legs. "Let's build one right here."

Instantly she was living it. In the angle between the logs she laid out an outline of twigs, exclaiming: "Here is my room, with low ceiling and exposed rafters and a big open fireplace. Not a single touch of pale pink or rosebuds!"

"Then here's my room, with a work-bench and a bed nine feet long that I can lose myself in."

"Then here outside my room," said Ruth, "I'm going to have a brick terrace, and all around it heliotrope growing in pots on the brick wall."

"I'm sorry, blessed, but you can't have a terrace. Don't you realize that every brick would have to be carted two hundred miles through this wilderness?"

"I don't care. If you appreciated me you'd carry them on your back, if necessary."

"Well, I'll think it over, but——Oh, look here, I'm going to have a porch made out of fresh saplings, outside of my room, and it 'll overlook the hills, and it 'll have outdoor cots with olive-gray army blankets over them, and when you wake up in the morning you'll see the hills in the first sunlight."

"Glorious! I'll give up my terrace. Though I do think I was w'eedled into it."

"Seriously, Ruth, wouldn't you like to have such a place, back in the wilderness?"

"Love it! I'd be perfectly happy there. At least for a while. I wouldn't care if I never saw another aigrette or a fat Rhine maiden singing in thirty sharps."

"Listen, how would this be for a site? (Let me stick some more wood there on your side of the fire.) Once when I was up in the high Sierras, in California, I found a wooded bluff—you looked a thousand feet straight down to a clear lake, green as mint-sauce pretty nearly, not a wrinkle on it. There wasn't a sound anywhere except when the leaves rustled. Then on the other side you looked way up to a peak covered with snow, and a big eagle sailing overhead—sailing and sailing, hour after hour. And you could smell the pine needles and sit there and look way off——Would you like it?"

"Oh, I can't tell you how much!"

"Have to go there some day."

"When you're president of the VanZile Company you must give me a Touricar to go in, and perhaps I shall let you go, too."

"Right! I'll be chauffeur and cook and everything." Quietly exultant at her sweet, unworded promise of liking, he hastily said, to cover that thrill, "Even a poor old low-brow mechanic like me does get a kind of poetic fervor out of a view like that."

"But you aren't a low-brow mechanic. You make me so dreadfully weary when you're mock-humble. As a matter of fact, you're a famous man and I'm a poor little street waif. For instance, the way you talk about socialism when you get interested and let yourself go. Really excited. I'd always thought that aviators and other sorts of heroes were such stolid dubs."

"Gee! it'd be natural enough if I did like to talk. Imagine the training in being with the English superintendent at the mine, that I was telling you about, and hearing Frazer lecture, and knowing Tony Bean with his South-American interests, and most of all, of course, knowing Forrest Haviland. If I had any pep in me——Course I'm terribly slangy, I suppose, but I couldn't help wading right in and wanting to talk to everybody about everything."

"Yes. Yes. Of course I'm abominably slangy, too. I wonder if every one isn't, except in books.... We've left our house a little unfinished, Carl."

"I'm afraid we'll have to, blessed. We'll have to be going. It's past seven, now; and we must be sure to catch the 8.09 and get back to town about nine."

"I can't tell you how sorry I am we must leave our house in the wilds."

"You really have enjoyed it?" He was cleaning the last of the dishes with snow, and packing them away. "Do you know," he said, cautiously, "I always used to feel that a girl—you say you aren't in society, but I mean a girl like you—I used to think it was impossible to play with such a girl unless a man was rich, which I excessively am not, with my little money tied up in the Touricar. Yet here we have an all-day party, and it costs less than three really good seats at the theater."

"I know. Phil is always saying that he is too poor to have a good time, and yet his grandmother left him fifteen thousand dollars capital in his own right, besides his allowance from his father and his salary from the law firm; and he infuriates me sometimes—aside from the tactlessness of the thing—by quite plainly suggesting that I'm so empty-headed that I won't enjoy going out with him unless he spends a lot of money and makes waiters and ushers obsequious. There are lots of my friends who think that way, both the girls and the men. They never seem to realize that if they were just human beings, as you and I have been to-day, and not hide-bound members of the dance-and-tea league, they could beat that beastly artificial old city.... Phil once told me that *no* man—mind you, no one at all—could possibly marry on less than fifteen thousand dollars a year. Simply proved it beyond a question."

"That lets me out."

"Phil said that no one could possibly live on the West Side—of course the fact that he and I are both living on the West Side doesn't count—and the cheapest good apartments near Fifth Avenue cost four thousand dollars a year. And then one can't possibly get along with less than two cars and four maids and a chauffeur. Can't be done!"

"He's right. Fawncy! Only three maids. Might as well be dead."

The pack was ready, now; he was swinging it to his back and preparing to stamp out the fire. But he dropped his burden and faced her in the low firelight. "Ruth, you won't make up your mind to marry Phil till you're *sure*, will you? You'll play with me awhile, won't you? Can't we explore a few more——"

She laughed nervously, trying to look at him. "As I said, Phil won't condescend to consider poor me till he has his fifteen thousand dollars a year, and that won't be for some time, I think, considering he is too well-bred to work hard."

"But seriously, you will——Oh, I don't know how to put it. You will let me be your playmate, even as much as Phil is, while we're still——"

"Carl, I've never played as much with any one as with you. You make most of the men I know seem very unenterprising. It frightens me. Perhaps I oughtn't to let you jump the fence so easily."

"You *won't* let Phil lock you up for a while?"

"No.... Mustn't we be going?"

"Thank you for letting the outlaw come to your party. The fire's out. Come."

With the quenching of the fire they were left in smothering darkness. "Where do we go?" she worried. "I feel completely lost. I can't make out a thing. I feel so lost and so blind, after looking at the fire."

Her voice betrayed that he was suddenly a stranger to her.

With hasty assurance he said: "Sit tight! See. We head for that tall oak, up the slope, then through the clearing, keeping to the right. You'll be able to see the oak as soon as you get the firelight out of your eyes. Remember I used to hunt every fall, as a kid, and come back through the dark. Don't worry."

"I can just make out the tree now."

"Right. Now for it."

"Let me carry my skees."

"No, you just watch your feet." His voice was pleasant, quiet, not too intimate. "Don't try to guide yourself by your eyes. Let your feet find the safe ground. Your eyes will fool you in the dark."

It was a hard pull, the way back. Encumbered with pack and two pairs of skees, which they dared not use in the darkness, he could not give her a helping hand. The snow was still falling, not very thick nor savagely wind-borne, yet stinging their eyes as they crossed open moors and the wind leaped at them. Once Ruth slipped, on a rock or a chunk of ice, and came down with an infuriating jolt. Before he could drop the skees she struggled up and said, dryly:

"Yes, it did hurt, and I know you're sorry, and there's nothing you can do."

Carl grinned and kept silence, though with one hand, as soon as he could get it free from the elusive skees, he lightly patted her shoulder.

She was almost staggering, so cold was she and so tired, and so heavy was the snow caked on her boots, when they came to a sharp rise, down which shone the radiance of an incandescent light.

"Road's right up there, blessed," he cried, cheerily.

"Oh, I can't——Yes, I will——"

He dropped the skees, put one arm about her shoulders and one about her knees, and almost before she had finished crying, "Oh no, *please* don't carry me!" he was half-way up the slope. He set her down safe by the road.

They caught the 8.09 train with two minutes to spare. Its warmth and the dingy softness of the plush seats seemed palatial.

Ruth rubbed her cold hands with a smile deprecating, intimate; and her shoulder drooped toward him. Her whole being seemed turned toward him. He cuddled her right hand within his, murmuring: "See, my hand's a house where yours can keep warm." Her fingers curled tight and rested there contentedly. Like a drowsy kitten she looked down at their two hands. "A little brown house!" she said.

CHAPTER XXXIV

While scientists seek germs that shall change the world, while war comes or winter takes earth captive, even while love visibly flowers, a power, mighty as any of these, lashes its human pack-train on the dusty road to futility. The Day's Work is the name of that power.

All these days of first love Carl had the office for lowering background. The warm trust of Ruth's hand on a Saturday did not make plans for the Touricar any the less pressing on a Monday. The tyranny of nine to five is stronger, more insistent, in every department of life, than the most officious oligarchy. Inspectors can be bribed, judges softened, and recruiting sergeants evaded, but only the grace of God will turn 3.30 into 5.30. And Mr. Ericson of the Touricar Company, a not vastly important employee of the mothering VanZile Corporation, was not entitled to go home at 3.30, as a really rational man would have done when the sun gold-misted the windows and suggested skating.

No longer was business essentially an adventure to Carl. Doubtless he would have given it up and have gone to Palm Beach to fly a hydro for Bagby, Jr., had there been no Ruth. Bagby wrote that he was coming North, to prepare for the spring's experiments; wouldn't Carl consider joining him?

Carl was now, between his salary and his investment in the Touricar Company, making about four thousand dollars a year, and saving nearly half of it, against the inevitable next change in his life, whatever that should be. He would probably climb to ten thousand dollars in five years. The Touricar was promising success. Several had been ordered at the Automobile Show; the Chicago, Boston, and Philadelphia agents of the company reported interest. For no particular reason, apparently, Milwaukee had taken them up first; three Milwaukee people had ordered cars.... An artist was making posters with beautiful gipsies and a Touricar and tourists whose countenances showed lively appreciation of the efforts of the kind Touricar manufacturers to please and benefit them. But the head salesman of the company laughed at Carl when he suggested that the Touricar might not only bring them money, but really take people off to a larger freedom:

"I don't care a hang where they go with the thing as long as they pay for it. You can't be an idealist and make money. You make the money and then you can have all the ideals you want to, and give away some hospitals and libraries."

They walked and talked, Ruth and Carl. They threaded the Sunday-afternoon throng on upper Broadway, where on every clear Sunday all the apartment-dwellers (if they have remembered to have their trousers pressed or their gloves cleaned in preparation) promenade like stupid black-and-white peacocks past uninteresting apartment-houses and uninspiring upper Broadway shops, while two blocks away glorious Riverside Drive, with its panorama of Hudson and hills and billowing clouds, its trees and secret walks and the Soldiers and Sailors Monument, is nearly deserted. Together they scorned the glossy well-to-do merchant in his newly ironed top-hat, and were thus drawn together. It is written that loving the same cause makes honest friendship; but hating the same people makes alliances so delightful that one can sit up late nights, talking.

At the opening of the flying season Carl took her to the Hempstead Plains Aviation Field, and, hearing his explanations, she at last comprehended emotionally that he really was an aviator.

They tramped through Staten Island; they had tea at the Manhattan. Carl dined with Ruth and her father; once he took her brother, Mason, to lunch at the Aero Club.

Ruth was ill in March; not with a mysterious and romantic malady, but with grippe, which, she wrote Carl, made her hate the human race, New York, charity, and Shakespeare. She could not decide whether to go to Europe, or to die in a swoon and be buried under a mossy headstone.

He answered that he would go abroad for her; and every day she received tokens bearing New York post-marks, yet obviously coming from foreign parts: a souvenir card from the Piræus, stating that Carl was "visiting cousin T. Demetrieff Philopopudopulos, and we are enjoying our drives so much. Dem. sends his love; wish you could be with us"; an absurd string of beads from Port Saïd and a box of Syrian sweets; a Hindu puzzle guaranteed to amuse victims of the grippe, and gold-fabric slippers of China; with long letters nonchalantly relating encounters with outlaws and wrecks and new varieties of disease.

He called on her before her nose had quite lost the grippe or her temper the badness.

Phil Dunleavy was there, lofty and cultured in evening clothes, apparently not eager to go. He stayed till ten minutes to ten, and, by his manner of cold surprise when Carl tried to influence the conversation, was able to keep it to the Kreisler violin recitals, the architecture of St. John the Divine's, and Whitney's polo, while Carl tried not to look sulky, and manœuvered to get out the excellent things he was prepared to say on other topics; not unlike the small boy who wants to interrupt whist-players and tell them about his new skates. When Phil was gone Ruth sighed and said, belligerently:

"Poor Phil, he has to work so hard, and all the people at his office, even the firm, are just as common as they can be; common as the children at my beastly old settlement-house."

"What do you mean by 'common'?" bristled Carl.

"Not of our class."

"What do you mean by 'our class'?"

And the battle was set.

Ruth refused to withdraw "common." Carl recalled Abraham Lincoln and Golden-Rule Jones and Walt Whitman on the subject of the Common People, though as to what these sages had said he was vague. Ruth burst out:

"Oh, you can talk all you like about theories, but just the same, in real life most people are common as dirt. And just about as admissible to Society. It's all very fine to be good to servants, but you would be the first to complain if I invited the cook up here."

"Give her and her children education for three generations——"

She was perfectly unreasonable, and right in most of the things she said. He was perfectly unreasonable, and right in all of the things he said. Their argument was absurdly hot, and hurt them pathetically. It was difficult, at first, for Carl to admit that he was at odds with his playmate. Surely this was a sham dissension, of which they would soon tire, which they would smilingly give up. Then, he was trying not to be too contentious, but was irritated into retorting. After fifteen minutes they were staring at each other as at intruding strangers, he remembering the fact that she was a result of city life; she the fact that he wasn't a product of city life.

And a fact which neither of them realized, save subconsciously, was in the background: Carl himself had come in a few years from Oscar Ericson's back yard to Ruth Winslow's library—he had made the step naturally, as only an American could, but it was a step.

She was loftily polite. "I'm afraid you can't quite understand what the niceties of life mean to people like Phil. I'm sorry he won't give them up to the first truck-driver he meets, but I'm afraid he won't, and occasionally it's necessary to face facts! Niceties of the kind he has gr——"

"*Nice!*"

"Really——" Her heavy eyebrows arched in a frown.

"If you're going to get 'nice' on me, of course you'll have to be condescending, and that's one thing I won't permit."

"I'm afraid you'll find that one has to permit a great many things. Sometimes, apparently, I must permit great rudeness."

"Have I been rude? Have——"

"Yes. Very."

He could endure no more. "Good night!" he growled, and was gone.

He was frightened to find himself out of the house; the door closed between them; no going back without ringing the bell. He couldn't go back. He walked a block, slow, incredulous. He stood hesitant before the nearest corner drug-store, shivering in the March wind, wondering if he dared go into the store and telephone her. He was willing to concede anything. He planned apt phrases to use. Surely everything would be made right if he could only speak to her. He pictured himself crossing the drug-store floor, entering the telephone-booth, putting five cents in the slot. He stared at the red-and-green globes in the druggist's window; inspected a display of soaps, and recollected the fact that for a week now he had failed to take home any shaving-soap and had had to use ordinary hand-soap. "Golly! I must go in and get a shaving-stick. No, darn it! I haven't got enough money with me. I *must* try to remember to get some to-morrow." He rebuked himself for thinking of soap when love lay dying. "But I must remember to get that soap, just the same!" So grotesque is man, the slave and angel, for while he was sick with the desire to go back to the one comrade, he sharply wondered if he was not merely acting all this agony. He went into the store. But he did not telephone to Ruth. There was no sufficiently convincing reason for calling her up. He bought a silly ice-cream soda, and talked to the man behind the counter as he drank it. All the while a tragic Ruth stood before him, blaming him for he knew not what.

He reluctantly went on, regretting every step that took him from her. But as he reached the next corner his shoulders snapped back into defiant straightness, he thrust his hands into the side pockets of his top-coat, and strode away, feeling that he had shaken off a burden of "niceness." He had, willy-nilly, recovered his freedom. He could go anywhere, now; mingle with any sort of people; be common and comfortable. He didn't have to take dancing lessons or fear the results of losing his job, or of being robbed of his interests in the Touricar. He glanced interestedly at a pretty girl; recklessly went into a cigar-store and bought a fifteen-cent cigar. He was free again.

As he marched on, however, his defiance began to ooze away. He went over every word Ruth or he had said, and when he reached his room he sat deep in an arm-chair, like a hurt animal crouching, his coat still on, his felt hat over his eyes, his tie a trifle disarranged, his legs straight out before him, his hands in his trousers pockets, while he disconsolately contemplated a photograph of Forrest Haviland in full-dress uniform that stood on the low bureau among tangled ties, stray cigarettes, a bronze aviation medal, cuff-buttons, and a haberdasher's round package of new collars. His gaze was steady and gloomy. He was dramatizing himself as hero in a melodrama. He did not know how the play would end.

But his dramatization of himself did not indicate that he was not in earnest.

Forrest's portrait suggested to him, as it had before, that he had no picture of Ruth, that he wanted one. Next time he saw her he would ask her.... Then he remembered.

He took out his new cigar, turned it over and over gloweringly, and chewed it without lighting it, the right corner of his mouth vicious in appearance. But his tone was plaintive as he mourned, "How did it all start, anyway?"

He drew off his top-coat and shoes, and put on his shabby though once expensive slippers. Slowly. He lay on his bed. He certainly did not intend to go to sleep—but he awoke at 2 A.M., dressed, the light burning, his windows closed, feeling sweaty and hot and dirty and dry-mouthed—a victim of all the woes since tall Troy burned. He shucked off his clothes as you shuck an ear of corn.

When he awoke in the morning he lay as usual, greeting a shining new day, till he realized that it was not a shining day; it was an ominous day; everything was wrong. That something had happened—really had—was a fact that sternly patrolled his room. His chief reaction was not repentance nor dramatic interest, but a vexed longing to unwish the whole affair. "Hang it!" he groaned.

Already he was eager to make peace. He sympathized with Ruth. "Poor kid! it was rotten to row with her, her completely all in with the grippe."

At three in the afternoon he telephoned to her house. "Miss Ruth," he was informed, "was asleep; she was not very well."

Would the maid please ask Miss Ruth to call Mr. Ericson when she woke?

Certainly the maid would.

But by bedtime Ruth had not telephoned. Self-respect would not let him call again, for days, and Ruth never called him.

He went about alternately resentful at her stubbornness and seeing himself as a lout cast out of heaven. Then he saw her at a distance, on the platform of the subway station at Seventy-second Street. She was with Phil Dunleavy. She looked well, she was talking gaily, oblivious of old sorrows, certainly not in need of Carl Ericson.

That was the end, he knew. He watched them take a train; stood there alone, due at a meeting of the Aeronautical Society, but suddenly not wishing to go, not wishing to go anywhere nor do anything, friendless, bored, driftwood in the city.

So easily had the Hawk swooped down into her life, coming by chance, but glad to remain. So easily had he been driven away.

For three days he planned in a headachy way to make an end of his job and join Bagby, Jr., in his hydroaeroplane experiments. He pictured the crowd that would worship him. He told himself stories unhappy and long about the renewed companionship of Ruth and Phil. He was sure that he, the stranger, had been a fool to imagine that he could ever displace Phil. On the third afternoon, suddenly, apparently without cause, he bolted from the office, and at a public telephone-booth he called Ruth. It was she who answered the telephone.

"May I come up to-night?" he said, urgently.

"Yes," she said. That was all.

When he saw her, she hesitated, smiled shamefacedly, and confessed that she had wanted to telephone to him.

Together, like a stage chorus, they contested:

"I was grouchy——"

"I was beastly——"

"I'm honestly sorry——"

"'ll you forgive——"

"What was it all about?"

"Really, I do—not—know!"

"I agree with lots of the things you——"

"No, I agree with you, but just at the time—you know."

Her lively, defensive eyes were tender. He put his arm lightly about her shoulders—lightly, but his finger-tips were sensitive to every thread of her thin bodice that seemed tissue as warmly living as the smooth shoulder beneath. She pressed her eyes against his coat, her coiled dark hair beneath his chin. A longing to cry like a boy, and to care for her like a man, made him reverent. The fear of Phil vanished. Intensely conscious though he was of her hair and its individual scent, he did not kiss it. She was sacred.

She sprang from him, and at the piano hammered out a rattling waltz. It changed to gentler music, and under the shaded piano-lamp they were silent, happy. He merely touched her hand, when he went, but he sang his way home, wanting to nod to every policeman.

"I've found her again; it isn't merely play, now!" he kept repeating. "And I've learned something. I don't really know what it is, but it's as though I'd learned a new language. Gee! I'm happy!"

CHAPTER XXXV

On an April Saturday morning Carl rose with a feeling of spring. He wanted to be off in the Connecticut hills, among the silvery-gray worm-fences, with larks rising on the breeze and pools a-ripple and yellow crocus-blossoms afire by the road, where towns white and sleepy woke to find the elms misted with young green. Would there be any crocuses out as yet? That was the only question worth solving in the world, save the riddle of Ruth's heart. The staid brownstone houses of the New York streets displayed few crocuses and fewer larks, yet over them to-day was the bloom of romance. Carl walked down to the automobile district past Central Park, sniffing wistfully at the damp grass, pale green amid old gray; marveling how a bare patch of brown earth, without a single blade of grass, could smell so stirringly of coming spring. A girl on Broadway was selling wild violets, white and purple, and in front of wretched old houses down a side-street, in the negro district, a darky in a tan derby and a scarlet tie was caroling:

"Mandy, in de springDe mocking-birds do sing,An' de flowers am so sweet along de ol' bayou——"

Above the darky's head, elevated trains roared on the Fifty-third Street trestle, and up Broadway streaked a stripped motor-car, all steel chassis and grease-mottled board seat and lurid odor of gasoline. But sparrows splashed in the pools of sunshine; in a lull the darky's voice came again, chanting passionately, "In de spring, spring, *spring*!" and Carl clamored: "I've *got* to get out to-day. Terrible glad it's a half-holiday. Wonder if I dare telephone to Ruth?"

At a quarter to three they were rollicking down the "smart side" of Fifth Avenue. One could see that they were playmates, by her dancing steps and his absorption in her. He bent a little toward her, quick to laugh with her.

Ruth was in a frock of flowered taffeta. "I won't wait till Easter to show off my spring clothes. It isn't done any more," she said. "It's as stupid as Bobby's not daring to wear a straw hat one single day after September fifteenth. Is an aviator brave enough to wear his after the fifteenth?... Think! I didn't know you then—last September. I can't understand it."

"But I knew you, blessed, because I was sure spring was coming again, and that distinctly implied Ruth."

"Of course it did. You've guessed my secret. I'm the Spirit of Spring. Last Wednesday, when I lost my marquise ring, I was the spirit of vitriol, but now——I'm a poet. I've thought it all out and decided that I shall be the American Sappho. At any moment I am quite likely to rush madly across the pavement and sit down on the curb and indite several stanzas on the back of a calling-card, while the crowd galumps around me in an awed ring.... I feel like kidnapping you and making you take me aeroplaning, but I'll compromise. You're to buy me a book and take me down to the Maison Épinay for tea, and read me poetry while I yearn over the window-boxes and try to look like Nicollette. Buy me a book with spring in it, and a princess, and a sky like this—cornflower blue with bunny-rabbit clouds."

At least a few in the Avenue's flower-garden of pretty débutantes in pairs and young university men with expensive leather-laced tan boots were echoing Ruth in gay, new clothes.

"I wonder who they all are; they look like an aristocracy, useless but made of the very best materials," said Carl.

"They're like maids of honor and young knights, disguised in modern costumes! They're charming!"

"Charmingly useless," insisted our revolutionary, but he did not sound earnest. It was too great a day for earnestness about anything less great than joy and life; a day for shameless luxuriating in the sun, and for wearing bright things. In shop windows with curtains of fluted silk were silver things and jade; satin gowns and shoe-buckles of rhinestones. The sleek motor-cars whisked by in an incessant line; the traffic policemen nodded familiarly to hansom-drivers; pools on the asphalt mirrored the delicate sky, and at every corner the breeze tasted of spring.

Carl bought for her Yeats's poems, tucked it under his arm, and they trotted off. In Madison Square they saw a gallant and courtly old man with military shoulders and pink cheeks, a debonair gray mustache, and a smile of unquenchable youth, greeting April with a narcissus in his buttonhole. He was feeding the sparrows with crumbs and smiled to see one of them fly off, carrying a long wisp of hay, bustling away to build for himself and his sparrow bride a bungalow in the foot-hills of the Metropolitan Tower.

"I love that old man!" exclaimed Ruth. "I do wish we could pick him up and take him with us. I dare you to go over and say, 'I prithee, sir, of thy good will come thou forthfaring with two vagabonds who do quest high and low the land of Nowhere.' Something like that. Go on, Carl, be brave. Pretend you're brave as an aviator. Perhaps he has a map of Arcadia. Go ask him."

"Afraid to. Besides, he might monopolize you."

"He'll go with us, without his knowing it, anyway. Isn't it strange how you know people, perfect strangers, from seeing them once, without even speaking to them? You know them the rest of your life and play games with them."

The Maison Épinay you must quest long, but great is your reward if you find it. Here is no weak remembrance of a lost Paris, but a French-Canadian's desire to express what he believes Paris must be; therefore a super-Paris, all in brown velvet and wicker tables, and at the back a long window edged with boxes red with geraniums, looking to a back-yard garden where rose-beds lead to a dancing-faun terminal in a shrine of ivy.

They sipped grenadine, heavy essence of a thousand berries. They had the place to themselves, save for Tony the waiter, with his smile of benison; and Carl read from Yeats.

He had heard of Yeats at Plato, but never had he known crying curlew and misty mere and the fluttering wings of Love till now.

His hand rested on her gloved hand.... Tony the waiter re-re-rearranged the serving-table.... When Ruth broke the spell with, "You aren't very reverent with perfectly clean gloves," they chattered like blackbirds at sunset.

Carl discovered that, being a New-Yorker, she knew part of it as intimately as though it were a village, and nothing about the rest. She had taught him Fifth Avenue; told him the history of the invasion by shops, the social differences between East and West; pointed out the pictures of friends in photographers' wall-cases. Now he taught her the various New Yorks he had discovered in lonely rambles. Together they explored Chelsea Village section, and the Oxford quadrangles of General Theological Seminary, where quiet meditation dwells in Tudor corridors; upper Greenwich Village, the home of Italian *tables d'hôte*, clerks, social-workers, and radical magazines, of alley rookeries and the ancient Jewish burying-ground; lower Greenwich Village, where run-down American families with Italian lodgers live on streets named for kings, in wooden houses with gambrel roofs and colonial fanlights. From the same small-paned windows where frowsy Italian women stared down upon Ruth, Ruth's ancestors had leaned out to greet General George Washington.

On an open wharf near Tenth Street they were bespelled by April. The Woolworth Tower, to the south, was an immortal shaft of ivory and gold against an unwinking blue sky, challenging the castles and cathedrals of the Old World, and with its supreme art dignifying the commerce which built and uses it. The Hudson was lustrous with sun, and a sweet wind sang from unknown Jersey hills across the river. Moored to the wharf was a coal-barge, with a tiny dwelling-cabin at whose windows white curtains fluttered. Beside the cabin was a garden tended by the bargeman's comely white-browed wife; a dozen daisies and geraniums in two starch-boxes.

Forging down the river a scarred tramp steamer, whose rusty sides the sun turned to damask rose, bobbed in the slight swell, heading for open sea, with the British flag a-flicker and men chanting as they cleared deck.

"I wish we were going off with her—maybe to Singapore or Nagasaki," Carl said, slipping his arm through hers, as they balanced on the stringpiece of the wharf, sniffing like deer at the breeze, which for a moment seemed to bear, from distant burgeoning woods, a shadowy hint of burning leaves—the perfume of spring and autumn, the eternal wander-call.

"Yes!" Ruth mused; "and moonlight in Java, and the Himalayas on the horizon, and the Vale of Cashmir."

"But I'm glad we have this. Blessed, it's a day planned for lovers like us."

"Carl!"

"Yes. Lovers. Courting. In spring. Like all lovers."

"Really, Carl, even spring doesn't quite let me forget the *convenances* are home waiting."

"We're not lovers?"

"No, we——"

"Yet you enjoy to-day, don't you?"

"Yes, but——"

"And you'd rather be loafing on a dirty wharf, looking at a tramp steamer, than taking tea at the Plaza?"

"Yes, just now, perhaps——"

"And you're protesting because you feel it's proper to——"

"It——"

"And you really trust me so much that you're having difficulty in seeming alarmed?"

"Really——"

"And you'd rather play around with me than any of the Skull and Bones or Hasty Pudding men you know? Or foreign diplomats with spade beards?"

"At least they wouldn't——"

"Oh yes they would, if you'd let them, which you wouldn't.... So, to sum up, then, we *are* lovers and it's spring and you're glad of it, and as soon as you get used to it you'll be glad I'm so frank. Won't you?"

"I will not be bullied, Carl! You'll be having me married to you before I can scream for help, if I don't start at once."

"Probably."

"Indeed you will not! I haven't the slightest intention of letting you get away with being masterful."

"Yes, I know, blessed; these masterful people bore me, too. But aren't we modern enough so we can discuss frankly the question of whether I'd better propose to you, some day?"

"But, boy, what makes you suppose that I have any information on the subject? That I've ever thought of it?"

"I credit you with having a reasonable knowledge that there are such things as marriage."

"Yes, but——Oh, I'm very confused. You've bullied me into such a defensive position that my instinct is to deny everything. If you turned on me suddenly and accused me of wearing gloves I'd indignantly deny it."

"Meantime, not to change the subject, I'd better be planning and watching for a suitable day for proposing, don't you think? Consider it. Here's this young Ericson—some sort of a clerk, I believe—no, don't *think* he's a university man——You know; discuss it clearly. Think it might be better to propose to-day? I ask your advice as a woman."

"Oh, Carl dear, I think not to-day. I'm sorry, but I really don't think so."

"But some time, perhaps?"

"Some time, perhaps!" Then she fled from him and from the subject.

They talked, after that, only of the sailors that loafed on West Street, but in their voices was content.

They crossed the city, and on Brooklyn Bridge watched the suburbanites going home, crowding surface-car and elevated. From their perch on the giant spider's web of steel, they saw the Long Island Sound steamers below them, passing through a maelstrom of light on waves that trembled like quicksilver.

They found a small Italian restaurant, free of local-color hounds and what Carl called "hobohemians," and discovered *fritto misto* and Chianti and *zabaglione*—a pale-brown custard flavored like honey and served in tall, thin, curving glasses—while the fat proprietress, in a red shawl and a large brooch, came to ask them, "Everyt'ing all-aright, eh?" Carl insisted that Walter MacMonnies, the aviator, had once tried out a motor that was exactly like her, including the Italian accent. There was simple and complete bliss for them in the dingy pine-and-plaster room, adorned with fly-specked calendars and pictures of Victor Emmanuel and President McKinley, copies of the *Bolletino Della Sera* and large vinegar bottles.

The theater was their destination, but they first loitered up Broadway, shamelessly stopping to stare at shop windows, pretending to be Joe the shoe-clerk and Becky the cashier furnishing a Bronx flat. Whether it was anything but a game to Ruth will never be known; but to Carl there was a hidden high excitement in planning a flower-box for the fire-escape.

Apropos of nothing, she said, as they touched elbows with the sweethearting crowd: "You were right. I'm sorry I ever felt superior to what I called 'common people.' People! I love them all. It's——Come, we must hurry. I hate to miss that one perfect second when the orchestra is quiet and the lights wink at you and the curtain's going up."

During the second act of the play, when the heroine awoke to love, Carl's hand found hers.

And it must have been that night when, standing between the inner and outer doors of her house, Carl put his arms about her, kissed her hair, timidly kissed her sweet, cold cheek, and cried, "Bless you, dear." But, for some reason, he does not remember when he did first kiss her, though he had looked forward to that miracle for weeks. He does not understand the reason; but there is the fact. Her kisses were big things to him, yet possibly there were larger psychological changes which occulted everything else, at first. But it must have been on that night that he first kissed her. For certainly it was when he called on her a week later that he kissed her for the second time.

They had been animated but decorous, that evening a week later. He had tried to play an improvisation called "The Battle of San Juan Hill," with a knowledge of the piano limited to the fact that if you struck alternate keys at the same time, there appeared not to be a discord.

"I must go now," he said, slowly, as though the bald words had a higher significance. She tried to look at him, and could not. His arms circled her, with frightened happiness. She tilted back her head, and there was the ever-new surprise of blue irises under dark brows. Uplifted wonder her eyes spoke. His head drooped till he kissed her lips. The two bodies clamored for each other. But she unwound his arms, crying, "No, no, no!"

He was enfolded by a sensation that they had instantly changed from friendly strangers to intimate lovers, as she said: "I don't understand it, Carl. I've never let a man kiss me like that. Oh, I suppose I've flirted, like most girls, and been kissed sketchily at silly dances. But this——Oh, Carl, Carl dear, don't ever kiss me again till—oh, not till I *know*. Why, I'm scarcely acquainted with you! I do know how dear you are, but it appals me when I think of how little background you have for me. Dear, I don't want to be sordid and spoil this moment, but I do know that when you're gone I'll be a coward and remember that there are families and things, and want to wait till I know how they like you, at the very least. Good night, and I——"

"Good night, dear blessed. I know."

CHAPTER XXXVI

There were, as Ruth had remarked, families.

When Carl was formally invited to dine at the Winslows', on a night late in April, his only anxiety was as to the condition of his dinner-coat. He arrived in a state of easy briskness, planning apt and sensible remarks about the business situation for Mason and Mr. Winslow. As the maid opened the door Carl was wondering if he would be able to touch Ruth's hand under the table. He had an anticipatory fondness for all of the small friendly family group which was about to receive him.

And he was cast into a den of strangers, most of them comprised in the one electric person of Aunt Emma Truegate Winslow.

Aunt Emma Truegate Winslow was the general-commanding in whatsoever group she was placed by Providence (with which she had strong influence). At a White House reception she would pleasantly but firmly have sent the President about his business, and have taken his place in the receiving line. Just now she sat in a pre-historic S chair, near the center of the drawing-room, pumping out of Phil Dunleavy most of the facts about his chiefs' private lives.

Aunt Emma had the soul of a six-foot dowager duchess, and should have had an eagle nose and a white pompadour. Actually, she was of medium height, with a not unduly maternal bosom, a broad, commonplace face, hair the color of faded grass, a blunt nose with slightly enlarged pores, and thin lips that seemed to be a straight line when seen from in front, but, seen in profile, puffed out like a fish's. She had a habit of nodding intelligently even when she was not listening, and another habit of rubbing her left knuckles with the fingers of her right hand. Not imposing in appearance was Aunt Emma Truegate Winslow, but she was born to discipline a court.

An impeccable widow was she, speaking with a broad A, and dressed exquisitely in a black satin evening gown.

By such simple-hearted traits as being always right about unimportant matters and idealistically wrong about important matters, politely intruding into everything, being earnest about the morality of the poor and auction bridge and the chaperonage of nice girls, possessing a working knowledge of Wagner and Rodin, wearing fifteen-dollar corsets, and believing on her bended knees that the Truegates and Winslows were the noblest families in the Social Register, Aunt Emma Truegate Winslow had persuaded the whole world, including even her near-English butler, that she was a superior woman. Family tradition said that she had only to raise a finger to get into really smart society. Upon the death of Ruth's mother, Aunt Emma had taken it as one of her duties, along with symphony concerts and committees, to rear Ruth properly. She had been neglecting this duty so far as to permit the invasion of a barbarian named Ericson only because she had been in California with her young son, Arthur. Just now, while her house was being opened, she was staying at the Winslows', with Arthur and a peculiarly beastly Japanese spaniel named Taka-San.

She was introduced at Carl, she glanced him over, and passed him on to Olive Dunleavy, all in forty-five seconds. When Carl had recovered from a sensation of being a kitten drowned in a sack, he said agreeable things to Olive, and observed the situation in the drawing-room.

Phil was marked out for Aunt Emma's favors; Mr. Winslow sat in a corner, apparently crushed, with restorative conversation administered by Ruth; Mason Winslow was haltingly attentive to a plain, well-dressed, amiable girl named Florence Crewden, who had prematurely gray hair, the week-end habit, and a weakness for baby talk. Ruth's medical-student brother, Bobby Winslow, was not there. The more he saw of Bobby's kind Aunt Emma, the more Carl could find it in his heart to excuse Bobby for having escaped the family dinner.

Carl had an uncomfortable moment when Aunt Emma and Mr. Winslow asked him questions about the development of the Touricar. But before he could determine whether he was being deliberately inspected by the family the ordeal was over.

As they went in to dinner, Mr. Winslow taking in Aunt Emma like a small boy accompanying the school principal, Ruth had the chance to whisper: "My Hawk, be good. Please believe I'm not responsible. It's all Aunt Emma's doing, this dreadfully stately family dinner. Don't let her bully you. I'm frightened to death and——Yes, Phil, I'm coming."

The warning did not seem justified in view of the attractive table—candles, cut glass, a mound of flowers on a beveled mirror, silvery linen, and grapefruit with champagne. Carl was at one side of Aunt Emma, but she seemed more interested in Mr. Winslow, at the end of the table; and on his other side Carl had a safe companion in Olive Dunleavy. Across from him were Florence Crewden, Phil, and Ruth—Ruth shimmering in a gown of yellow satin, which broke the curves of her fine, flushed shoulders only by a narrow band.

The conversation played with people. Florence Crewden told, to applause and laughter, of an exploratory visit to the College of the City of New York, and her discovery of a strange race, young Jews mostly, who went to college to study, and had no sense of the nobility of "making" fraternities.

"Such outsiders!" she said. "Can't you imagine the sort of a party they'd have—they'd all stand around and discuss psychology and dissecting puppies and Greek roots! Phil, I think it would be a lovely punishment for you to have to join them—to work in a laboratory all day and wear a celluloid collar."

"Oh, I know their sort; 'greasy grinds' we used to call them; there were plenty of them in Yale," condescended Phil.

"Maybe they wear celluloid collars—if they do—because they're poor," protested Ruth.

"My dear child," sniffed Aunt Emma, "with collars only twenty-five cents apiece? Don't be silly!"

Mr. Winslow declared, with portly timidity, "Why, Em, my collars don't cost me but fifteen——"

"Mason dear, let's not discuss it at dinner.... Tell me, all of you, the scandal I've missed by going to California. Which reminds me; did I tell you I saw that miserable Amy Baslin, you remember, that married the porter or the superintendent or something in her father's factory? I saw her and her husband at Pasadena, and they seemed to be happy. Of course Amy would put the best face she could on it, but they must have been miserably unhappy—such a sad affair, and she could have married quite decently."

"What do you mean by 'decently'?" Ruth demanded.

Carl was startled. He had once asked Ruth the same question about the same phrase.

Aunt Emma revolved like a gun-turret getting Ruth's range, and remarked, calmly: "My dear child, you know quite well what I mean. Don't, I beg of you, bring any socialistic problems to dinner till you have really learned something about them.... Now I want to hear all the nice scandals I have missed."

There were not many she had missed; but she kept the conversation sternly to discussions of people whose names Carl had never heard. Again he was obviously an Outsider. Still ignoring Carl, Aunt Emma demanded of Ruth and Phil, sitting together opposite her:

"Tell me about the good times you children have been having, Ruthie. I am so glad that Phil and you finally went to the William Truegates'. And your letter about the Beaux Arts festival was charming, Ruthie. I quite envied you and Phil."

The dragon continued talking to Ruth, while Carl listened, in the interstices of his chatter to Olive:

"I hope you haven't been giving all your time and beauty-sleep doing too much of that settlement work, Ruthie—and Heaven only knows what germs you will get there—of course I should be the first to praise any work for the poor, ungrateful and shiftless though they are—what with my committees and the Truegate Temperance Home for Young Working Girls—it's all very well to be sympathetic with them, but when it comes to a settlement-house, and Heaven knows I have given them all the counsel and suggestions I could, though some of the professional settlement workers are as pert as they can be, and I really do believe some of them think they are trying to end poverty entirely, just as though the Lord would have sent poverty into the world if He didn't have a very good reason for it—you will remember the Bible says, 'The poor you always have with you,' and as Florence Barclay says in her novels, which may seem a little sentimental, but they are of such a good moral effect, you can't supersede the Scriptures even in the most charming social circles. To say nothing of the blessings of poverty, I'm sure they're much happier than we are, with our onerous duties, I'm sure that if any of these ragamuffin anarchists and socialists and anti-militarists want to take over my committees they are welcome, if they'll take over the miserable headaches and worried hours they give me, trying to do something for the poor, they won't even be clean but even in model tenements they will put coal in the bath-tubs. And so I do hope you haven't just been wearing yourself to a bone working for ungrateful dirty little children, Ruthie."

"No, auntie dear, I've been quite as discreet as any Winslow should be. You see, I'm selfish, too. Aren't I, Carl?"

"Oh, very."

Aunt Emma seemed to remember, then, that some sort of a man, whose species she didn't quite know, sat next to her. She glanced at Carl, again gave him up as an error in social judgment, and went on:

"No, Ruthie, not selfish so much as thoughtless about the duties of a family like ours—and I was always the first to say that the Winslows are as fine a stock as the Truegates. And I am going to see that you go out more the rest of this year, Ruthie. I want you and Phil to plan right now to attend the Charity League dances next season. You must learn to concentrate your attention——"

"Auntie dear, please leave my wickedness till the next time we——"

"My dear child, now that I have the chance to get all of us together—I'm sure Mr. Ericson will pardon the rest of us our little family discussions—I want to take you and Master Phil to task together. You are both of you negligent of social duties—duties they are, Ruthie, for man was not born to serve alone—though Phil is far better than you, with your queer habits, and Heaven only knows where you got them, neither your father nor your dear sainted mother was slack or selfish——"

"Dear auntie, let's admit that I'm a black sheep with a little black muzzle and a habit of butting all sorts of ash-cans; and let Phil go on his social way rejoicing."

Ruth was jaunty, but her voice was strained, and she bit her lip with staccato nervousness when she was not speaking. Carl ventured to face the dragon.

"Mrs. Winslow, I'm sure Ruth has been better than you think; she has been learning all these fiendishly complicated new dances. You know a poor business man like myself finds them——"

"Yes," said Aunt Emma, "I am sure she will always remember that she is a Winslow, and must carry on the family traditions, but sometimes I am afraid she gets under bad influences, because of her good nature." She said it loudly. She looked Carl in the eye.

The whole table stopped talking. Carl felt like a tramp who has kicked a chained bulldog and discovers that the chain is broken.

He wanted to be good; not make a scene. He noticed with intense indignation that Phil was grinning. He planned to get Phil off in a corner, not necessarily a dark corner, and beat him. He wanted to telegraph Ruth; dared not. He realized, in a quarter-second, that he must have been discussed by the Family, and did not like it.

Every one seemed to be waiting for him to speak. Awkwardly he said, wondering all the while if she meant what her tone said she meant, by "bad influences":

"Yes, but——Just going to say——I believe settlement work is a good influence——"

"Please don't discuss——" Ruth was groaning, when Aunt Emma sternly interrupted:

"It is good of you to take up the cudgels, Mr. Ericson, and please don't misjudge me—of course I realize that I am only a silly old woman and that my passion to see the Winslows keep to their fine standards is old-fashioned, but you see it is a hobby of mine that I've devoted years to, and you who haven't known the Winslows so very long——" Her manner was almost courteous.

"Yes, that's so," Carl mumbled, agreeably, just as she dropped the courtesy and went on:

"———you can't judge—in fact (this is nothing personal, you know) I don't suppose it's possible for Westerners to have any idea how precious family ideals are to Easterners. Of course we're probably silly about them, and it's splendid, your wheat-lands, and not caring who your grandfather was; but to make up for those things we do have to protect what we have gained through the generations."

Carl longed to stand up, to defy them all, to cry: "If you mean that you think Ruth has to be protected against me, have the decency to say so." Yet he kept his voice gentle:

"But why be narrowed to just a few families in one's interests? Now this settlement———"

"One isn't narrowed. There are plenty of *good* families for Ruth to consider when it comes time for my little girl to consider alliances at all!" Aunt Emma coldly stated.

"I *will* shut up!" he told himself. "I will shut up. I'll see this dinner through, and then never come near this house again." He tried to look casual, as though the conversation was safely finished. But Aunt Emma was waiting for him to go on. In the general stillness her corsets creaked with belligerent attention. He played with his fork in a "Well, if that's how you feel about it, perhaps it would be better not to discuss it any further, my dear madam," manner, growing every second more flushed, embarrassed, sick, angry; trying harder every second to look unconcerned.

Aunt Emma hawked a delicate and ladylike hawk in her patrician throat, prefatory to a new attack. Carl knew he would be tempted to retort brutally.

Then from the door of the dining-room whimpered the high voice of an excited child:

"Oh, mamma, oh, Cousin Ruthie, nurse says Hawk Ericson is here! I want to see him!"

Every one turned toward a boy of five or six, round as a baby chicken, in his fuzzy miniature pajamas, protectingly holding a cotton monkey under his arm, sturdy and shy and defiant.

"Why, Arthur!" "Why, my son!" "Oh, the darling baby!" from the table.

"Come here, Arthur, and let's hear your troubles before nurse nabs you, old son," said Phil, not at all condescendingly, rising from the table, holding out his arms.

"No, no! You just let me go! I want to see Hawk Ericson. Is that Hawk Ericson?" demanded the son of Aunt Emma, pointing at Carl.

"Yes, sweetheart," said Ruth, softly, proudly.

Running madly about the end of the table, Arthur jumped at Carl's lap.

Carl swung him up and inquired, "What is it, old man?"

"Are you Hawk Ericson?"

"At your commands, cap'n."

Aunt Emma rose and said, masterfully, "Come, little son, now you've seen Mr. Ericson it's up to beddie again, up—to—beddie."

"No, no; please no, mamma! I've never seen a' aviator before, not in all my life, and you promised me 'cross your heart, at Pasadena you did, I could see one."

Arthur's face showed signs of imminent badness.

"Well, you may stay for a while, then," said Aunt Emma, weakly, unconscious that her sway had departed from her, while the rest of the table grinned, except Carl, who was absorbed in Arthur's ecstasy.

"I'm going to be a' aviator, too; I think a' aviator is braver than anybody. I'd rather be a' aviator than a general or a policeman or anybody. I got a picture of you in my scrap-book—you got a funny hat like Cousin Bobby wears when he plays football in it. Shall I get you the picture in my scrap-book?... Honest, will you give me another?"

Aunt Emma made one more attempt to coax Arthur up to bed, but his Majesty refused, and she compromised by scolding his nurse and sending up for his dressing-gown, a small, blue dressing-gown on which yellow ducks and white bunny-rabbits paraded proudly.

"Like our blue bowl!" Carl remarked to Ruth.

Not till after coffee in the drawing-room would Arthur consent to go to bed. This real head of the Emma Winslow family was far too much absorbed in making Carl tell of his long races, and "Why does a flying-machine fly? What's a wind pressure? Why does the wind shove up? Why is the wings curved? Why does it want to catch the wind?" The others listened, including even Aunt Emma.

Carl went home early. Ruth had the opportunity to confide:

"Hawk dear, I can't tell you how ashamed I am of my family for enduring anybody so rude and opinionated as Aunt Emma. But—it's all right, now, isn't it?... No, no, don't kiss me, but—dear dreams, Hawk."

Phil's voice, from behind, shouted: "Oh, Ericson! Just a second."

Carl was not at all pleased. He remembered that Phil had listened with obvious amusement to his agonized attempt to turn Aunt Emma's attacks.

Said Phil, while Ruth disappeared: "Which way you going? Walk to the subway with you. You win, old man. I admire your nerve for facing Aunt Emma. What I wanted to say——I hope to thunder you don't think I was in any way responsible for Mrs. Winslow's linking me and Ruth that way and——Oh, you understand. I admire you like the devil for knowing what you want and going after it. I suppose you'll have to convince Ruth yet, but, by Jove! you've convinced me! Glad you had Arthur for ally. They don't make kiddies any better. God! if I could have a son like that——I turn off here. G-good luck, Ericson."

"Thanks a lot, Phil."

"Thanks. Good night, Carl."

CHAPTER XXXVII

Long Beach, on the first hot Sunday of May, when motorists come out from New York, half-ready to open asphalt hearts to sea and sky. Carl's first sight of it, save from an aeroplane, and he was mad-happy to find real shore so near the city.

Ruth and he were picnicking, vulgar and unashamed, among the dunes at the end of the long board-walk, like the beer-drinking, pickle-eating parties of fishermen and the family groups with red table-cloths, grape-basket lunches, and colored Sunday supplements. Ruth declared that she preferred them to the elegant loungers who were showing off new motor-coats on the board-walk. But Carl and she had withdrawn a bit from the crowds, and in the dunes had made a nest, with a book and a magazine and a box of chocolates and Carl's collapsible lunch-kit.

Not New York only, but all of Ruth's relatives were forgot. Aunt Emma Truegate Winslow was a myth of the dragon-haunted past. Here all was fresh color and free spaces looking to open sea. Behind the dunes, with their traceries of pale grass, reveled the sharp, unshadowed green of marshes, and an inland bay that was blue as bluing, a startling blue, bordered by the emerald marshes. To one side—afar, not troubling their peace—were the crimson roofs of fantastic houses, like chalets and California missions and villas of the Riviera, with gables and turrets of red tiles.

Before their feet was the cream-colored beach, marked by ridges of driftwood mixed with small glistening shells, long ranks of pale-yellow seaweed, and the delicate wrinkles in the sand that were the tracks of receding waves. The breakers left the beach wet and shining for a moment, like plates of raw-colored copper, making one cry out with its flashing beauty. Then, at last, the eyes lifted to unbroken bluewater—nothing between them and Europe save rolling waves and wave-crests like white plumes. The sea was of a diaphanous blue that shaded through a bold steel blue and a lucent blue enamel to a rich ultramarine which absorbed and healed the office-worn mind. The sails of tacking sloops were a-blossom; sea-gulls swooped; a tall surf-fisherman in red flannel shirt and shiny black hip-boots strode out into the water and cast with a long curve of his line; cumulus clouds, whose pure white was shaded with a delicious golden tone, were baronial above; and out on the sky-line the steamers raced by.

Round them was the warm intimacy of the dune sands; beyond was infinite space calling to them to be big and unafraid.

Talking, falling into silences touched with the mystery of sun and sea, they confessed youth's excited wonder about the world; Carl sitting cross-legged, rubbing his ankles, a springy figure in blue flannel and a daring tie; while Ruth, in deep-rose linen, her throat bright and bare, lay with her chin in her hands, a flush beneath the gentle brown of her cheeks, her white-clad ankles crossed under her skirt, slender against the gray sand, thoughtful of eye, lost in happiness.

"Some day," Carl was musing, "your children and mine will say, 'You certainly lived in the most marvelous age in the world.' Think of it. They talk about the romance of the Crusades and the Romans and all that, but think of the miracles we've seen already, and we're only kids. Aviation and the automobile and wireless and moving pictures and electric locomotives and electric cooking and the use of radium and the X-ray and the linotype and the submarine and the labor movement—the I. W. W. and syndicalism and all that—not that I know anything about the labor movement, but I suppose it's the most important of all. And Metchnikoff and Ehrlich. Oh yes, and a good share of the development of the electric light and telephone and the phonograph.... Golly! In just a few years!"

"Yes," Ruth added, "and Montessori's system of education—that's what I think is the most important.... See that sail-boat, Hawk! Like a lily. And the late-afternoon gold on those marshes. I think this salt breeze blows away all the bad Ruth.... Oh! Don't forget the attempts to cure cancer and consumption. So many big things starting right now, while we're sitting here."

"Lord! what an age! Romance—why, there's more romance in a wireless spark—think of it, little lonely wallowing steamer, at night, out in the dark, slamming out a radio like forty thousand tigers spitting—and a man getting it here on Long Island. More romance than in all the galleons that ever sailed the purple tropics, which they mostly ain't purple, but dirty green. Anything 's possible now. World cools off—a'right, we'll move on to some other planet. It gets me going. Don't have to believe in fairies to give the imagination a job, to-day. Glad I've been an aviator; gives me some place in it all, anyway."

"I'm glad, too, Hawk, terribly glad."

The sun was crimsoning; the wind grew chilly. The beach was scattered with camp-fires. Their own fire settled into compact live coals which, in the dusk of the dune-hollow, spread over the million bits of quartz a glow through which pirouetted the antic sand-fleas. Carl's cigarette had the fragrance that comes only from being impregnated with the smoke of an outdoor fire. The waves were lyric, and a group at the next fire crooned "Old Black Joe." The two lovers curled in their nest. Hand moved toward hand.

Ruth whispered: "It's sweet to be with all these people and their fires.... Will I really learn not to be supercilious?"

"Honey! You—supercilious? Democracy—— Oh, the dickens! let's not talk about theories any more, but just about Us!"

Her hand, tight-coiled as a snail-shell, was closed in his.

"Your hand is asleep in my hand's arms," he whispered. The ball of his thumb pressed her thumb, and he whispered once more: "See. Now our hands are kissing each other—we—we must watch them better.... Your thumb is like a fairy." Again his thumb, hardened with file and wrench and steering-wheel, touched hers. It was startlingly like a kiss of real lips.

Lightly she returned the finger-kiss, answering diffidently, "Our hands are mad—silly hands to think that Long Beach is a tropical jungle."

"You aren't angry at them?"

"N-no."

He cradled her head on his shoulder, his hand gripping her arm till she cried, "You hurt me." He kissed her cheek. She drew back as far as she could. Her hand, against his chest, held him away for a minute. Her defense suddenly collapsed, and she was relaxed and throbbing in his arms. He slipped his fingers under her chin, and turned up her face till he could kiss her lips. He had not known the kiss of man and woman could be so long, so stirring. Yet at first he was disappointed. This was, after all, but a touch—just such a touch as finger against finger. But her lips grew more intense against his, returning and taking the kiss; both of them giving and receiving at once.

Wondering at himself for it, Carl thought of other things. He was amazed that, while their lips were hot together, he worried as to what train Ruth ought to take, after dinner. Yet, with such thoughts conferring, he was in an ecstasy beyond sorrow; praying that to her, as to him, there was no pain but instead a rapture in the sting of her lips, as her teeth cut a little into them.... A kiss—thing that the polite novels sketch as a second's unbodied bliss—how human it was, with teeth and lips to consider; common as eating—and divine as martyrdom. His lips were saying to her things too vast and extravagant for a plain young man to venture upon in words:

"Lady, to you I chant my reverence and faith everlasting, in such unearthly music as the angels use when with lambent wings they salute the marching dawn." Such lyric tributes, and an emotion too subtle to fit into any words whatever, his lips were saying....

Then she was drawing back, rending the kiss, crying, "You're almost smothering me!"

With his arms easily about her, but with her weight against his shoulder, they and their love veiled from the basket-parties by the darkness, he said, quiveringly: "See, my arms are a little house for you, just as my hand was a little house for your hand, once. My arms are the walls, and your head and mine together are the roof."

"I love the little house."

"No. Say, 'I love *you*.'"

"No."

"Say it."

"No."

"Please——"

"Oh, Hawk dear, I couldn't even if—just now, I do want to say it, but I want to be fair. I am terribly happy to be in the house of Hawk's arms. I'm not afraid in it, even out here on the dark dunes—which Aunt Emma wouldn't—somehow—approve! But I do want to be fair to you, and I'm afraid I'm not, when I let you love me this way. I don't want to hurt you. Ever. Perhaps it's egotistical of me, but I'm afraid you would be hurt if I let you kiss me and then afterward I decided I didn't love you at all."

"But can't you, some day——"

"Oh, I don't know, I don't *know*! I'm not sure I know what love is. I'm not sure it's love that makes me happy (as I really am) when you kiss me. Perhaps I'm just curious, and experimenting. I was quite conscious, when you kissed me then; quite conscious and curious; and once I caught myself wondering for half a second what train we'd take. I was ashamed of that, but I wasn't ashamed of taking mental notes and learning what these 'kisses,' that we mention so glibly, really are. Just experimenting, you see. And if you were *too* serious about our kiss, it wouldn't be at all fair to you."

"I'm glad you're frank, blessed, and I guess I understand pretty well how you feel, but, after all, I'm fairly simple about such things. Blessed, blessed, I don't really know a thing but 'I love you.'"

His arms were savage again; he kissed her, kissed her lips, kissed the hollow of her throat. Then he lifted her from the ground and would not set her down till she had kissed him back.

"You frightened me a lot, then," she said. "Did the child want to impress Ruth with his mighty strength? Well, she shall be impressed. Hawk, I do hope—I do hate myself for not knowing my mind. I will try not to experiment. I want you to be happy. I do want to be honest with you. If I'm honest, will you try not to be too impatient till I do know just what I want?... Oh, I'm sick of the modern lover! I talk and talk about love; it seems as though we'd lost the power to be simple, like the old ballads. Or weren't the ballad people really simple, either? You say you are; so I think you will have to run away with me.... But not till after dinner! Come."

The moon was rising. Swinging hands, they tramped toward the board-walk. The crunch of their feet in the sand was the rhythmic spell of a magician, which she broke when she sighed:

"Should I have let you kiss me, out here in the wilds? Will you respect me after it?"

"Princess, you're all the respect there is in the world."

"It seems so strange. We were absorbed in war and electricity and then——"

"Love is war and electricity, or else it's dull, and I don't think we two 'll ever get dull—if you do decide you can love me. We'll wander: cabin in the Rockies, with forty mountains for our garden fence, and an eagle for our suburban train."

"And South Sea islands silhouetted at sunset!... Look! That moon!... I always imagine it so clearly when I hear Hawaiian singers on the Victrola—and a Hawaiian beach, with fireflies in the jungle behind and a phosphorescent sea in front and native girls dancing in garlands."

"Yes! And Paris boulevards and a mysterious castle in the Austrian mountains, with a hidden treasure in dark, secret dungeons, and heavy iron armor; and then, bing! a brand-new prairie town in Saskatchewan or Dakota, with brand-new sunlight on the fresh pine shacks, and beyond the town the plains with brand-new grass rolling."

"But seriously, Hawk, would you want to go to all those places, if you were married? Would you, practically? You know, even rich globe-trotters go to the same sorts of places, mostly. And we wouldn't even be rich, would we?"

"No, just comfortable; maybe five thousand a year."

"Well, would you really want to keep on going, and take your wife? Or would you settle down like the rest, and spend money so you could keep in shape to make money to spend to keep in shape?"

"Seriously I would keep going—if I had the right girl to go with me. It would be mighty important which one, though, I guess—and by that I mean you. Once, when I quit flying, I thought that maybe I'd stop wandering and settle down, maybe even marry a Joralemon kind of a girl. But I was meant to hike for the hiking's sake.... Only, not alone any more. I *need* you.... We'd go and go. No limit.... And we wouldn't just go places, either; we'd be different things. We'd be Connecticut farmers one year, and run a mine in Mexico the next, and loaf in Paris the next, if we had the money."

"Sometimes you almost tempt me to like you."

"Like me now!"

"No, not now, but—— Here's the board-walk."

"Where's those steps? Oh yes. Gee! I hate to leave the water without having had a swim. Wish we'd had one. Dare you to go wading!"

"Oh, ought I to, do you think? Wading would be silly. And nice."

"Course you oughtn't. Come on. Don't you remember how the sand feels between your toes?"

The moon brooded upon the lulled waves, and quested among the ridges of driftwood for pearly shells. The pools left by the waves were enticing. Ruth retreated into the shelter of the board-walk and came shyly out, clutching her skirts, her feet and ankles silver in the light.

"The sand does feel good, but uh! it's getting colder and colder!" she wailed, as she cautiously advanced into the water. "I'll think up punishments for you. You've not only caused me to be cold, but you've made me abominably self-conscious."

"Don't be self-conscious, blessed. We are just children exploring." He splashed out, coat off, trousers rolled to the knee above his thin, muscular legs, galloping along the edge of the water like a large puppy, while she danced after him.

They were stilled to the persuasive beauty of the night. Music from the topaz jeweled hotels far down the beach wove itself into the peace on land and sea. A fish lying on shore was turned by the moon into ivory with carven scales. Before them, reaching to the ancient towers of England and France and the islands of the sea, was the whispering water. A tenderness that understood everything, made allowance for everything in her and in himself, folded its wings round him as he scanned her that stood like a slender statue of silver— dark hair moon-brightened, white arms holding her skirts, white legs round which the spent waves sparkled with unworldly fire. He waded over to her and timidly kissed the edge of her hair.

She rubbed her cheek against his. "Now we must run," she said. She quickly turned back to the shadow of the board-walk, to draw on her stockings and shoes, kneeling on the sand like the simple maid of the ballads which she had been envying.

They tramped along the board-walk, with heels clicking like castanets, conscious that the world was hushed in night's old enchantment.

As they had answered to companionship with the humble picnic-parties among the dunes, so now they found it amusing to dine among the semi-great and the semi-motorists at the Nassau. Ruth had a distinct pleasure when T. Wentler, horse-fancier, aviation enthusiast, president of the First State Bank of Sacramento, came up, reminded Carl of their acquaintanceship at the Oakland-Berkeley Aero Meet, and begged Ruth and Carl to join him, his wife, and Senator Leeford, for coffee.

As they waited for their train, quiet after laughter, Ruth remarked: "It was jolly to play with the Personages. You haven't seen much of the frivolous side of me. It's pretty important. You don't know how much soul satisfaction I get out of dancing all night and playing tennis with flanneled oafs and eating *marrons glacés* and chatting in a box at the opera till I spoil the entire evening for all the German music-lovers, and talking to all the nice doggies from the Tennis and Racquet Club whenever I get invited to Piping Rock or Meadow Brook or any other country club that has ancestors. I want you to take warning."

"Did you really miss Piping Rock much to-day?".

"No—but I might to-morrow, and I might get horribly bored in our cabin in the Rockies and hate the stony old peaks, and long for tea and scandal in a corner at the Ritz."

"Then we'd hike on to San Francisco; have tea at the St. Francis or the Fairmont or the Palace; then beat it for your Hawaii and fireflies in the bush."

"Perhaps, but suppose, just suppose we were married, and suppose the Touricar didn't go so awfully well, and we had to be poor, and couldn't go running away, but had to stick in one beastly city flat and economize! It's all very well to talk of working things out together, but think of not being able to have decent clothes, and going to the movies every night—ugh! When I see some of the girls who used to be so pretty and gay, and they went and married poor men—now they are so worn and tired and bedraggled and perambulatorious, and they worry about Biddies and furnaces and cabbages, and their hair is just scratched together, with the dubbest hats—I'd rather be an idle rich."

"If we got stuck like that, I'd sell out and we'd hike to the mountain cabin, anyway, say go up in the Santa Lucias, and keep wild bees."

"And probably get stung—in the many subtle senses of that word. And I'd have to cook and wash. That would be fun *as* fun, but to have to do it——"

"Ruth, honey, let's not worry about it now, anyhow. I don't believe there's much danger. And don't let's spoil this bully day."

"It has been sweet. I won't croak any more."

"There's the train coming."

CHAPTER XXXVIII

While the New York June grew hotter and hotter and stickier and stickier, while the crowds, crammed together in the subway in a jam as unlovely as a pile of tomato-cans on a public dump-heap, grew pale in the damp heat, Carl labored in his office, and almost every evening called on Ruth, who was waiting for the first of July, when she was to go to Cousin Patton Kerr's, in the Berkshires. Carl tried to bring her coolness. He ate only poached eggs on toast or soup and salad for dinner, that he might not be torpid. He gave her moss-roses with drops of water like dew on the stems. They sat out on the box-stoop—the unfriendly New York street adopting for a time the frank neighborliness of a village—and exclaimed over every breeze. They talked about the charm of forty degrees below zero. That is, sometimes. Their favorite topic was themselves.

She still insisted that she was not in love with him; hooted at the idea of being engaged. She might some day go off and get married to some one, but engaged? Never! She finally agreed that they were engaged to be engaged to be engaged. One night when they sought the windy housetop, she twined his arms about her and almost went to sleep, with her hair smooth beneath his chin. He sat motionless till his arms ached with the strain, till her shoulder seemed to stick into his like a bar of iron; glad that she trusted him enough to doze into warm slumber in the familiarity of his arms. Yet he dared not kiss her throat, as he had done at Long Beach.

As lovers do, Carl had thought intently of her warning that she did care for clothes, dancing, country clubs. Ruth would have been caressingly surprised had she known the thought and worried conscientiousness he gave to the problem of planning "parties" for her. Ideas were always popping up in the midst of his work, and never giving him rest till he had noted them down on memo.-papers. He carried about, on the backs of envelopes, such notes as these:

Join country clb take R dances there?
Basket of fruit for R
Invite Mason W lunch
Orgnze Tcar tour NY to SF
Newspaper men on tour probly Forbes
Rem Walter's new altitude 16,954
R to Astor Roof
Rem country c

He did get a card to the Peace Waters Country Club and take Ruth to a dance there. She seemed to know every other member, and danced eloquently. He took her to the Josiah Bagbys' for dinner; to the first-night of a summer musical comedy. But he was still the stranger in New York, and "parties" are not to be had by tipping waiters and buying tickets. Half of the half-dozen affairs which they attended were of her inspiration; he was invited to go yachting at Larchmont, motoring, swimming on Long Island, with friends of herself and her brothers.

One evening that strikes into Carl's memories of those days of the *pays du tendre* is the evening on which Phil Dunleavy insisted on celebrating a Yale baseball victory by taking them to dinner in the oak-room of the Ritz-Carlton, under whose alabaster lights, among the cosmopolites, they dined elaborately and smoked slim, imported cigarettes. The thin music of violins took them into the lonely gray groves of the Land of Wandering Tunes, till Phil began to talk, disclosing to them a devotion to beauty, a satirical sense of humor, and a final acceptance of Carl as his friend.

A hundred other "parties" Carl planned, while dining alone at inferior restaurants. A hundred times he took a ten-cent dessert instead of an exciting fifteen-cent strawberry shortcake, to save money for those parties. (Out of such sordid thoughts of nickel coins is built a love enduring, and even tolerable before breakfast coffee.)

Yet always to him their real life was in simple jaunts out of doors, arranged without considering other people. Her father seemed glad of that. He once said to Carl (giving him a cigar), "You children had better not let Aunt Emma know that you are enjoying yourselves as you want to! How is the automobile business going?"

It would be pleasant to relate that Carl was inspired by love to put so much of that celebrated American quality "punch" into his work that the Touricar was sweeping the market. Or to picture with quietly falling tears the pathos of his business failure at the time when he most needed money. As a matter of fact, the Touricar affairs were going as, in real life, most businesses go— just fairly well. A few cars were sold; there were prospects of other sales; the VanZile Corporation neither planned to drop the Touricar, nor elected our young hero vice-president of the corporation.

In June Gertrude Cowles and her mother left for Joralemon. Carl had, since Christmas, seen them about once a month. Gertie had at first represented an unhappy old friend to whom he had to be kind. Then, as she seemed never to be able to give up the desire to see him tied down, whether by her affection or by his work, Carl came to regard her as an irritating foe to the freedom which he prized the more because of the increasing bondage of the office. The last stage was pure indifference to her. Gertie was either a chance for simple sweetness which he failed to take, or she was a peril which he had escaped, according to one's view of her; but in any case he had missed—or escaped—her as a romantic hero escapes fire, flood, and plot. She meant nothing to him, never could again. Life had flowed past her as, except in novels with plots, most lives do flow past temporary and fortuitous points of interest.... Gertie was farther from him now than those dancing Hawaiian girls whom Ruth and he hoped some day to see. Yet by her reaching out for his liberty Gertie had first made him prize Ruth.

The 1st of July, 1913, Ruth left for the Patton Kerrs' country house in the Berkshires, near Pittsfield. Carl wrote to her every day. He told her, apropos of Touricars and roof-gardens and aviation records and Sunday motor-cycling with Bobby Winslow, that he loved her; he even made, at the end of his letters, the old-fashioned lines of crosses to represent kisses. Whenever he hinted how much he missed her, how much he wanted to feel her startle in his arms, he wondered what she would read out of it; wondered if she would put the letter under her pillow.

She answered every other day with friendly letters droll in their descriptions of the people she met. His call of love she did not answer—directly. But she admitted that she missed their playtimes; and once she wrote to him, late on a cold Berkshire night, with a black rain and wind like a baying bloodhound:

It is so still in my room & so wild outside that I am frightened. I have tried to make myself smart in a blue silk dressing gown & a tosh lace breakfast cap, & I will write neatly with a quill pen from the Mayfair, but just the same I am a lonely baby & I want you here to comfort me. Would you be too shocked to come? I would put a Navajo blanket on my bed & a papier maché Turkish dagger & head of Othello over my bed & pretend it was a cozy corner, that is of course if they still have papier maché ornaments, I suppose they still live in Harlem & Brooklyn. We would sit *very* quietly in two wicker chairs on either side of my fireplace & listen to the swollen brook in the ravine just below my window. But with no Hawk here the wind keeps wailing that Pan is dead & that there won't ever again be any sunshine on the valley. Dear, it really *isn't* safe to be writing like this, after reading it you will suppose that it's just you that I am lonely for, but of course I'd be glad for Phil or Puggy Crewden or your nice solemn Walter MacMonnies or *any* suitor who would make foolish noises & hide me from the wind's hunting. Now I will seal this up & *NOT* send it in the morning.

Your playmate Ruth

Here is one small kiss on the forehead but remember it is just because of the wind & rain.

Presumably she did mail the letter. At least, he received it.

He carried her letters in the side-pocket of his coat till the envelopes were worn at the edges and nearly covered with smudged pencil-notes about things he wanted to keep in mind and would, of course, have kept in mind without making notes. He kept finding new meanings in her letters. He wanted them to indicate that she loved him; and any ambiguous phrase signified successively that she loved, laughed at, loathed, and loved him. Once he got up from bed to take another look at a letter and see whether she had said, "I hope you had a dear good time at the Explorers' Club dinner," or "I hope you had a good time, dear."

Carl was entirely sincere in his worried investigation of her state of mind. He knew that both Ruth and he had the instability as well as the initiative of the vagabond. As quickly as they had claimed each other, so quickly could either of them break love's alliance, if bored. Carl himself, being anything but bored, was as faithfully devoted as the least enterprising of moral young men, He forgot Gertie, did not write to Istra Nash the artist, and when the VanZile office got a new telephone-girl, a tall, languorous brunette with shadowy eyes and fine cheeks, he did not even smile at her.

But—was Ruth so bound? She still refused to admit even that she could fall in love. He knew that Ruth and he were not romantic characters, but every-day people with a tendency to quarrel and demand and be slack. He knew that even if the rose dream came true, there would be drab spots in it. And now that she was away, with Lenox and polo to absorb her, could the gauche, ignorant Carl Ericson, that he privately knew himself to be, retain her interest?

Late in July he received an invitation to spend a week-end, Friday to Tuesday, with Ruth at the Patton Kerrs'.

CHAPTER XXXIX

The brief trip to the Berkshires was longer than any he had taken these nine months. He looked forward animatedly to the journey, remembering details of travel—such trivial touches as the oval brass wash-bowls of a Pullman sleeper, and how, when the water is running out, the inside of the bowl is covered with a whitish film of water, which swiftly peels off. He recalled the cracked white paint of a steamer's ventilator; the abruptly stopping zhhhhh of a fog-horn; the vast smoky roof of a Philadelphia train-shed, clamorous with the train-bells of a strange town, giving a sense of mystery to the traveler stepping from the car for a moment to stretch his legs; an ugly junction station platform, with resin oozing from the heavy planks in the spring sun; the polished binnacle of the S.S. *Panama*.

He expected keen joy in new fields and hills. Yet all the way north he was trying to hold the train back. In a few minutes, now, he would see Ruth. And at this hour he did not even know definitely that he liked her.

He could not visualize her. He could see the sleeve of her blue corduroy jacket; her eyes he could not see. She was a stranger. Had he idealized her? He was apologetic for his unflattering doubt, but of what sort *was* she?

The train was stopping at her station with rattling windows and a despairing grind of the wheels. Carl seized his overnight bag and suit-case with fictitious enthusiasm. He was in a panic. Emerging from the safe, impersonal train upon the platform, he saw her.

She was waving to him from a one-seated phaeton, come alone to meet him—and she was the adorable, the perfect comrade. He thought jubilantly as he strode along the platform: "She's wonderful. Love her? Should say I do!"

While they drove under the elms, past white cottages and the village green, while they were talking so lightly and properly that none of the New England gossips could be wounded in the sense of propriety, Carl was learning her anew. She was an outdoor girl now, in low-collared blouse and white linen skirt. He rejoiced in her modulating laugh; the contrast of blue eyes and dark brows under her Panama hat; her full dark hair, with a lock sun-drenched; her bare throat, boyishly brown, femininely smooth; the sweet, clean, fine-textured girl flesh of the hollow of one shoulder faintly to be seen in the shadow of her broad, drooping collar; one hand, with a curious ring of rose quartz and steel points, excitedly pounding a tattoo of greeting with the whip-handle; her spirited irreverences regarding the people they passed; chatter which showed the world transformed as through ruby glass—a Ruth radiant, understanding, his comrade. She was all that he had believed during her absence and doubted while he was coming to her. But he had no time to repent of his doubt, now, so busily was he exulting to himself, slipping a hand under her arm: "Love her? I—should—say—I—do!"

The carriage rolled out of town with the rhythmic creak of a country buggy, climbed a hill range by means of the black, oily state road, and turned upon a sandy side-road. A brook ran beside them. Sunny fields alternated with woods leaf-floored, quiet, holy—miraculous after the weary city. Below was a vista of downward-sloping fields, divided by creeper-covered stone walls; then a sun-meshed valley set with ponds like shining glass dishes on a green table-cloth; beyond all, a long reach of hillsides covered with unbroken fleecy forest, like green down....

"So much unspoiled country, and yet there's people herded in subways!" complained Carl.

They drove along a level road, lined with wild raspberry-bushes and full of a thin jade light from the shading maples. They gossiped of the Patton Kerrs and the Berkshires; of the difference between the professional English week-ender and the American, who still has something of the naïve provincial delight of "going visiting"; of New York and the Dunleavys. But their talk lulled to a nervous hush. It seemed to him that a great voice cried from the clouds: "It is beside *Ruth* that you are sitting; Ruth whose arm you feel!" In silence he caught her left hand.

As he slowly drew back her hand and the reins with it, to stop the ambling horse, the two children stared straight at each other, hungry, tremulously afraid. Their kiss—not only their lips, but their spirits met without one reserve. A straining long kiss, as though they were forcing their lips into one body of living flame. A kiss in which his eyes were blind to the enchantment of the jade light about them, his ears deaf to brook and rustling forest. All his senses were concentrated on the close warmth of her misty lips, the curve of her young shoulder, her woman sweetness and longing. Then his senses forgot even her lips, and floated off into a blurred trance of bodiless happiness—the kiss of Nirvana. No foreign thought of trains or people or the future came now to drag him to earth. It was the most devoted, most sacred moment he had known.

As he became again conscious of lips and cheek and brave shoulders and of her wide-spread fingers gripping his upper arm, she was slowly breaking the spell of the kiss. But again and again she kissed him, hastily, savage tokens of rejoicing possession.

She cried: "I do know now! I do love you!"

"Blessed——"

In silence they stared into the woods while her fingers smoothed his knuckles. Her eyes were faint with tears, in the magic jade light.

"I didn't know a kiss could be like that," she marveled, presently. "I wouldn't have believed selfish Ruth could give all of herself."

"Yes! It was the whole universe."

"Hawk dear, I wasn't experimenting, that time. I'm glad, glad! To know I can really love; not just curiosity!... I've wanted you so all day. I thought four o'clock wouldn't ever come—and oh, darling, my dear, dear Hawk, I didn't even know for sure I'd like you when you came! Sometimes I wanted terribly to have your silly, foolish, childish, pale hair on my breast—such hair! lady's hair!—but sometimes I didn't want to see you at all, and I was frightened at the thought of your coming, and I fussed around the house till Mrs. Pat laughed at me and accused me of being in love, and I denied it—and she was right!"

"Blessed, I was scared to death, all the way up here. I didn't think you could be as wonderful as I knew you were! That sounds mixed but—— Oh, blessed, blessed, you really love me? You really love me? It's hard to believe I've actually heard you say it! And I love you so completely. Everything."

"I love you!... That is such an adorable spot to kiss, just below your ear," she said. "Darling, keep me safe in the little house of arms, where there's only room for you and me—no room for offices or Aunt Emmas!... But not now. We must hurry on.... If a wagon had been coming along the road——!"

As they entered the rhododendron-lined drive of the Patton Kerr place, Carl remembered a detail, not important, but usual. "Oh yes," he said, "I've forgotten to propose."

"Need you? Proposals sound like contracts and all those other dull forms; not like—that kiss.... See! There's Pat Kerr, Jr., waving to us. You can just make him out, there on the upper balcony. He is the darlingest child, with ash-blond hair cut Dutch style. I wonder if you didn't look like him when you were a boy, with your light hair?"

"Not a chance. I was a grubby kid. Made noises.... Gee! what a bully place. And the house!... Will you marry me?"

"Yes, I will!... It *is* a dear place. Mrs. Pat is——"

"When?"

"——always fussing over it; she plants narcissuses and crocuses in the woods, so you find them growing wild."

"I like those awnings. Against the white walls.... May I consider that we are engaged then, Miss Winslow—engaged for the next marriage?"

"Oh no, no, not engaged, dear. Don't you know it's one of my principles——"

"But look——"

"——not to be engaged, Hawk? Everybody brings the cunnin' old jokes out of the moth-balls when you're engaged. I'll marry you, but——"

"Marry me next month—August?"

"Nope."

"September?"

"Nope."

"Please, Ruthie. Aw yes, September. Nice month, September is. Autumn. Harvest moon. And apples to swipe. Come on. September."

"Well, perhaps September. We'll see. Oh, Hawk dear, can you conceive of us actually sitting here and solemnly discussing being *married*? Us, the babes in the wood? And I've only known you three days or so, seems to me.... Well, as I was saying, *perhaps* I'll marry you in September (um! frightens me to think of it; frightens me and awes me and amuses me to death, all at once). That is, I shall marry you unless you take to wearing pearl-gray derbies or white evening ties with black edging, or kill Mason in a duel, or do something equally disgraceful. But engaged I will not be. And we'll put the money for a diamond ring into a big davenport.... Are we going to be dreadfully poor?"

"Oh, not pawn-shop poor. I made VanZile boost my salary, last week, and with my Touricar stock I'm getting a little over four thousand dollars a year."

"Is that lots or little?"

"Well, it 'll give us a decent apartment and a nearly decent maid, I guess. And if the Touricar keeps going, we can beat it off for a year, wandering, after maybe three four years."

"I hope so. Here we are! That's Mrs. Pat waiting for us."

The Patton Kerr house, set near the top of the highest hill in that range of the Berkshires, stood out white against a slope of crisp green; an old manor house of long lines and solid beams, with striped awnings of red and white, and in front a brick terrace, with basket-chairs, a swinging couch, and a wicker tea-table already welcomingly spread with a service of Royal Doulton. From the terrace one saw miles of valley and hills, and villages strung on a rambling river. The valley was a golden bowl filled with the peace of afternoon; a world of sun and listening woods.

On the terrace waited a woman of thirty-five, of clever face a bit worn at the edges, carefully coiffed hair, and careless white blouse with a tweed walking-skirt. She was gracefully holding out her hand, greeting Carl, "It's terribly good of you to come clear out into our wilderness." She was interrupted by the bouncing appearance of a stocky, handsome, red-faced, full-chinned, curly-black-haired man of forty, in riding-breeches and boots and a silk shirt; with him an excited small boy in rompers—Patton Kerr, Sr. and Jr.

"Here you are!" Senior observantly remarked. "Glad to see you, Ericson. You and Ruthie been a deuce of a time coming up from town. Holding hands along the road, eh? Lord! these aviators!"

"Pat!"

"Animal!"

——protested Mrs. Kerr and Ruth, simultaneously.

"All right. I'll be good. Saw you fly at Nassau Boulevard, Ericson. Turned my horn loose and hooted till they thought I was a militant, like Ruthie here. Lord! what flying, what flying! I'd like to see you race Weymann and Vedrines.... Ruthie, will you show Mr. Ericson where his room is, or has poor old Pat got to go and drag a servant away from reading *Town Topics*, heh?"

"I will, Pat," said Ruth.

"I will, daddy," cried Pat, Jr.

"No, my son, I guess maybe Ruthie had better do it. There's a certain look in her eyes——"

"Basilisk!"

"Salamander!"

Ruth and Carl passed through the wide colonial hall, with mahogany tables and portraits of the Kerrs and the sword of Colonel Patton. At the far end was an open door, and a glimpse of an old-fashioned garden radiant with hollyhocks and Canterbury bells. It was a world of utter content. As they climbed the curving stairs Ruth tucked her arm in his, saying:

"Now do you see why I won't be engaged? Pat Kerr is the best chum in the world, yet he finds even a possible engagement wildly humorous—like mothers-in-law or poets or falling on your ear."

"But gee! Ruth, you *are* going to marry me?"

"You little child! My little boy Hawk! Of course I'm going to marry you. Do you think I would miss my chance of a cabin in the Rockies?... My famous Hawk what everybody cheered at Nassau Boulevard!" She opened the door of his room with a deferential, "Thy chamber, milord!... Come down quickly," she said. "We mustn't miss a moment of these days.... I am frank with you about how glad I am to have you here. You must be good to me; you will prize my love a little, won't you?" Before he could answer she had run away.

After half home-comings and false home-comings the adventurer had really come home.

He inspected the gracious room, its chintz hangings, four-poster bed, low wicker chair by the fireplace, fresh Cherokee roses on the mantel; a room of cheerfulness and open spaces. He stared into woods where a cool light lay on moss and fern. He did not need to remember Ruth's kisses. For each breath of hilltop air, each emerald of moss, each shining mahogany surface in the room, repeated to him that he had found the Grail, whose other name is love.

Saturday, they loafed over breakfast, the sun licking the tree-tops in the ravine outside the windows; and they motored with the Kerrs to Lenox, returning through the darkness. Till midnight they talked on the terrace. They loafed again, the next morning, and let the fresh air dissolve the office grime which had been coating his spirit. They were so startlingly original as to be simple-hearted country lovers, in the afternoon, declining Kerr's offer of a car, and rambling off on bicycles.

From a rise they saw water gleaming among the trees. The sullen green of pines set off the silvery green of barley, and an orchard climbed the next rise; the smoky shadow of another hill range promised long, cool forest roads. Crows were flying overhead, going where they would. The aviator and the girl who read psychology, modern lovers, stood hand in hand, as though the age of machinery were a myth; as though he were a piping minstrel and she a shepherdess. Before them was the open road and all around them the hum of bees.

A close, listless heat held Monday afternoon, even on the hilltop. The clay tennis-court was baking; the worn bricks of the terrace reflected a furnace glow. The Kerrs had disappeared for a nap. Carl, lounging with Ruth on the swinging couch in the shade, thought of the slaves in New York offices and tenements. Then, because he would himself be back in an office next day, he let the glare of the valley soothe him with its wholesome heat.

"Certainly would like a swim," he remarked. "Couldn't we bike down to Fisher's Pond, or maybe take the Ford?"

"Let's. But there's no bath-house."

"Put a bathing-suit under your dress. Sun 'll dry it in no time, after the swim."

"As you command, my liege." And she ran in to change.

They motored down to Fisher's Pond, which is a lake, and stopped in a natural woodland-opening like a dim-lighted greenroom. From it stretched the enameled lake, the farther side reflecting unbroken woods. The nearer water-edge was exquisite in its clearness. They saw perch fantastically floating over the pale sand bottom, among scattered reeds whose watery green stalks were like the thin columns of a dancing-hall for small fishes. The surface of the lake, satiny as the palm of a girl's hand, broke in the tiniest of ripples against white quartz pebbles on the hot shore. Cool, flashing, golden-sanded, the lake coaxed them out of their forest room.

"A lot like the Minnesota lakes, only smaller," said Carl. "I'm going right in. About ready for a swim? Come on."

"I'm af-fraid!" She suddenly plumped on the earth and hugged her skirts about her ankles.

"Why, blessed, what you scared of? No sharks here, and no undertow. Nice white sand——"

"Oh, Hawk, I was silly. I felt I was such an independent modern woman a-a-and I aren't! I've always said it was silly for girls to swim in a woman's bathing-suit. Skirts are so cumbersome. So I put on a boy's bathing-suit under my dress—and—I'm terribly embarrassed."

"Why, blessed——Well, I guess you'll have to decide." His voice was somewhat shaky. "Awful scared of Carl?"

"Yes! I thought I wouldn't be, with you, but I'm self-conscious as can be."

"Well, gee! I don't know. Of course——Well, I'll jump in, and you can decide."

He peeled off his white flannels and stood in his blue bathing-suit, not statue-like, not very brown now, but trim-waisted, shapely armed, wonderfully clean of neck and jaw. With a "Wheee!" he dashed into the water and swam out, overhand.

As he turned over and glanced back, his heart caught to see her standing on the creamy sand, a shy, elfin figure in a boy's bathing-suit of black wool, woman and slim boy in one, silken-throated and graceful-limbed, curiously smaller than when dressed. Her white skirt and blouse lay tumbled about her ankles. She raised rosy arms to hide her flushed face and her eyes, as she cried:

"Don't look!"

He obediently swam on, with a tenderness more poignant than longing. He heard her splashing behind him, and turned again, to see her racing through the water. Those soft yet not narrow shoulders rose and fell sturdily under the wet black wool, her eyes shone, and she was all comradely boy save for her dripping, splendid hair. Singing, "Come on, lazy!" she headed across the pond. He swam beside her, reveling in the well-being of cool water and warm air, till they reached the solemn shade beneath the trees on the other side, and floated in the dark, still water, splashing idle hands, gazing into forest hollows, spying upon the brisk business of squirrels among the acorns.

Back at their greenwood room, Ruth wrapped her sailor blouse about her, and they squatted like un-self-conscious children on the beach, while from a field a distant locust fiddled his August fandango and in flame-colored pride an oriole went by. Fresh sky, sunfish like tropic shells in the translucent water, arching reeds dipping their olive-green points in the water, wavelets rustling against a gray neglected rowboat, and beside him Ruth.

Musingly they built a castle of sand. An hour of understanding so complete that it made the heart melancholy. When he sighed, "Getting late; come on, blessed; we're dry now," it seemed that they could never again know such rapt tranquillity.

Yet they did. For that evening when they stood on the terrace, trying to forget that he must leave her and go back to the lonely city in the morning, when the mist reached chilly tentacles up from the valley, they kissed a shy good-by, and Carl knew that life's real adventure is not adventuring, but finding the playmate with whom to quest life's meaning.

CHAPTER XL

After six festival months of married life—in April or May, 1914—the happy Mrs. Carl Ericson did not have many "modern theories of marriage in general," though it was her theory that she had such theories. Like a majority of intelligent men and women, Ruth was, in her rebellion against the canonical marriage of slipper-warming and obedience, emphatic but vague. She was of precise opinion regarding certain details of marriage, but in general as inconsistent as her library. It is a human characteristic to be belligerently sure as to whether one prefers plush or rattan upholstery on car seats—but not to consider whether government ownership of railroads will improve upholstering; to know with certainty of perception that it is a bore to have one's husband laugh at one's pet economy, of matches or string or ice—but to be blandly willing to leave all theories of polygamy and polyandry, monogamy and varietism, to the clever Russian Jews.

As regards details Ruth definitely did want a bedroom of her own; a desire which her mother would have regarded as somehow immodest. She definitely did want shaving and hair-brushing kept in the background. She did not want Carl the lover to drift into Carl the husband. She did not want them to lose touch with other people. And she wanted to keep the spice of madness which from the first had seasoned their comradeship.

These things she delightfully had, in May, 1914.

They were largely due to her own initiative. Carl's drifting theories of social structure concerned for the most part the wages of workmen and the ridiculousness of class distinctions. Reared in the farming district, the amateur college, the garage, and the hangar, he had not, despite imagination, devoted two seconds to such details as the question of whether there was freedom and repose—not to speak of a variety of taste as regards opening windows and sleeping diagonally across a bed—in having separate bedrooms. Much though he had been persuaded to read of modern fiction, his race still believed that marriage bells and roses were the proper portions of marriage to think about.

It was due to Ruth, too, that they had so amiable a flat. Carl had been made careless of surroundings by years of hotels and furnished rooms. There was less real significance for him in the beauty of his first home than in the fact that they two had a bath-room of their own; that he no longer had to go, clad in a drab bath-robe, laden with shaving materials and a towel and talcum powder and a broken hand-mirror and a tooth-brush, like a perambulating drug-store toilet-counter, down a boarding-house hall to that modified hall bedroom with a tin tub which his doctor-landlord had called a bath-room.

Pictures, it must be admitted, give a room an air; pleasant it is to sit in large chairs by fireplaces and feel yourself a landed gentleman. But nothing filled Carl with a more delicate—and truly spiritual—satisfaction than having a porcelain tub, plenty of hot water, and the privilege of leaving his shaving-brush in the Ericson bath-room with a fair certainty of finding it there when he wanted to shave in a hurry.

But, careless of surroundings or not, Carl was stirred when on their return from honeymooning in the Adirondacks he carried Ruth over the threshold and they stood together in the living-room of their home.

It was a room to live in and laugh in. The wood-work was white-enameled; the walls covered with gray Japanese paper. There were no portières between living-room and dining-room and small hall, so that the three rooms, with their light-reflecting walls, gave an effect of spaciousness to rather a cramped and old-fashioned apartment. There were not many pictures and no bric-à-brac, yet the rooms were not bare, but clean and trim and distinguished, with the large davenport and the wing-chair, chintz-cushioned brown willow chairs, and Ruth's upright piano, excellent mahogany, and a few good rugs. There were only two or three vases, and they genuinely intended for holding flowers, and there was a bare mantelpiece that rested the eyes, over the fuzzily clean gas-log. The pictures were chosen because they led the imagination on—etchings and color prints, largely by unknown artists, like windows looking on delightful country. The chairs assembled naturally in groups. The whole unit of three rooms suggested people talking.... It was home, first and last, though it was one cell in one layer of a seven-story building, on a street walled in with such buildings, in a city which lined up more than three hundred of such streets from its southern tip to its northern limit along the Hudson, and threw in a couple of million people in Brooklyn and the Bronx.

They lived in the Nineties, between Broadway and Riverside Drive; a few blocks from the Winslow house in distance, but one generation away in the matter of decoration. The apartment-house itself was comparatively old-fashioned, with an intermittent elevator run by an intermittent negro youth who gave most of his time to the telephone switchboard and mysterious duties in the basement; also with a down-stairs hall that was narrow and carpeted and lined with offensively dark wood. But they could see the Hudson from their living-room on the sixth floor at the back of the house (the agent assured them that probably not till the end of time would there be anything but low, private houses between them and the river); they were not haunted by Aunt Emma Truegate Winslow; and Ruth, who had long been oppressed by late-Victorian bric-à-brac and American Louis XVth furniture, so successfully adopted Elimination as the key-note that there was not one piece of furniture bought for the purpose of indicating that Mr. and Mrs. Carl Ericson were well-to-do.

She dared to tell friends who before the wedding inquired what she wanted, that checks were welcome, and need not be monogrammed. Even Aunt Emma had been willing to send a check, provided they were properly married in St. George's Church. Consequently their six rooms showed a remarkable absence of such usual wedding presents as prints of the smugly smiling and eupeptic Mona Lisa, three muffin-stands in three degrees of marquetry, three electroliers, four punch-bowls, three sets of almond-dishes, a pair of bird-carvers that did not carve, a bust of Dante in New Art marble, or a de luxe set of De Maupassant translated by a worthy lady with a French lexicon. Instead, they bought what they wanted—rather an impertinent thing to do, but, like most impertinences, thoroughly worth while. Their living-room was their own. Carl's bedroom was white and simple, though spotty with aviation medals and silver cups and monoplanes sketchily rendered in gold, and signed photographs of aviators. Ruth's bedroom was also plain and white and dull Japanese gray, a simple room with that simplicity of hand-embroidery, real lace, and fine linen appreciated by exclamatory women friends.

She taught Carl to say "dahg" instead of "dawg" for "dog"; "wawta" instead of "wotter" for "water." Whether she was more correct in her pronunciation or not does not matter; New York said "dahg," and it amused him just then to be very Eastern. She taught him the theory of house-lighting. Carl had no fanatical objection to unshaded incandescent bulbs glaring from the ceiling. But he came to like the shaded electric lamps which Ruth installed in the living-room. When she introduced four candles as sole lighting of the dining-room table, however, he grumbled loudly at his inability to see what he was eating. She retired to her bedroom, and he huffily went out to get a cigar. At the cigar-counter he repented of all the unkind things he had ever done or could possibly do, and returned to eat humble pie—and eat it by candle-light. Inside of two weeks one of the things which Carl Ericson had always known was that the harmonious candle-light brought them close together at dinner.

The teaching, in this Period of Adjustments, was not all on Ruth's part. It was due to Carl's insistence that she tried to discover what her theological beliefs really were. She admitted that only at twilight vespers, with a gale of violins in an arched roof, did she really worship in church. She did not believe that priests and ministers, who seemed to be ordinary men as regards earthly things, had any extraordinary knowledge of the mysteries of heaven. Yet she took it for granted that she was a good Christian. She rarely disagreed with the Dunleavys, who were Catholics; or her Aunt Emma, who regarded anything but High Church Episcopalianism as bad form; or her brother Mason, who was an uneasy Unitarian; or Carl, who was an unaggressive agnostic.

Of the four it was Carl who seemed to have the greatest interest in religions. He blurted out such monologues as, "I wonder if it isn't pure egotism that makes a person believe that the religion he is born to is the best? *My* country, *my* religion, *my* wife, *my* business—we think that whatever is ours is necessarily sacred, or, in other words, that we are gods—and then we call it faith and patriotism! The Hindu or the Christian is equally ready to prove to you—and mind you, he may be a wise old man with a beard—that his national religion is obviously the only one. Find out what you yourself really do think, and if you turn out a Sun-worshiper or a Hard-shell Baptist, why, good luck. If you don't think for yourself, then you're admitting that your theory of happiness is the old dog asleep in the sun. And maybe he is happier than the student. But I think you like to experiment with life."

His arguments were neither original nor especially logical; they were largely given to him by Bone Stillman, Professor Frazer, and chance paragraphs in stray radical magazines. But to Ruth, politely reared in a house with three maids, where it was as tactless to discuss God as to discuss sex, his defiances seemed terrifyingly new.... She was not the first who had complacently gone to church after reading Bernard Shaw.... But she did try to follow Carl's loose reasoning; to find out what she thought and what the spiritual fashions of her neighborhood made her think she thought.

The process gave her many anxious hours of alternating impatience with fixed religious dogmas, and loneliness for the comfortable refuge of a personal God, whose yearning had spoken to her in the Gregorian chant. She could never get herself to read more than two chapters of any book on the subject, nor did she get much light from conversation. One set of people supposed that Christianity had so entirely disappeared from intelligent circles that it was not worth discussion; another set supposed that no one but cranks ever thought of doubting the essentials of Christianity, and that, therefore, it was not worth discussion; and to a few superb women whom she knew, their religion was too sweet a reality to be subjected to the noisy chatter of discussion. Gradually Ruth forgot to think often of the matter, but it was always back in her mind.

They were happy, Carl and Ruth. To their flat came such of Ruth's friends as she kept because she liked them for themselves, with a fantastic assortment of personages and awkward rovers whom the ex-aviator knew. The Ericsons made an institution of "bruncheon"—breakfast-luncheon—at which coffee and eggs and deviled kidneys, a table of auction bridge and a davenport of talk and a wing-chair of Sunday papers, were to be had on Sunday morning from ten to one. At bruncheon Walter MacMonnies told to Florence Crewden his experiences in exploring Southern Greenland by aeroplane with the Schliess-Banning expedition. At bruncheon Bobby Winslow, now an interne, talked baseball with Carl. At bruncheon Phil Dunleavy regarded cynically all the people he did not know and played piquet in a corner with Ruth's father.

Carl and Ruth joined the Peace Waters Country Club, and in the spring of 1914 went there nearly every Saturday afternoon for tennis and a dance. Carl refused golf, however; he always repeated a shabby joke about the shame of taking advantage of such a tiny ball.

He seemed content to stick to office, home, and tennis-court. It was Ruth who planned their week-end trips, proposed at 8 A.M. Saturday, and begun at two that afternoon. They explored the tangled rocks and woods of Lloyd's Neck, on Long Island, sleeping in an abandoned shack, curled together like kittens. They swooped on a Dutch village in New Jersey, spent the night with an old farmer, and attended the Dutch Reformed church. They tramped from New Haven to Hartford, over Easter. Carl was always ready for their gipsy journeys; he responded to Ruth's visions of foaming South Sea isles; but he rarely sketched such pictures himself. He had given all of himself to joy in Ruth. Like many men called "adventurers," he was ready for anything but content with anything.

It was Ruth who was finding new voyages. She kept up her settlement work and progressed to an active interest in the Women's Trade Union League and took part in picketing during a Panama Hat-Workers' strike. She may have had more curiosity than principle, but she did badger policemen pluckily. She was studying Italian, the Montessori method, cooking. She taught new dishes to her maid. She adopted a careless suggestion of Carl and voluntarily increased the maid's salary, thereby shaking the rock-ribbed foundations of Upper West Side society.

In nothing did she find greater satisfaction than in being neither "the bride" nor "the little woman" nor any like degrading thing which recently married girls are by their sentimental spinster friends expected to be. She did not whisper the intimate details of her honeymoon to other young married women; she did not run about quaintly and tinily telling her difficulties with household work.

When a purring, baby-talking acquaintance gurgled: "How did the Ruthie bride spend her morning? Did she cook some little dainty for her husband? Nothing bourgeois, I'm *sure!*" in reply Ruth pleasantly observed: "Not a chance. The Ruthie bride cussed out the janitor for not shooting up a dainty cabbage on the dumb-waiter, and then counted up her husband's cigarette coupons and skipped right down to the premium parlors with 'em and got him a pair of pale-blue Boston garters and a cunning granite-ware stew-pan, and then sponged lunch off Olive Dunleavy. But nothing bourgeois!"

Such experiences, told to Carl, he found diverting. He seemed, in the spring of 1914, to want no others.

CHAPTER XLI

The apparently satisfactory development of the Touricar in the late spring of 1914 was the result of an uneconomical expenditure of energy on the part of Carl. Personally he followed by letter the trail of every amateur aviator, every motoring big-game hunter. He never let up for an afternoon. VanZile had lost interest in the whole matter. Whenever Carl thought of how much the development of the Touricar business depended upon himself, he was uneasy about the future, and bent more closely over his desk. On his way home, swaying on a subway strap, his pleasant sensation of returning to Ruth was interrupted by worry in regard to things he might have done at the office. Nights he dreamed of lists of "prospects."

Late in May he was disturbed for several days by headaches, lassitude, nausea. He lied to Ruth: "Guess I've eaten something at lunch that was a little off. You know what these restaurants are." He admitted, however, that he felt like a Symptom. He stuck to the office, though his chief emotion about life and business was that he wished to go off somewhere and lie down and die gently.

Directly after a Sunday bruncheon, at which he was silent and looked washed out, he went to bed with typhoid fever.

For six weeks he was ill. He seemed daily to lose more of the boyishness which all his life had made him want to dance in the sun. That loss was to Ruth like a snickering hobgoblin attending the specter of death. Staying by him constantly, forgetting, in the intensity of her care, even to want credit for virtue, taking one splash at her tired eyes with boric acid and dashing back to his bed, she mourned and mourned for her lost boy, while she hid her fear and kept her blouses fresh and her hair well-coiffed, and mothered the stern man who lay so dreadfully still in the bed.... He was not shaved every day; he had a pale beard under his hollow cheeks.... Even when he was out of delirium, even when he was comparatively strong, he never said anything gaily foolish for the sake of being young and noisy with her.

During convalescence Carl was so wearily gentle that she hoped the little boy she loved was coming back to dwell in him. But the Hawk's wings seemed broken. For the first time Carl was afraid of life. He sat and worried, going over the possibilities of the Touricar, and the positions he might get if the Touricar failed. He was willing to loaf by the window all day, his eyes on a narrow, blood-red stripe in the Navajo blanket on his knees, along which he incessantly ran a finger-nail, back and forth, back and forth, for whole quarter-hours, while she read aloud from Kipling and London and Conrad, hoping to rekindle the spirit of daring.

One sweet drop was in their cup of iron. As woodland playmates they could never have known such intimacy as hovered about them when she rested her head lightly against his knees and they watched the Hudson, the storms and flurries of light on its waves, the windy clouds and the processional of barges, the beetle-like ferries and the great steamers for Albany. They talked in half sentences, understanding the rest: "Tough in winter——" "Might be good trip——" Carl's hand was always demanding her thick hair, but he stroked it gently. The coarse, wholesome vigor was drained from him; part even of his slang went with it; his "Gee!" was not explosive.

He took to watching her like a solemn baby, when she moved about the room; thus she found the little boy Carl again; laughed full-throated and secretly cried over him, as his sternness passed into a wistful obedience. He was not quite the same impudent boy whose naughtiness she had loved. But the good child who came in his place did trust her so, depend upon her so....

When Carl was strong enough they went for three weeks to Point Pleasant, on the Jersey coast, where the pines and breakers from the open sea healed his weakness and his multitudinous worries. They even swam, once, and Carl played at learning two new dances, strangely called the "fox trot" and the "lu lu fado." Their hotel was a vast barn, all porches, white flannels, and handsome young Jews chattering tremendously with young Jewesses; but its ball-room floor was smooth, and Ruth had lacked music and excitement for so long that she danced every night, and conducted an amiable flirtation with a mysterious young man of Harvard accent, Jewish features, fine brown eyes, and tortoise-shell-rimmed eye-glasses, while Carl looked on, a contented wall-flower.

They came back to town with ocean breeze and pine scent in their throats and sea-sparkle in their eyes—and Carl promptly tied himself to the office desk as though sickness and recovery had never given him a vision of play.

Ruth had not taken the Point Pleasant dances seriously, but as day on day she stifled in a half-darkened flat that summer, she sometimes sobbed at the thought of the moon-path on the sea, the reflection of lights on the ball-room floor, the wavelike swish of music-mad feet.

The flat was hot, dead. The summer heat was unrelenting as bedclothes drawn over the head and lashed down. Flies in sneering circles mocked the listless hand she flipped at them. Too hot to wear many clothes, yet hating the disorder of a flimsy negligée, she panted by a window, while the venomous sun glared on tin roofs, and a few feet away snarled the ceaseless trrrrr of a steam-riveter that was erecting new flats to shut off their view of the Hudson. In the lava-paved back yard was the insistent filelike voice of the janitor's son, who kept piping: "Haaay, Bil-lay, hey; Billy's got a girl! Hey, Billy's got a girl! Haaay, Bil-lay!" She imagined herself going down and slaughtering him; vividly saw herself waiting for the elevator, venturing into the hot sepulcher of the back areaway, and there becoming too languid to complete the task of ridding the world of the dear child. She was horrified to discover what she had been imagining, and presently imagined it all over again.

Two blocks across from her, seen through the rising walls of the new apartment-houses, were the drab windows of a group of run-down tenements, which broke the sleek respectability of the well-to-do quarter. In those windows Ruth observed foreign-looking, idle women, not very clean, who had nothing to do after they had completed half an hour of slovenly housework in the morning. They watched their neighbors breathlessly. They peered out with the petty virulent curiosity of the workless at whatever passed in the streets below them. Fifty times a day they could be seen to lean far out on their fire-escapes and follow with slowly craning necks and unblinking eyes the passing of something—ice-wagons, undertakers' wagons, ole-clo' men, Ruth surmised. The rest of the time, ragged-haired and greasy of wrapper, gum-chewing and yawning, they rested their unlovely stomachs on discolored sofa-cushions on the window-sills and waited for something to appear. Two blocks away they were—yet to Ruth they seemed to be in the room with her, claiming her as one of their sisterhood. For now she was a useless woman, as they were. She raged with the thought that she might grow to be like them in every respect—she, Ruth Winslow!... She wondered if any of them were Norwegians named Ericson.... With the fascination of dread she watched them as closely as they watched the world with the hypnotization of unspeakable hopelessness.... She had to find her work, something for which the world needed her, lest she be left here, useless and unhappy in a flat. In her kitchen she was merely an intruder on the efficient maid, and there was no nursery.

She sat apprehensively on the edge of a chair, hating the women at the windows, hating the dull, persistent flies, hating the wetness of her forehead and the dampness of her palm; repenting of her hate and hating again—and taking another cold bath to be fresh for the home-coming of Carl, the tired man whom she had to mother and whom, of all the world, she did not hate.

Even on the many cool days when the streets and the flat became tolerable and the vulture women of the tenements ceased to exist for her, Ruth was not much interested, whether she went out or some one came to see her. Every one she knew, except for the Dunleavys and a few others, was out of town, and she was tired of Olive Dunleavy's mirth and shallow gossip. After her days with Carl in the valley of the shadow, Olive was to her a stranger giggling about strange people. Phil was rather better. He occasionally came in for tea, poked about, stared at the color prints, and said cryptic things about feminism and playing squash.

Her settlement-house classes were closed for the summer. She brooded over the settlement work and accused herself of caring less for people than for the sensation of being charitable. She wondered if she was a hypocrite.... Then she would take another cold bath to be fresh for the home-coming of Carl, the tired man whom she had to mother, and toward whom, of all the world's energies, she knew that she was not hypocritical.

This is not the story of Ruth Winslow, but of Carl Ericson. Yet Ruth's stifling days are a part of it, for her unhappiness meant as much to him as it did to her. In the swelter of his office, overlooking motor-hooting, gasoline-reeking Broadway, he was aware that Ruth was in the flat, buried alive. He made plans for her going away, but she refused to desert him. He tried to arrange for a week more of holiday for them both; he could not; he came to understand that he was now completely a prisoner of business.

He was in a rut, both sides of which were hedged with "back work that had piled up on him." He had no desire, no ambition, no interest, except in Ruth and in making the Touricar pay.

The Touricar Company had never paid expenses as yet. How much longer would old VanZile be satisfied with millions to come in the future—perhaps?

Carl even took work home with him, though for Ruth's sake he wanted to go out and play. It really was for her sake; he himself liked to play, but the disease of perpetual overwork had hold of him. He was glad to have her desert him for an evening now and then and go out to the Peace Waters Country Club for a dance with Phil and Olive Dunleavy. She felt guilty when she came home and found him still making calculations. But she hummed waltzes while she put on a thin, blue silk dressing-gown and took down her hair.

"I *can't* stand this grubby, shut-in prison," she finally snapped at him, on an evening when he would not go to the first night of a roof-garden.

He snarled back: "You don't have to! Why don't you go with your bloomin' Phil and Olive? Of course, I don't ever want to go myself!"

"See here, my friend, you have been taking advantage for a long time now of the fact that you were ill. I'm not going to be your nurse indefinitely." She slammed her bedroom door.

Later she came stalking out, very dignified, and left the flat. He pretended not to see her. But as soon as the elevator door had clanged and the rumbling old car had begun to carry her down, away from him, the flat was noisy with her absence. She came home eagerly sorry—to find an eagerly sorry Carl. Then, while they cried together, and he kissed her lips, they made a compact that no matter for what reason or through whose fault they might quarrel, they would always settle it before either went to bed.... But they were uncomfortably polite for two days, and obviously were so afraid that they might quarrel that they were both prepared to quarrel.

Carl had been back at work for less than one month, but he hoped that the Touricar was giving enough promise now of positive success to permit him to play during the evening. He rented a VanZile car for part time; planned week-end trips; hoped they could spend——

Then the whole world exploded.

Just at the time when the investigation of Twilight Sleep indicated that the world might become civilized, the Powers plunged into a war whose reason no man has yet discovered. Carl read the head-lines on the morning of August 5th, 1914, with a delusion of not reading "news," but history, with himself in the history book.

Ten thousand books record the Great War, and how bitterly Europe realized it; this is to record that Carl, like most of America, did not comprehend it, even when recruits of the Kaiser marched down Broadway with German and American flags intertwined, even when his business was threatened. It was too big for his imagination.

Every noon he bought half a dozen newspaper extras and hurried down to the bulletin-boards on the *Times* and *Herald* buildings. He pretended that he was a character in one of the fantastic novels about a world-war when he saw such items as "Russians invading Prussia," "Japs will enter war," "Aeroplane and submarine attack English cruiser."

"Rats!" he said, "I'm dreaming. There couldn't be a war like that. We're too civilized. I can prove the whole thing 's impossible."

In the world-puzzle nothing confused Carl more than the question of socialism. He had known as a final fact that the alliance of French and German socialist workmen made war between the two nations absolutely impossible—and his knowledge was proven ignorance, his faith folly. He tentatively bought a socialist magazine or two, to find some explanation, and found only greater confusion on the part of the scholars and leaders of the party. They, too, did not understand how it had all happened; they stood amid the ruins of international socialism, sorrowing. If their faith was darkened, how much more so was Carl's vague untutored optimism about world-brotherhood.

He had two courses—to discard socialism as a failure, or to stand by it as a course of action which was logical but had not, as yet, been able to accomplish its end. He decided to stand by it; he could not see himself plunging into the unutterable pessimism of believing that all of mankind were such beast fools that, after this one great sin, they could not repent and turn from tribal murder. And what other remedy was there? If socialism had not prevented the war, neither had monarchy nor bureaucracy, bourgeois peace movements, nor the church.

With a whole world at war, Carl thought chiefly of his own business. He was not abnormal. The press was filled with bewildered queries as to what would happen to America. For two weeks the automobile business seemed dead, save for a grim activity in war-trucks. VanZile called in Carl and shook his head over the future of the Touricar, now that all luxuries were threatened.

But the Middle West promised a huge crop and prosperity. The East followed; then, slowly, the South, despite the closed outlet for its cotton crop. Within a few weeks all sorts of motor-cars were selling well, especially expensive cars. It was apparent that automobiles were no longer merely luxuries. There was even a promise of greater trade than ever, so rapidly were all the cars of the warring nations being destroyed.

But, once VanZile had considered the possibility of letting go his Touricar interest in order to be safe, he seemed always to be considering it. Carl read fate in VanZile's abstracted manner. And if VanZile withdrew, Carl's own stock would be worthless. But he stuck at his work, with something of a boy's frightened stubbornness and something of a man's quiet sternness. Fear was never far from him. In an aeroplane he had never been greatly frightened; he could himself, by his own efforts, fight the wind. But how could he steer a world-war or a world-industry?

He tried to conceal his anxiety from Ruth, but she guessed it. She said, one evening: "Sometimes I think we two are unusual, because we really want to be free. And then a thing like this war comes and our bread and butter and little pink cakes are in danger, and I realize we're not free at all; that we're just like all the rest, prisoners, dependent on how much the job brings and how fast the subway runs. Oh, sweetheart, we mustn't forget to be just a bit mad, no matter how serious things become." Standing very close to him, she put her head on his shoulder.

"Sure mustn't. Must stick by each other all the more when the world takes a run and jumps on us."

"Indeed we will!"

Unsparingly the war's cosmic idiocy continued, and Carl crawled along the edge of a business precipice, looking down. He became so accustomed to it that he began to enjoy the view. The old Carl, with the enthusiasm which had served him for that undefined quality called "courage," began to come to life again, laughing, "Let the darned old business bust, if she's going to."

Only, it refused to bust.

It kept on trembling, while Carl became nervous again, then gaily defiant, then nervous again, till the alternation of gloom and bravado disgusted him and made Ruth wonder whether he was an office-slave or a freebooter. As he happened to be both at the time, it was hard for him to be either convincingly. She accused him of vacillating; he retorted; the suspense kept them both raw....

To add to their difficulties of adjustment to each other, and to the ego-mad world, Ruth's sense of established amenities was shocked by the reappearance of Carl's pioneering past as revealed in the lively but vulgar person of Martin Dockerill, Carl's former aviation mechanic.

Martin Dockerill was lanky and awkward as ever, he still wrote post-cards to his aunt in Fall River, and admired burlesque-show choruses, but he no longer played the mouth-organ (publicly), for he had become so well-to-do as to be respectable. As foreign agent for the Des Moines Auto-Truck Company he had toured Europe, selling war-trucks, or lorries, as the English called them, first to the Balkan States, then to Italy, Russia, and Turkey. He was for a time detailed to the New York office.

It did not occur either to him nor to Carl that he was not "welcome to drop in any time; often as possible," to slap Carl on the back, loudly recollect the time when he had got drunk and fought with a policeman in San Antonio, or to spend a whole evening belligerently discussing the idea of war or types of motor-trucks when Ruth wistfully wanted Carl to herself. Martin supposed, because she smiled, that she was as interested as Carl in his theories about aeroplane-scouting in war.

Ruth knew that most of Carl's life had been devoted to things quite outside her own sphere of action, but she had known it without feeling it. His talk with Martin showed her how sufficient his life had been without her. She began to worry lest he go back to aviation.

So began their serious quarrels; there were not many of them, and they were forgotten out of existence in a day or two; but there were at least three pitched battles during which both of them believed that "this ended everything." They quarreled always about the one thing which had intimidated them before—the need of quarreling; though apropos of this every detail of life came up: Ruth's conformities; her fear that he would fly again; her fear that the wavering job was making him indecisive.

And Martin Dockerill kept coming, as an excellent starting-point for dissension.

Ruth did not dislike Martin's roughness, but when the ex-mechanic discovered that he was making more money than was Carl, and asked Carl, in her presence, if he'd like a loan, then she hated Martin, and would give no reason. She became unable to see him as anything but a boor, an upstart servant, whose friendship with Carl indicated that her husband, too, was an "outsider." Believing that she was superbly holding herself in, she asked Carl if there was not some way of tactfully suggesting to Martin that he come to the flat only once in two weeks, instead of two or three times a week. Carl was angry. She said furiously what she really thought, and retired to Aunt Emma's for the evening. When she returned she expected to find Carl as repentant as herself. Unfortunately that same Carl who had declared that it was pure egotism to regard one's own religion or country as necessarily sacred, regarded his own friends as sacred—a noble faith which is an important cause of political graft. He was ramping about the living-room, waiting for a fight—and he got it.

Their moment of indiscretion. The inevitable time when, believing themselves fearlessly frank, they exaggerated every memory of an injury. Ruth pointed out that Carl had disliked Florence Crewden as much as she had disliked Martin. She renewed her accusation that he was vacillating; scoffed at Walter MacMonnies (whom she really liked), Gertie Cowles (whom she had never met), and even, hesitatingly, Carl's farmer relatives.

And Carl was equally unpleasant. At her last thrust he called her a thin-blooded New-Yorker and slammed his bedroom door. They had broken their pledge not to go to bed on a quarrel.

He was gone before she came out to breakfast in the morning.

In the evening they were perilously polite again. Martin Dockerill appeared and, while Ruth listened, Carl revealed how savagely his mind had turned overnight to a longing for such raw adventuring as she could never share. He feverishly confessed that he had for many weeks wavered between hating the whole war and wanting to enlist in the British Aero Corps, to get life's supreme sensation—scouting ten thousand feet in air, while dozens of batteries fired at him; a nose-to-earth volplane. The thinking Carl, the playmate Carl that Ruth knew, was masked as the foolhardy adventurer—and as one who was not merely talking, but might really do the thing he pictured. And Martin Dockerill seemed so dreadfully to take it for granted that Carl might go.

Carl's high note of madness dropped to a matter-of-fact chatter about a kind of wandering which shut her out as completely as did the project of war. "I don't know," said he, "but what the biggest fun in chasing round the country is to get up from a pile of lumber where you've pounded your ear all night and get that funny railroad smell of greasy waste, and then throw your feet for a hand-out and sneak on a blind and go hiking off to some town you've never heard of, with every brakie and constabule out after you. That's living!"

When Martin was gone Carl glanced at her. She stiffened and pretended to be absorbed in a magazine. He took from the mess of papers and letters that lived in his inside coat pocket a war-map he had clipped from a newspaper, and drew tactical lines on it. From his room he brought a small book he had bought that day. He studied it intently. Ruth managed to see that the title of the book was *Aeroplanes and Air-Scouting in the European Armies*.

She sprang up, cried: "Hawk! Why are you reading that?"

"Why shouldn't I read it?"

"You don't mean to—— You——"

"Oh no, I don't suppose I'd have the nerve to go and enlist now. You've already pointed out to me that I've been getting cold feet."

"But why do you shut me out? Why do you?"

"Oh, good Lord! have we got to go all over that again? We've gone over it and over it and over it till I'm sick of telling you it isn't true."

"I'm very sorry, Hawk. Thank you for making it clear to me that I'm a typical silly wife."

"And thank you for showing me I'm a clumsy brute. You've done it quite often now. Of course it doesn't mean anything that I've given up aviation."

"Oh, don't be melodramatic. Or if you must be, don't fail to tell me that I've ruined your life."

"Very well. I won't say anything, then, Ruth."

"Don't look at me like that, Hawk. So hard. Studying me.... Can't you understand—— Haven't you any perception? Can't you understand how hard it is for me to come to you like this, after last night, and try——"

"Very nice of you," he said, grimly.

With one cry of "Oh!" she ran into her bedroom.

He could hear her sobbing; he could feel her agony dragging him to her. But no woman's arms should drug his anger, this time, to let it ache again. For once he definitely did not want to go to her. So futile to make up and quarrel, make up and quarrel. He was impatient that her distant sobs expressed so clearly a wordless demand that he come to her and make peace. "Hell!" he crawked; jerked his top-coat from its nail, and left the flat—eleven o'clock of a chilly November evening.

CHAPTER XLII

Dizzy with all the problems of life, he did not notice where he went. He walked blocks; took a trolley-car; got off to buy a strong cigar; took the next trolley that came along; was carried across the Fifty-ninth Street bridge to Long Island. At the eighth or tenth stop he hurried out of the car just as it was starting again. He wondered why he had been such a fool as to leave it in a dark street of flat-faced wooden houses with dooryards of trampled earth and a general air of poverty, goats, and lunch-pails. He tramped on, a sullen and youthless man. Presently he was in shaggy, open country.

He was frightened by his desertion of Ruth, but he did not want to go back, nor even telephone to her. He had to diagram where and what and why he was; determine what he was to do.

He disregarded the war as a cause of trouble. Had there been no extra business-pressure caused by the war, there would have been some other focus for their misunderstandings. They would have quarreled over clothes and aviation, Aunt Emma and Martin Dockerill, poverty and dancing, quite the same.

Walking steadily, with long periods when he did not think, but stared at the dusty stars or the shaky, ill-lighted old houses, he alined her every fault, unhappily rehearsed every quarrel in which she had been to blame, his lips moving as he emphasized the righteous retorts he was almost certain he had made. It was not hard to find faults in her. Any two people who have spent more than two days together already have the material for a life-long feud, in traits which at first were amusing or admirable. Ruth's pretty manners, of which Carl had been proud, he now cited as snobbish affectation. He did not spare his reverence, his passion, his fondness. He mutilated his soul like a hermit. He recalled her pleasure in giving him jolly surprises, in writing unexpected notes addressed to him at the office, as fussy discontent with a quiet, normal life; he regarded her excitement over dances as evidence that she was so dependent on country-club society that he would have to spend the rest of his life drudging for her.

He wanted to flee. He saw the whole world as a conspiracy of secret, sinister powers that are concealed from the child, but to the man are gradually revealed by a pitiless and never-ending succession of misfortunes. He would never be foot-loose again. His land of heart's desire would be the office.

But the ache of disappointment grew dull. He was stunned. He did not know what had happened; did not even know precisely how he came to be walking here. Now and then he remembered anew that he had sharply left Ruth— Ruth, his dear girl!—remembered that she was not at hand, ready to explain with love's lips the somber puzzles of life. He was frightened again, and beginning to be angry with himself for having been angry with Ruth.

He had walked many miles. Brown fields came up at him through the paling darkness. A sign-board showed that he was a few miles from Mineola. Letting the coming dawn uplift him, he tramped into Mineola, with a half-plan of going on to the near-by Hempstead Plains Aviation Field, to see if there was any early-morning flying. It would be bully to see a machine again!

At a lunch-wagon he ordered buckwheat-cakes and coffee. Sitting on a high stool before a seven-inch shelf attached to the wall, facing an array of salt-castors and catsup-bottles and one of those colored glass windows with a portrait of Washington which give to all lunch-wagons their air of sober refinement, Carl ate solemnly, meditatively.... It did not seem to him an ignoble setting for his grief; but he was depressed when he came out to a drab first light of day that made the street seem hopeless and unrested after the night. The shops were becoming visible, gray and chilly, like a just-awakened janitor in slippers, suspenders, and tousled hair. The pavement was wet. Carl crossed the street, stared at the fly-specked cover of a magazine six months old that lay in a shop window lighted by one incandescent. He gloomily planned to go back and have another cup of coffee on the shelf before Washington's glassy but benign face.

But he looked down the street, and all the sky was becoming a delicate and luminous blue.

He trotted off toward Hempstead Plains.

The Aviation Field was almost abandoned. Most of the ambitious line of hangars were empty, now, with faded grass thick before the great doors that no one ever opened. A recent fire had destroyed a group of five hangars.

He found one door open, and three sleepy youngsters in sweaters and khaki trousers bringing out a monoplane.

Carl watched them start, bobbed his chin to the music of the motor, saw the machine canter down the field and ascend from dawn to the glory of day. The rising sun picked out the lines of the uninclosed framework and hovered on the silvery wing-surface. The machine circled the field at two hundred feet elevation, smoothly, peacefully. And peace beyond understanding came to Carl.

He studied the flight. "Mm. Good and steady. Banks a little sharp, but very thorough. Firs' rate. I believe I could get more speed out of her if I were flying. Like to try."

Wonderingly he realized that he did not want to fly; that only his lips said, "Like to try." He was almost as much an outsider to aviation as though he had never flown. He discovered that he was telling Ruth this fact, in an imaginary conversation; was commenting for her on dawn-sky and the plains before him and his alienation from exploits in which she could not share.

The monoplane landed with a clean volplane. The aviator and his mechanicians were wheeling it toward the hangar. They glanced at him uninterestedly. Carl understood that, to them, he was a Typical Bystander, here where he had once starred.

The aviator stared again, let go the machine, walked over, exclaiming: "Say, aren't you Hawk Ericson? This is an honor. I heard you were somewhere in New York. Just missed you at the Aero Club one night. Wanted to ask you about the Bagby hydro. Won't you come in and have some coffee and sinkers with us? Proud to have you. My name 's Berry."

"Thanks. Be glad to."

While the youngsters were admiring him, hearing of the giants of earlier days, while they were drinking inspiration from this veteran of twenty-nine, they were in turn inspiring Carl by their faith in him. He had been humble. They made him trust himself, not egotistically, but with a feeling that he did matter, that it was worth while to be in tune with life.

Yet all the while he knew that he wanted to be by himself, because he could thus be with the spirit of Ruth. And he knew, subconsciously, that he was going to hurry back to Mineola and telephone to her.

As he dog-trotted down the road, he noted the old Dutch houses for her; picked out the spot where he had once had a canvas hangar, and fancied himself telling her of those days. He did not remember that at this hangar he had known Istra, Istra Nash, the artist, whose name he scarce recalled. Istra was an incident; Ruth was the meaning of his life.

And the solution of his problem came, all at once, when suddenly it was given to him to understand what that problem was.

Ruth and he had to be up and away, immediately; go any place, do anything, so long as they followed new trails, and followed them together. He knew positively, after his lonely night, that he could not be happy without her as comrade in the freedom he craved. And he also knew that they had not done the one thing for which their marriage existed. They were not just a man and a woman. They were a man and a woman who had promised to find new horizons for each other.

However much he believed in the sanctity of love's children, Carl also believed that merely to be married and breed casual children and die is a sort of suspended energy which has no conceivable place in this over-complex and unwieldy world. He had no clear nor ringing message, but he did have, just then, an overpowering conviction that Ruth and he—not every one, but Ruth and he, at least—had a vocation in keeping clear of vocations, and that they must fulfil it.

Over the telephone he said: "Ruth dear, I'll be right there. Walked all night. Got straightened out now. I'm out at Mineola. It's all right with me now, blessed. I want so frightfully much to make it all right with you. I'll be there in about an hour."

She answered "Yes" so non-committally that he was smitten by the fact that he had yet to win forgiveness for his frenzy in leaving her; that he must break the shell of resentment which would incase her after a whole night's brooding between sullen walls.

On the train, unconscious of its uproar, he was bespelled by his new love. During a few moments of their lives, ordinary real people, people real as a tooth-brush, do actually transcend the coarsely physical aspects of sex and feeding, and do approximate to the unwavering glow of romantic heroes. Carl was no more a romantic hero-lover than, as a celebrated aviator, he had been a hero-adventurer. He was a human being. He was not even admirable, except as all people are admirable, from the ash-man to the king. There had been nothing exemplary in his struggle to find adjustment with his wife; he had been bad in his impatience just as he had been good in his boyish affection; in both he had been human. Even now, when without reserve he gave himself up to love, he was aware that he would ascend, not on godlike pinions, but by a jerky old apartment-house elevator, to make peace with a vexed girl who was also a human being, with a digestive system and prejudices. Yet with a joy that encompassed all the beauty of banners and saluting swords, romantic towers and a fugitive queen, a joy transcending trains and elevators and prejudices, Carl knew that human girl as the symbol of man's yearning for union with the divine; he desired happiness for her with a devotion great as the passion in Galahad's heart when all night he knelt before the high altar.

He came slowly up to their apartment-house. If it were only possible for Ruth to trust him, now——

Mingled with his painfully clear remembrance of all the sweet things Ruth was and had done was a tragic astonishment that he—this same he who was all hers now—could possibly have turned impatiently from her sobs. Yet it would have been for good, if only she would trust him.

Not till he left the elevator, on their floor, did he comprehend that Ruth might not be awaiting him; might have gone. He looked irresolutely at the grill of the elevator door, shut on the black shaft.

"She was here when I telephoned——"

He waited. Perhaps she would peep out to see if it was he who had come up in the elevator.

She did not appear.

He walked the endless distance of ten feet to their door, unlocked it, labored across the tiny hall into the living-room. She was there. She stood supporting herself by the back of the davenport, her eyes red-edged and doubtful, her face tightened, expressing enmity or dread or shy longing. He held out his hands, like a prisoner beseeching royal mercy. She in turn threw out her arms. He could not say one word. The clumsy signs called "words" could not tell his emotion. He ran to her, and she welcomed his arms. He held her, abandoned himself utterly to her kiss. His hard-driving mind relaxed; relaxed was her body in his arms. He knew, not merely with his mind, but with the vaster powers that drive mind and emotion and body, that Ruth, in her disheveled dressing-gown, was the glorious lover to whom he had been hastening this hour past. All the love which civilization had tried to turn into Normal Married Life had escaped Efficiency's pruning-hook, and had flowered.

"It's all right with me, now," she said; "so wonderfully all right."

"I want to explain. Had to be by myself; find out. Must have seemed so unspeakably r——"

"Oh, don't, don't explain! Our kiss explained."

While they talked on the davenport together, reaching out again and again for the hands that now really were there, Ruth agreed with Carl that they must be up and away, not wait till it should be too late. She, too, saw how many lovers plan under the June honeymoon to sail away after a year or two and see the great world, and, when they wearily die, know that it will still be a year or two before they can flee to the halcyon isles.

But she did insist that they plan practically; and it was she who wondered: "But what would happen if everybody went skipping off like us? Who'd bear the children and keep the fields plowed to feed the ones that ran away?"

"Golly!" cried Carl, "wish that were the worst problem we had! Maybe a thousand years from now, when every one is so artistic that they want to write books, it will be hard to get enough drudges. But now—— Look at any office, with the clerks toiling day after day, even the unmarried ones. Look at all the young fathers of families, giving up everything they want to do, to support children who'll do the same thing right over again with *their* children. Always handing on the torch of life, but never getting any light from it.

People don't run away from slavery often enough. And so they don't ever get to do real work, either!"

"But, sweetheart, what if we should have children some day? You know——— Of course, we haven't been ready for them yet, but some day they might come, anyhow, and how could we wander round———"

"Oh, probably they will come some day, and then we'll take our dose of drudgery like the rest. There's nothing that our dear civilization punishes as it does begetting children. For poisoning food by adulterating it you may get fined fifty dollars, but if you have children they call it a miracle—as it is— and then they get busy and condemn you to a lifetime of being scared by the boss."

"Well, darling, please don't blame it on me."

"I didn't mean to get so oratorical, blessed. But it does make me mad the way the state punishes one for being willing to work and have children. Perhaps if enough of us run away from nice normal grinding, we'll start people wondering just why they should go on toiling to produce a lot of booze and clothes and things that nobody needs."

"Perhaps, my Hawk.... Don't you think, though, that we might be bored in your Rocky Mountain cabin, if we were there for months and months?"

"Yes, I suppose so," Carl mused. "The rebellion against stuffy marriage has to be a whole lot wider than some little detail like changing from city to country. Probably for some people the happiest thing 'd be to live in a hobohemian flat and have parties, and for some to live in the suburbs and get the missus elected president of the Village Improvement Society. For us, I believe, it's change and *keep going*."

"Yes, I do think so. Hawk, my Hawk, I lay awake nearly all night last night, realizing that we *are* one, not because of a wedding ceremony, but because we can understand each other's make-b'lieves and seriousnesses. I knew that no matter what happened, we had to try again.... I saw last night, by myself, that it was not a question of finding out whose fault a quarrel was; that it wasn't anybody's 'fault,' but just conditions.... And we'll change them.... We won't be afraid to be free."

"We won't! Lord! life's wonderful!"

"Yes! When I think of how sweet life can be—so wonderfully sweet—I know that all the prophets must love human beings, oh, so terribly, no matter how sad they are about the petty things that lives are wasted over.... But I'm not a prophet. I'm a girl that's awfully much in love, and, darling, I want you to hold me close."

Three months later, in February, 1915, Ruth and Carl sailed for Buenos Ayres, America's new export-market. Carl was the Argentine Republic manager for the VanZile Motor Corporation, possessed of an unimportant salary, a possibility of large commissions, and hopes like comets. Their happiness seemed a thing enchanted. They had not quarreled again.

The S.S. *Sangrael*, for Buenos Ayres and Rio, had sailed from snow into summer. Ruth and Carl watched isles of palms turn to fantasies carved of ebony, in the rose and garnet sunset waters, and the vast sky laugh out in stars. Carl was quoting Kipling:

"The Lord knows what we may find, dear lass,And the deuce knows what we may do—But we're back once more on the old trail, our own trail, the out trail,We're down, hull down on the Old Trail—the trail that is always new."

"Anyway," he commented, "deuce only knows what we'll do after Argentine, and I don't care. Do you?"

Her clasping hand answered, as he went on:

"Oh, say, bles-sed! I forgot to look in the directory before we left New York to see if there wasn't a Society for the Spread of Madness among the Respectable. It might have sent us out as missionaries.... There's a flying-fish; and to-morrow I won't have to watch clerks punch a time-clock; and you can hear a sailor shifting the ventilators; and there's a little star perched on the fore-mast; singing; but the big thing is that you're here beside me, and we're *going*. How bully it is to be living, if you don't have to give up living in order to make a living."

THE END